# MYTHOS SEAS
# MOVING
# SEAMOUNTS

BOOK FOUR

# MYTHS SEAS
# MOVING SEAMOUNTS

JEREMY J. DAVIDSON

*To my aunts, for their help and support with these novels*

This is a work of fiction.
The story, all names, characters, and incidents portrayed in this production are fictitious. No identification with actual persons (living or deceased), places, buildings, and products is intended or should be inferred.

© 2023 Jeremy J. Davidson
All rights reserved.

No part of this book may be reproduced, transmitted, or stored in an information retrieval system in any form or by any means; graphic mechanical, electronic, or mechanical including photocopying, taping, and recording without prior written permission from the author.
No part of this publication is to be used to train generative AI technologies and machine learning language models without prior written permission from the author.

Identifiers: ISBN 979-8-9891162-6-3 (Paperback) | ISBN 979-8-9891162-7-0 (ebook) | Library of Congress Control Number: 2023923649
Printed & Published in the United States of America
Dayton, NV.

Check out Mythosseas.com

Cover art by Jeremy J. Davidson
Design by Jeremy J. Davidson

# CONTENTS

*Chapter One*
ON THE WIND. . . . . . . . . . . . . . . . . . . . . . . . . . . . .1

*Chapter Two*
WARNINGS. . . . . . . . . . . . . . . . . . . . . . . . . . . . . . . .13

*Chapter Three*
GOODBYE AND HELLO. . . . . . . . . . . . . . . . . . . . . .32

*Chapter Four*
TRAVELING IN TEAMS. . . . . . . . . . . . . . . . . . . . . . .40

*Chapter Five*
FROM THE SEAGULL'S BEAK. . . . . . . . . . . . . . . . . 58

*Chapter Six*
ANCIELLON ISLE. . . . . . . . . . . . . . . . . . . . . . . . . . .65

*Chapter Seven*
SNAPPING TURTLE INN. . . . . . . . . . . . . . . . . . . . . 88

# CONTENTS

*Chapter Eight*
AUNTIE ANCIE..............................114

*Chapter Nine*
SIGNS OF DARKNESS........................127

*Chapter Ten*
SIRENS SONG..............................132

*Chapter Eleven*
THE TEST.................................155

*Chapter Twelve*
ENCOUNTER WITH HISTORY...................164

*Chapter Thirteen*
TIME TO ACT..............................178

*Chapter Fourteen*
THE DARK PILLAR..........................191

*Chapter Fifteen*
THE WEAPON...............................205

*Chapter Sixteen*
SAVING SERPENTS..........................217

*Chapter Seventeen*
UNFINISHED BUSINESS......................225

## CONTENTS

*Chapter Eighteen*
GATHERING SHADOWS. . . . . . . . . . . . . . . . . . . . . . .231

*Chapter Nineteen*
THE LAST LIGHT. . . . . . . . . . . . . . . . . . . . . . . . . . . . 241

EPILOGUE. . . . . . . . . . . . . . . . . . . . . . . . . . . . . . . . .266

GLOSSARY. . . . . . . . . . . . . . . . . . . . . . . . . . . . . . . . 281

SNEAK PEEK OF MYTHOS SEAS BEYOND . . . . . . 301

# CHAPTER ONE
# ON THE WIND

A loud howl rang out through the trees as Jackson ran through the first of the morning light. His heart pounded in his chest as he skidded around an immense old oak tree while a growl echoed out of the underbrush!

"Spells, spells, SPELLS!!" Jackson huffed when more growls joined the first. Leaping into the air, he quickly engulfed himself in a sphere of water, shooting towards the canopy as several wolflike forms shot out of the bushes.

"DON'T LET HIM ESCAPE!"

Jackson dove and dodged between the branches as one of the creatures jumped against the trunk of a tree, dug its claws in deep, and shot upwards! He spun to the side before the creature flew by him, growling in frustration before it hit the ground. As it snarled, Jackson darted between the great trees of the forest, fleeing towards the shore beyond.

"Almost there." Jackson gasped when he flew over a rocky outcropping as the shoreline came into view up ahead. He suddenly yelped, flipping around just before two more dark shapes pounced from their hiding places in the rocks below him!

Jackson barely dodged the creatures' attacks, wincing when they smashed into each other with whining yelps before he shot

# MYTHOS SEAS: MOVING SEAMOUNTS

forward, staying as close to the top of the canopy as he could. Suddenly, there was a loud howl, and he was blasted out of the air by a surge of magical sound waves that sent him spinning down towards the ground, landing in a big pile of bushes with a crash!

"OWOWOWOwowowowwww...." Jackson grumbled as he sat up and rubbed his left arm, which was likely to bruise later, while four shapes snuck up behind him with their teeth bared.

Jackson felt a shiver go down his spine before the creatures charged! He screamed when he was tackled to the ground as their mouths opened wide and—

"AHAHAhaha!! Stop it. Stop!" Jackson laughed as four excited cadolin puppies happily licked his face and hands. "Hey come-on, do you have to rub it in?" He gently pushed them away, their tails thrashing about joyfully while Daychaser, his father, and a few other members of the pack came strolling over with amused looks on their snouts.

"I thought for sure you'd make it that time." Draflor, Jackson's Dra Na Ko fish friend, came floating out from the staff while he inspected a map of Starkelp Isle. "You were smart to follow the smaller streamlet towards shore, rather than the main river like you had before."

"It took us a while to track you down because of that." Daychaser's father, Squallrunner, put in. "I wasn't aware that you knew of the island's smaller waterways."

"He didn't." Everyone looked over to see a smugly grinning Spinescale slither out of the undergrowth. "I helped him map out this route while you lot were off on another hunting trip." The purple and yellow, winged sea snake's eyes sparkled mischievously. "Which is also how he knew about the hiding spots in the rocks, he was going to hide there himself."

# ON THE WIND

"Spinescale!" Jackson's cheeks turned red in embarrassment while Draflor gave him an amused look. "You didn't have to tell them that part."

"What? You weren't able to do it anyway." Spinescale teased, making Jackson mutter something that made Daychaser meet his father's eye and wink.

"I guess we can include that in today's report to Leavamentee." Daychaser said innocently as he stretched his long legs with a yawn.

"WHAT, NONONono I—!" Jackson's face paled and everyone burst out laughing.

"So THAT'S why you didn't want me to tell anyone about your hiding spots!" Spinescale giggled. "Oh, did I mention the one by the—"

"SSSssshhhh!" Jackson hurriedly made vines grow up from the ground and wrap around Spinescale's snout. "Spinescale!!!"

"HALT."

Jackson winced when the magical form of Leavamentee herself charged over, coming to a quick about face as she looked from Squallrunner and Draflor. "So, how'd he do today? I take it this is as far as he got?"

"He performed much better today." Squallrunner sat down in his confident, calm way. "He found a path we didn't think he'd use, and threw us off his trail for a good fifteen minutes before we caught his scent and were able to locate him."

"He also never flew over the tree-line, kept away from the cliffs—where the wind wouldn't take his scent to where the pack was searching—didn't hide himself in the rocky outcropping like before, and..." Draflor got a wry look on his face. "He kept his usage of the water-travel spell to a minimum. As you'd insisted."

"Good."

# MYTHOS SEAS: MOVING SEAMOUNTS

Jackson tensed when Leavamentee leveled him with her ever-intense gaze. "I'm glad to hear you're learning. Though it's not as fast as I'd like, it'll have to do." Jackson cringed as her eyes slid down to Spinescale, who had managed to free herself from Jackson's entangling vines. "What's this about?"

"Oh nothing, we were just giving Jackson a hard time." Spinescale nonchalantly stretched her wings and smirked a bit. "Just having a little bit of fun."

Leavamentee didn't look impressed as she turned her piercing eyes back to Squallrunner and the other members of the pack. "Meet me in the main cavern in thirty minutes, I want a full report." When the seawolf nodded, her form promptly vanished away and Squallrunner slowly got to his feet and let out a howl. The rest of the pack echoed the call before the entire group set off towards the sea, weaving in and out of the trees.

Squallrunner gave his son a head-rub while they wandered off, but after a moment, Daychaser turned and gave Jackson a concerned look. "You ok?"

Jackson let out the breath he'd been unconsciously holding and sat down with a thunk. "I... don't know." He looked over to Draflor with a thoughtful frown. "Has she always been like this?"

"Leavamentee?" Draflor looked up from the scroll he'd been using to track Jackson's progress and lessons and rolled his eyes. "I think that old manatee's been sour and stern since the day she was born." The scroll rolled shut. "If you think she's bad now, you should've been around when she and her husband did drills together. I swear they could shatter stone just from their calls alone."

"I seem to remember hearing that they did shatter a bunch of stones when you were here for your training."

# ON THE WIND

Jackson looked up to see an amused looking Serphere come floating over with the water-travel spell she'd taught him.

"What? How could I possibly help myself when I discovered an enchantment that could make normal rocks look just like the Starkelp Warrior Trainees?" Draflor looked up towards the sky innocently. "Not like it was my fault the rocks don't know how to take orders."

"I seem to recall that Leavamentee and her mate chased you around the sanctuary a few times for that one." Serphere's mate, Longspar, said wryly as he came whipping over. "I'm honestly surprised that's all they did to you."

"Can't do anything, if you can't catch your target." Draflor grinned impishly. "I led them on a merry chase that ended with them destroying ten rocky outcroppings, three battlements, and scattering the schools of fish around the sanctuary to the far currents from their rage." His eyes gleamed with mischief. "And all they had to show for it was magically bright purple skin, sea-flowers growing from their noses, and a lot of explaining to do to the council."

Spinescale gave a single snicker and threw a wing over her mouth to keep from laughing too loud. Jackson put his head in his hand, shaking his head and smiling while Daychaser's jaw dropped open in shock.

"And THAT was part of why you were assigned to be tutored by the Staff of Solarswell." Serphere gave a weary, but slightly amused sigh. "It was the only way to keep your mischief under control."

"Solarswell would claim otherwise." Draflor laughed as the group headed towards the ocean, only to pause when a loud whinny and a deep hiss echoed through the trees.

Jackson looked over and waved when his horse friend, Thorra, and his venstorn friend, Toxun, came running through the

# MYTHOS SEAS: MOVING SEAMOUNTS

underbrush. A moment later his aluran friend, Courser, rushed out after them on his two long legs, letting out a happy call. For most of his journey Jackson hadn't really had a good opportunity to release his old friends from their magical stasis inside a special gemstone his family had left him. However, now that they were staying on a large island with plenty of food and water, Jackson had felt comfortable setting them free.

"Hey Thorra, Courser, morning Toxun." Jackson ran over to give them a quick hug as Thorra shoved him playfully with his head while Toxun gave him a gentle, friendly nip.

"Morning Jackson." Thorra whinnied as Courser ran over to give him a light headbutt. "How'd your training go?"

"Didss yous pass?" Toxun asked in his strange serpentine voice.

"Jackson still has a bit more to learn before he can outwit seawolves." Spinescale smirked.

"I think he could, if he was allowed to use all his magic." Daychaser smiled as his seawolf friend, Skycaller, came back to check and see what was taking them all so long.

"While I agree," said Skycaller, glancing in confusion out to sea. "Why does Leavamentee give him so many handicaps in her training sessions? Stonecurrent, Koiwae, and the medians training sessions are much less…" Her ears flicked back uncertainly. "Torturous."

"You're telling me…" Jackson sighed tiredly. "I hate Leavamentee's training sessions, they always stress me out so bad."

"And you never did perform well when you were stressed out, or had a harsh teacher." Thorra bobbed his head in agreement. "I remember that's why Grandpa Spencer took over your training with riding in races, the other people who coached riders in the tribe

# ON THE WIND

always made you so nervous you couldn't remember anything they taught you."

"THORRA." Jackson said, his cheeks turning red. "You didn't have to mention that!"

Serphere chuckled. "Don't be ashamed Jackson, everyone learns a little bit differently." She glanced out to see. "Like your friends Blade and Shadowtorrent for example, they thrive under Leavamentee's training style, while Startide is blossoming under Koiwae's wisdom and guidance."

"And Daychaser and Skycaller are learning a great deal from Docion's tutelage." Longspar continued with a quick glance towards Spinescale. "And you seem to be learning much from both Koiwae and Falganous."

"Who are two opposites in personality..." Draflor added wryly as he made a quick note on his ever-increasing lists.

Jackson shrugged sheepishly. "I guess, but I really wish I could have more lessons from Stonecurrent, Koiwae, or Oceaono..." He sighed. "Especially Stonecurrent, even if his training sessions are really hard, I love them." He gave a self-condoning grin. "I'd take a whole week's worth of Stonecurrent's lessons over one of Leavamentee's drills any day."

"Which is why you only have a finful of her drills to deal with." Longspar said kindly. "The medians quickly noticed who was best suited to teaching you, especially Seanel. She was once the head of the academy at Mythos Pearl before her duties as a median required her to put her focus elsewhere."

"She was?" Jackson asked in surprise, only to get distracted when a strong blast of wind shot by. His head flew up as the wind rushed past his ears, a beautiful, yet sad, melody flying along with it. "Huh? Did you guys hear that?"

"Yeah." Thorra's ears perked up and he turned to look in the direction Jackson was looking.

"Hear what?" Daychaser asked, his ears swiveling around while the others all glanced about with confused expressions.

"What is it?" Courser questioned.

"There it is again." Thorra trotted forward as Jackson looked around while more wind whipped around him, bringing more of the melody along with it.

"I wonder…" Draflor mused as Jackson hurried over and jumped onto Thorra's back.

"Go that way Thorra, follow the wind." Jackson said, grabbing onto the stallion's mane while the wind rushed past them, heading into the thick of the forest. Thorra neighed, slightly rearing before taking off after the leaves blowing through the air as the haunting melody continued.

Jackson held tightly as Thorra galloped through the forest while the song grew louder and more poignant, strange words and messages mixed in with the melody. There were times when the wind would fade away slightly, but the second Jackson used his wind magic the call would return. He and Thorra raced after the calling wind while the others struggled to follow them.

"JACKSON, HOLD UP WILL YA?!" Spinescale called when Thorra suddenly swooped up a long ledge, galloping to the top of a tall rise while the wind grew weaker, but the song grew louder. Once Jackson and Thorra crested the rise, they skidded to a stop and Courser raced up behind them.

*Whoa…* Jackson thought as he, Courser, and Thorra looked down over the expansive tree covered island that hid part of the Starkelp Strand Sanctuary. The cliff-face beneath them sharply dropped towards the forest below, and the sight made Jackson shiver slightly. He suddenly looked up, his breath catching when he

# ON THE WIND

felt the wind return with greater force, whipping around him, Courser, and Thorra.

"It's like it's calling to me..." Thorra whispered, taking another step forwards, while Courser stepped back. "Like it wants me to jump off the cliff and follow it."

Jackson had the same feeling and frowned uncertainly. He reached out to the wind with his own magic as Toxun came rushing up towards them, the others hot on his tail. Jackson watched as his magic went spiraling out of his hands and spread through the air in a wild, long line. The magic almost seemed to form a pathway into the sky, heading towards the top of the mountain in the middle of the island.

"Thorra..." Jackson said, feeling the stallion shift in anticipation. "Do it!"

Thorra whinnied excitedly and reared again before he leapt off the cliff towards the spiraling magic. Jackson let out a surprised and delighted whoop as they flew through the air before the wind surged up beneath them, carrying them upwards!

Thorra neighed in excitement as he began to run through the air while the wind below his hooves glowed brightly with magic! The magical wind shot ahead of them and Thorra raced up it, making Jackson laugh happily as they raced past the cliffs, sending a small flock of seabirds that were resting along the edges into flight. Up and around they raced, chasing the magical wind through the air while the pure white seabirds flew past them, letting out wild, surprised cries.

With the loud melody ringing in his ears, which was turning from sad to hopeful, Jackson reached out and grabbed a feather that fell from one of the seabirds. Thorra suddenly leapt forward, soaring over a tall rocky spire before landing on the magical wind and racing forwards again, following the breeze towards a tall peak where a gentle blue glow of magic could be seen.

Thorra was breathing heavily as his hooves clattered onto the polished stone just outside the entrance to a mountaintop cave, which was slightly aglow with light blue and white magic. The stallion let out a long, happy whinny while Jackson quickly dismounted and took a few tentative steps forwards.

"Where are we?" Jackson asked quietly as the wind gently danced around his shoulders while he and Thorra wandered into the cavern.

The song grew louder and louder until they came into a large room that sparkled with magical water droplets, which were spinning around in the air. Jackson's breath caught in his throat as Thorra let out an impressed snort at the scene in front of them.

The white statue of a tall, finely dressed woman, with huge wings stretched out behind her, was reaching forward with her right arm and hand extended. A statue of a Sonaekian man, with a white tail, reached up towards her outstretched hand with his, as if he was handing something to her. A strong looking hippocampus curved around the man while a brilliant pegasus, its wings spread majestically, stood behind the woman.

Jackson's eyes widened when a brilliant spiral crystal—that hovered between the statues—pulsed in time with the melody ringing in his and Thorra's ears.

Just below the crystal, a large sun shaped gemstone shimmered brightly, the shining symbols inside it morphing and changing between a multitude of different creatures, never settling on one form.

Draflor let out a low, impressed whistle when he, Longspar, and Serphere—who were using their water travel magic to carry themselves and the others—came swooping in behind Jackson and

## ON THE WIND

Thorra. "One of the Windspiral's. I'd wondered if there was one on this island."

"Windspiral?" Daychaser huffed the question while he and the rest of the group got their bearings, only to go quiet as they took in the sight before them.

"Wow…" Spinescale hissed. "That's a gorgeous bunch of statues."

"And look what the Windspiral is guarding…" Longspar smiled in relief. "The Key of Creature's Light, one of the artifacts the medians wanted Jackson to find."

Jackson took a few steps forward when the call turned longing and the crystals suddenly began flashing brightly.

"Jasssonsss bes carefulss." Toxun hissed worriedly when Jackson walked towards the crystals.

"It's ok." Serphere said, quietly hushing him. "Watch."

Jackson reached out with both his water and wind magic as the magical wind formed into steppingstones below his feet, leading up to where the two crystals were hovering. When he reached the artifacts, he slowly reached out his hand and formed a symbol for wind magic in front of him.

Immediately the spiral crystal floated over and began swirling around him before the Star of the Sea and the Earthcore came flashing out of his hands. All three crystals began flashing wildly before they all suddenly shot into Jackson's hands, and he took a deep breath.

Reaching up, Jackson gently picked the Key of Creature's Light from the air and grasped it to his chest. As the magical item touched his shirt, the music and wind in the chamber stilled and the magical water droplets slowly evaporated into a warm mist. The blue glow of the walls dimmed away to nothing, and only moments later the statues seemed to fade out of view before they vanished, leaving the cavern empty, like they had never been there in the first place.

"What... just happened?" Spinescale asked as Draflor suddenly started chuckling to himself.

Jackson hopped down from the steps before the magical platforms seemed to blow away.

"I believe Jackson's just acquired another aspectrial stone." Serphere said with a smirk before Draflor burst out laughing.

"HAHAHAHAHAHAHAHA!!! AND I CAN'T WAIT TO SEE THE LOOK ON LEAVAMENTEE'S FACE WHEN SHE AND THE OTHERS FIND OUT!" Draflor howled.

Jackson paled at Draflor's words and looked anxiously towards the exit.

"You ok son?" Longspar asked.

"I just realized we're gonna be late for Leavamentee's meeting." Jackson facepalmed. "She's gonna kill me!"

"Oh, I think she'll be a bit more understanding once she finds out what you got." Serphere said wryly as she turned towards the exit. "But you're right, we should get back before she sends Blade and Shadowtorrent out to find us."

## CHAPTER TWO
# WARNINGS

Jackson had quickly helped Draflor and the whipfins lower everyone down from the mountain and find their way back to the seashore. Once they reached the beach, he gave Thorra, Courser, and Toxun a quick goodbye, promising to come back later before he and the others dashed into the sea.

"Spells, spells, spells!" Jackson muttered as he shot off ahead of the group, Spinescale clinging tightly to his bag.

"Aw, come on Jackson." Spinescale said as she tightened her coils around the straps of the bag. "I'm sure you won't be in too much trouble, remember what Serphere said?"

"You're not the one who'll have to sit through one of Leavamentee's lectures!" Jackson groaned worriedly while he whipped around a large strand of starkelp.

Draflor looked up from the map he was looking over. "Don't worry, we'll help get you out of it." His eyes twinkled mischievously. "Although… I can't promise I'll help Leavamentee's mood any, but I can quickly get her focus off of you."

"Is that good or bad?" Daychaser asked as he and Skycaller came swimming up next to Jackson, their tails pumping.

# MYTHOS SEAS: MOVING SEAMOUNTS

*Depends on what Draflor does.* Jackson managed a small, wry smile which quickly faded once he saw Blade, Shadowtorrent, and Startide swimming towards them.

"THERE you are." Startide said with a relieved sigh. "Leavamentee sent us out looking for you when she couldn't find you around the island. Where were you guys?"

"Oh, you know..." Draflor started before Jackson could explain. "Just building Jackson's legend, that's all."

"Buildin what now?" Blade asked while Shadowtorrent and Startide exchanged perplexed looks.

"We'll explain at the sanctuary!" Jackson said as he darted forwards. "I don't want to push Leavamentee's patience anymore than I have."

"If I missed something good again, I swear..." Startide muttered as the entire group turned and hurried towards the entrance to the sanctuary.

They were shocked when they found Longspar and Serphere already at the entrance, quietly talking to Leavamentee who glanced over at Jackson with a half-lidded look, though she seemed impressed.

"So..." She said and Jackson slowed nervously. "You found the Key of Creature's Light all on your own. You're more resourceful than I give you credit."

Jackson wasn't sure whether Leavamentee was complimenting him or not, and shrugged uncertainly. "Um... yes?"

"The meeting with the seawolves will wait." Leavamentee flipped around. "Everyone, to the Communication Chamber, post haste."

"Yes Mam!" Draflor said from the staff, making Leavamentee level it with a tight glare.

"And take your annoying Dra Na Ko with you." She grumbled.

# WARNINGS

"I go wherever the staff goes!" Draflor called in a singing tone.

"The day you finish your studies I'll..." Leavamentee left her threat unfinished, which only made Draflor chuckle more as her form promptly vanished away.

Startide rolled her eyes. "Would it kill her to relax?" She whispered just loud enough for Jackson and the others to hear.

"I have a feeling that's not her style." Shadowtorrent chuckled.

"Maybe after this is all over, she'll calm down?" Skycaller offered hopefully.

Draflor and the whipfins all exchanged a quick, disbelieving look.

"Nah." Draflor said as a loud bell-like sound suddenly rang out through the hold, letting everyone know they needed to hurry up. "I'd say that's not likely."

*Ya think?* Jackson shook his head tiredly and shot through the doors and down the hallway, aiming for the Communication Chamber.

"You know that old manatee well, don't ya?" Blade asked Draflor as the group hurried after Jackson.

Draflor gave a short nod. "She was a good friend of my grandsire. They fought in many battles together back in the day, and I often came here to visit when I was younger."

Blade hmphed. "Explains why ya like flarin her fins so much and don't get beaten to fishfood."

"Maybe that's the reason." Draflor grinned. "Or maybe it's just too much fun to irk her when I know exactly what to do to escape scar-free."

Jackson rolled his eyes while he hurried towards the meeting room. After he'd rounded a large bend the hallway made, he waved to a group of sharks and a number of immense goliathan whales, one of which being his friend, Granitebow.

# MYTHOS SEAS: MOVING SEAMOUNTS

While the Starkelp Sanctuary hadn't had many creatures that Jackson could free from the rogue petrifying magic, there were still a large number of animals that were now living there. Most of them were creatures Jackson's friends had rallied and gathered together after he'd been kidnapped and dragged to Shieldguard. However, there were still plenty of Sonaekian creatures whom Jackson had freed, including a good number of Shieldguard Knights, though all of them were animals, not Sonaekian waterborn.

Reaching the doors to the Communication Chamber, Jackson nodded to a couple of sharks outfitted in brightly polished stilven armor. The sharks saluted him and his friends before the doors swung open and Jackson hurried inside. He was greeted excitedly by Stonecurrent while Leavamentee, Depthcall, Squallrunner, Oceaono, the other medians, and Koiwae all turned towards him.

"There he is!" Stonecurrent smiled. "Went on ahead and figured out how to find the next key on your own did you? Not a bad morning's work." He gave Leavamentee a sly look. "Especially since some creatures thought you weren't quite ready for the challenge."

"Never said that." Leavamentee retorted sharply. "Just wasn't sure he'd know how to break the enchantments, his training hadn't covered that yet."

"How DID you know how to break those enchantments, young Jackson?" Koiwae asked, looking perplexed. "We hadn't taught you any such things yet."

"I was wondering that myself…" Oceaono smiled curiously, giving Jackson a questioning look.

"My dad and his brothers are talented at breaking enchantments. I learned a lot from them." Jackson shrugged, "and I didn't have to do that much, the secret on how to undo them was in the song."

# WARNINGS

Everyone in the room seemed confused before Draflor laughed. "Of course, that's what you and Thorra kept talking about." He looked over at Oceaono with a grin. "The Windspiral guarding the key must've been singing a melody only an aspect guardian or a pure wind creature could hear."

"Wait…" Fulrion gave Jackson a shocked look. "Windspiral? Don't tell me…"

When Jackson smiled sheepishly Stonecurrent and Draflor busted up laughing at the other's stunned expressions.

After a few moments Oceaono chuckled quietly to himself. "Full of surprises, aren't you Jackson?"

"B—but one person guarding three aspects!" Falganous stuttered. "That's… that's unheard of."

"So is someone who can use every element, old friend." Seanel said with a small smile while Depthcall giggled. "There is always more to learn."

"And it's not all good."

Everyone turned in surprise when the magical form of Lorgeo—a sapphire golem Jackson had helped at the Jewel Isles—suddenly appeared, his expression grim. "Oceaono, guardians, we have a problem, a big one."

"What happened?" Koiwae asked worriedly.

"That fleet of Toxicshade ships Jackson had warned me about months ago just tried to sail through here this morning." Lorgeo said darkly but held up a hand to silence Jackson when he saw the boy's frightened look. "Don't worry, I took care of them, their stone bodies are now decorating the seafloor of the canyon."

Startide, Spinescale, and Daychaser grimaced at Lorgeo's description, but didn't comment before the sapphire golem continued.

# MYTHOS SEAS: MOVING SEAMOUNTS

"Once I took care of the men and their ships, I sensed something strange within one of the vessels and decided to investigate." Lorgeo's mouth twisted into a disapproving scowl as he bent over to pick up a couple items. "And found these."

Seanel, Depthcall, and Stonecurrent let out alarmed bellows while Koiwae's fins flashed out in surprise as Fulrion and Falganous growled. Docion, Oceaono, and Sharval all looked shocked while Draflor's face darkened.

"Are those what I think they are?" Draflor asked, his voice low, a slightly angry edge to it.

"They are." Lorgeo held up one of the strange items. "These artifacts are weapons once used by the Ironmamba in the Great War over two hundred years ago." He met Oceaono's gaze as the median tried to calm himself. "And I found a message in one of the ships talking about taking these, and other dark weapons from that time, to the old battle grounds outside Great Ghost Point."

Oceaono let his breath out very slowly while Jackson looked over to his friends and shrugged uncertainly. "Um... I take it you know those weapons?" He asked Oceaono.

"We do." Oceaono's face was tight. "They were part of a set of five magical artifacts that became corrupted after the Ironmamba took them." He took a deep breath. "The power of those artifacts was part of what led our nation to summon the colossals."

"Mind you, they were part of the reason." Docion added. "Though the destruction of one of our coastal cities on the Northern Continent was directly tied to these artifacts."

"Thank the heavens we had enough warning to evacuate..." Sharval shook her head. "Or more than just the city would've been lost."

# WARNINGS

"But those were supposed to have been destroyed long ago!" Depthcall said, looking stunned. "How did those two...?" She went quiet. "My father led the team that destroyed them..."

Stonecurrent's eyes suddenly widened. "You mean the team my brother was apart of?" He and Depthcall locked gazes before both their eyes hardened.

"Traitor in more than one sense of the word." Depthcall said bitterly as Stonecurrent huffed in disgust.

"Young Jackson?" Koiwae suddenly asked. "Do you know of these artifacts? You seemed to recognize them as well."

"Of course." Jackson answered with a shrug. "They were the same ones used to destroy the towns along the entire length of the Viperio Stretch."

"The Spherefang's old home?" Spinescale asked.

Jackson looked over at her and nodded. "Yep, that's how the emperor laid waste to the cities in such a way that the other nations couldn't tell what exactly had destroyed them. That's how my family was so easily blamed for it." He scowled unhappily. "They had one more of those though... I remember the letters my Dad recovered had three different items drawn on them."

"And we only have two..." Depthcalled groaned. "Bottomkillers."

"Lorgeo?" Stonecurrent asked. "You said the message you found mentioned they were taking those artifacts to the area just outside of Great Ghost Point?"

"These and more from what I read." Lorgeo's form faded away as he left to put down the items before he returned and folded his arms. "The message clearly mentioned that other fleets were bringing more powerful artifacts, at least one or two tied to the Ironmamba."

Seanel closed her eyes tiredly. "Of course, and the stronghold around that area is where the last key is hidden." She shook her head, "and now we have this going on too."

"Lorgeo, would you like me to send Cora over to retrieve those artifacts?" Koiwae asked. "I should have the facilities here to properly destroy them, this time for good."

"I'd love nothing more." Lorgeo said in his curt way. "Don't want them to suddenly react and mess up all my hard work here. I've had more than enough trouble these last few centuries."

"Did... The messages say anything else?" Jackson asked worriedly.

Lorgeo looked at him out of the corner of his eye. "Mentioned a war with the Fire Tribes, and that the Toxicshade Emperor was gathering his forces together with the artifacts for some purpose around the Point. Whatever that purpose is, the orders indicated it was to be taken care of before they commenced their attacks. Beyond that, nothing solid. I assume the captain of the ship already knew about the particulars before he got these orders."

Jackson looked down thoughtfully, his features tightening while Stonecurrent and his friends gave him worried looks.

"What's wrong?" Daychaser asked, swimming up next to Jackson.

"My aunt and some of my other relatives are originally from the Fire Tribes..." Jackson said, glancing up. "Some of their family came to visit us once when I was little, so I know a lot of my relatives from there."

"And you're worried about your family." Stonecurrent nodded before he glanced over at the medians. "I think we're out of time to focus on training."

"I know, but we had to try and make some time for it." Oceaono sighed as he swam forward, "and the darkness we've been

## WARNINGS

sensing is only growing stronger, we can no longer even sense what's going on around Abyssward Pass." He took a deep breath. "That and we've felt strange dark energies building around the stronghold as well. So..." He lifted his head determinedly as he turned to Leavamentee. "Guardian Leavamentee, please get to work at once with getting the teleportation pool connected to the Clawwake Pillar activated and working, you have two nights before we move."

"Understood." Leavamentee said. "If Koiwae is willing to aid me, I can have it working by tomorrow evening." She glanced over to Koiwae who nodded before she turned back to Oceaono. "What teams need to prepare for departure?"

"Depthcall." Oceaono turned to her. "Ready the knights and your Whaleguard and select a couple members to stay behind to help Leavamentee protect the strand. Blade..." He looked over to Sharval who flicked her fins in agreement. "Blade will be leading the team of sharks he's in charge of, and if Squallrunner be willing, we'd appreciate the help of his podpack in this endeavor."

"You have it." Squallrunner said, having remained silent for most of the meeting. He and Daychaser locked eyes before they nodded. "Just tell us when, where, and what."

"Thank you." Oceaono nodded to Squallrunner gratefully. "Stonecurrent, I want you to help me finish with Jackson's training over the next day or so." He said firmly. "There are a few things we need to wrap up before he goes. Serphere and Longspar..."

Both whipfins raised a brow expectantly.

"I'll ask that your clans remain here to help at Starkelp." Oceaono's tone softened a bit. "I know your kind aren't made for battle, and you and your clans are the last of your kind to remain. If you were lost, it'd be a true tragedy for the seas." He smiled a bit teasingly. "Especially with the return of the lisheave that your kind love so much."

Serphere and Longspar only nodded before Oceaono turned to Jackson and his friends.

"Startide, Shadowtorrent, Spinescale, and Draflor." Oceaono said, his voice holding a hint of question. "You may stay if you wish and remain here where you'll be safe. Those that leave here will likely end up accompanying Jackson to the capital and must... face the unknown dangers of the darkness we've been sensing. There's no promise that you'll return."

"I'm going." Startide said determinedly, giving Jackson a nod. "We've been through too much together to back out now."

"Same." Shadowtorrent added while Spinescale smirked.

"Now that Jackson has his new bag and access to fresh water, good luck stopping me." She said with a bit of sass in her tone.

Draflor chuckled. "You know I'm going, there's no need to ask." He gave Jackson a nudge. "Someone has to keep an eye on these guys."

"Excuse me?" Startide gave Draflor a half-lidded look. "I think we're the ones having to keep an eye on **you**!"

"Only when I let you." Draflor smirked, only to roll his eyes when Solarswell flashed. "No, I'm NOT gathering magic for you now. It can wait until after the meeting."

Jackson and his friends snickered while the other creatures gave an assortment of exasperated responses.

"Very well." Oceaono nodded with a contented smile. "Then we'll give you all the details of your orders the day of departure." He turned back towards the communication orb. "We'll be back soon, there's matters we must check on before the morrow." His form vanished away, quickly followed by the other medians, Lorgeo, and Koiwae.

# WARNINGS

Stonecurrent huffed a bit. "Jackson, meet me in the usual training room in an hour please, we'll try to get a few things with your training done before Oceaono comes back."

Jackson nodded as he saw his hands flash faintly. "Ok. If my bag's there, but I'm not, jostle it. I gotta check something."

Stonecurrent nodded his understanding as Jackson flipped around and dashed out of the chamber before Leavamentee could nab him for the seawolves report on his training. Once he arrived in the training room where he usually had his lessons, he teleported himself into his new bag.

"Mind hanging out here for a bit?" He asked Spinescale as she unwrapped herself from his back.

"Sure, not like I have anything crazy to train for." Spinescale smirked as she slithered down and made for her favorite basking rock. "Off to check on you and Draflor's mysterious secret, are you?"

"If we are…" Draflor smirked. "Could we tell you?"

Spinescale rolled her eyes while she coiled atop the rock, "and that's a yes." She settled down for a nap. "Have fun, don't get lost."

Jackson laughed. "We won't."

"At least not too badly." Draflor joked before Jackson teleported them into his personal bag.

Seconds later, the Star of the Sea, Earthcore, and—to Jackson's faint surprise—the Windspiral all came flying out of his hands and danced around him.

"Ready to do a little more training?" The Star of the Sea asked. "Our friend, and the Windspiral, have a few things they'd like to teach you as well, just in case."

"Of course!" Jackson said enthusiastically, making the Star of the Sea and the Earthcore chuckle slightly.

"I'll let y'all know when we're due back for Stonecurrent's lesson." Draflor smiled as Solarswell floated over to watch from the sidelines. Draflor had finally been given permission to watch Jackson's training sessions with the aspect stones, and had been enjoying himself immensely. "At least you know, if I don't get to caught up in trying to figure out the crazy spells you've all been working on."

"Ever the magic loving creature, aren't we?" The Star of the Sea asked wryly.

Draflor shrugged his fins with a smirk. "What can I say, it's a gift." He gave Jackson a friendly wink. "As Jackson well knows."

Jackson laughed before he was enveloped in a bright sphere of energy as the aspectrial stones whirled around him.

"Now then." The Star of the Sea said. "Let's begin where we left off last time…"

A little over three hours later, Jackson was breathing heavily as he dodged another of Stonecurrent's attacks while simultaneously making a current lift a number of rocks off the seafloor.

"I'm calling a break!" Draflor shouted from the sidelines once he saw Jackson flag.

"Got it." Stonecurrent immediately backed off, letting Jackson relax.

Jackson let out a sigh, and the rocks promptly began sinking down towards the bottom while he swam over to the bench to rest for a second.

# WARNINGS

"You're doing good." Draflor complimented as Stonecurrent came over, "but you're still struggling with multitasking under stress."

"I wish I could get that new type of barrier down." Jackson gasped a bit, feeling winded after doing both the aspect's lessons and Stonecurrent's back-to-back.

Stonecurrent chuckled. "Never fear Jackson, I think you'll get it eventually. These things take time; a city isn't built in a day, as the land dwellers say. Now..." He came in front of Jackson. "We've been practicing different spells and situations that help you with control, dealing with swiftly changing surges of magic, and..." He fell silent to see if Jackson could finish the thought.

"And you've been going over the spell Oceaono and the others have come up with that should reverse the Great Petrifying." Jackson held up one finger then flicked up a second one. "And you and Koiwae have been teaching me how to undo the enchantments and spells protecting the final key hidden in the Stronghold around Great Ghost Point."

He led up a third finger. "Koiwae has also made sure I know where the key's located and how to find it when we get there." A fourth finger flicked up. "And you've also been teaching me other spells that have to do with ocean travel, defense, and using magic that helps me navigate more easily by using the enchantments on the glove you gave me."

"Excellent." Stonecurrent grinned, "and you survived Leavamentee's test this morning, though I still expect some improvement on her next one." His eyes sparkled mischievously. "If you need to know where you need to improve there, Draflor has your charts."

"Should I pull them out now?" Draflor teased and Jackson rolled his eyes.

"I think I'll worry about that, once I hear if she's actually giving me another test before we go." Jackson said wryly, but Stonecurrent shook his head.

"Remember what I said about the unseen enemy?" Stonecurrent asked with a smile.

Jackson groaned. "I know, I know, but you also made the distinction to 'beware of the unseen enemy' in battle."

"Aaaaand do you think Leavamentee has ever truly left the battle?" Stonecurrent smirked.

"Spells..." Jackson moaned, his shoulders slumping while he rolled his eyes. "No, I guess not."

"Then maybe you'd better go over your charts." Stonecurrent chuckled as he turned to leave. "I'll be back in twenty minutes, don't forget to eat a little while Draflor's droning over your paperwork."

"Excuse me?" Draflor gave Stonecurrent a mock look of insult as the whale started to vanish away. "Since when do I drone?"

"When you're acting out the 'Overly Studious Scholar!'" Stonecurrent laughed before he disappeared.

Draflor smirked a bit before he let out a huff of laughter. "Did I ever mention he was my favorite teacher?" He asked, pulling out the all too familiar lists and charts documenting Jackson's progress.

"Maybe once or twice." Jackson smiled. "Sometimes I think you're trying to flatter him." He teased.

"Oh yes," Draflor laughed. "I'm hoping that if I flatter Stonecurrent enough, that he'll ask Solarswell to upgrade his orb to include a snack bar. The eating here is terrible, the food has no flavor whatsoever."

"Would help if there was food." Jackson rolled his eyes.

# WARNINGS

"Exactly my point." Draflor replied before they both laughed and got down to the business of going over the different things Jackson needed to work on.

When Jackson's break was done, Stonecurrent swiftly returned to resume the training session. Jackson trained until it was almost sunset and was wondering when he'd be finished when Draflor and the staff suddenly swooped over to the opposite side of the room from Stonecurrent.

Jackson quickly blocked a barrage of attacks from Stonecurrent as Draflor smirked. *What's going on?* He wondered when he saw Draflor's eye twinkle in anticipation as the Dra Nah Ko swam away from Solarswell before they both began glowing.

"Beware." Stonecurrent grinned.

Jackson's eyes widened once he realized what was about to happen. "Spells."

He quickly dashed upwards as Solarswell and Draflor fired their attack towards him, while Stonecurrent swooped up from the other side. As a multitude of magical whales formed and let out deafening bellows Jackson flipped around to a stop when Draflor surged in to block his escape.

"Where you think you're going?!" Draflor shouted with a grin as magical energy formed over his fins, turning them into long, sharp magical blades.

Jackson formed a huge barrier around himself before Draflor slashed his attacks against it as one of the magical whales crashed into the other side.

*Too much at once!* Jackson cried out mentally as he shot out the top of his protective barrier and fired a multitude of attacks in all directions. His ploy made some of the whales' swoop to the side, only for Solarswell's attack to smack Jackson on the back of his tail. *Spells!!!*

# MYTHOS SEAS: MOVING SEAMOUNTS

Jackson spun away, diving around Draflor's next attack while simultaneously trying to figure out what to do about the whales, Stonecurrent, and Solarswell. The huge number of assailants suddenly became too much for him and Jackson inwardly screamed as he started casting a spell. *GAAAAHHH! I NEED MORE OF ME.*

Stonecurrent and the others paused when Jackson's body flashed brightly before three large spheres shot out of him and morphed into some oddly familiar forms.

"What the dragon!?" Draflor exclaimed in shock when four Jackson's turned to look at him, while Solarswell flashed in surprise.

"What?" Jackson and his copies all asked, feeling a bit confused as to why everyone had stopped.

Stonecurrent's jaw dropped open while he looked between Jackson and his copies until Jackson and his duplicates all turned to see what everyone was staring at.

"AAAAHHH!!" The Jacksons all shot backwards before looking at each other wildly. Finally, they all turned to look at Stonecurrent, who was still too surprised to speak. "Um... Stonecurrent?" They all asked in unison. "What's going on?"

Stonecurrent made a strangled sounding bellow while Draflor just stared, his fins drooping. "Ok... well I'll add that to your list of abilities."

The Jacksons all gave Draflor a quick, slightly disapproving, look. "Wait... you've been documenting all my abilities?" They asked and Draflor grimaced uneasily.

"Maybe... Uh ok..." Draflor looked over at Stonecurrent. "Stonecurrent, can you please teach Jackson how to combine back into one? This is starting to creep me out."

"I..." Stonecurrent shook his head. "Yes. Jackson..." His fins slumped a bit when all the boys looked at him. "Uh..." The whale

# WARNINGS

sighed, shaking his head tiredly. "You never cease to surprise, don't you?"

The Jacksons all looked at each other uncertainly before they smiled sheepishly. "Well, I didn't plan this one." They all answered.

"Ok seriously, can the real Jackson please be the only one to speak." Draflor pleaded as the door opened and Leavamentee came swimming in. "You're freaking me out."

"Soldiers, Stonecurrent, what's the holdup? You were supposed to be done with training two minutes ago I—WHAT IN THE WHALES MAW!!!" Her eyes bugged out as she looked between the Jacksons. "What—howdid—whereinthe—isthat—I…" She shut her mouth "You know what…" She flipped around. "Nevermind, let me know what happened later. I'm out." She swam back out the door which promptly closed behind her.

"Um… Stonecurrent?" The Jacksons all asked. "I take it this is a spell like what the goliathan whales can do?"

"If it is, it's your own version of it." Stonecurrent let out an amused huff. "Your copies seem all too aware and connected to your spirit. For goliathan whales, our copies and real self never speak all at once, it's usually one at a time."

"PLEASE tell me the others are actually copies and not clones!" Draflor pled. "I don't know if my brain could handle cloning magic."

"They're copies Draflor." Stonecurrent reassured as he swam up to the Jacksons. "No magic can clone another living creature, at least, not in a true and living form. A fake one, maybe, but not a true and living one. Now Jackson." He instructed. "Focus, identify which one of you is the real Jackson."

The Jackson's all exchanged a quick look before they shrugged and closed their eyes. After a few moments of silence, three of the

# MYTHOS SEAS: MOVING SEAMOUNTS

Jacksons pointed to the one in the back who opened his eyes and looked up at Stonecurrent.

"Good." Stonecurrent sighed. "Now, I'll tell you how to end the spell in such a way that you'll only feel slightly ill, and not actual pain."

"WAIT PAIN?!" All the Jacksons eyes flipped open and widened in alarm.

"For a spell of this type..." Stonecurrent said wryly. "The user pays a price, nothing long-term or permanent, but a price."

"Well... ok..." The Jacksons all said nervously before they closed their eyes again and listened as Stonecurrent instructed them on how to safely break the spell.

Once the spell broke, the other Jacksons bodies began to glow before condensing down into large glowing water droplets. The droplets suddenly flew into Jackson's body and he grimaced when the magic swept over him, making him dizzy before he started sinking.

"I got you." Stonecurrent quickly came up beneath him and caught him. "You ok?"

"Dizzy..." Jackson mumbled. "So many... thoughts... memories."

"That's normal." Stonecurrent reassured. "Your brain is just processing all the memories and sensations you and your other selves just made. It'll take you a bit more training with this spell before the feeling becomes less..." He chuckled a bit when Jackson lurched, his face turning green as he covered his mouth. "Nauseating."

"Well, I'm glad that's over." Draflor sighed as he and Solarswell floated over. "Seeing the goliathan whales and goliathan-whaleborn knights do that is one thing, but seeing one of your best friends in the quadruple is a whole n'other squid to swallow."

# WARNINGS

"I think it'd be best if we save the training for this type of magic for a later time." Stonecurrent counseled as Jackson managed to get to his fins. "This magic is tricky to master in its completeness and very draining." He gave Jackson a serious look. "For now, I'd recommend you not use it, unless of course you are in dire danger and must have more than just one of you to work with..." He got a conflicted look in his eyes. "But still, I'd advise against it for now, and if you do... please be careful. The damage your copies get will, in the end, affect you. Though not in the exact same way as it did them."

"I kinda figured." Jackson replied tightly, still feeling queasy. "Um, do you mind if I go and rest onshore a bit? I think some fresh air will help—" He covered his mouth again as he dry-heaved.

"Go right ahead." Stonecurrent agreed. "I think that's an excellent idea."

"Thank you." Jackson mumbled through his fingers and slowly swam out of the room, aiming for the sanctuary's entrance.

## CHAPTER THREE
# GOODBYE AND HELLO

A while later, Jackson sighed tiredly while he lay on the soft sand of the beach on the south side of Starkelp Isle. The stars were twinkling above him, Toxun, Courser, and Thorra, as they looked out towards the brightly glimmering starkelp.

"Where are all the others?" Thorra asked while he scratched his head with his foreleg.

"Yeah, usually some of your other friends come to join us." Courser added.

Jackson shrugged. "Daychaser's spending some last-minute quality time with his podpack, Draflor and Solarswell are going over something with Koiwae, and Blade and Granitebow are off training with the troops. I don't know where Spinescale is…" He smirked a bit. "And Startide and Shadowtorrent said something about doing a little patrol around the island."

Toxun snorted. "Theyss nots foolingss anybodys."

"I wish they'd fool somebody!" The four friends looked over as Spinescale came slithering out of the surf with a sour look on her snout. "Startide's been acting weirder than an eel in a quiver of sea snakes since Shadowtorrent offered to take her wake surfing three days after he got here."

# GOODBYE AND HELLO

"Ah… young love." Thorra nickered in amusement. "Isn't it wonderful?"

Spinescale got a disgusted look in her eyes. "About as wonderful as a stuck shed…" She hissed as she coiled up on the sand next to Jackson, who gave her a wry look.

"Does it really bother you that much?" Jackson asked, slightly concerned by Spinescale's disapproval.

"She could do better than an ex-honored killer whale." Spinescale muttered pensively. "She shouldn't be crushing on a bad boy, believe me."

"Isss thiissss the voice of exssperience talkings?" Toxun lifted a scalebrow in question, although his eyes sparkled impishly.

"Rather not talk about it." Spinescale hissed.

"Sounds like a yes…" Courser teased, making Spinescale puff in annoyance and turn away.

Jackson huffed in amusement, wondering what kinda snake Spinescale's ex-crush was like as he looked up at the sky above them and frowned.

Worries over the darkness he'd kept hearing about tumbled around in his mind. Despite Stonecurrent's previous reassurances that he and the medians would tell Jackson more about it, he hadn't been able to learn much, other than it was growing and becoming more of a threat. The medians seemed afraid to even breach the topic when he was around, which made Jackson even more worried and confused as to why no one was trusting him with the information.

He'd also overheard the medians talking about there being old, damaged artifacts and weapons around the Stronghold that could pose a problem if messed with. That brought forth his worries about the war and his relatives in the fire tribes, but also brought back memories of his family.

## MYTHOS SEAS: MOVING SEAMOUNTS

"I miss them..." Jackson whispered to himself as he and the others watched a shooting star race across the sky.

"Ssssooss do I'ss" Toxun hissed, having settled down in the sand next to Jackson, looking melancholy. "We'ss all usseed to gatherssss ans watch thee sssstarss."

"Every night we could." Thorra nickered as he lifted his head high to listen to the waves crashing against the cliffs further down the coast.

Courser crooned sadly. "It's so strange to think they're almost half a world away and trapped in stone."

Jackson sighed as he looked down at the waves, which glowed with the multitude of shining starkelp pods. "Are you guys going to be ok?"

"We'll be fine." Thorra reassured, stamping his hoof in emphasis. "It's you that we're worried about."

"Itssss a longss journeyss aheads." Toxun rumbled as he looked out over the seas.

"So why aren't you three coming?" Spinescale asked, looking perplexed.

"Because we're the... last plan." Thorra gave a horsey frown. "If... anything happens to Jackson, we're..."

"The onesss whosss wills helps others find hisss family to frees them." Toxun finished with a frown while Courser lowered his head, looking uncomfortable.

"Oh..." Spinescale gave Jackson an apologetic look. "I... I'm sorry."

Jackson shrugged uneasily. "We just... wanted to be sure that the original reason for me starting this whole thing isn't, um, well." He shook his head. "Yeah."

"Yeah." Spinescale answered before she looked out towards the waves. "You know, Thorra could at least come along. Koiwae

# GOODBYE AND HELLO

talked about a spell that can be used on horses so they can take a waterborn form like a hippocampus."

"I know." Thorra nickered. "But we all talked about it, and I keep feeling it'd best for me to stay here with Courser and Toxun." His tail switched back and forth unhappily. "It'd take awhile for me to get used to underwater travel, and the spell might not even work on me." He motioned towards the mountain behind them with his head. "I have strong wind magic in my bloodline, not water."

"Jussst the sssamess." Toxun added. "We'll beess helpings the creaturesss heres with trainings before goings toosss Jewel islessss for a bits to sseeess if the ssspherefangssss needsss helps."

Courser chittered sadly. "I wish Jackson was on a land-based quest. We've been so... useless."

"You haven't been useless." Jackson shook his head. "Even if I never dared free you, because I was worried about... making sure you'd be ok. I've always known you three were there for me." Jackson reached up and patted Thorra's flank. "That's been more help than you know." He leaned his chin on his arms. "I nearly summoned you multiple times throughout the journey, but I never did because I felt like you'd just have to just ride along in my bag the entire time. It didn't seem fair to any of you, to make you just sit in the bag forever without anything to do but wait."

"Evenss though that's sssorta whatss we wasss doings anywaysss." Toxun snorted.

"I'm tempted to come along in one of your bags now..." Thorra huffed worriedly. "I don't like letting you leave without us."

"Neither do I..." Jackson sighed. "I guess I should've let you guys out sooner, so you could've tried getting used to underwater life before we had to leave again."

"You'll love the Jewel Isle's though." Spinescale said, trying to cheer Thorra, Courser, and Toxun up. "And going through the portal pools isn't nearly as frightening as you might think." She got a smug look on her face. "It's actually pretty fun, I wanted to go back and forth a couple times, but Leavamentee got all grouchy about it and turned the pool off."

Jackson laughed. "I was just happy to see you again." He frowned thoughtfully. "Wish we could get Zepherdust and Avavo here too." He leaned forwards. "Zepherdust was one of my first traveling companions... it'd be nice to have her with us again."

"I'm sure she wishes the same thing." Thorra reassured as the form of Leavamentee came floating up from the waves like a stern, armor-clad ghost.

"Jackson!" She called curtly. "Tell your friends goodbye and head into your quarters to rest for the night soldier. You'll be in training all day tomorrow and then leaving before the sun comes up the next day. No time for last minute goodbyes."

"Oh... ok." Jackson called as he stiffly got to his feet, brushing the sand off his legs and trousers. "Be there in a minute."

He went over and grabbed Thorra, Courser, and Toxun in a big hug. "Bye you guys, love you." He whispered as Toxun and Courser curled their necks around him while Thorra ruffled his hair with his chin. "I'm... going to miss you so much. If anything happens, tell the family I love them."

"We will." Thorra nickered sadly. "Please be careful, and we love ya to."

"Jacksonss." Toxun said with a pained look in his eyes. "Beforess you goess." He glanced over to Thorra.

"Your parents and grandparents believed in you." Thorra caught Jackson's gaze and held it. "Before they sent us into the crystal..." Thorra choked up a bit.

Courser nudged Thorra as he gave Jackson a serious look. "They made sure that if we saw you, that we'd let you know."

# GOODBYE AND HELLO

"Andss theyss knew you'd dos the rights thingsss." Toxun added. "Your mother ssssaid you'd madess her a promisesss, and she knew you'ds keeps it."

Tears stung Jackson's eyes and he bit his lip to try and keep from crying. "I... needed that. Thanks you guys." He grabbed them in a hug again. "See you soon."

"You'd better." Thorra neighed as Courser crooned while Toxun gave Jackson a friendly nip on the shoulder.

As Jackson soberly swam back into the sanctuary for the night, Spinescale slithering along beside him. He was surprised when he ran into Startide, Shadowtorrent, Granitebow, Daychaser, Draflor, and Blade.

"Hey, you guys..." Jackson gave them a perplexed look when he noticed Startide and Daychaser exchange a quick smirk. "What's going on?"

"Got somethin Leavamentee wants us to all check on." Blade said, sounding bored, motioning towards one of the areas of the sanctuary that had large tracts of shoreline.

"Come on!" Daychaser squeed, coming forward to shove Jackson in the direction Blade had indicated as Draflor and Solarswell floated over.

"But what is it?" Jackson asked, feeling immensely perplexed as he let the others guide him in the general direction.

"Beats me." Granitebow said, sounding perplexed as well. "Leavementee just said something about more troops arriving this evening."

"But why would we need to check on the new troops?" Jackson asked as they neared a large sandy section of seafloor that quickly rose up to the shore. He paused for a second when he heard a barking sound and his eyes widened when two familiar shapes split

from a huge group of creatures and raced towards them.
"ZEPHERDUST?! AVAVO?"

Jackson let out a wild happy yell before he shot forwards as Zepherdust let out a happy call.

"HEY!!!" She shouted, swooping in to give Jackson a quick hug as Avavo, Startide, and Daychaser hurried in to join them.

The five friends all began laughing and talking at once until Zepherdust pulled back, still laughing happily. "It's so good to see you guys again."

"It's so good to see you too!" Startide said, glancing down at her flipper, "how's your flipper?"

"Good as new." Zepherdust extended it out, showing a thin scar that was the only indication of the injury she'd gotten all those months ago.

"But how did you guys get here?" Jackson asked, giving Startide and the others a suspicious look. "And why do I get the feeling I was the only one who didn't know about you all coming?"

Daychaser and the others all chuckled before Draflor swooped over. "They got here through the portal pools just a little bit ago."

"But how?" Jackson asked. "The Mistsurge Isle Outpost's magic had died…"

"It did…" Avavo began as a few more of the colorfully furred seals from Mistsurge Isle came swimming over, Leavamentee, Stonecurrent, and Koiwae in tow. "But only for a month or so. One day when we swam by, we found the magic was working again."

"At which point, your young friends reached out to the medians." Koiwae took up the explanation with a fond look at Zepherdust and Avavo. "They and the other seals and creatures around the Isle had heard about the danger you and your other friends were facing, as well as your kidnapping…"

## GOODBYE AND HELLO

"And since they were able to contact them, the medians and other guardians have been training them remotely, until the outpost got enough juice to teleport them here." Stonecurrent smiled, looking pleased and amused by the shocked and thrilled expression on Jackson's face.

"But that doesn't mean you all get to chit-chat and catch up tonight." Leavamentee snipped as she gave Jackson a firm look. "You need to get off to sleep, soldier. You're hard enough to wake up when you've got enough sleep, and I'm not having you drowsy-eyed and half asleep for training tomorrow."

"B-but—" Jackson started to protest, only for Leavamentee to give him a pointed glare.

Startide, Draflor and a few others rolled their eyes while Stonecurrent gave Leavamentee a wry look. "Now really old girl, you seriously think Jackson'll be able to fall asleep after news like this?"

"Don't matter, he's heading off to bed." Leavamentee insisted and Zepherdust and Avavo looked over at Jackson and shrugged uncertainly.

"We'll try to catch up tomorrow." Zepherdust whispered before Leavamentee spun Jackson around in a current of water, facing him towards the sleeping quarters.

## CHAPTER FOUR
# TRAVELING IN TEAMS

The next morning Jackson got another confirmation that Leavamentee didn't kid around as he barely had enough time to grab some food before he was rushed off to train with Oceaono and Stonecurrent. He had a quick break for lunch before Leavamentee surprised him with another test, much to Jackson's chagrin.

Once that ordeal was finally over, Jackson was then given another short break, which wasn't much since the aspects decided to train him during that.

He had a few minutes to talk with Zepherdust and Avavo between training sessions, and found out his old friends had been learning the ancient magic the seals of Mistsurge Isle were once feared for. Before he had to leave for his lesson with Stonecurrent, Jackson made them promise to show him some of their magic later. He then trained hard until he crashed into his bed for the night, utterly exhausted.

He was woken long before the sun rose when Draflor, with an evil twinkle in his eyes, made a huge vortex of icy water encase Jackson while he slept.

# TRAVELING IN TEAMS

"GAAAAAH!!!" Jackson shot up from his bed and darted around for a minute while he tried to escape the icy water that Draflor made surge after him.
"Draflor stop it! I'm up, I'm up!" Jackson cried before he teleported himself into his bag. He popped out a moment later with a disapproving frown, forcefully using his magic to make a bubble of air around his torso and head before he lit a large number of flickering flames as he shivered.
Draflor snickered a bit while Leavamentee looked on thoughtfully.
"Hm… a bit unorthodox." She said primly, "but more effective than anything I've tried to wake him."
"Effective my tail…" Jackson grumbled unhappily as his skin started to thaw out a bit.
"Can you teach me how to do that, so we can wake him later?" Startide asked Draflor while she, Spinescale, Zepherdust, Blade, Shadowtorrent, and Daychaser peeked in the doorway. "We've all been trying to figure out a way to quickly wake Jackson up for months now, and nothing seems to consistently work."
"And that would've been useful a long time ago…" Zepherdust added with a small smile.
"I don't know if y'all could muster the ice magic for the job." Draflor smirked, ending his spell and letting the icy slush and miniature icebergs slowly rise towards the top of the room. "But I know a water spell that might do the trick, though I can't guarantee that'll work as fast."
Jackson gave him a tart look while he tried to rub feeling back into his tail. "Um, could you please not freeze me almost solid next time? Please!?"
"Not his fault, soldier." Leavamentee lifted a brow meaningfully. "It still took Draflor two minutes to wake you, if

freezing you solid is what it takes, then we'll do it every-time." She flipped around and headed towards the doorways while Jackson gave her an unhappy look. "Back in my day, no-one slept as deep as you do. Daychaser has your breakfast, eat it on your way to the meeting chamber. You leave in less than an hour."

After Leavamentee had left, Daychaser leaned over to Jackson. "You have no idea how much she used the phrase, 'In my day,' before you got here." He whispered. "It about drove us whirlpools."

"I stopped counting once I reached one hundred..." Startide added in a long-suffering tone.

"Could drive a shark to shore..." Blade grumbled.

"I imagine she's gotten worse since she's been locked down for two hundred years." Draflor commented thoughtfully. "She's saying it more often than I remember."

"Well, it could be worse I guess..." Jackson said. "Though I'll take it over a lady in my tribe who loved to try matchmaking. There wasn't a festival, celebration, or party where she wasn't trying to hook some girl and guy up, or convince some boy to dance with the girl she thought was 'perfect for him.'" He rolled his eyes. "It was terrible."

"Ugh!" Draflor winced. "You win, that would be much worse."

"Come on." Skycaller called as she quickly swam over with Avavo. "Oceaono and the medians briefing is about to start."

"Yeah, Granitebow and the others are already waiting for us." Avavo added.

Jackson was still shivering while he hurried after his friends as they rushed out into the hallway. As they quickly swam through the hold Daychaser tossed him a large lisheave, which Jackson quickly scarfed down while the others talked.

"I wonder how this'll all work?" Shadowtorrent asked. "I heard Depthcall mention that there's a lot of dishonored and some of the

# TRAVELING IN TEAMS

Fallen who are still looking for Jackson. Maybe they're sending us all out in one big team."

"It'd be nice if we all traveled together." Zepherdust said, giving Jackson, Daychaser, and Startide a warm smile. "It's been too long."

"It would be nice if we all traveled with each other..." Startide said, giving Jackson, Zepherdust, and the others a grin before she and Shadowtorrent locked gazes for a second.

Spinescale hmphed when she saw the two oroca blush. "I'm hoping they split us all up a bit..." She moved closer to Jackson before she muttered quietly to him. "The less lovey-dovey eyes the better."

"We'll find out soon enough." Draflor said as they entered the meeting chamber to find everyone waiting for them.

"Good." Oceaono nodded. "You're all here." He crossed his arms behind his back as he swam a bit higher in the water column. "As you all know." His voice carried strongly throughout the chamber. "There are a number of things that still need to be accomplished before we can free the Sonaeko Nation. On top of that, there is the threat of dishonored, the Toxicshade's tampering with ancient artifacts from the Steelserpent War, and the darkness that's... taking over parts of our seas." He took a deep breath. "Which... is why we'll be splitting everyone into teams."

"Teams?!" Jackson and his friends all asked in surprise before Leavamentee sternly shushed them.

"Depthcall." Oceaono said firmly. "You will be leading a team including the knights, your Whaleguard, ex-fallen, and other honorable whales who've joined us. You'll be taking a longer route that runs along the southeastern current before you turn up to the stronghold by Great Ghost point. On your way, you'll be looking into a couple matters that we'd like to keep private as of now."

# MYTHOS SEAS: MOVING SEAMOUNTS

"Shadowtorrent and Avavo, while I know you both wished to join your friend Jackson this trip, I'm sorry to say that won't be the case." Oceaono gave them a nod. "You will both be traveling with a mixed group of honorable creatures from here and the Mistsurge Outpost, who will take their own route before meeting up with Squallrunner and the seawolf podpacks..." He glanced over to Squallrunner. "Who are forming their own team, and once they regroup with you, you'll all combine with Depthcall's group at a later point."

"Blade." Oceaono gave Blade a quick look. "You'll be leading your own team, and taking a different route entirely. You'll be taking the most direct route, but arguably the most dangerous. It will be your team's responsibility to scout out potential dangers and problems along the way, and around Great Ghost Point once you reach it. You are to relay anything you find to Leavamentee, who will then warn the other teams."

"Startide, Zepherdust, and Daychaser." Oceaono gave them both a small smile. "You three have been a constant support to both us and Jackson this whole journey, and because of that, you will be going as your own team this time."

"HUH?!" Startide, Daychaser, Zepherdust, and Jackson all exchanged a confused look before looking back up at Oceaono.

"B-but..." Startide began. "We've always traveled with Jackson before..."

"And in a way you will." Oceaono smirked as he motioned to Koiwae, who came swimming forward with five odd looking gems that sparkled with a strange light. The water particles around the gems began glowing before they formed into shapes that made many of the creatures' gasp in surprise.

"As you can see." Oceaono said, motioning to the images of white-tailed boys—that bore only a passing resemblance to

# TRAVELING IN TEAMS

Jackson—as their forms solidified around the stones. "Each team will be taking one of these special gems along with them." He crossed his arms behind his back. "We're doing this to try and confuse and throw off any dishonored, or if the darkness proves to be..." He cleared his throat uneasily before he shook his head. "This will help keep the real whereabouts of Jackson a secret because...." He turned to Jackson. "You will be leading your own team, and taking a different route to the Point."

"Me?" Jackson pointed at himself in surprise. "But—"

Oceaono held up a hand to silence him. "Your team will consist of you, Draflor, and Spinescale." Oceaono smiled at Jackson's reaction before he gently cleared his throat. "You will be taking a route to the Stronghold that should get you there after Blade, but around the same time as the other teams. You'll be taking a route that's more about stealth than speed."

He let out a sigh. "We want to make sure that there are as many reports of you all over the eastern Centurian Sea as possible, so dishonored creatures and other forces are left confused and unaware of where to look first. Your team will head out second to last, Draflor is already aware of the route and will show you it as you go."

Jackson glanced over at Draflor who gave him a small, slightly apologetic smile, but didn't respond as Oceaono continued. "Depthcall, your team will enter the portal pool first, please make sure to report back as soon as possible on your findings."

"Affirmative." Depthcall said before she headed towards the exit. "My team and I will leave immediately." She let out a long loud bellow as she left the meeting chamber, and Jackson watched as a huge group of creatures quickly followed after her. Granitebow gave Jackson and the others a quick farewell before he rushed after them, falling into place next to his brother.

# MYTHOS SEAS: MOVING SEAMOUNTS

Only a minute later, the group Shadowtorrent and Avavo were a part of, suddenly began gathering and they quickly said goodbye to Jackson and the others. Avavo and Zepherdust exchanged a fond smile while Shadowtorrent and Startide gave each other a quick head rub.

Startide was blushing a bit as Shadowtorrent and Avavo left, that is until she noticed Jackson, Daychaser, and Draflor smirking at her.

"What?" She asked, turning a little red in embarrassment while Zepherdust got a small, knowing smile on her snout.

"Nothing…" Daychaser smirked a bit. "Tell me, how many dates has he taken you on?"

Startide blushed even deeper when Draflor, Skycaller, and Jackson snickered a bit, while Spinescale just scowled in annoyance.

Squallrunner' group moved out next. The seawolf let out a loud ringing call to gather the members of his podpack who were going, as well as two other podpacks who had joined the Sonaekian cause. Daychaser swam forward to give his father and the rest of his family a quick goodbye which made Jackson's eyes water a bit.

Daychaser and Skycaller gave each other a quick tail slap and she smiled warmly at him before she followed after the others. Daychaser watched her go with a slightly dreamy look in his eyes, which he quickly removed when he saw Startide and Zepherdust watching him with smug expressions.

"Uh… what?"

"Oh you know, **nothing**…" Startide said slyly.

"So Daychaser, how many dates have you taken her on?" Zepherdust added, a similarly sly look in her eyes.

"WHAT?" Daychaser turned deep red in embarrassment, and Jackson raised a brow in interest while Draflor, and this time

# TRAVELING IN TEAMS

Spinescale, chuckled. "N-none... I'm not old enough for that... and she's... just... a friend..." He muttered defensively, his cheeks still burning as Startide and Zepherdust got smug looks in their eyes when he glanced away.

"Mm hmm, suuure that's what they all say." Startide giggled as she and Zepherdust slapped fins. Daychaser turned to glare at them while Jackson smirked a bit, wondering how long it'd be until Daychaser was old enough to take Skycaller on a date.

"Another two years." Draflor whispered and Jackson gave him a startled look.

"How'd you know?" Jackson whispered back.

"I could see it in your expression." Draflor snickered until Sharval motioned for Blade who saluted to Jackson and the others before he swam off to join his team.

Jackson shifted his bag on his shoulders as Stonecurrent looked over to him and grinned. "Your turn."

"Bye you guys." Jackson's voice caught a bit as he hugged Startide, Zepherdust, and Daychaser. "See you soon."

"Be careful." Startide said as Daychaser and Zepherdust nodded.

"Can't guarantee that..." Spinescale hissed in amusement. "This is Jackson we're talking about."

Jackson gave Spinescale a blank look before he swam out towards the hallway, heading down towards the largest cavern in the sanctuary. When the doors to the main cavern opened, he was met with the sight of buildings, statues, and petrified coral gardens that coated the seafloor. The buildings and statues glimmered in the early morning glow of the sunlight stones.

As they swam towards the far side of the cavern, Jackson could see the whipfins had gathered to send them off. He glanced over when Stonecurrent and some of the others suddenly floated up alongside him.

Stonecurrent must've noticed the confused look on Jackson's face, because he gave Jackson a questioning look. "Why the look Jackson?"

"I was just wondering…" He began. "I've heard of teleportation spells, portals, doors, and even a window." Jackson tilted his head sideways. "And Spinescale, Zepherdust, and the others have talked about teleportation pools, but what exactly are they? And how do they work underwater?"

Everyone went silent for a moment before Stonecurrent laughed. "I guess I've been trapped away at the bottom of the sea too long. I forgot that someone born on land might find the concept strange." He looked over at Leavamentee who came floating over. "Shall we show him?"

"That's why we're here." Leavamentee said dryly, giving Stonecurrent a half-lidded look. "Or did you have some other way to teleport them across the sea?"

"If I did, I wouldn't of bothered helping you get the pool set-up." Stonecurrent responded wryly. "Where's your sense of humor old girl?"

"Don't have time for it." Leavamentee said firmly and swam on ahead, ignoring the dubious look that Draflor and Stonecurrent exchanged at her reply. The manatee led the group through a tall, wide archway that led into a giant room and Jackson gasped.

A huge, highly detailed map decorated the entire spherical chamber, which was crisscrossed with runes and lines showing ocean currents, air currents, and even magical ones that pulsed across the map. Around the huge room there were a couple of large dark purple pools of liquid that danced in large basins which floated around in the middle of the water column.

# TRAVELING IN TEAMS

Jackson was surprised to still see Blade and his team in the room, and when he turned around, he saw Startide, Zepherdust, and Daychaser come up behind them.

Startide's eyes widened when she saw the teleportation pool. "Is this what a pool of water looks like from above?" She asked Jackson.

"Yep, although why is it purple?" Jackson asked.

"This is a special type of magically enchanted liquid used only by the Sonaeko for teleportation spells." Koiwae came up beside Startide. "The enchantments turn it a purple color, and when magic is coursing through it, you'll see beautiful streams of brilliant gold flowing inside." He looked over at Jackson. "Some land dwellers would say it looks like glowing honey."

"What's honey?" Blade asked, looking back at them as the portal began to glow.

"A type of sweet tasting liquid made by bugs called bees." Draflor said. "Humans and many other land-dwelling creatures love to eat it."

"Humans get weirder and weirder..." Blade grumbled.

"Hey, I can hear you, you know." Jackson called.

"Do the portals only lead to specific places?" Daychaser asked.

"Each portal is set up with a magical connection to a sister portal in another location." Oceaono gestured to the map covering the walls. "Mostly to major cities, holds, and sanctuaries, but certain portals can also send you to areas around special towers that were built in places without major cities and the like."

"Uh… then why not just send us to where we need to go to fix this mess?" Spinescale suggested as Blade and his team suddenly dove through the gold-gilded purple waters.

"We would if we could, but the force of the Great Petrifying either destroyed or disrupted the teleportation pools that were located beyond the Great Abyssal drop off." Koiwae answered with a frown. "It seems only those in these more protected waters were able to survive the destructive forces of the Great Petrifying. I'm afraid we can only send you to a finful of places."

The gold streams of color in the pools suddenly died down after Blade and his team had vanished and Draflor gave Leavamentee a startled look. "What's wrong?"

"Not enough power to keep it on constantly." Leavamentee answered with a tight, disapproving frown. "That's why we're spacing you all out so much, the sanctuary is still recovering from all the years of damage and neglect."

"Jackson!"

While Leavamentee drew more power in preparation to reopen the portal pool, Serphere, Longspar, Slickhide, Traildrop, Flashtail and some of the other whipfins came hurrying over.

"Here." Serphere handed Jackson a large dead fullbud lisheave. "For the trip, don't forget to get enough to eat as you travel." She said in a mothering tone as she and the other whipfins quickly said their goodbyes.

"Be careful son." Longspar said firmly.

"And thanks for everything." Flashtail added.

"Don't be stupid." Slickhide yawned before he was slapped by Traildrop.

"What he means..." She gave him a tart look. "Is, be careful."

"We're rooting and praying for you." Serphere said kindly. "Come back to see us soon."

"Jackson!" Leavamentee called. "You and your team are up, soldier. Hurry it up."

"Coming." Jackson quickly grabbed the whipfins in a hug. "Bye you guys and thank you."

# TRAVELING IN TEAMS

Jackson took a deep breath as he came up to the portal and gave Draflor a quick look. He gave him an encouraging nod and Jackson's mouth tightened into a determined line before he swam upwards and quickly dove into the swirling gold and purple liquid. As the magical liquid flowed around him, Jackson felt like he was swimming through space and time before he suddenly burst out from a gently spinning pool into the bright morning light. As he turned and looked behind him, he saw the magical waters suddenly seem to evaporate away and frowned uncertainly. "Where's the tower?"

"I was just about to ask the same question." Spinescale piped up, searching the clear waters around them. "I don't see nothin that looks Sonaekian made."

"The tower is probably quite far away." Draflor commented as his magical map came spiraling out to fill the water around them. "It's really just a magical crystal spire that allows teleportation pools to open up anywhere within a set distance around it." He moved a couple glowing dots around on the map. "Oceaono and the others were planning to teleport us as far as they could to the west of the tower."

"Jackson, you guys get there ok?"

Jackson looked down as his glove flashed a bit before the form of Stonecurrent appeared. "Yep, we're good." Jackson replied. "Draflor's just getting his mapping spell ready."

"Excellent." Stonecurrent smiled. "Then I won't keep you, good luck, and check in with me soon." His form promptly vanished away, and Jackson glanced over at Draflor.

"You got it?"

"Yes-sir." Draflor grinned at him as the map grew slightly bigger and he pointed southwards. "Let's get moving, I'll show you the route as we go."

# MYTHOS SEAS: MOVING SEAMOUNTS

"Then come on!" Spinescale urged as she wrapped her tail around Jackson's backpack. "Let's go."

Jackson activated his quick current spell and shot off through the water. As they traveled, Draflor helped Jackson and Spinescale learn their route and where they were supposed to stop and check in with the medians and guardians. They took quick stops throughout the day so Jackson could refresh his magical reserves and rest. However, while they were traveling, Jackson and Spinescale were awed by the immense size and breadth of the great underwater seagrass prairies they were quickly traveling over.

As a day of travel turned into four, Jackson had seen a large number of creatures who called the oceanic prairies home. There were herds of dugongs and other manatee like creatures, beautiful sea turtles, tiger sharks and a wide assortment of fish that had watched curiously as Jackson had sped past.

Very early the morning of the fifth day, Jackson and his friends were shooting over another large stretch of the never-ending underwater grasslands when Jackson saw something that made him pause a moment.

"Are those hippocampi?" He asked once he noticed a huge herd of creatures not too far off while the sun began peeking over the horizon.

"Hm?" Draflor poked his head out of the staff while Spinescale roused herself from a nap inside Jackson's backpack.

"Strangest looking horses I've ever seen…" Spinescale hissed groggily, still trying to shake the sleep from her eyes.

Draflor laughed. "They're a closely related species, but…" He shook his head. "They look a **little** different than normal horses."

"No kidding…" Jackson whispered when he saw one had a bright orange coat with green stripes up its forelegs and along the long fin at the end of its powerful tail.

# TRAVELING IN TEAMS

Some of the other hippocampi had more normal colored coats, but others had more striking colors like green, yellow, and even red. There also seemed to be a wide range of patterns that Jackson had never seen on normal horses, and he shook his head before he activated his own map spell to check his course. "Is that what Thorra would've looked like if he'd used the spell Koiwae had talked about?"

"No..." Draflor shook his head. "The spell Koiwae was talking about is basically the same spell you used to awaken as a waterborn, or in your case, a lightborn." He flipped a page in the book he was reading. "Thorra would've awoken with a tail of some type of ocean creature he had a strong connection to." He glanced over at the herd as Jackson reactivated his quick current spell and shot off. "Though, horses only ever awaken as fish, dolphin, manatee, shark, or whaleborn, or maybe an icthyoborn or some other sea reptile, though I'd have to check a couple records to confirm that last one." His eyes returned to his book. "You'll never see a horse awaken as a crabborn or octopusborn for example, don't ask me why though, that's just how it's always worked."

Jackson hummed thoughtfully as he flew past a large group of dugongs, some of whom lifted their heads quickly, strands of seagrass still in their mouths as they watched him race off. "Are hippocampi just descendants of horses that became waterborn?"

"Not... that I know of." Draflor frowned a bit as he quickly licked the tip of his fin before using it to turn another page. "I think they came into being not long after the Creation, when there was still all that wild elemental magic that changed some of the first humans into the elves, dwarves, and fairies and the like." He hmphed thoughtfully. "That was a few centuries or more before awakening magic was discovered by humans, though the aspects themselves had been aware of and guarding the magic for a long time."

"Forgive me…" Spinescale asked, looking completely lost, "but what exactly are the aspects again?"

"I don't know if I've ever been told either…" Jackson added as he swerved around a huge rocky outcropping. "Though I know I'm guarding and helping them, I don't really know what they are."

Draflor gave Jackson a stunned look before he huffed a bit in amusement. "Well… first time for everything I guess." His book snapped shut before he reached over to grab another one out of seemingly nowhere. "The aspects are ancient creatures created by the Creator to maintain balance of the world's magic and to preserve the creatures connected to those magics."

He opened the new book and quickly leafed through it. "Each element had a specific aspect species tied to it, though I'm a bit fuzzy on the names of the species themselves." He flipped his book around to show an image of the whole world of Mythos with a large number of animal shaped symbols around it.

"Huh…" Spinescale puffed as Jackson lifted a brow curiously. "I wonder why I've never heard of them before?"

"The knowledge was likely lost with the Great Petrifying." Draflor said sadly. "As was the Alliance of Aspect Guardians, a group of people from many races and nations who helped the aspects in their tasks." He flipped the page to show a number of people of many different races who stood in different positions. Each person had a glowing symbol connected to a specific element above their hands. "From what I've gleaned, the Great Petrifying also wiped out the other nations who were allied to the Sonaeko, including the elves, dwarves and other races." He brought the book back over to him as he flipped a page. "Those races were all once a

# TRAVELING IN TEAMS

part of the huge alliance known as The United Nations of Nature's Balance."

"That would explain a few things." Jackson muttered, cautiously soaring closer to the surface when he saw a large tiger—that had a strong shark-like tail instead of back legs—patrolling the seagrass prairie below. "I haven't heard of any elves or dwarves since before the war. I know they fled these western lands during the war, but then they were never heard of more."

"Wait…" Spinescale's eyes widened. "Are you saying that the fate of all those nations and races depends on…" She gave Jackson a long look. "Um, us?"

Jackson groaned, slowing slightly when he suddenly felt an already immense weight of responsibility increase on his shoulders.

Draflor winced. "Sorry… that's why the medians and I never brought it up before, we didn't want to stress you more."

"It's ok." Jackson muttered as he gave a passing glance at his map to see if he was still on course. "Is that why no-one is telling me about the darkness either?"

Draflor went quiet for a minute. "Probably, but I don't know."

"Do you know what it is?" Spinescale asked shrewdly, eyeing Draflor intently.

"Maybe." Draflor answered, "but I'm not completely sure, and I'm not risking Oceaono's ire by worrying you guys with what I've heard and my theory." His focus returned to another book as Jackson let his spell end when he neared a large rocky outcropping.

Spinescale slithered out of her place in Jackson's backpack as he clambered out of the water and settled in on the large outcropping to rest and have an early breakfast. After he and Spinescale were settled, Jackson sat his backpack down and vanished into the larger of his two bags.

## MYTHOS SEAS: MOVING SEAMOUNTS

He stretched before he dove around the newly established lisheave jungle to look for something to eat. Quickly selecting some fronds from a kelp-like variety of lisheave and a large fullbud one for himself, Jackson then nabbed a good sized fullbud for Spinescale. He surfaced and was just about to teleport back out when the aspect stones flashed out of his hands.

"Huh?" Jackson blinked in surprise as the stones twirled around him and he laid the lisheave down on the shore. "What's up? Are you guys wanting to do a training session now?"

"No, there isn't time." The Earthcore said gruffly. "Though we would've liked to get more training in before now."

"We actually have something we need to tell you." The Windspiral said, a melodic soft feminine voice ringing out from the crystal.

"Now that Draflor has told you more about what the aspects are…" The Star of the Sea continued. "We felt like we needed to let you know that, as one who guards aspects and the crystals they're bonded with, a status that was once known as an aspect guardian, you have the ability to borrow our power."

"Or a portion of it." The Earthcore added dryly. "Depends on the situation."

"But you can only ask to borrow our power when you truly need it, and we must approve before we share it with you." The Windspiral said.

Jackson's eyes widened and he nodded. "Oh, ok."

"We realize this is a bit out of the blue, but we felt it best to tell you now." The Star of the Sea said. "You won't likely have any down time to speak with us here soon, there is too much at stake."

"Remember our words and the things we've taught ya." The Earthcore said before the stones all spiraled towards Jackson's hands.

## TRAVELING IN TEAMS

"Good luck, we're here when you need us." The Windspiral said before they vanished into Jackson's hands.

## CHAPTER FIVE
# FROM THE SEAGULL'S BEAK

"Oooo!" Spinescale hissed in delight when Jackson teleported himself back out and held the smaller lisheave out to her. "Don't mind if I do."

Jackson winced when she suddenly struck before dragging the lisheave back into her coils. Gulping slightly and feeling a touch ill, Jackson moved off to the side to cook his own lisheave while Spinescale worked on swallowing hers. After Jackson had settled in to eat his own breakfast, he saw Draflor come out from the staff curiously.

"Why'd you go into the bag?" Draflor asked. "You know you can just use the crystals in the seafloor around the bag to look inside and see what's swimming around them."

"I know." Jackson said before he took a big bite out of his own breakfast. "But I like going in to harvest it myself if I can."
*Although I wasn't expecting the aspect stones to appear when I was there...*

"Huh, well to all their own." Draflor grinned before he glanced up to the rocks above them and frowned. "Looks like we could have some visitors…"

# FROM THE SEAGULL'S BEAK

"And I'm glad my meal is already finished." Spinescale said wryly while she came slithering over, a large bulge around her middle. "I don't care to share with seagulls." She muttered as she followed Draflor's gaze to a few seabirds who were busy arguing over a scrap of something on the top of the outcropping.

Jackson inched back to hide what was left of his own meal from the greedy gulls. The birds screamed loudly as they fought for the piece of food before a giant shadow fell over them and they scattered.

"Albatross!" One of the gulls shouted before a huge white bird dove into the throng and snatched up the morsel the gulls were squabbling over. Jackson and his friends watched while the large bird swallowed the treat smugly before it soared away, a couple of gulls angrily flying after it.

"Stupid albatross…" One of the gulls muttered sourly. "I fought hard to catch that fish earlier."

"It'd be easier if those ships we saw heading to the island hadn't been poisoning the food they threw over!" Another gull grumbled and Jackson's eyes widened curiously.

"Humph, I hate that nation, always making life harder on us wiser creatures." Another gull spat before he took wing. "I'm heading out to try and see if there's a meal somewhere else."

A few other gulls took flight and followed after the first, all except one, who was looking around the outcropping stubbornly, as if hoping a tiny piece of flesh had been dropped. One of the other gulls swooped back and called to the lone gull questioningly.

"Hey Blistercall, you comin?"

"In a minute, I'm sure I saw a piece of that fish fall around here somewhere…" The black headed gull replied quickly while he pecked around.

## MYTHOS SEAS: MOVING SEAMOUNTS

"Suit yourself." The other gull called before it flew off. "Don't blame me if you miss out on something better!"

"I'd of had something better if those horrid Toxicshade ships hadn't poisoned those stale rolls." The gull muttered.

"WHO?!" Jackson exclaimed and the gull let out a loud cry before flying into the air.

"Aaaand you scared it off." Spinescale smirked. "I'm not sure if I'm disappointed or thrilled."

"Don't shed your skin yet." Draflor said, pointing to the gull who had circled back with a suspicious look in his eyes. "He's coming back."

Jackson closed his eyes so he could use his connection to his new bag to see into the ocean inside it. After a second, he found what he was after and looked up at the gull hopefully when a fullbud lisheave appeared in his hands. Settling down on the rock, Jackson slowly watched as the gull's eyes gleamed hungrily while he dove closer.

"Hungry?" Jackson asked when the gull got within hearing range and shook the lisheave temptingly in his hands.

"Humph, he has no idea." The gull muttered to himself, unaware that Jackson could understand him.

Jackson smirked. "I might have a slight idea."

The gull let out a shocked cry and flew back a bit, giving Jackson a piercing look. "Can you understand me?"

"I can." Jackson said, tossing the lisheave on the ground in front of him. "And I'm more than willing to share my food with you, though I'd ask you to tell me more about these ships you and the other gulls were complaining about."

"Deal!" The gull darted down and began tearing into the lisheave hungrily. "We saw the ships a few days ago." The gull began between large beak-fulls of flesh. "Oh this is good. Mm, the

# FROM THE SEAGULL'S BEAK

ships..." He ripped off a fin and swallowed it. "Were from the Venom Nations, Toxicshade vessels." He took another large bite. "Horrid people, have no respect for seabirds." He squawked contently as he dug into the lisheave, making Jackson wince a bit. "Don't know where they're going, but they stopped at a large island a little over a day or two's flight from here and seemed to be staying to try and stock up before sailing to feathers knows where."

Jackson and his friends exchanged a quick look before Jackson turned back to the gull. "Would you be willing to lead us to this island?"

The gull stopped eating long enough to give Jackson a searching look with its beady black eyes. "What's in it for me?" He asked before diving back into his meal.

"Another meal." Draflor said, picking up on where Jackson was going. "We have lisheave even bigger than that one."

"Could take a few days to get there..." The gull said betwixt bites, a shrewd look in his eyes. "I'll need more food to get me through the trip."

"You said around a day or two's flight from here." Jackson responded firmly. "I'm willing to give you a small meal for the first day of travel, and then a very large final meal as payoff for your help if there are actually Toxicshade ships at this island you talked about."

"Final offer." Spinescale added quickly. "I doubt you'll find a better deal anywhere else out here."

The sly look in the gull's eyes didn't diminish while he seemed to consider the offer. "Oh, very well." He answered. "I agree, but only if the final payoff is bigger than this one!" He greedily dug into what remained of the lisheave as Jackson rolled his eyes.

"Fine, do we have a deal?" Jackson asked.

"We do." The gull burped before he promptly sat down on the hard stone, his stomach bugling. "And I'll start leading you there, right after I can digest enough to get myself airborne."

"Should I threaten to eat him if he doesn't hurry it up?" Spinescale whispered to Draflor and Jackson when Blistercall's eyes half closed while he dozed.

"Best not push it." Draflor sighed. "I think we'll have our fins full just making sure he doesn't try to lead us on a wild goose chase in the hopes of getting another free meal."

"Well hopefully we won't have to wait too long..." Jackson whispered.

As it turned out, the group had to wait until nearly lunchtime before Blistercall finished "digesting" his meal and finally began leading them towards the island. Jackson swiftly kept up with the gull for the rest of the day, using his magic to race just under the surface of the waves. However, when night fell, he found he had to use his water travel spell to fly just over the surface so he could see the bird, and come morning he was utterly exhausted.

Draflor helped him with his spells until the group took a quick stop for lunchtime and Jackson tossed a hand sized lisheave up to Blistercall, who quickly tore it apart. Jackson had a feeling the gull would've complained about the size of the lisheave if he hadn't noticed Spinescale glaring at his feathered hide intently, as if she was daring him to complain and see how it worked out for him.

Jackson was just finishing up his own meal when he heard an oddly familiar sounding call and quickly dunked his head under the water.

# FROM THE SEAGULL'S BEAK

"Startide?" Jackson asked as he submerged to see Startide, Daychaser, Zepherdust, and the fake crystal Jackson, who was hanging onto Startide's dorsal fin, rushing towards them.
"Are you guys ok?" Startide called worriedly when they neared. "I detected you with my magic just this morning."
"Yeah, and you guys are way off course." Daychaser added in concern.
"We really shouldn't of been able to find you this easy." Zepherdust said, mirroring Daychaser's concerned look as she swooped closer.
"We're following a lead on the Toxicshade." Spinescale answered, pointing up to Blistercall as he circled them. "Jackson wants to see if this other fleet some gulls were talking about has more weapons or info on what they're planning."
"Oh..." Startide glanced up to the circling bird with a conflicted expression. "Well. Ok."
"That explains why you veered so far off course..." Zepherdust followed Startide's gaze.
Daychaser gave Jackson a once over before he squinted his eyes suspiciously. "Let me guess, you didn't sleep at all last night, did you?"
Jackson grimaced, shrugging sheepishly before a traitorous yawn escaped his throat. "Is it that obvious?"
Startide, Zepherdust, and Daychaser locked gazes for a minute before Startide huffed a bit, letting out a little squee before she swam over to Jackson. "Grab on, we'll help you follow the gull to the island so you can get a bit of sleep."
"How long do you have to go?" Daychaser asked as Jackson gratefully came over and strapped himself in on the opposite side of the fake Jackson.

## MYTHOS SEAS: MOVING SEAMOUNTS

"Another day…" Draflor looked up at Blistercall. "If the gull doesn't try to stall for another free snack."

"A free snack?" Zepherdust asked.

"We'll explain after I let him know we're ready to continue." Spinescale hissed before she untangled herself from Jackson's backpack and hurried up to the surface. After she'd called to Blistercall she hurried back to dive into Jackson's backpack while Startide let out a creaking sound and hurried after the seabird. As Draflor and Spinescale filled the others in, Jackson gratefully closed his eyes and passed out.

## CHAPTER SIX
# ANCIELLON ISLE

The following morning, after a wonderful night's sleep, Jackson was slowly following the seagull: the others a few tail lengths behind him as the bird dipped and soared above the choppy waves.

"You sure he knows where he's going?" Spinescale asked from her place on Jackson's pack. "This seems like an odd way to go to find an island."

"I agree, there isn't a single tall seamount for hundreds of whale lengths." Startide said as she sounded the seafloor with her magic before she peered up at the bird doubtfully. "I still think we're being led into trouble; seagulls aren't known for their honesty."

Jackson rolled his eyes. "I doubt Blistercall would be lying to us about where some of the Toxicshade had stopped to gather supplies. I know the seabirds back home hated the Toxicshade for poisoning some of their fellow birds, and these ones here had a similar story."

"Besides, what would a seagull get from leading us astray? I mean, beyond a free meal. They're only truly loyal to their own kind, or sea magi from what I understand." Daychaser said as he dove back into the water.

# MYTHOS SEAS: MOVING SEAMOUNTS

"I'm sure it'll be fine." Zepherdust said, spinning around Startide swiftly. "It's not like we couldn't get away easily if things go south."

Jackson quickly swam up to the surface and shot into the air, using his water travel magic to dart up next to the black headed seagull.

"Squa!!" Blistercall flapped away from Jackson before giving him a long look. "Can you warn me before you do that?" He insisted. "I'm not used to humanoids flying into my aircurrent."

"Sorry." Jackson gave him a sheepish smile and lifted his shoulders in an apologetic shrug. "I was just wondering where we're going exactly? Startide said something about there not being any large seamounts for quite a ways."

Blistercall gave a creaking laugh. "That's the problem with you surface dwellers, you have no sense of imagination." He got a smug, slightly haughty look in his eye. "We aren't going to a normal island. Anciellon Isle isn't a seamount."

Jackson blinked, a perplexed expression sweeping over his face. "Huh? Then what is it?"

The gull snickered. "That for me to know, and you surface dwellers to find out."

Jackson and the others fell silent for a moment.

"Ok, when do you think we'll get there then?" Jackson asked.

"A few slides of the sun past midday." Blistercall's shrewd beady eyes drifted over to a group of gulls in the distance. "Provided, they aren't heading to a feeding gathering."

Jackson gave the gull a scathing glance which the bird returned with a stubborn look. "What? A bird has to eat."

"And yet just the other day you ate so much you couldn't take off." Draflor moved to Jackson's right and gave the gull a sly smirk.

# ANCIELLON ISLE

"Surely you aren't trying to get Jackson to give you an extra free meal, are you? I seem to recall that wasn't the deal."

The gull muttered under his breath. "Fine, we'll get there before noon, but I'm getting a big one of those lisheave you got before we part ways."

"Only after we see the Toxicshade ships in the harbor." Jackson said firmly. "I'm not trying to be rude, but that was the deal. We're going way off course coming this way, and I'm only doing this to try and find out why the Toxicshade Emperor is bringing artifacts from the Steelserpent War to the old battlefields."

"And if there's no Toxicshade there won't be any information to find, so we're heading off and you're not getting another free meal." Spinescale hissed, sounding a touch angry.

"Ok, ok, I get it." The gull flew ahead, grumbling under his breath.

Jackson let out a quiet sigh, "some creatures kids…" He closed his eyes and let himself drop back to the sea.

"You're telling me." Spinescale added before they splashed back under the water.

"So, what did the greedy gull say?" Daychaser asked while they all picked up the pace to keep up with Blistercall.

"We should get there about noon, now that he knows we won't be willing to give him a free lunch if he tries to stall." Draflor grinned. "Poor thing, acts like he hasn't had a good meal in hours, he must be starving."

"Oh yeah, poor thing." Startide rolled her eyes. "I'm sure he'll wither away to nothing."

Jackson, Zepherdust, and Daychaser chuckled, while a small smirk shone in Spinescale's eyes.

They followed the gull dutifully for the rest of the morning until he let out a call to Jackson as he dropped to just above the surface. After a quick nod to his friends Jackson quickly shot out of the water to see what was going on.

"See the spot of green up ahead? That's Anciellon Isle." Blistercall soared upwards a bit when Daychaser and Startide began breaching to listen in as Zepherdust porpoised next to them. "It's one of the largest isles on the centurion sea."

"Isn't it the home of the Centel Nation?" Jackson felt a light orb go off in his mind, "and that's why it's not an actual seamount."

"Wondered how long it'd take for one of you to figure it out." Blistercall continued after an exasperated squark. "Yes, its home to the Centel's, they've lived in this part of the sea for a few years now."

"Mind filling the rest of us in?" Startide asked as she soared out of the water.

"Yes, I don't think I've ever heard of the Centel's." Zepherdust added.

"The Centel Nation's island is famous for being the only floating island in the Centurian Sea." Jackson said. "No one knows how or why it floats, though some say the island itself is alive and moves around the sea on its own. Others claim that the Centel's control where the island goes, and that they move their island to the best areas for trading."

"Weird..." Daychaser seemed curious. "The island doesn't stay in one place then?"

"Sometimes for a few days, sometimes for months, sometimes for years." Blistercall cut in. "Can I have my lunch n..." His voice dropped out when both Spinescale and the others stared at him disapprovingly, making him close his beak and keep flying towards the island.

# ANCIELLON ISLE

Jackson looked over at Draflor, who had gone uncharacteristically quiet all of the sudden. "Something wrong Draflor?"

"Hm?" Draflor's eyes lost their faraway look. "Oh, nothing, don't worry about it. Something about this whole Anciellon Isle just sounds familiar that's all." He vanished back into the staff, muttering something about going back to read some old texts.

The group stuck close to Blistercall as the island got bigger and bigger and Jackson could see the signs of large rivers and waterfalls. He marveled at the strangely shaped mountain on the southern side of the island while the group neared the shoreline. A few minutes later they all submerged when a large ship sailed by, heading for a bustling line of docks up ahead.

"The Toxicshade ships are on the east side of the harbor." Blistercall said after he perched on Startide's dorsal fin once the group slowed down when they neared a large port.

"Zepherdust and I will go check it out, you guys wait here." Daychaser said before they both swept off into the blue.

Jackson peeked out of the water to get a better look at the harbor and the huge number of ships that were traveling around it. "Looks like a trading port all right." He groaned once he made out the movements of crowds of people milling about the docks and streets.

"Not one for big cities I take it?" Draflor asked as he came popping out of the staff, a book floating in the water next to him.

Jackson shook his head. "I've always hated them, too many people, too much going on, and there's always trouble."

## MYTHOS SEAS: MOVING SEAMOUNTS

"Hm, no argument there, although I love visiting libraries in large cities, good reading." Draflor looked back at his book and made a tisking noise before another one appeared next to him. "Maybe it's in this one."

"Mind if I take a look?" Startide asked. "I take it you're looking for any mention of this Anciellon Isle?"

Draflor nodded. "Or anything about Anciellon, the name sounds familiar to me for some reason." A book appeared in front of Startide's snout which she began eagerly looking through. She'd maybe gone through three pages when Zepherdust came shooting over, swiftly followed by Daychaser.

"We found them!" Zepherdust called as Daychaser nodded.

"There's a number of ships with the Toxicshade insignia on their hulls on the far side of the harbor." Daychaser gave the gull a dip of his snout. "The gull was right."

"Of course I was." Blistercall looked offended. "What could possibly give you any idea otherwise?"

"How about—" Spinescale was stopped by a raised hand from Jackson before he teleported a very large fullbud lisheave from his pack.

He quickly checked to make sure it wasn't going to seed before he held it out to the gull. "Thank you Blistercall, here's our end of the deal."

The gull gave a greedy scream as he swooped over and snatched the lisheave from Jackson's hand, taking off into the sky towards the open sea.

"Good riddance." Spinescale said with a puff.

Draflor looked up from his book with a rueful smirk. "Don't count on him not coming back. I can already hear the other seabirds who've noticed his prize. He'll be lucky to keep it all to himself."

# ANCIELLON ISLE

"Should we head off towards the ships then?" Daychaser watched the flurry of a small group of seabirds as they took off from the docks and rushed in the direction Blistercall was flying. "If we stay here, they might swarm us, hoping for a handout of their own."

"Good enough reason for me." Startide nosed the book back to Draflor.

"Me too." Zepherdust added, flipping around. "Come on, we'll show you what we found."

"Hold on." Jackson's eyes slitted when he saw a white bird swoop towards the small group of seabirds.

"What's wrong? Just another seabird." Spinescale slithered off his shoulder and began swimming in the direction Daychaser and Zepherdust had returned from, "and I've had enough of those to last me for a shed or two."

Jackson watched suspiciously while the large white bird swiftly soared above the flock of seabirds. "That's no seabird..." He said before the bird dove into the flock, causing them to scatter in all directions with wild screeching calls. The attack revealed a small black bird that had been hidden in the seabirds' midst and the large white bird immediately snatched it from the air.

"What in the currents?" The book Draflor was reading snapped shut as he watched.

The white bird reached down with its large beak and plucked something off the struggling black bird. It suddenly let its captive go, a trail of black feathers scattering from the little bird when it careened away.

"What's going on?" Daychaser asked as the white bird flew back towards the island.

"That's a gleam eagle." Jackson swam forward to try and see where the bird was flying to. "They're very rare and only attach themselves to light mages…" He frowned, "and I think that one just stole something from a messenger bird."

"Couldn't it just be hunting here?" Startide asked.

"No, it definitely took something from that bird." Draflor said, "and if I remember correctly, wild gleam eagles never live this close to villages and cities. They like high mountains or isolated valleys."

Spinescale suddenly shuddered. "Please tell me we aren't going after that thing; I can't stand eagles."

Jackson felt bad for Spinescale, who had been hunted by eagles before. He shook his head. "No, I don't think it concerns us, it's just… odd."

Draflor flicked his fins in agreement. "Very odd."

"Well, we aren't gonna find any information just floating here." Daychaser swam around them before making his way back into the dock. "Come-on, I think you'll want to see what we found."

Jackson and the others followed Daychaser and Zepherdust deeper into the harbor, Startide slowly dodging a large piece of floating debris.

"This harbor is a lot dirtier than the one at the Jewel Isles…" She ducked beneath a large crate hanging low in the water. "Don't they ever clean up after themselves?"

"I remember some of my distant relatives saying that the harbors humans trade at aren't known for being very clean…" Daychaser spun lazily around a barnacle encrusted beam that was holding up an end to one of the docks.

"A harbor my family used to trade at was worse than this, but it was owned by a clan that joined up with the Toxicshade so…" Jackson shrugged.

"I wonder if it was the one my mom told me about…" Zepherdust mused as she dodged away from what looked like a

algae covered blanket that was being swept around in the current.
"She said she'd been to one once that was absolutely filthy."
"Lot of good places to hide though." Spinescale suddenly vanished through a hole in a large sunken barrel only to dart out with a startled hiss when an annoyed lobster chased her off, snapping his claws angrily.
"No snoopin missy! This is my barrel!"
"Hmph! Wasn't looking for a home, just a snack." Spinescale hissed as she darted back over to the others.
"You ok?" Zepherdust asked.
"I'm fine." Spinescale did her version of an eyeroll. "I'm just not used to such big lobsters, I've seen a couple giant crabs, but no lobsters that large."
The group wound their way over to where six huge ships were marooned, slowly drifting up and down in the gentle current of the harbor.
"I didn't expect six of these ships…" Jackson whispered, looking at the purple, black, red, and gold painted into the markings on their hulls. "These are some of the emperor's royal fleet."
"There's more." Daychaser led them over to where the largest ship was docked and pointed to the large number of men on board with his snout. "There was a break in the men earlier, and I saw some strange looking thing behind them. I don't know what it was though."
"I wasn't able to see anything except soldiers on the other boats…" Zepherdust added.
Jackson watched the guards quietly for a minute, they were all wearing the armor of the Toxicshade's elite force.
"What'cha thinking?" Spinescale gave Jackson a tap with her tail.

# MYTHOS SEAS: MOVING SEAMOUNTS

"I... don't know..." Jackson glanced back at the other ships. "But those are some of the emperor's elite, if they're here and all heading the same way the other ships are..."

"Then they're planning something big." Draflor finished. "The question is, what?"

"Should I sneak aboard and do a bit of spying?" Spinescale giggled enthusiastically, "and maybe have a bit of fun while I'm up there?"

Jackson shook his head. "They'd likely kill you if they saw you." He looked up to see the sun hovering in the sky. "I think I'd better try to do a fly over tonight, maybe I can see what Daychaser saw. I doubt they're worried about guarding from people spying in the sky."

Spinescale slashed her tail in annoyance. "I forget these guys are so scaleless, but what do we do in the meantime? We don't really have time to just sit and wait..."

"I think Startide, Zepherdust, and I should probably leave you early this evening, we're supposed to by acting as a decoy, not traveling with you." Daychaser flared his flippers slightly in regret. "The plan was for us to meet up with Blade and his team before meeting up with you."

Startide nodded. "Perhaps we should go now, we have some current to make up if we are going to meet up with Blade and the others on time."

Jackson's mouth twisted in a frown. "I guess... I didn't know you guys were meeting up with Blade though."

"Why don't you hang around for a bit and help me go through some of my books first?" Draflor floated another volume over to Startide. "I really feel like there is something important about the name of this isle."

# ANCIELLON ISLE

Jackson looked over at Spinescale. "Maybe while you guys do that, Spinescale and I could go ashore for a bit, maybe we can find something that will help us figure out what's going on."

Spinescale's eyes twinkled in anticipation. "I'm game."

Daychaser looked like he might protest Jackson's plan but finally shook his head. "If you are heading ashore, I think Startide, Zepherdust, and I should go. If we don't meet up with Blade here soon, the guardians and medians might start getting worried..." He gave Jackson an imploring look. "Just be careful, would you?"

"We'll try." Jackson gave a sheepish grin as he shrugged. "I don't want to get into any more trouble."

"Yet you seem to have a talent for finding it..." Daychaser rolled his eyes with a sigh. "We'll see you soon, you know how to get to the meeting place?"

"And the different seamarks?" Startide added as Zepherdust got a thoughtful look on her snout.

"If he doesn't, I do." Draflor piped up as he rolled a long scroll closed. "We'll get there."

"Maybe I should stay here and just make sure you guys get back safe?" Zepherdust suddenly interjected, giving Daychaser and Startide a quick look. "I know that's not the original plan but..." She glanced over to Jackson. "If you're going ashore, maybe it'd be best for someone to stick around, just to make sure nothing bad happens." She flicked her flipper forward to show a fetching band that matched one that Daychaser and Startide were both wearing. "If something happened, I could alert Startide and Daychaser with this."

"I don't plan to do anything crazy..." Jackson lightly protested with a small smile.

"It's not a bad idea though..." Startide agreed with Zepherdust.

"It's your call Jackson." Draflor glanced over to him with a wry grin. "You're in charge of our team."

Jackson was quiet for a moment before he sighed and looked over to Zepherdust. "Ok, but don't stay too close to the main area of the harbor. I don't plan to come back to the ocean here." He pointed further down the coast. "Let's head further down that way before I go ashore."

"Sounds good." Zepherdust nodded with a smile, though she glanced back at Daychaser and Startide. "We'll see you at the meeting place."

Daychaser bobbed his head in acknowledgement while he tapped Jackson on the shoulder with his flipper. "See you soon."

"Be careful!" Startide called before they vanished through the murky blue water of the harbor.

Jackson waved goodbye before he slipped off his backpack and secured it to a portion of the dock that wasn't near the Toxicshade and went into his first bag to change.

"Surprised you kept your Sonaekian clothes on." Spinescale commented, noticing Jackson had only switched out his clothes for a tunic with a hood and a different pair of shoes.

Zepherdust gave Jackson a quick look as they swiftly made their way to an area beyond the docks, where an abundance of wave washed boulders allowed them to scramble ashore unseen. "True, I would've thought you'd choose some of your old clothes." she added, looking perplexed.

"My other clothes are all too worn, or they have my tribe's markings on them." Jackson explained while he crawled ashore behind a large outcropping. "I'd rather attract attention with these clothes, than have the Toxicshade discover me."

"I guess..." Spinescale gave him a once over, "but I doubt you'll be able to hide in the crowd very easily. I don't think those shades of blue are popular here."

"Which is where the color change comes in." Jackson dried himself off enough for his legs to return and slowly stood up. He changed his skin color to a light tan and turned the hues of his clothes from blues and whites to deep greens and muted browns, the colors a nature mage would often wear. "Better?" He asked while he crouched down so Spinescale could climb up on his outstretched arm.

"Hm, well you won't make any large catches with it, but it'll do." Spinescale slithered up his arm to perch on his shoulder as he flicked the hood over his head.

"I'll see you guys when you get back!" Zepherdust called from the surf. When Jackson waved at her she turned and dove back into the shallows, swimming further out to hide amongst some rocky offshore outcroppings.

As Jackson walked along the beach, he passed a good number of large odd-looking rocks. About halfway down the beach, one of the large rocks suddenly moved and Jackson yelped as he jumped to the side.

"Toxic! Now that's a **huge** tortoise." Spinescale commented when a tired, but curious, looking turtle poked its head out from its shell.

"There's more than one." Jackson whispered as he realized many of the other rocks along the shoreline were really shells. "Holy Hippocampus, that one's as big as a small horse!"

"I wouldn't ride one though." Spinescale snickered, "too slow."

"Way to slow." Draflor added from the staff.

# MYTHOS SEAS: MOVING SEAMOUNTS

Avoiding the curious glances of the tortoises, Jackson cautiously made his way to the edge of the harbor. The trip took a few minutes, but it took even longer for Jackson to convince himself to walk out into the crowd. He only managed to step out when he saw Draflor peek out from the staff and give him an encouraging look.

"I hate, hate, hate big crowds." Jackson muttered quietly before he tried to weave through the hustle and bustle without crashing into anyone, which he failed at miserably. The noise, smells, and sights of the docks were almost overwhelming as vendors called out over the murmuring roar of people talking and bartering for goods. The smells of cooking food, strange spices, and unwashed men was very strong and tormented Jackson's nose after so many months at sea, forcing him to hold back a gag when he bumped into a particularly pungent individual.

Jackson tried to ignore the curious looks or calculating stares some people gave him when they saw his clothes. He had to force himself to keep his head up, reminding himself the hood hid most of his face from view.

"Sir, could I interest you in some of the rarest shells? Collected on my journeys through the southern reefs!"

Jackson shied, shaking his head when one merchant reached for his sleeve, which resulted in him nearly crashing into an older woman who gave him a cross look before she huffed by. *Why did I think it was a good idea to come ashore again?*

Letting out a terse breath while he made his way towards the entrance to the large seaside town, Jackson glanced around him uneasily. He skirted to the far side of the street with a group of other people once they noticed a few Toxicshade soldiers coming out through the gates.

# ANCIELLON ISLE

Many a distrustful glare followed the men as they walked off and Jackson breathed a sigh of relief. At least the people here weren't allies to the Toxicshade.

He slightly paused once he realized that he'd likely have to check in at the gates. The Centel's might be a trading nation, but they also did a lot to try and keep their kingdom safe and crime free. That often meant making sure any unusual characters were checked at the gates, and unfortunately for Jackson, his unusually styled clothes fit that scroll exactly.

He joined up with a group of people as they made their way through the gates, hoping he might slip through with the crowd without any issues.

"You there, in the strange green clothes, and your hood up."

Jackson barely stopped the groan that rumbled in his chest. He felt Spinescale snicker when he looked over at the guards, the older of which had his finger pointed at him. "Come over here please."

Slowly, Jackson came over to where the guards were posted. One of them motioned for him to head to an area where other people who had caught notice were either waiting or talking to other guards or gatekeepers that were questioning them.

A balding middle-aged gatekeeper turned, his eyebrows shooting up in surprise once he noticed Jackson's appearance. The man turned and whispered to a woman who sat at the table behind him who gave Jackson a single stare. She promptly made a small stone in her hand and threw it over to where a group of guards were standing and waiting.

The stone hit a small plate with a strange symbol on it, making a distinct sound that caught the attention of a couple of guards who came marching over. As the men took their places next to the gatekeeper and the woman Jackson felt his pulse start to pound in his ears while the lady motioned him forward.

# MYTHOS SEAS: MOVING SEAMOUNTS

"Name and tribe or clan please, and your business here. Also please remove your hood." The women said curtly as Jackson came walking nervously over.

"J-Jackson, of the clan Suncrest..." Jackson silently thanked Stonecurrent for helping him discover one of his ancestral clan names while cursing himself for being so nervous as he pulled his hood back. "I-I'm just p-passing through."

He saw the guards make eye contact and he knew he seemed quite suspicious.

The woman leaned back a bit as the man spoke. "You wouldn't happen to have anything of value on you by chance? Everything you have on you is yours?"

Jackson was so nervous he shook his head and nodded at the same time. "I j-just have my staff, backpack, and a-armband on me."

"And they're all yours? Seems kinda strange that someone so young would have such a powerful looking staff." The woman crossed her arms.

"They're m-mine." Jackson said, making eye contact with the woman.

"I'm afraid I don't believe you young man." The man said. "We'd better take that staff and keep you here until we can find out who's it is."

"Draflor help me out a bit, will you?" Jackson whispered urgently when one of the guards moved forward, his eyes focused on Solarswell.

"Oh, for currents sake!" Draflor came flashing out of the staff with steam fairly pouring out his gills. "Can't a guy go through sixty-eight volumes of Mythos Island History without getting interrupted?"

# ANCIELLON ISLE

Draflor gave Jackson a quick wink before he turned and glared at the dumbfounded gatekeepers and guards, whose mouths had dropped open in shock. "Seriously, one only has so many years to study before he goes into the next life."

The balding gatekeeper made a gurgling noise in his throat while the woman struggled to speak.

"I-I beg your pardon uh..." She gave Draflor a flabbergasted look. "Sir, but is this young man your... uh."

"Jackson?" Draflor pointed to Jackson with a fin. "Oh, him and I go way back, he's the caretaker of this staff after all, you could say he's heir to it." Draflor was enjoying himself immensely as he gave the woman a wink. "Good guy he is, a bit quiet, but—" Draflor feigned shock. "Great dragons, you didn't think he'd stolen the staff now did you!?" Draflor made a tisking sound before he swam in front of one of the guards and opened his mouth wide, making the man flinch.

"Shame, shame, shame. I mean it's not his fault you all don't have the same fashion sense as his clan."

Jackson could feel Spinescale laughing from her pouch in his backpack, and he had to work hard to hide a smile himself while Draflor continued his "tirade."

"I mean really, you've only seen him for what? Maybe a finful of minutes, and you're already trying to take something from him just because he's a bit different and uneasy in all this hustle and bustle. Not everyone is comfortable in these crazy trading towns." He waggled a fin in front of the lady's face.

"I..." The lady blinked before she smacked her quill on the counter and leaned forward to try and look Draflor in the eye, though he didn't make it easy on her. "Now see here sir, how could the young man not arouse suspicion? He's in the strangest clothes

I've seen in ages, and he had his hood up and was tripping all over his words. We're only trying to do our jobs here."

Jackson bit his tongue when he saw Draflor's eyes sparkle with mischief. *Wonder if I should intervene...? Draflor might be having a bit too much fun.*

"Isn't your job to listen, and make sure that justice is served?" Draflor moved forward until he was nearly "nose to nose" with the woman. "If I remember correctly, before he even came over you summoned guards to stand with you. Which made him even more nervous, then you asked him three questions: which he answered nervously, yet honestly, and yet after those three questions you and your lover boy here suddenly decide you are going to take his stuff away without questioning him further. Doesn't the law of your people say innocent until proven guilty?"

One of the guards guffawed a bit when the woman and the balding man both turned bright red at Draflor's words. Jackson glanced behind him with a tiny smirk when Spinescale tumbled out of the bag, wreathing in laughter.

A deep rumbling laugh pulled everyone's attention away when a large, stocky man slowly clapped his hands as he came walking over, a large yellow a black terrapin crawling beside him. "I say young man, you have quite the little defense consultant on you; I haven't enjoyed my shift this much in ages."

"S-sir I—" The woman stopped when the man held up his palm. "Don't worry Athinel, I'll handle this one. You're doing your best out here, and we've all been a bit tense since a certain venom nation arrived..." The man shrugged as he leaned over and looked at the section of the scroll Athinel had written Jackson's information.

"Clan Suncrest huh? Haven't heard of that one, you must be from one of those wandering clans that doesn't show up much?"

# ANCIELLON ISLE

Jackson felt some of the tension release from his shoulders and nearly sighed. "Y-yes, my family doesn't do m-much in the way of trading, we have all we n-need to care for ourselves."

"Pick up your snake friend and follow me young man. I have some questions I'd like to ask you, and you two, come along with me." The man motioned to the guards. "Let's go into my office." While Jackson bent over to pick up Spinescale, Draflor gave Athinel and the balding man an intimidating look. As Jackson hurried after the man a book appeared next to Draflor before he vanished back into the staff, muttering smugly. "Now then, back to volume thirty-five..."

Jackson was led to a small room where the large man picked up his terrapin friend and sat him on the table. He then settled into his chair and tapped a writing quill against a stretch of scroll. "Now Jackson, I'd like to know where your clan had last settled, it just makes things a bit easier on me." He gave the staff a wry look as his turtle friend dipped one of its claws in an inkwell and scratched a couple letters on the scroll. "And I've seen enough to know that staff is yours, but I'd still like to know what else you have on you, just for our records."

"The last place my family settled was the Northern Continent." Jackson said hesitantly, not sure what to make of the turtle, who was also making notes. "But the Toxicshade changed that."

"Hm, my apologies, we aren't thrilled to have them here ourselves. The merchants are especially livid about it, bad for business." The man gave Jackson an understanding frown while he made a few notes. "Now what do you have on you?"

"I have my stilvan armband, casting glove and armguards, my pack and..." Jackson quickly teleported some seeds into the bag, "and some seeds."

# MYTHOS SEAS: MOVING SEAMOUNTS

"Seeds?" The quill hovered over the scroll and the man looked up without raising his head.

"I'm a nature mage sir, and seeds are easier to transport than full grown food." Jackson explained as the turtle's eyes gleamed in interest.

"Would you show me the seeds?" The man asked.

Jackson pulled the container of seeds out and opened it to show the man.

"Quite a collection, are you sure you don't plan to do a bit of trading in the farmer's district?" The man grinned when he asked the question. "There's some seeds there I don't even recognize."

The turtle clacked its beak in emphasis.

Jackson shook his head. "I don't need any money right now, and some of these seeds are my clans' special stock. It'd be the death of me if I traded some of them."

"Fair enough." The man chuckled and made a few more notes while the turtle looked disappointed. "Mind showing me the stilven armband? I haven't seen one in a bit, and I assume you have a stone in there?"

Jackson wasn't sure which stone he had in the armband and pulled up his sleeve to show it and froze when he saw he'd put his moonstone in there at some point. He wasn't sure who was more surprised at the sight of the moonstone, him, or the men in the room.

"Spells..." Jackson whispered, realizing the men would quickly connect the dots that he was a light user.

One of the guards immediately went over and shut the door, which instantly put Jackson on the defensive! His hands crackled with a spell as Spinescale shot up from the bag, hissing dangerously.

"Easy, easy!!" The large man said, holding up his hands while the turtle shot into its shell. "You have nothing to fear here, show him Reyold."

# ANCIELLON ISLE

The remaining guard came forward and held out his hands, forming a glowing white symbol above them, which made Jackson relax slightly, although he still gave the man a suspicious look.

"Prove it." Jackson said, his eyes slitted, while Spinescale flared out her wings and hissed in emphasis.

The man's eyes widened at Jackson's challenge, but he quickly formed a light barrier around himself. Jackson sent a beam of his own magic against the barrier before he finally relaxed as the light died away.

"You're a touchy one, now aren't ya?" The large man said as the turtle peeked out from its shell.

"If you'd been in the Toxicshade's territories when the bounty was placed, you'd be to." Jackson said, quickly removing the moonstone and putting it into his bag. "And I hadn't heard what stance your nation had taken on light mages since you still maintained open trade with the Toxicshade, a couple other nations had put a bounty on them as well."

"You won't come to harm here for your light magic." The man reassured. "Although, the fact that your clan was around when the bounty was first set in place explains a lot of your behaviors today." He shook his head while the turtle came out again. "And we'd never hurt good people. True light magic is only wielded by those who are good, we have no reason to turn against them."

"Some of my relatives escaped from the Northeastern lands, you were lucky you and your family escaped as well." The guard said, putting his weapon back to his side.

Jackson's head immediately started to droop a bit at the mention of his family, and he saw the guard's eyes widen a bit. "Didn't your family escape too?"

"I am the last of my family who walk this earth." Jackson said, holding back the pain when the words left his mouth.

# MYTHOS SEAS: MOVING SEAMOUNTS

"I... I see." The guard said. "I'm sorry."

Jackson pinched his lips in a tiny smile and nodded before he looked back to the large man. "Do you know why the Toxicshade are here? I've heard more of their ships are heading down towards the Fire Tribes land as they prepare for war."

"All I know is they are gathering some supplies while here." The man said as he rolled up the scroll before the turtle grabbed it in its jaws. "I know they plan to stay here for maybe another week to wait out a storm that's coming, and that they are guarding something on their ships that seems to have great value." He looked Jackson in the eyes while the turtle walked over and put the scroll on the top of a large pile of unsorted scrolls. "But you should know better than to try to interfere with the Toxicshade son, you know how ruthless they are."

Jackson held the man's gaze. "I know better than I want to, but I also have some extended family in the Fire Tribes, and I'm heading that way."

"I see..." The man seemed to be deep in thought. "Yet I'm afraid I don't have anything more to tell you, they keep their plans a secret."

Jackson stood silently for a minute. "Do you know anyone who might know more information on them? Someone who wouldn't try to kill me preferably."

"You're serious about this aren't you?" A thread of weariness touched the man's words. "I'm telling you son; this isn't something you want to get mixed up in."

"I'm already more mixed up in it then you'll ever know." Jackson pressed as he saw the man's eyes widen. "I don't plan to do anything stupid, and nothing here. I just need information."

# ANCIELLON ISLE

The curiosity of the men in the room was tangible while Jackson held the man's gaze. Finally, the head gatekeeper sighed and sat back in his seat. "Reyold?"

"If you are that serious, go to the milk bar on the other side of town. Snapping Turtle Inn, is the name." The guard said, "and talk to Ofnik, the owner, he might have information for you." The guard held up a hand, "but let me warn you, while Ofnik is a good man, he's a bit peculiar and won't give information to you easily. He's risking a lot to find the information he does, and he doesn't part with it to just anyone."

"Tell him we sent you, that'll at least tip him off." The head gatekeeper said as the turtle bobbed its head in a nod. "But you'll likely have to prove yourself to him, and even then, he might not be willing to give you any information."

Jackson nodded. "Thank you, may I go now?"

# CHAPTER SEVEN
# SNAPPING TURTLE INN

"Snapping Turtle Inn huh?" Spinescale looked around curiously while Jackson wound his way through town. "Kinda an odd name if you ask me."

"There does seem to be a lot of turtle themed stores and merchandise." Jackson replied as they passed a store named "Tinyshell Bakery," which had a variety of turtle shaped pastries lining the outside display. A number of small box turtles were quietly browsing through the flowerbed in front of the shop. "And just a lot of turtles, period."

"Care for a sweet cake stranger?" A portly lady who was keeping watch over the display of goodies asked with a smile.

Jackson shook his head. "I'm not really hungry right now, but thank you." He looked over the display. "They do look delicious though, perhaps I'll stop by later."

The woman grinned. "We'll be open until right before sunset, but then we all normally head over to the milk bar to socialize for a bit. It's kinda a custom we have here."

"Are turtles a custom too? I've noticed there seems to be a lot of turtles… on everything." Jackson pointed to the other stores on the street, all of which had something turtle themed.

# SNAPPING TURTLE INN

The lady laughed while another woman walked out of another store with a large tortoise in tow. "We do love our turtles here, there's a long-standing tradition that the turtles came to this isle many years ago and taught us how to move it so we could go to better waters. We consider turtles to be symbols of prosperity, protection, and peace." She pointed to one of the turtle shell shaped cookies. "Why don't you take one, it's on the house, business has been a bit slow lately and I hate to throw these out tonight if they don't get sold."

"Thank you." He picked up a cookie and took a big bite, sighing in delight. "Mmmm, it's really good."

"Well thank you young man, I do pride myself in having the best baked goods on the isle." She waved him off. "Now I can see you have places to be, but stop by again anytime, and tell your friends."

Jackson waved his thanks as he made his way down the street towards a very large building, avoiding a large tortoise that had decided to doze in the middle of the street.

"I didn't think the name would fit the building itself…" Draflor said when he looked out from the staff to inspect the turtle shell shaped sign that had "Snapping Turtle Inn" written on it. "That roof is quite the feat of craftsmanship."

Jackson agreed, the whole roof of the building was shaped and patterned after a large turtle shell, and even the entrance was covered with what looked like the top of a snapping turtle head. "That lady wasn't kidding when she said they like turtles here." He glanced at the large pond along the right side of the building, where a number of snapping turtles were calmly basking on rocks or logs.

"Hm…" Draflor's eyes suddenly lit up. "Wait! That gives me an idea." He then scowled at Solarswell when the staff flashed. "Well, you could've said something earlier. Not like you've been much help lately, you've been too busy with your own research." Draflor grumbled to the staff while he vanished from view.

"I swear, those two act like an old, mated pair of albatross." Spinescale slithered partway out of the bag so she could get a better look at the building. "Big place, but what the venom is a milk bar exactly?"

"Milk bars are quite common in larger cities and towns." Jackson whispered as they got closer to the building, drawing the attention of some of the snapping turtles. "They're where people go to socialize and visit with one another."

"Ok, but why is it called a 'milk bar?'"

"Well, most of what they offer is milk: cow, camel, belhurran, horse, you name it, they probably have it. They turn the milk to cream, make sweet cold cream, ferment it, boil it, and make cheese. If you can do something to milk to make it taste better, or different, they do it. It draws quite a crowd. They're known for their large assortments of good food too."

Spinescale didn't look impressed. "Must be a mammal thing."

Jackson hesitated a dolphin-length from the entrance. He took a deep breath before walking underneath the large wooden beak covering the double doors and slipped through them. His arrival drew some attention when a few people saw his attire, and he kept his head slightly down while he walked around the dining area to the counter and pulled up a stool to take a seat.

"What'll it be stranger?" An intimidatingly large and very stocky man with a thick, dark brown goatee asked as he finished cleaning out a large mug and came walking over.

"J-just a chilled glass of belhurran milk please." Jackson said, quickly teleporting a small coin from his bag when he noticed the man kept a long dagger at his side.

# SNAPPING TURTLE INN

"Not from around here, are ya?" The man placed down a tall glass of cold milk in front of Jackson and took the coin.

"I'm... I'm just passing through." Jackson said quietly when he noticed a few of the nosier customers trying to eavesdrop as an utterly huge alligator snapping turtle—who was dozing in a water basin by a wood stove—opened an eye curiously. Jackson pulled his hood back a bit and took a long slow drink, relishing the flavor he hadn't had for so long. "Oh, that's good."

The man snorted. "I'm Ofnik, if ya need anything more just holler. It's been slow lately, and the rush doesn't hit until around sunset."

"Actually, um..." Jackson took a deep breath to try and steady his nerves, why was talking to creatures so much easier? "Reyold and one of the other men at the gate said to come here. I'm looking for some information."

The man went back to cleaning a cup and Jackson was beginning to wonder if he'd been heard when the man snorted in a slightly disbelieving type of way. "Doubt someone like you could handle the information I like to collect. You look like you'd get blown over in a stiff wind."

Jackson chafed at the man's words and took another deep breath, hoping he wouldn't regret what he said next. "I was told you'll sometimes try to see if the person can prove themselves."

The man finished washing the glass and slipped it back onto its stack before a hard smirk crossed his face. "You got some guts for a scrawny kid. Do you even know the nature of my 'tests?'"

"No..." Jackson suddenly felt a bit small as his voice squeaked, "but whether I know or not, I still need information."

The man's chest began to shake before he threw his head back as a roaring laugh escaped his throat, getting the attention of nearly everyone in the inn. "Alright then kid, we haven't had some excitement of this type in a while. It'll do me good." He cupped a hand to his mouth. "Hey Ferson, go grab that brother of yours, this scrawny kid wants a challenge. Spread the word and grab a couple of the others too, this should be fun!"

Jackson shrunk in on himself when a group of men went running out the door as the conversation in the inn suddenly turned loud and excited.

"I think you just caught more than you could swallow." Spinescale said, and Jackson glared back at her. "I think I might enjoy this, wonder if I should try to get Draflor's attention...?"

"You're a big help."

"I try."

One of the waitresses ran into the back and pounded on the door to the large kitchen. "Hey Nikal, have Boren grab a few glasses of belhurren milk. There's been a challenge!"

Jackson heard an exclamation of excited surprise before the door opened and the waitress was nearly yanked through it by an excited older woman. A few men began getting up to move tables and chairs around as Ofnik vanished into the back while the alligator snapping turtle lifted its head with an interested gleam in its eye. Jackson really began wondering what he'd gotten himself into as the men formed a large semicircle of chairs and tables in the room.

"Uh... what is this challenge exactly?" Jackson asked once Ofnik came back out with a couple large boxes.

The man only grinned. "You'll find out soon enough."

"Oh, you're in so much trouble." Spinescale said just as Draflor came swooping out of the staff.

"I found it I—!!" Draflor looked around the room with wide eyes. "Uh, is this a bad time?" He asked when Ofnik blinked at his appearance, the man's eyebrows shooting up in surprise.

# SNAPPING TURTLE INN

"Probably, but if you hang around you might get some entertainment." Spinescale cooed, coming halfway out of Jackson's pack. "Jackson accepted the challenge, and whatever it is, it looks like it's quite the little event. Haven't seen this much action in awhile now."

Jackson had the sudden urge to teleport Spinescale into the bag, but had the sneaking suspicion she'd bite him later if he did. "Hey, I'm the one who's going to be competing here."

Spinescale shrugged her wings. "Oh, don't be a fang in the sand. I don't want to see you get hurt, but can you blame me for wanting a bit of mischief? This has been the most stressful turn of my life. That, and I know if it gets too bad you could just use your magic to escape; no one here knows a thing about water magic."

Jackson slumped in the stool a bit and gave Spinescale a pensive look, unsure of what to say. Meanwhile, a couple snapping turtles came scrambling in through a turtle sized entrance, all of them eyeing the goings-on with interest.

"I wonder what this competition is…?" Draflor wondered quietly after he'd snuck back into the staff to avoid the questioning gaze of Ofnik. "It doesn't seem like anything I've ever seen."

A large group of men came rushing into the inn, many of whom were carrying some large bags of strange tubers as they came rushing over.

"This is the kid?" One man asked before he gave a scornful laugh. "Oh, he's not going to last a minute, he'll faint at the first bite."

"Bite?" Jackson asked before he was suddenly urged from his stool and placed down in a chair on the open side of the semi-circle. A couple more men and a few women quickly took some seats next to him while the tables and chairs surrounding them filled nigh to bursting.

# MYTHOS SEAS: MOVING SEAMOUNTS

"Welcome all to the Challenge of Plantfire." Ofnik called out as he entered the semi-circle, rapping a cup against a turtle-shell shaped bell. "As you all recall, the last new contestant left us on his way to the healer's, nearly in a coma, and this time we'll see who of these daring folks lasts the longest."

"Anyone who wishes to forfeit now, may, otherwise you are committing to the remainder of the contest or until you can no longer function." Ofnik said before he turned to look at Jackson. "You can leave now if ya want kid."

Jackson broke out in a cold sweat when he felt the weight of an entire room full of eyes rest on him, but he clenched his fists and shook his head. "I-I'm staying."

"It'll be your funeral!" One man hollered, making several people laugh while the alligator snapping turtle tilted its head thoughtfully.

"Very well. We will start off our contestants with the coolest tubers we have, and then we will double the heat from there." Ofnik proclaimed. "Now then." He turned to Jackson and the contestants. "Under no circumstances is magic to be used, which means you, young man, have to remove all the spells you have active on you at this time." He held out a large light crystal that was glowing like mad, "and judging by the light, it's quite a few." A few snapping turtles snapped their jaws in emphasis.

Jackson could hear Draflor whisper something to the staff, which instantly dimmed, and Jackson took a deep breath. "F-Fine, I'm already the c-center of attention anyway." He let his color-change spell drop and heard several gasps once the brilliant blues and whites of his clothes flashed into view, as well as his white skin.

"Very good." Ofnik barely raised a brow when the crystal stopped glowing, though the turtles all seemed very intrigued. "Now pass out the portion these crazy men and women are to consume."

# SNAPPING TURTLE INN

The chef and some of the waitresses came forward with large trays, each one with a long line of different types of garlic-like roots and placed them before the contestants.

"You will start with the leftmost cloves and work your way up to the hottest." Ofnik instructed. "The last one standing wins the battle."

Jackson picked up a clove and sniffed it, making him cough, which prompted some laughter.

"What's the matter kid, never seen a spitfire clove before?" The rude man who mocked Jackson earlier snorted.

"This is a spitfire clove?" Jackson asked in disbelief. "It doesn't look like any I've ever seen."

"You must be from the northern lands, they don't grow these there." A woman commented.

"You may begin." Ofnik said as a judge and a snapping turtle came up next to each contestant to watch. "And you must keep each clove in your mouth for ten seconds before you swallow, if you don't make it that long, you automatically forfeit."

Jackson stared at the spitfire clove for a few seconds after the other people had quickly thrown them into their mouths. "I wonder..."

"Do you know what that is?" Draflor inquired. "You seem more curious than nervous."

"Yes... and the first bite is always the worst one." Jackson gingerly popped the first clove into his mouth and immediately coughed when the burning magical juices of the clove attacked his tongue. "Yep, first bite is always the worst, not a bad flavor though."

Jackson noticed that most people, including the other contestants and the turtles, were watching his reactions closely.

# MYTHOS SEAS: MOVING SEAMOUNTS

"If you think that one is bad you won't like the next one." One lady prodded before she put a third one in her mouth.

"I d-didn't say the clove was bad, I said the first bite was always the worst." Jackson replied thoughtfully as he lifted the second one to his mouth, popped it in, and began chewing. "Flavor's ok on this one…" He muttered quietly to himself after he swallowed.

He heard groaning to his right and saw a woman, who had eaten up to six of the tubers, swaying back and forth in her seat. Meanwhile, a man who'd gotten through his fifth one had bent over before he could pop the sixth one in his mouth.

"Ok folks, it looks like we are nearing our first drop out, who will it be Mr. Dorill at five or Mrs.…"

Jackson ignored the guy who had begun commenting on the competition as the bent-over man crumpled, hitting the floor with a thunk. A snapping turtle, who was helping judge, walked over and snapped its jaw nine times while the man tried to get up. When the turtle snapped the tenth time the man groaned, raising a trembling hand in defeat. One of the waitresses came running over with a glass of nearly frozen milk and handed it to him. The snapping turtle got a disappointed look in its eyes while the man immediately began drinking, swishing the liquid around in his mouth as tears ran down his cheeks.

Jackson glanced down at an unused plate and counted twelve different cloves. He looked over to see some of the other contestants had made it to nearly their eighth or ninth clove. Those competitors who had made it that far had begun the strangest of things to try and calm the fire in their mouth, some pounding the table with their fists, while others kicked their legs wildly.

"I'm not sure whether I'm amused or concerned by these people's choice of entertainment…" Draflor said, watching a man

# SNAPPING TURTLE INN

with tears pouring down his cheeks collapse to the floor after eating his tenth clove. The man didn't even wait for the snapping turtle to stop snapping before waving his hand weakly for milk.

"I apologize for everything I said earlier..." Spinescale muttered while people began cheering wildly for their favorite contestant as more and more people began working their way up to the hottest cloves. "This has to be the strangest competition I've ever seen."

"I've heard of eating competitions, but this is ridiculous." Draflor commented. "If they want to test their strength, why not with races, mock duels, or other competitions?"

"I wonder if the flavor just keeps getting blander with each clove?" Jackson mumbled to himself after he popped his fourth one in, having eaten the third while Draflor and Spinescale were taking.

"Flavor? Are you kidding me, people are nearly spitting fire over there and you're concerned about flavor?" Spinescale thwacked Jackson with her tail. "I think you better stop before you burn your brains out."

With a small eyeroll, Jackson popped the fifth into his mouth before he groaned, drawing the attention of many different people and turtles who were watching eagerly for his reaction.

"That tastes so bad..." Jackson shuddered once he'd swallowed. "That's the worst one."

"You think that's bad, try the next one!" Someone mocked and a turtle seemed to smirk.

Jackson rolled his eyes again as he popped in the sixth root and began chewing while three more people tapped out. Leaving two men and one woman, each on their eleventh clove, all of whom were trying desperately to finish chewing without collapsing on the floor.

# MYTHOS SEAS: MOVING SEAMOUNTS

Jackson popped in the seventh as one of the men crumbled, the woman holding an arm up in triumph while her other arm was clenched to her waist.

While Jackson threw in his next clove, the other two contestants took a few seconds to breathe before they gave each other a fierce look. They then threw in their last cloves and began chewing, their faces nearly fire red from the heat.

As the seconds ticked by, Jackson bit into his ninth one while the man and women stared each other down amidst the wild yells of the onlookers. Just before they reached ten, the woman's eyes rolled back in her head and she collapsed to the floor, a waitress running over to revive her and force some milk down the fainted lady's throat.

The man gave a triumphant grin and pumped his fist in the air. "Beat that, Darla, I WI—"

"OH YUCK!" Jackson made a face after he bit down on the tenth one and unintentionally interrupted the gloating man.

The room went deathly quiet for a moment before Ofnik spoke. "What do you mean by, 'yuck?'"

Jackson held up a hand so he could finish his ten seconds and swallowed, a single tear running down his cheek. "Sorry, I didn't mean to say that out loud…" He picked up the eleventh one to look it over and was just about to put it in his mouth when Ofnik stopped him.

"What did you mean by 'yuck,' kid?"

"Huh?" Jackson paused, his face turning a deeper shade of red than it was. "I… uh… I… n-nothing, sorry I'll keep going."

"No…" Ofnik pressed, the alligator snapping turtle leaning forward intently. "I want an answer to my question first."

Jackson gave a nervous laugh. "Uh, I d-don't mean to be rude b-but the tenth one…" He tapped the place where the tenth one had been. "T-the flavor was uh... well terrible, I didn't like it at all." He popped the eleventh one in his mouth and grimaced. "Oh help! This one's worse!"

Jackson suddenly became aware that everyone in the room was staring at him, and it was so quiet you could hear a cockatrice feather hit the floor. He swallowed the clove slowly before reaching for the twelfth one. "Sorry, I guess that was kinda rude of me..."

He popped the last clove in his mouth and began chewing, wrinkling his nose as a few tears escaped his eyes. "Whew, this one does have a kick to it doesn't it?" He frowned once he swallowed it. "Is the flavor always that bland though? Maybe I just got a bad clove."

A couple turtles' beaks fell open.

Jackson reached over and took the twelfth clove off another tray and popped it in his mouth. "No... about the same really, you ever thought about crossing them with some more flavorful varieties? This wouldn't be any good for cooking a good Fire Festival stew."

"Yo-your disappointed in the FLAVOR!?" The other remaining contestant roared! Looking fit to blow steam out of his bright red ears. "This isn't no cooking competition, it's a battle of wills!"

Jackson blinked before he laughed in embarrassment. "Eheheh... Sorry... I wasn't trying to be rude, err." He gave an Ofnik an imploring glance as he shivered from the bad taste in his mouth. "Guh! By chance do you have a really hot one that tastes good? I need to get the taste of the last three out of my mouth, and I have a feeling milk just won't cut it."

"You want MORE?" Ofnik, the turtles, and the remaining people looked dumbfounded, while Spinescale went limp as Draflor stared in shock.

Jackson's eyes widened until he saw Draflor and Spinescale's expressions and busted up laughing. "I never thought I'd see the day when I made you two speechless!" He kept laughing until he noticed everyone was still watching and tried to turn his laugh into a cough. "Huh, eheh, sorry. I guess that's it then?"

"THIS! That's it? No pain, no nothing!" The other remaining contestant raged. "That's the second hottest variety we have, and you just brush it off because of the FLAVOR!?"

"Y-you do have a hotter one? Can I try that? I want to see how it compares to my family's variety." Jackson jumped up from his seat while Draflor smacked a fin against his snout and shook his head.

Jackson slowly sat back down when no one spoke, until finally Ofnik said. "Your family raises spitfire plants kid?"

"Well… yeah, but I don't think they're the same varieties you all have here. They don't look at all alike."

"If we bring out our hottest variety for you to try, can you show us your family's?" Ofnik was looking both intensely curious and stunned as he motioned to one of the waitresses to bring him a glass of milk.

Jackson tilted his head while he slipped off his backpack. "I guess so, it'll take me a minute to grow one though: do you have a large bowl I could use?"

Jackson teleported a small tuber from his bag that he then pretended to remove from his pack. Someone came over with a large bowl and handed it to him while someone else brought out a small bag of tubers.

"Folks, I never thought I'd say this, but we have a second portion to our competition." Ofnik said, motioning a couple people forward. "Can someone go grab my brother from the back please? He'll want to be part of this."

# SNAPPING TURTLE INN

A lady vanished into the back as a couple of men and a single woman, one of the cooks, came up to the counter where Jackson was pouring some water from a cup onto the clove and began growing the tuber. A couple turtles scampered closer to watch, and even the giant alligator snapping turtle lifted itself from its water basin to come over.

The small tuber flashed in response to Jackson's magic and began growing wildly before the bowl filled with roots as the leafy foliage twisted up into the air while little fire-colored buds formed. As the woman came back with Ofnik's brother, Jackson reached out and tapped one of the buds, which opened with a brilliant flash as fire shot from its petals.

"Yep, should be r-ready to harvest a tuber or two I think." Jackson grinned, reaching down to twist a couple of fire orange and red cloves off the bottom of the plant. Almost immediately, the top began to shrivel up, the plant wilting away like it was being burned up by flames. Jackson collected the remaining tubers and put them in his bag before teleporting them into his backpack while he gave the stunned onlookers a shy smile.

"W-what? I'm a nature mage, what d-did you expect?"

Ofnik shook his head a bit. "You got a good one on me kid." He pulled a clumped-up bundle of cloves out of the small bag and broke off a small tuber, which he handed to Jackson. "Tell us what you think."

Jackson sniffed the clove, which was a pale yellow, before he took a small bite off the end and chewed a minute before eating the whole thing. "Not as bad as the last one, but the flavor could still be improved a bit."

Many a head began shaking at his response, while some of the turtles gave him impressed looks. The last remaining contestant began uttering angrily as he stomped over for a closer look at the cloves Jackson had placed on the counter.

"Now, let us try yours." The lady who was one of the cooks said, reaching out and grabbing one of Jackson's cloves.

"Whoa, whoa w-wait!" Jackson quickly pulled it away. "Let me cut a small piece for you to try."

The alligator snapping turtle crawled closer and gave Jackson's boot a soft bite.

"Ouch!" Jackson jumped a bit. "What?"

"Cut a piece for him too." Ofnik said as Jackson took the knife he was offered.

After checking for any unusual spells, Jackson cut some thin slices off and handed them out to each of the four people, and one turtle, who were waiting. Ofnik's brother gave Jackson an offended look when he handed him the thin slice.

"Now look here kid, I think you're being a bit insulting by giving us this thin of a slice. We have each handled a whole clove of the hottest variety we know of."

"If you want a whole clove after this, I'll let you have one to eat. I promise." Jackson said, "but you might want to just try what I gave you first."

There was a moment of silence as each person placed their respective piece in their mouths, while the turtle reached his jaws forward and snapped up his piece.

"The flavor truly is wonderful…" The chef praised, "but where is the—OH GREAT TURTLE SHELLS!" She fell off her seat as her face turned bright red and a small flame escaped her mouth. "MILK I NEED MILK! NOW!"

She scrambled to her feet and tore into the kitchen while another stream of fire escaped her mouth! One of the men who tried

## SNAPPING TURTLE INN

the tuber covered his mouth as his eyes bugged out before he charged after the chef.

Meanwhile, Ofnik and his brother each let out a yell, tumbling over each other as they lunged for a glass of milk. When they hit the floor, bursts of flames ballooned from their mouths while a waitress ran over with two sloshing glasses of iced milk and shoved it into their flailing hands! Not a second later the alligator snapping turtle's eyes widened before he shot off and dove into his pool, fire spouting from the sides of his beak!

Jackson tried, but failed, to hold back a snicker at the sight of the men chugging the milk down their throats before they hollered for more. His snicker seemed to break the dam and Spinescale and Draflor suddenly began howling while four people, and one turtle, worked to calm the literal and figurative flames in their mouths.

Jackson giggled as men rushed over with buckets of water that they used to quickly douse the fire started by Ofnik's brother, who had accidently breathed too hard next to a wooden table, quickly setting it aflame. Meanwhile, steam rose from the alligator snapping turtle's water basin as he tried to still the flames in his beak.

"Remind me never to eat your family's cooking at a Fire Festival!" Draflor howled, making the staff whirl with color as he flipped around.

"My uncle and Aunt do put the 'fire' in the festival." Jackson smirked while the flames died out. "Although we use stone tables and chairs when we eat their cooking."

"BWAHAHISSSSHAAHAHISSHAHISS!! I WONDER WHY!" Spinescale was laughing so hard her hissing had somehow become loud enough for people to hear across the room.

"I-I've never had anything quite like that!" The chef gasped as she stumbled out of the kitchen while Ofnik's brother was helped up into a chair. "Now **that's** a spitfire plant."

"T-that wasn't even the hottest variety, I'm n-not allowed to grow those." Jackson went over and helped lift Ofnik from the floor. "W-well, I mean I could, b-but the last time I did that I accidently s-set my mom's garden on fire sooo…" He shrugged, "you could say I was b-banned from them."

"That might be a good thing for us kid." Ofnik said, patting him on the back in thanks as he was hauled into a chair. "Does your mouth ever stop feeling like a burnt piece of charcoal?"

"Give it an hour or t-two and you'll be fine, although things m-might taste a bit burnt until morning." Jackson said as he went over and popped the rest of the clove into his mouth, much to the horror of everyone watching.

"Are you INSANE KID!" Ofnik's brother cried while a few turtles ducked into their shells. "Get outside before you set the whole place on fire!"

"I can do fire magic, calm down." Jackson said as he chewed through the tuber, relishing the taste and barely noticing the flames. "Just give me some room please." When the magical flames of the tuber ignited he squinted, squelching the flames inside his mouth before they could escape. However, a surge of hot, magical air still swept out from him, making a few people's eyes widen in surprise.

"Aaahh, I haven't had one of those in so long." He sighed before muttering quietly to himself. "That tastes so much better than fish or seaweed…"

"Well Jackson, I didn't expect to see this when I got here." Reyold said as he came out from the crowd, clapping his hands. "I was expecting you to be crumpled down on the ground or at the infirmary."

"Reyold?" Jackson paused after he teleported the remaining tuber into his bag.

# SNAPPING TURTLE INN

"The very same. You made quite a show, although I don't remember you mentioning you could use fire magic at the gate." Jackson opened his mouth and then closed it again. "W-weeell... I did mention I have relatives among the Fire Tribes." Jackson cringed at how lame his response was.

Reyold laughed, although the inquisitive look in his eye remained. "That you did, you also weren't wearing blue earlier."

*I think I should've stayed at sea today...* Jackson shrunk into himself a bit as Ofnik came over and patted his back. "Come-on kid, you've proven yourself enough for me. Let's go have a chat about this business you mentioned. You coming Reyold?"

"I wouldn't miss it Uncle."

Jackson gave Reyold a long, leery look while he followed Ofnik into the back of the building as people gathered and began chatting excitedly, looks of wonder on many of their faces. Reyold leaned over to whisper a few things into Ofnik's ear as they quickly led Jackson into a large room that was full of books and maps and had a big window looking out over the city.

"So, what is this information you're looking for kid?" Ofnik asked while the large alligator snapping turtle swam into the room through a specially made pool system.

"He's wanting information on the Toxicshade and why they're here." Reyold said as he sat down in a large comfy-looking chair in the corner of the room.

Ofnik's eyes slitted and he stared at Jackson for a long time. "Now why would someone like you want information on the Toxicshade?" He asked as the snapping turtle poked his head out of the water to listen.

"M-my family was hunted by them in the north." Jackson had to rally his courage, which had fled during the walk into the back room. "And I have family in the f-fire tribes to the south, I want to know what their plans are so I can be better p-prepared when I go that way."

"You're not telling me something kid."

"What he's not telling, you truly don't need to know." Draflor slipped out into the open, ready to come to Jackson's defense.

"You really do like a good spat, don't you?" Reyold commented.

Draflor shrugged. "I'm not fond of this type of spat personally, but it is what it is."

Ofnik sighed. "I don't wish to get into a spat, I assure you, but I do feel like I need to know a bit about you before I commit to giving you any information."

The alligator snapping turtle snapped its jaws loudly in emphasis, making Jackson jump.

"Then what are you wanting to know?" Jackson asked. "I'm telling the truth about my family."

"But yet I can tell there is something more, your clothes don't match any fire tribe, and neither does your form of magic. While I'm sure during wartime any allies of the United Fire Tribes would want to know what the Toxcishade's plans are, you aren't old enough to be involved with war plans or other such things."

"Then what are you wanting to know?"

"Why did you come here looking for this information, and why do you, a lone kid with no family, need it?"

"As far as coming here looking for information, a little bird told me." Jackson saw Draflor grin slightly at the irony of the phrase, since a bird did tell them. "And I need it to help my friends, the Toxcishade are all converging on one point for some reason before they'll even start fighting the Fire Tribes that I'm assuming have gathered in the area, and I need to know why."

# SNAPPING TURTLE INN

"Does this point have any significance?" Reyold asked, leaning forward to have his arms rest on his knees.

"Yes, but we don't know exactly what. It's a place where major battles were fought in the Steelserpent War and there have been strange energies building there." Jackson said. "I know there are some powerful artifacts around that area from the war, but I don't know if the Toxicshade know about them, or if they plan to do something with them if they do."

Ofnik and Reyold gave each other a worried look.

"You weren't kidding when you said you were more involved than we could expect. How do you know all that?" Reyold asked.

"That's our secret." Draflor said. "We aren't at liberty to say."

Ofnik looked down at the table for a few moments. "What do your sources think the Toxicshade might be planning? Or what this build-up of strange energies could mean?"

Jackson bit his lip uncertainly, unsure of what else they could say, and looked over at Draflor who gave a slight nod and "swam" forward a bit.

"We don't know what the Toxicshade are planning, that's what we are trying to find out." Draflor's tone was serious, at odds with his normal jovial persona. "The place they are heading towards is where a couple of powerful venom and water creatures were turned to stone, and it's also where a large number of Ironmamba ships were destroyed or sunk, along with their weapons and artifacts. Though I understand that is not common knowledge."

Draflor formed a map of energy in front of him, showing the area he was talking about. "This entire area has seen a powerful increase in dark or tainted energy that has been spreading throughout the waters." Draflor's tone was foreboding. "This type of tainted energy can appear from a number of factors; a sharp change in the magic of an area, large cataclysmic events, the clashing of powerful magics, but it is also occasionally associated with very powerful beings with dark intentions, it affects their magic which spreads around them—"

"I am aware of such things." Ofnik interrupted as he looked up from the table, his gaze nearly stern. "What do you think it means?"

If Draflor was taken-aback by the interruption he didn't show it, and simply met the men's gaze. "I honestly don't know what it is. There have been no cataclysmic events in this area for centuries, same with sharp changes in the magic of the land and sea. That leaves two options, but I've yet to hear of any being in that area powerful enough to cause such a surge, as to the clashing of powerful magics…" Draflor shifted as if in regret. "I know of none since the Steelserpent War."

Ofnik let out a frustrated breath. "I was hoping you'd have some idea that would help me explain the meaning of this letter." He pulled a long, slightly water damaged scroll from his desk and rolled it out on the table, motioning for Jackson and Draflor to come read.

"Magic cannons?" Jackson whispered, "and the empire's magic core. What on Mythos are they taking those there for?" Jackson couldn't believe his eyes and reread the first part of the missive. "Wha??"

"Now you know why I hoped you had some insight on what was going on there." Ofnik scooted back in his chair and grabbed another missive hidden behind a set of books. "And what we found in this one, makes things even more confusing."

Jackson took a seat as the second scroll was rolled out and began reading in earnest while thoughts spun in his head. As he read through the latter part of the missive his breath caught. "They are planning to destroy some of their forces as an example to the Fire Tribes?"

# SNAPPING TURTLE INN

Jackson put his hand on the missive as he scrutinized the names of the captains of some of the example vessels. "I know that name…" He quietly ran his fingers over one of the names. "He's of the old kingdoms…" Jackson pondered over some of the other names. "And some of these names are from old venom clan families too… they're related to the Spherefangs."

"What in the turtle shell are you talking about?" Reyold moved his chair over to get a better look. "Old clans?"

Jackson touched a couple names thoughtfully with his fingers. "These family names are from the older Venom Kingdoms, kingdoms the Toxicshade coerced into joining them years ago." Jackson's fingers began thrumming on the table. "There's been a lot of unrest associated with those factions the last few years…"

"Huh, trying to crush a revolt and send a message to the Fire Tribes at the same time then." Ofnik said. "Smart, even if it's dirty, mean, and nasty."

"That still doesn't answer any questions as to why they're gathering there." Draflor snapped his mouth shut in frustration. "It can't be a coincidence; Oceaono said Great Ghost Point is right next to the center of the tainted energy in that area."

"Great Ghost point? You didn't mention that earlier." Reyold seemed to be getting distrustful.

"I showed you the area." Draflor said. "I would've shown the rest if you'd asked."

Ofnik sat back heavily in his seat. "The Toxicshade have the ability to sink many ships to their deaths if they use magic cannons powered by their throne core. Perhaps the emperor and his men have been in that area with the core for long enough to cause the taint?"

# MYTHOS SEAS: MOVING SEAMOUNTS

"The taint started well over a year ago." Draflor tapped the date of the letter with his tail. "The emperor hasn't been hovering there with his fleet all this time, has he?"

"No, not that I'm aware of." Ofnik leaned back and slung one leg over the other, "and using a throne core to sink a few fleets of ships is a bit overkill."

"It also wouldn't be effective." Reyold added as the alligator snapping turtle lifted his head up higher to listen. "The core could only let out that much power for a short time, though it would be more than long enough to sink a few fleets."

Jackson's eyes widened once he got to the bottom of the second missive and he nudged Draflor, who looked down to where Jackson's fingers were hovering.

"What?" Ofnik leaned forward, noticing Jackson's expression.

"I didn't know Great Ghost point was a nesting ground for sea-serpents..." Jackson met Draflor's gaze. "Did it used to be?"

"It was before the Steelserpent War..." Draflor pulled out another book, "but during the war they had no choice but to nest elsewhere, it was too dangerous for their young. They nested along the Great Abyssal Drop-off during that time."

"Would they have anything to do with why the Toxicshade would gather there?"

"... No, not that I can think of." Draflor was flipping through another book urgently. "This species of sea serpent don't have any connection to the venom, they are purely water magic users, although the occasional one can use some nature magic." Draflor looked confused as he tossed the book away and returned to the missive. "I honestly think they'd keep the Toxicshade from going there, Great Ghost Point got its name from their territorial nature in the first place."

# SNAPPING TURTLE INN

"Ok, are you part elf or something." Reyold suddenly demanded, smacking his hands on the table as he rose to his feet. His sudden outburst caused Jackson and Draflor to look up in surprise. "You know way too much for a young kid. You say you're from the Northern Continent, but yet you know more about what is going on around Great Ghost Point and this area than our whole network of people combined, and we've been at this for years!" He pointed a finger at Jackson. "I think you better start talking and telling the truth."

Jackson bristled at his words. "I'm not part elf, at least not that I know of, and I have been telling the truth, just not everything about me."

"I'm not from the northern lands however, and neither are those we are aligned to, which is how Jackson knows more than you think he should." Draflor added.

"It's also why he's able to do so much crazy magic." Spinescale suddenly grinned, although she knew only Jackson and Draflor could understand her. "Can I pretend to bite him? Just to make him rethink his temper a bit? All this talking, while interesting, is getting a bit dull."

Reyold opened his mouth to say more but was interrupted by Ofnik. "That's enough Reyold." He folded his arms. "Kid, I don't like not knowing who you are, or who you are helping, but you seem to be doing good." He sighed. "Although, I wish you had more answers, but you've only prompted a lot more questions."

"To be fair we know little of you, and you've given us more questions than answers as well." Draflor pointed out. "Let's call it even."

Ofnik chuckled. "Scrappy one, aren't you?"

"Only if I need to be." Draflor looked smug. "Which is quite often."

# MYTHOS SEAS: MOVING SEAMOUNTS

The turtle snapped his jaws as if he approved of Draflor's sentiments.

"Do you mind if I take this?" Jackson asked, pointing to the missive as he remembered something. "There is someone I'd like to show it to if we can find him."

Reyold leaned over and whispered urgently in Ofnik's ear before Ofnik shoved the scroll over to Jackson. "Go ahead, I have two of these scrolls, but I will ask a couple things in return."

"Ok…" Jackson slowly took the scroll and rolled it up. "What would that be?" He placed the scroll in his bag.

"When you find the answers to your questions, somehow let me know, I'm curious." Ofnik grinned, "and I get the feeling you will find out more than we will." He whistled long and loud.

Jackson flipped his head to the side when the large window in the room suddenly swung open. With a loud cry the large gleam eagle from earlier came swooping in and landed on Ofnik's arm.

"Two and three." His words snapped Jackson out of his shock at seeing the large eagle while Spinescale shrunk into the bag a bit. "I want to know how you got to our little Island. Reyold here said someone of your description couldn't be found on any of the ships in port, and three." He leaned forward, his eagle friend leaning forward as well, clapping its beak in emphasis. "Who is the group you are aligned to?"

Jackson, Draflor, and Spinescale all exchanged a long look, before Spinescale motioned towards the large open window. "Why don't ya show him the way you got here?" Her eyes gleamed in anticipation as she pointed to the window. "It's getting late enough not many people would see you fly over anyways."

Daflor snickered. "I love the way you think, I'll answer the third question."

# SNAPPING TURTLE INN

Jackson shook his head while a small smile crossed his lips. "Well... as to how I got here." He wandered over to the window, making sure he wasn't too close to any paper products. "Let's just say..." He quickly cast his water travel spell.

Ofnik, Reyold, and the snapping turtle all lunged backwards while the eagle screeched in surprise when a column of water cascaded into existence around Jackson. "The ocean is our road."

"And as for who we are aligned to, look in your ancient records about the Sonaeko!" Draflor called before Jackson's legs turned into his tail and he darted out of the window. He soared into the evening sky as Spinescale hissed her approval of the shocked expressions on Ofnik's and Reyold's faces.

## CHAPTER EIGHT
# AUNTIE ANCIE

Jackson flew over the town as quickly as he could, going higher and higher into the sky in an effort to stay as unidentifiable as possible to any onlookers down below.

"Head that way, towards the front of the island." Draflor swooped off in the indicated direction.

"What about Zepherdust?" Jackson asked as he hurried after Draflor.

"I'll let her know where to meet us." Draflor smirked, a shimmering swirl of magic flowing out from his fins before it raced down towards the shoreline next to the harbor. As Jackson quickly followed Draflor he looked down every now and again at the beautiful island below. "This really is a pretty island." He commented when they passed over a large meadow surrounded by tall waving trees.

"Oh, it's more than an island." Draflor said mysteriously once the sea came into view up ahead.

"What you mean by that?" Spinescale got a funny look on her snout. "How can something be more than an island?"

Draflor refused to say more as he led Jackson back into the water with a splash. He had them follow him along the shoreline which suddenly seemed to cave inwards as night fell. A few

# AUNTIE ANCIE

moments later, Zepherdust, who was encased in brightly glowing magic, came whipping over.

"What's going on?" She asked, the magic around her fading away as she coasted next to them.

"Beats me..." Spinescale puffed.

"Draflor... where are you leading us?" Jackson shuddered, casting his biolumina spell to illuminate the water around him. His light revealed an utterly huge cavern that he regarded with dread. "You know I hate giant dark caverns." He gave Draflor a pleading look. "Please tell me we aren't going in there."

"It would be a bad idea if we did." Draflor began forming a strange symbol in front of him. "Remember when I said I figured out something?"

"Right in the midst of the milkbar?" Spinescale gave him a teasing look as Zepherdust got a perplexed expression on her snout. "Yes, I remember it well."

Draflor stuck his tongue out. "Smart seal," he rolled his eyes sarcastically. "Yes that. Let's just say I figured out the true nature of Anciellon Isle." As the symbol finished forming he, Jackson, Zepherdust, and Spinescale were enveloped in a bright green-blue bubble.

"Anciellon!" Draflor yelled, his voice roaring through the water. "Auntie Ancie! I know you're in there, you better wake up and come out here, or I'll start singing a song I know will get stuck in your head and drive you nuts for the next century." Draflor's tone was somehow serious and teasing at the same time.

Jackson, Zepherdust, and Spinescale both looked around wildly when a deep rumble shook the water as light green magic pulsed from the cave and raced out across the rock of the island. As the magic passed over the stone it changed, forming into a shiny material that gleamed from the light of Draflor's spell.

## MYTHOS SEAS: MOVING SEAMOUNTS

Jackson and his friends gasped when the head of a behemoth sized, slightly disgruntled turtle came sliding out of the cavern into view. The turtle's eyes slowly opened while she focused on the bubble, turning her head very slowly for a closer look.

"Draflor." The turtle's tired and ancient sounding voice made the water rumble. "I've gone two centuries without you and your kins nonsense, couldn't you give me another century to recoup?"

"Oh, Auntie Ancie, you flatter me so!" Draflor perked up. "You mean we only wore you and your kin out enough for you to only have to rest for three centuries? We'll have to try harder next time; I was expecting four at least."

"Why do I get a feeling there is more to Draflor than he's told us?" Spinescale whispered in Jackson's ear.

"Could be that every time we meet someone from before the Great Petrifying, they know him by name..." Jackson whispered back, "and seem to know about his mischievous side."

"If he's been doing more major mischief in the past then he's let on, he better tell me about it later. I feel like I keep missing out on something good."

The great turtle sighed, closing her eyes and pulling her head back slightly. "You haven't changed a bit, perhaps I should be grateful that you and your kin haven't been able to come for a visit, but..." Her eyes opened. "I know the circumstances as to why." Her voice was sad, longing. "I am the only of my kind to have survived the petrifying, as I assume, are you?"

"I've been stuck within the Staff of Solarswell for the last two centuries, it's been a pleasure I assure you." Draflor looked back when Solarswell flashed. "What? Don't give me that, you've been too busy helping the medians this last little while to pay any attention to us, but you can hound me when I make a joke like that?"

# AUNTIE ANCIE

The Auntie Ancie breathed out heavily, making a sound almost like a chuckle as she shifted her ancient gaze over to Jackson for a closer look.

"You look a lot like your ancient Uncle, Prince Theren, young man." She said approvingly. "I am relieved to see one of his brother's posterity has finally heeded the call of the sea."

Jackson's mouth opened, utterly speechless while Draflor suddenly stopped his conversation with the staff. "What was that Auntie?" Draflor asked, his eyes bugging out in shock.

"After the Petrifying, those who have been called the Lost Ones stayed with me for a time, Prince Theren and his eldest brother being among them." Auntie Ancie looked off into the sea as if pulling the memory from the ocean itself. "I was too weak to do more than offer them a safe home. It took all my strength to fight off the magic of the Petrifying, and my dear mate drained his magic to help me before he succumbed. I had gone towards the Northern Continent to escape the threat of the Dark One, as she still patrolled the seas at that time."

She seemed to let out a soft sigh. "While I lingered there to graze on the great kelp, Theren, his brother, and a small group of others who had found me decided to go ashore to see if there was any chance of help from the surviving nations."

She shook her head sadly. "But there was none, those nations were too caught up in their own efforts and the Lost Ones returned in sorrow. All save the eldest daughter of Theren's older brother, who had fallen madly in love with a man from the Northern Continent. She chose to stay, and the Star of the Sea and Book of the Sonaeko stayed with her, much to the shock of Theren and the others."

"What... what happened to Theren and the others?" Jackson asked, a deep pang in his chest.

# MYTHOS SEAS: MOVING SEAMOUNTS

"I took them as far as could to the south, far from the reaches of the Dark One." Her eyes grew mournful. "The Star of the Sea had told Theren of a place he and his followers could go to safely join with their nation in their slumber, if they so wished to seal their fate to them. The power of the Dark One and the war were too great at that point to restore the Sonaeko, so Theren and the others decided it would be best to wait, rather than live out their lives without their loved ones."

Her old eyes returned to Jackson. "Years later, Theren's niece, one of your ancestors, sent a call out to me that she wished to take some of her tribe, who were not blessed with the long life of the Sonaeko, to join Theren and the others. Her children were then grown, with families of their own, and she feared that she and her husband and some of their friends, who had been blessed with the blessing of longevity, would have to see their children and grandchildren die long before they ever grew old. Her father and the Star of the Sea had told her where to go to join her nation and family later, if she so chose."

She had a fond look in her eyes as she looked behind her. "At that point, I had found a group of people who had been displaced from the war, and they had made an alliance with me. In which, if I would give them protection and shelter, they would take care of my distant kin, the health of my great shell, and the life that grows thereon. If they kept their word, I would guide them to plentiful waters and the magic of my shell would bless them and their children. Even though they had settled here for many years, I heeded the call of Theren's niece and took her and her family as far as I could before she and her loved ones took a ship south, to where I don't know."

She got a thoughtful look on her beaked face. "Months later Theren's niece, Nelva, and some of the others returned and I took

## AUNTIE ANCIE

them back to the Northern Continent. I heard nothing from them until many years later, when I once again headed Nelva's call and took her and more of her tribe south once again before we parted ways..."

Her eyes refocused on Jackson. "I've not seen another Sonaeko, till now."

Jackson felt like he'd sink to the seafloor. "You mean that... you mean my Third Great Grandma and Grandpa and all my grandpa's family, and the members of my tribe that vanished are still alive?"

She nodded. "They are in stone, having joined their nation and the other nations in their eternal slumber, and I have remained in these oceans, far from where the Dark One used to swim."

"Auntie Ancie, do you know what happened to the Dark One?" Draflor interjected. "Is she still alive?"

"I do not know my child; her patrols ceased many decades ago." Auntie Ancie turned her head to look behind her. "I have not dared to go close enough to those seas to find out if she still remains or has perished with time. Her kind don't live as long as I when the blessing of longevity has been broken."

"There has been a darkness growing south of here, around Great Ghost Point, there is also darkness growing in the abyss that has covered the ruins of Abyssal City." Draflor quickly said. "And darkness has spread over other areas of the sea as well, and a current above Starkelp Strand has died."

Auntie Ancie's eyes slowly widened, her immense pupils shrinking. "I had doubted her ability to persevere this long." She looked at Jackson. "Take care young lightborn, if the Dark One still lives, your life will be in great danger. She seeks to bring all the seas to her reign and destroy the nation that swam in her way."

"But who is she exactly? No one has told me anything about her, or this darkness." Jackson quenched the shiver that threatened to go down his spine as he gave Draflor a sideways glance.

Auntie Ancie looked surprised. "Draflor, is this true?"

"It is, but I don't know the reason why, but I have been forbidden to tell Jackson anything either." Draflor shifted uncomfortably. "Though I wasn't sure of what the darkness was exactly until you mentioned… well her."

"By whom have you been forbidden?" Auntie Ancie pressed, giving him a slitted gaze.

"By the Sonaeko Medians, and Guardians." Draflor said.

"Oceaono?" She asked and Draflor gave his version of a nod. "Very well, I will respect their choice, although I question their reasoning." She turned to Jackson. "Remember child, darkness cannot destroy light, it is only when the light dims and fades away that darkness gains power." She moved her head back to Draflor. "You say there is a darkness growing at Great Ghost Point?"

"Yes, but we don't know why, or what is causing it." Draflor said. "Only that a corrupt nation is gathering there for some reason."

"A fleet of which has taken a rest break on your shell." Spinescale said while Zepherdust looked troubled. "They likely have some powerful weapons on their ships too."

"Oh, do they now…" Auntie Ancie got a dangerously disapproving look in her eyes. "I might have to do something about that…" She gave Draflor a mothering expression. "Be careful little scamp, though it pains me to admit, I hope to see you once again here soon."

Her old eyes focused on Jackson. "And you young lightborn, remember what I said about the darkness. Be wise, and if life becomes too hard, you are always welcome on my shell, as are you, young sea snake and young sea lion. Now I must go, I must remove

# AUNTIE ANCIE

my people from the darkness and build my strength for the future when the seas roll with war betwixt dark and light once again."

Draflor shoved the bubble to the side, throwing Jackson, Zepherdust, and Spinescale around in a jumble while a loud water vaporizing bellow rang through the sea. Light green magic spread out from Auntie Ancie's head to cover her body as her great webbed feet came moving out from where they were tucked into her shell. She shoved her immense bulk forward through the water, starting slowly but gaining speed as she surged past Jackson and the others.

"Where is she going?" Zepherdust asked worriedly as she righted herself.

"Yeah..." Spinescale shook herself when they surfaced and watched as the island aback the great turtle went coasting past. "Weren't we still talking?"

"Auntie Ancie does things her own way." Draflor said quietly as the part of the island where the city was flew into view. "She and her mate are the oldest of their kind, my sire said they were born at the creation. I never doubt her judgment, even if she does sometimes act oddly."

*Must be a water creature trait...* Jackson thought wryly while the harbor passed by. Many of the ships were surrounded by the glowing green magic which safely encased them as they were towed along.

However, the Toxicshade ships had no such protection, and were being battered by the waves, a couple near sinking as they lurched in the water. It looked like many, if not all the men had made for the docks, fear plastered on their faces while they watched the water crash into their ships. One of the largest vessels, the one Jackson and the others spied on earlier, suddenly tilted dangerously to one side before crashing over when the hull collapsed as some of the green magic pierced into its side.

# MYTHOS SEAS: MOVING SEAMOUNTS

"Let's go!" Jackson dove into the water towards the sinking ship while the remaining men and the captain scrambled from within and made a break for shore. "I want a better look at what they had on there, maybe they were guarding one of those cannons we read about."

"Send me into the bag please, I really need air!" Spinescale called and Jackson hurriedly teleported her in before he and the others dove towards the ship as it dropped under the waves, a couple other ships following it down.

"Over there Jackson, look!"

Jackson followed Draflor's gaze and saw a huge concave circle that was crisscrossed with runes, a large purple gem within the middle, and a ring of smaller ones around it.

"That's a magical cannon alright." Jackson called as it broke through the ropes and cords holding it onto the deck and began to sink quickly towards the bottom. Jackson quickly formed a symbol on it before it could vanish into the depths and it popped out of sight and into his bag.

Zepherdust gave him a surprised look. "Why did you do that?"

"I once overheard my grandpa talking about how many of the old venom clan's magical gems and other items had been stolen by the Toxcishade. I'm hoping to return a few." Jackson explained while he dove towards the captain's quarters, his body still faintly aglow.

Water had yet to fill the room when he busted the door down and rushed around, looking for anything that could be important or contain any information. Zepherdust scampered in behind him, giving the place a confused look.

"Better just send a bunch of things into your bag, I doubt we have enough time to be picky." Draflor pointed to the desk and other items that had been tossed around. "It still wouldn't be too good of an idea for you to go too deep, you haven't had a lot of experience with deep-water magic."

"That and it's dark." Jackson added before a whole slew of things in the room disappeared. He rushed around the room, throwing open drawers and even tried using his nature magic to break off a section of the cupboards before they vanished away.

"Nothing in here!" Zepherdust called as she used her nose to shut a cupboard that had slipped open.

"Just a thought, but why not send the whole ship into your bag?" Draflor suggested. "The new bag is big enough to hold a couple dozen of these things."

Jackson facepalmed. "You know, you could've mentioned that before I started breaking the thing apart."

"Sorry, it didn't really occur to me either, until I saw you smash that cupboard." Draflor ducked into a drawer. "This one has paperwork in it though."

Jackson hurried and sent the paperwork into his original bag and quickly looked around for a bit more before the hold started creaking from pressure. "They just had to use metal to fortify the exterior." Jackson frowned. "Doesn't do them much good, and earth or metal-based magic could still tear it apart."

"They're going against the Fire Tribes, remember?" Draflor pointed out with a smirk. "I do believe there's some benefit from metal in that case. Something about the boat not catching fire or what not."

"Ok, ok, I'll send the boat into the bag now." Jackson twisted around and placed the symbol on the ceiling. An immense flash of bubbles was released when the ship vanished, and Jackson immediately made a frantic dash to the surface as darkness closed in around him. Zepherdust wasn't a second behind him as he darted towards the waves.

"Hate, hate, hate, the dark!" Jackson shivered before he shot out of the water, breathing a huge sigh of relief at the sight of the sky above. "I'll never get used to that…" He muttered as he splashed back under the waves.

"I think we missed the other boats…"

Jackson followed Draflor's gaze and…. saw absolutely nothing. "Wow, she can really book it when she wants to."

"Better try your mapping magic, maybe we can still grab another ship or two." Draflor said.

"You know how weird it sounds when you say that?" Jackson laughed while he formed the mapping sphere around him after a quick look up at the sky.

Draflor gave a maniacal chuckle. "Why yes, yes I do! Shall we go make another name for you? Stealer of sinking ships?"

"Oh, please no, that's a horrible title." Jackson waved a hand as Zepherdust snickered while intricate maps began forming across the sphere as pulses of magic coursed into the water.

"There could be worse titles…" Zepherdust pointed out teasingly.

Jackson rolled his eyes before he looked back at his map. "There are a couple ships over there…" Jackson turned to inspect that area of the map before he looked up at the sky. "But… I don't know if we should head that way…"

"Why not?" Zepherdust gave the map a curious look.

"What's up?" Draflor came over only for his fins to flare out slightly. "Wow, Auntie can still whip up a nasty storm if she wants to."

"**She** summoned that storm?" Jackson was aghast.

"Why?" Zepherdust added.

"I'm guessing she's hoping to make sure those ships sink as deeply as possible." Draflor seemed amused, "and she's trying to

# AUNTIE ANCIE

prevent anyone from leaving her presence for a while. The Toxicshade can't find out what happened if their men can't figure out where they are."

"She's…. uh, thorough." Jackson blinked. "I guess we'd better make bubbles south."

"Um, maybe we should see if Spinescale wants back out here first." Zepherdust reminded him.

"Oops, hope that ship didn't land on her." Jackson winced.

When a very angry Spinescale reappeared Jackson cringed as she leveled him with a glare. "If we weren't on a time crunch, you'd be getting bitten very hard mister! What's the meaning of having a broken ship pop into the bag and causing a wave big enough to wash me off my resting spot? I've never been more startled in all my LIFE!"

"Sorry…" Jackson apologized. "I wasn't really thinking…"

"Horrible idea…" Draflor said innocently.

"HEY! It was your idea to send the whole ship into the bag in the first place!"

"ME? Why would I tell you to do such a thing?"

"You did to tell me to do that you twirp! Don't make me get Solarswell involved in this, and Zepherdust can back me up."

"O-ho are you threatening me?"

"Yes, I am, and don't make me do it." Jackson smirked. "I'm sure there is more magic the staff could use from the seas."

Draflor waggled a fin at him. "You sure you want to play hard-fin?"

"Ok, ok boys stop." Spinescale hissed in exasperation, throwing her wings out between them. "I can already see this is going to be a long journey the rest of the way south. If ya don't stop, I'M going to be telling Oceaono and Stonecurrent on the next check-in."

"Oh, we're just having some fun." Draflor laughed before giving Jackson a look, "but don't you dare get Solarswell involved in this."

"I don't have to." Jackson smiled smugly before he swam off in a southward direction. "I can already tell from the faint flashes he's well aware of everything that just happened."

"Dragonscales…" Draflor muttered when the flashing got more prominent and Zepherdust giggled. "Hey, I was only joking, you know that. No, I am not going to gather more magic right now, we have more important things to take care of!"

Jackson, and Spinescale, who had hitched a ride on his shoulder, snickered as they swam south with Zepherdust, following Jackson's map while Draflor and Solarswell squabbled.

## CHAPTER NINE
# SIGNS OF DARKNESS

The group traveled hard for a few days as they continued south, Jackson using a sea-sail spell he'd learned to help him and Zepherdust ride the currents as they continued onward. The sea once again became shallower as they neared their destination, much to Jackson, Zepherdust, and Spinescale's relief.

However, as they traveled further into the shallower seas the morning of the fourth day, something made Jackson pause and he slowed his pace slightly.

"Something wrong?" Zepherdust asked as she flipped around. Draflor peeked out from the staff as a groggy looking Spinescale woke up from a nap.

Jackson frowned uncertainly as he inspected the waters around them uncertainly. "I… I'm not sure…" He tilted his head when he noticed something in the water seemed off and squinted. "Does something about the water here seem off to anybody?"

Draflor came all the way out of the staff as Zepherdust's eyes glistened faintly with magic. Meanwhile, Spinescale came partway out of the bag, looking around them intently. Suddenly Zepherdust eyes widened at the same moment as Draflor's slitted.

"GET BACK!" Draflor shouted when dark shapes swept through the water towards them! Zepherdust let out a warning bark

# MYTHOS SEAS: MOVING SEAMOUNTS

as Jackson threw up a barrier around them and the dark forms banked away. A spell crackled around Jackson's hands, only for him to look over in surprise when Zepherdust shot past him, her flippers aglow.

As the dark mass swooped back towards them, Zepherdust flipped around, letting out an ear-splitting bark as magic raced from her flippers, forming into a shimmering shoal of tiny, magical fish that she catapulted forwards! Jackson watched in shock as the magical fish shot into the dark mass, flashing brightly before they shattered, sending a spray of shimmering magical particles flying in all directions.

The dark mass immediately broke apart as Zepherdust's magic sliced through it. Jackson shook off his own shock long enough to send a barrage of his own attacks firing at the remaining smaller masses that had started dashing towards them.

As Jackson and Zepherdust's attacks obliterated the darkness, Draflor shot forwards, rushing over to quickly trap a large glob of the darkness in a bright sphere.

"Thanks Zepherdust." Jackson breathed, still feeling a bit stunned.

"I... had no idea you could do that." Spinescale said, sounding impressed.

"Well…" Zepherdust looked a bit sheepish, but proud, as she swam back over. "Fulrion was a good teacher. He taught Avavo, some of the other sea lions, and I a lot about the old magic of the Mistsurge Isle seals."

"That was amazing." Jackson said, giving Zepherdust a wry grin. "Uh, you think you could show me that spell again sometime?"

Zepherdust giggled. "Sure, although Fulrion indicated it's easier for Sonaekian sealborn to learn."

# SIGNS OF DARKNESS

"Guys, you'd better come look at this..." Draflor called, having been busy inspecting the dark mass he'd trapped.

"What is it?" Zepherdust asked as they swam over, and Jackson's eyes widened.

"Is that a jellyfish?" Jackson asked.

"What? It can't be, I've never seen a jellyfish like that!" Spinescale said, giving the dark glob a confused look as she swam closer.

"It **was** a jellyfish..." Draflor commented as Jackson frowned, leaning forward for a closer look.

The creature had the curved bell of a normal jellyfish, except it seemed to be made of dark, inky looking gel. Dark shadows spread out from the bell, and Jackson saw small thin black tendrils waving slightly in the shadows. He gave Draflor a puzzled look. "What do you mean that this 'was a jellyfish?'"

"When creatures embrace dark magic, they... change." Draflor commented quietly as a stream of light reached out from the barrier he'd encased the creature in. The jellyfish seemed to try and propel itself away from the light and Draflor's eyes slitted. "This is bad." He backed away when the dark jellyfish suddenly seemed to melt into shadows before his barrier flashed brightly, dispelling the remains of the shadowy jellyfish completely.

"The Dark One?" Jackson asked worriedly.

"She's been here." Draflor whispered, looking disturbed, "and some creatures here joined her cause..." He glanced back to where the remnants of the dark mass Zepherdust and Jackson had destroyed were seeming to evaporate away.

"What do we do?" Zepherdust asked worriedly while Spinescale got a troubled look in her eyes.

"Get out of this area, quickly." Draflor gave Jackson a serious look before he glanced back at Zepherdust, "and have that fin band of yours alert Startide and Daychaser so they can join us soon." He swam up towards the surface. "Come on, we need to get out of this area before it gets dark, no telling if there might be another group of dark creatures around here."

Jackson watched Zepherdust glance down at the band around her flipper before it glowed faintly and she made a soft, approving sound. He glanced back at the dying shadows from the dark swarm of jellyfish and felt his stomach clench in worry.

With one final look, he hurried after the others as Spinescale slipped back into his bag, giving him a worried look.

"You ok?" She whispered.

Jackson shrugged his shoulders. "It's just sad to see creatures choosing bad things."

"It always is…" Spinescale replied, glancing back slightly. "That's why I worry about Startide with Shadowtorrent."

"The sea snake you had a crush on?" Jackson whispered back, his eyes widening.

Spinescale nodded. "If he hadn't of gotten eaten by a shark, he'd of been one of the first truly dishonored snakes in the Jewel Isles…" She got a sober look in her eyes. "Served him right, glad I wasn't that close to him, but it still affected all of us when he chose darkness." She got a wry look in her eyes. "That snake has a brother who's pretty cute though." She closed her eyes, "and it hit him pretty hard when his brother fell…"

"But Shadowtorrent isn't like that snake you knew…" Jackson reassured quietly. "He's doing just the opposite of what that snake did."

Spinescale sighed. "I know… but I worry, I don't want to see any of you guys get hurt."

## SIGNS OF DARKNESS

"Trust takes time." Zepherdust said shyly, glancing over. "Take it from me. Give it some time and see what you think, you don't have to make a final choice about Shadowtorrent now."

Spinescale gave Zepherdust a wry frown. "I guess so... but I still don't know, something about Shadowtorrent still rubs my scales the wrong way." She slipped back into Jackson's bag and used her tail to yank it shut.

Jackson, Draflor, and Zepherdust all exchanged an uncertain look before Jackson gave a slight shrug.

"Give her time." Draflor wrote in the water with his magic.

## CHAPTER TEN
# SIRENS SONG

Very late that night, after a long day of traveling as fast and as far as they could, Jackson dragged himself atop a rocky outcropping to sleep for what remained of the night. After securing his bag, he teleported in for a well-deserved rest and a quick look through the rest of the captain's quarters of the ship he'd nabbed. He wasn't able to find anything else of much informational value and truly didn't care about the other things, so he went back to bed for the night.

He was woken the next morning by an alarmed Spinescale, who came whipping over and smacked him across the face with her tail!

"WAKE UP!" She hollered, likely for the fifth or sixth time as Jackson yelped in pain from the smack of her tail.

"Ow! What the spe—"

"No time, I just saw Zepherdust dash into the water when a ship passed by the rock you secured the bag on!"

Jackson didn't even get to wipe the sleep from his eyes before he teleported them out of the bag and hunkered down on the outcropping, looking carefully about.

"Zepherdust?" Jackson whispered worriedly, only to sigh when she poked her head out of the water, looking startled and alarmed.

# SIRENS SONG

"I think those were Toxicshade ships!" Zepherdust whispered urgently.

"Over there." Draflor tilted his body for a better look in the early morning mist. "I can make out a few ships heading off that way."

Jackson threw on his bag as he held out his arm for Spinescale. Once she'd raced up his arm and coiled around his shoulders he ran across the brown-gray stone and dove into the water before he and Zepherdust swiftly stroked after the ships.

It only took them a minute or so to catch up to the vessels, and Jackson quietly surfaced alongside the last one in the fleet. "It's a Toxicshade vessel alright..." He whispered, aware of how well sound traveled over water. "One of the newer ones to, not an Old Kingdom vessel."

"Is that good?" Zepherdust asked in a hushed voice.

"I... don't know..." Jackson sank under the surface, swimming over to inspect all the other ships in the fleet, half of whom were older vessels from the old venom clans.

"Those the ships that are going to be sunk?" Spinescale asked while Jackson and Zepherdust dove under one of the last ships.

"I think so..." Jackson paused when he heard someone talking and quickly resurfaced. "Shh."

He cupped a hand over his ear before he smacked his hands against the surface in frustration. Zepherdust dove below him before they slithered quickly through the water towards one of the newer ships. Jackson used his water magic to lift himself, Zepherdust, and the others up alongside the vessel as he followed the sound that was coming from a cracked window further down.

"I don't know what happened to the fleet that was coming from Bolithy." A man growled as Jackson and the others sidled up next to the window to eavesdrop. "They should've met up with one of the other fleets already, but there hasn't been any word from them at all."

"The emperor is growing impatient, your ships are already behind schedule."

Jackson saw the flash of a communication mirror.

"If that fleet has been sunk, we will need all three of the cannons you are carrying to release the power the Ironmamba Emperor left us."

Jackson and the others exchanged an alarmed look.

"We will be there as soon as possible; the weather has held us back." The man was sounding frustrated. "I've been doing all I can."

There was a moment of silence. "Are the ships from the old clans still with you?"

"Of course they are, and they don't expect a thing. It's all going according to plan." The man assured. "The other fleet of old clan vessels isn't far behind us and should meet up with ours anytime now."

"Good, see that they don't get tipped off to our plans, and give them their orders."

"I'll make sure they get into position." He said.

"See that you do."

Jackson's nose scrunched up in disgust as the men ended their conversation and he let his spell end, dropping him and the others back into the sea.

"Lovely guy this Emperor…" Spinescale added. "Remind me how he got to where he is now?"

"By a lot of treachery, force, and flattery." Jackson grumbled sourly.

"Do you think there might be a way to warn the old clans?" Draflor asked.

# SIRENS SONG

"I have the scroll we got from Ofnik." Jackson hooked his thumb back at his bag. "But I don't know if I'll recognize anyone enough to be sure they would be the one who I should give the scroll to."

"Don't forget we are supposed to meet up with Blade at Vigilwave Rock here soon." Zepherdust said, glancing behind her. "Though, I'm surprised that Startide and Daychaser haven't found us yet."

"I think it's time we reach out to Oceaono and Stonecurrent." Jackson brought up his gloved hand as he let himself sink deeper into the water.

"Stonecurrent, Oceaono." He called into the stone in the glove. "It's Jackson."

Magic swirled around in the stone for a time before it slowly petered out. "That's odd." Jackson said with a frown.

"They must be doing something that's preventing them from answering right now..." Draflor said. "That's not a good sign."

"Sure it's something they're doing, and not someone preventing us from reaching them?" Spinescale questioned uneasily.

Jackson and Zepherdust exchanged a worried look when Draflor didn't respond immediately. Finally, he shook his head. "No, if there was... someone preventing them from reaching us, the magic would've felt different."

"Oh... well, maybe we should see about those other vessels that guy mentioned." Spinescale said, giving Jackson a meaningful look. "Can't hurt."

"We do have a bit of time..." Zepherdust commented, "but not a lot."

Draflor looked around at the mist uncertainly as Jackson moved off, casting his mapping spell to help them find the other ships. "Let's hurry, this mist reminds me of sirens, and I don't enjoy dealing with them."

"Sirens? Here?" Jackson halted. "There are sirens in this part of the sea?"

"Beats me, they don't like to stay in the same territories for more than a couple decades." Draflor gave the mist a second look, "but that mist does look suspicious to me."

"Spells." Jackson swam off while the first fleet of ships carried on further into mist.

"Um, just a question, but what will happen to the ships if there are sirens here?" Spinescale asked.

"Would they endanger the old clan ships?" Zepherdust wondered.

Jackson bit his lip worriedly as Draflor took note of the last ship they passed.

"Well…" Draflor frowned, "hopefully a few of the old clan ships won't end up wrecking on the rocks. Sirens don't take well to trespassing vessels."

"And here I was worried about the sea serpents." Jackson grumbled, darting towards a small number of dots heading their way.

"That was quick." Draflor commented not even a minute later. "Guess that guy wasn't kidding when he said 'anytime now.'"

"I get the feeling that the Toxicshade don't kid around." Spinescale responded as her dark eyes ran over the hull of one of the ships. "Recognize any of these?"

"They're old clan ships." Jackson said, skirting around one vessel. He quickly changed his hide to dark gray before he porpoised out of the water alongside the ship for a minute to listen and watch.

# SIREN'S SONG

He could make out the sight of armored men and women walking about on the ship, while sailors went about their tasks. He quickly went over to another ship to listen for a minute. He ended up swallowing a mouthful of water when he heard a voice he recognized right as he plunged back into the waves.

"You ok?" Draflor asked as Jackson hacked for a moment.

"I-cough-I know that voice-COUGH!" Jackson pounded his chest lightly with his fist. "I didn't know I could still choke on water like that."

"Ironic huh?" Draflor was only slightly sympathetic, "but who was that you heard?"

"It was—" Jackson stopped, glancing behind him when a beautiful song suddenly came dancing across the waves. "What on Mythos?"

"UGH! It had to be siren mist." Draflor groaned before turning towards where the sound came from. "SHUT IT WILL YOU?! WE DON'T HAVE TIME FOR THIS."

Jackson quickly plugged his ears. "It isn't going to make me go all googly eyed and the like, is it?"

"What? Good seas no." Draflor motioned angrily. "It's just their warning calls, it's the mirages you have to be careful of."

"Mirages?" Zepherdust asked worriedly as the band around her flipper glistened slightly.

"JACKSON?" A voice called out, making Jackson and the others whip around to see Daychaser, Startide, Blade and his shiver, and a small pod of light gray and yellow dolphins come racing towards them.

"Daychaser! Startide, there you are!" Zepherdust called in relief, swimming closer while Jackson gave Blade a surprised look.

"Blade? You're here too?" Jackson called as they got closer while the singing increased in beauty and volume.

## MYTHOS SEAS: MOVING SEAMOUNTS

"Yeah, I thought we were supposed to meet you at Vigilwave Rock..." Spinescale pointed out, looking perplexed.

"We sent a call to Blade to try and find us, once we received Zepherdust's warning." Startide explained as Blade swooped in closer, revealing a bright band on his dorsal fin as well.

"Me and my team hurried to meet up with them before we started lookin for ya." Blade continued.

"And Startide sounded you with her magic right after we ran into Sunstream and her pod." Daychaser came up and tapped Jackson on the shoulder with his snout. "They said this was where a large façade of sirens were living."

Draflor was nearly steaming in annoyance. "I keep telling them over and over again, if they want to scare humans off to just use their usual screeches and screams, but NooOOoo! They use their beautiful warning songs instead." He swam off towards where the mist had been growing even thicker. "FOR THE LAST WING WHIPPING TIME! YOU'RE ONLY GOING TO MAKE THEM COME TOWARDS YOU!!" The fish's voice was nearly a roar.

"Um... what's gotten into Draflor?" Startide whispered, her voice squeaking a bit. "I've never heard him roar like that."

Blade just flared his fins slightly. "Didn't know the fish hated sirens."

"Draflor, calm down will you?" Jackson tapped the staff. "Solarswell! Are you there? Draflor has gone whirlpool."

The staff suddenly flashed like mad and Draflor's form was suddenly yanked back through the water and sucked into the staff just before he could let out another yell.

"..."

"Well... that was unexpected." Spinescale said, while Zepherdust just looked stunned.

# SIRENS SONG

Daychaser blinked before he whipped himself out of his stupor. "We need to get you out of here Jackson. Sunstream says the sirens have their whelps this time of year and are even more moody than normal."

"They truly won't react kindly, especially with this many ships." Sunstream, a young female dolphin said worriedly. "They've already driven many pods out of this area. They have the nastiest tempers and their shadow and water magic make it hard for us to defend ourselves against them."

"Shadow magic? Oh spells..." Jackson looked over his shoulder as another ship vanished into the mist. "That could be bad."

"Won't be now." Blade, his brightly polished armor shimmered as he came up and nudged Jackson from behind. "We need to get ya out of here."

"I can't, Mavous and his brother are on one of those ships." Jackson protested as he was shoved again.

"Shed skin... You're kidding..." Spinescale groaned.

Blade stopped. "The venom guys related to the Spherefangs?"

"Yes, I heard Mavous's voice just before the sirens started calling." Jackson insisted firmly.

Blade slashed the water with his teeth in annoyance. "Course he was, out of all the ships." He lashed the water a couple more times and a number of armored sharks came swimming into view. "Guess we got our work cut out for us boys. Form a perimeter."

As Jackson watched Blade command his shiver of sharks while they formed a protective barrier around him and the others, he inwardly shook his head. *I still think it's strange to see Blade acting so... military...*

"Sunstream, you know how to deal with these sirens?" Blade asked.

The dolphin had a look of alarm cross her eyes. "No, not at all, that's why we fled. It was just too dangerous here for us."

"Then what do we do?" Zepherdust asked as the group moved off.

"Jackson can deal with the sirens with his light magic." Draflor appeared before the staff started to pull him back in. "Hey, I'm calm now, but you try working with the siren peace teams for months to convince the sirens that their warning calls sound beautiful and wonderful to humans instead of frightening, only to have them think you're crazy. That façade's entire nest sight was destroyed because they wouldn't listen to reason and then they demanded I fix the damage, NO WING WIPP—" Draflor was promptly sucked back into the staff.

"OK... well, we now know why Draflor hates sirens." Spinescale said with a rueful look in her eyes. She glanced over to Jackson uncertainly. "We sure we want to go chasing after these ships if these creatures are that unreasonable?"

"I made a promise to Mavous's family." Jackson started swimming after the ships even faster, a light spell forming around him. "Come on, we have to hurry before they get too close to the rocks!"

Once Jackson and his friends entered into the reach of the sirens' mist, he had to spread out his light spell around him once he began noticing weird things forming in the darkening water. He heard the shouts of men and women up ahead and popped his head out of the water.

As Daychaser, Startide, and Zepherdust poked their heads up next to him, Jackson squinted. He could barely make out the hull of a ship that looked like it had slid too close to one of the others and was now somewhat stuck.

"Draflor, what should I do?" Jackson asked quietly.

# SIRENS SONG

"Find the sirens and ask them to stop, if that doesn't work encase them in a light barrier! It should make all this mist and the mirages disappear."

"Giant shark!" Sunstream suddenly cried before she and her pod took off into the water as Jackson looked under the surface and saw... nothing.

"My guess is a mirage." Daychaser sounded around, looking a bit confused. "I thought I saw another shattered one earlier, but since I'd heard about the whole mirage thing..." He shrugged. "Didn't bother me much, and it vanished soon after."

"What does the siren's magic conjure up anyways?" Startide asked. "Something you fear?"

"It's honestly quite random." Draflor said from the confines of the staff. "It varies from images of terrifying things, random memories, or things you or the sirens have seen."

"That explains the ophiotaurus I saw just a second ago..." Zepherdust inched behind Daychaser, looking slightly paler than usual.

"Then why the stories of beautiful women leading men to their deaths?" Jackson asked, remembering the tales he'd heard from some old sailors while there was a loud groaning crack when the stuck ships managed to break free of one another. A feeling of uneasiness settled in the air when he heard more sailors and warriors cry out in alarm.

"It's really a bunch of twisted myths." Draflor's face appeared on the orb and he rolled his eyes, "but I guess the sirens do look somewhat humanlike... Although if the sailors piloting the ships get freaked out or enchanted by the songs, they usually do wreak their vessels."

When Blade and his shiver suddenly tightened the circle, everyone stopped talking and tensed defensively. Jackson's eyes narrowed nervously when a strange creature darted past and another loud, but beautiful, cry rang out through the mist. A moment later, more shapes darted around them, prompting Startide and Daychaser to sound the water heavily as Spinescale and Zepherdust began forming spells around themselves.

"LeeEEAAVvvee heerree, ooorr wee wiiiilll EEENDD YOoouu!" A weezy voice cried out.

"Not until you stop and let these ships pass." Jackson responded. "Please, there're good people on boats, they don't deserve to be killed by crashing onto the rocks here."

"WeeEEee guuaaard OOOUUuur YyyyOOOOUuuung. TttHHhhheeeessssee ssSSOOUNNnnddds HhhUUUummMMMAAaanns FEAR!"

"I'm a human, and the only sound that's freaking me out right now is you talking, the singing warning sounds are pretty." Jackson replied matter-of-factly, feeling a touch annoyed.

"NNNnnnOOOOOOooo HHHuummaanns DDDddooonNnn'TTtt HHhhhavvveee FLliiipppeerrrs. Hhhuuummmannnsss ssCCCAaaRREeeed of WwwwAAaarrnnning criiillllEEESSSss."

"Oh for spells sake!" Jackson sighed and glanced over to Startide. "Could you give me a lift up, please?"

Startide obliged and Jackson carefully clambered up onto her back while she lifted him from the water. He quickly dried himself off enough for his legs to return, ignoring the mirages of a fallen whale charging through the air towards him as he stood up on Startide's back. "See? I'm a human, and none of these sounds are scary, very nice in fact. Like something I'd want to hear."

Some of the singing ceased. "Huuummaaan thiiinnkk warning ssoong nniicccee?"

## SIRENS SONG

"Yes, it's the mirages that are sometimes scary, although the dancing dolphin over there is kinda cute." Jackson smiled a bit at the sight of a spinning green dolphin. "Although, really, the mirages would be more effective at scaring humans away if you could make it seem like something scary is coming at them from the direction you don't want them to go."

More of the singing died down and the mist lightened up behind Jackson but got thicker in the direction he was facing. Before the mist thickened, Jackson managed to make out silhouettes of strange looking creatures perched on some rocky outcroppings.

"IIiiifFFff SSssoOOnnggg nnooottt sssccaaarrree yyyooouuu wWWEEEEeeeEE DddRrivvee aaawaayy Bbbbyyy FOORRRCCEEE!"

Jackson yelped when a multitude of dark creatures suddenly began leaping from the rocks into the water. His eyes widened once shadow energy formed around their webbed hands as their cries suddenly turned vicious and frightening.

"GET READY FOR BATTLE!" Blade shouted as Jackson dove into the water and quickly formed a light barrier around him and his friends. Not a second later a barrage of shadowy attacks crashed into the shield with small blasts before they dissipated into nothingness.

"Blade, let me shine some lights on you and the others, I know a trick or two." Draflor called as the staff began glowing wildly. "This'll bide us some time!"

Blade and his shiver slowed before a multitude of lights came flashing forth from Solarswell's orb to ricochet off the armor of the sharks! The light reflected and flashed in every direction as Jackson and the others covered their eyes while the sirens screamed in pain and fright, darting away as quickly as they could.

# MYTHOS SEAS: MOVING SEAMOUNTS

"Swim, SWIM!" Draflor cried, shaking Jackson and the others into action. They quickly turned and fled towards where the fleet of ships had regrouped before making a break in the opposite direction of where the sirens were.

Jackson porpoised out of the water a couple times to look behind them when the mist seemed to try and follow. A few small black forms jumped from the water a ways back, giving him quick hard stares as they leapt. *Their faces really do look a lot like humans...* Jackson thought as they neared the fleeing ships.

Once they came up behind the vessels, Jackson could hear the captains and leaders yelling firm, but anxious, orders to their men while they tried to get as far away from the sirens as possible.

"Well, that's that." Blade said. "Let's get you off to the meetin place."

Jackson gave Blade a quick look. "There's something I need to give to Mavous before we go."

"Then you better hurry." Startide gave a wary glance behind her. "We're being followed. I think some of the older sirens noticed the color of your hide."

Jackson looked down at his bright white tail and groaned. "Why does that color change spell nearly always break when I get spooked?"

"Blade, you and your shiver make sure the sirens don't sneak up on us." Daychaser said, taking charge. "Startide, use your magic to help them know where the sirens might come from, Zepherdust, you guard Startide's back, the others and I will go with Jackson to keep watch."

Jackson changed his hide back to a dark gray as Blade and his shiver spread out while Startide's eyes flashed with magic.

"Ready?" Daychaser came up beside Jackson as Zepherdust swooped over the hover behind Startide.

"Ready." Jackson shot forwards towards the ships, using his magic to skim the surface of the water while he listened, trying to make out any familiar sounding voice as he neared. He dove when one of the men on lookout spotted him and gave a panicked shout, bringing a group of mages and archers to the sides, ready to fire at any strange sight.

"Try weaving underneath the ships for a bit." Draflor suggested from the staff.

Jackson nodded, diving deeper before coming up beside the first ship to listen for a moment until he gave up and darted over to the next one. It wasn't until the third ship that he recognized not only Mavous's voice, but also his brother and Captain Venmoral's.

"I need a distraction on the other side of the ship." Jackson met Daychaser and Spinescale's eyes.

"Oh, I think we can manage something." Spinescale flashed her fangs enthusiastically. "Ready for a bit of mischief, Daychaser?"

Daychaser grinned, although his eyes were worried. "Yep, let's go. Don't get caught Jackson, I'll let out a call when you're clear."

"K." Jackson looked up at the deck high above him nervously as they swooped off. While the ships creaked and groaned in the slightly rough surf, Jackson watched nervously. His eyes followed the tilt and sway of the boats, rocking back and forth slightly in the water as he began his spell.

"There's the signal." Draflor said when a loud howl echoed in their ears before a thunder of feet rolled across the deck as men and women ran to the opposite side.

Jackson took a deep breath and cast his spell, shooting into the air before he quickly made it to the edge of the deck. He hovered nervously along the railing of the ship as he peered through the wooden rails, searching anxiously for Mavous or the others.

## MYTHOS SEAS: MOVING SEAMOUNTS

He finally saw the man further down the deck, urgently talking with none other than the captain of the ship, Captain Venmoral, and Mavous's brother. Jackson rushed along the length of the deck before he shot up to eye height with Mavous and Captain Venormal and the group of men and a single woman whipped around in alarm.

"You, YOU!? How did? Is this another mirage?" Mavous half stuttered, half cried.

"There isn't time to explain Mavous, the sirens are still coming this way." Jackson brought the scroll out of his bag and threw it towards Mavous, "and you have bigger worries ahead than sirens." He flipped backwards and dove into the sea as Mavous stumbled forward to grab the scroll.

As the captain of the ship yelled for backup, Jackson quickly met up with Daychaser and Spinescale. Daychaser let out a loud trill-bark to Startide, and only a few moments later she, Zepherdust, and the shiver of sharks came charging into view.

"Let's get out of here!!" Startide called, pausing out of habit so Jackson could grab her dorsal fin. "They're getting bolder by the second."

"Lead the way." Jackson started his quick current spell and coursed after Daychaser when a small swarm of sirens appeared in the dark water, their eyes latched on him.

Startide quickly took the lead as Blade and a Darktyr shark touched fins. As one the sharks slashed their tails in the direction of the sirens, causing long curved blades of water to fly into the swarm, scattering the siren in all directions.

While the siren's enraged cries rang out behind them, Startide swiftly led them away from the fleeing ships! Jackson's chest relaxed ever so slightly when the water grew lighter with the rising sun as they escaped the reaches of the sirens mist.

# SIRENS SONG

The sirens however, hadn't given up completely and were still following the group from a distance, although they couldn't match the speed of Jackson and his friends.

When the water below them began to deepen and the sun rose higher into the sky, most of the sirens finally broke off their attack.

After a few more minutes of hard swimming, Startide turned to check the water behind them. "They're still there. They're getting really far behind us, but they're still there."

"How many?" Zepherdust asked.

"Three." Startide said.

"Odd." Draflor commented as he made an appearance, a journal on the history and behavior of sirens in fin. "Sirens detest deep water; they'll normally only chance a crossing of deep oceans with their entire façade." He flipped through a few more pages while Daychaser came over for a look at what he was reading. "Although, from personal experience, I do know a few daring individuals will choose to go into deeper water if they so desire."

"Should we stop to see why they are still chasing us?" Jackson asked after reading a paragraph or so in Draflor's book. "From what this indicates, we're a lot further out than they're usually comfortable with, even if they're being driven from the shallows."

"It might not hurt..." Daychaser considered. "We do have an advantage out here if things take a dive."

"I'm not so sure, their shadow magic was really making it hard to figure out what was going on back there." Startide put in and Zepherdust nodded.

"Shadow magic isn't as potent in broad daylight." Jackson pointed up to the sun. "Even then, I should be able to use my light magic to counter their spells since I can see them."

"Won't hurt to know why they're chasin us." Blade added. "B-sides, we know how to battle out here." He turned to his shiver. "Darktyr and deeptyr, deeper water and get into position. Highwater sharks you're with me." The shiver broke apart as the large darktyr and deeptyr sharks slowly cruised into the depths, while Blade and the other sharks took their places around Jackson and his friends.

"No wonder Leavamentee likes him so much…" Jackson whispered to Startide.

"Yeah, I know, he was driving us snappers back at Starkelp…" She rolled her eyes. "He took to her lessons like a seagull to the air."

"Could we focus on the task at hand?" Spinescale interrupted, giving them a wry look. "We do have a small group of sirens on the way."

"We have a few flashes of the sun before they get within sight." Startide looked into the deep with her magic. "Maybe more, they seem to be getting a bit bite-shy, they keep hesitating."

"I would be too, if I was out in deep water without you guys." Spinescale looked around uncertainly. "I like having seafloor not too far away…"

"I agree with that." Jackson commented. "I think I'll get a few light spells ready, just in case."

"No argument there…" Zepherdust said, casting an uneasy glance below her at the dark waters.

The group waited while the minutes slowly passed by, everyone alert and anxious. Jackson knew the sirens were getting closer when Startide tensed slightly, and the shark's speed increased.

# SIRENS SONG

"Ready or not..." Draflor said when the forms of the three sirens, a male and two females, came into view. Daychaser swam in front of Jackson and Startide while the sharks all closed in around the sirens, who cried out with their melodic warning calls.

"Good afternoon, sirens of the southern waters." Daychaser called. "Might I ask why you have been following us?"

One of the females bared her teeth as the water darkened around her, only for her to let out a beautiful cry when Jackson surrounded her with a sphere of light magic.

"We don't wish to cause you any harm." Daychaser's calm voice carried clearly through the water as the other two sirens prepared to attack. "We only wish to know why you have followed us. If you do try anything however, we have a light mage who can stop you in your trails."

The sirens exchanged a long, uneasy look at the mention of a light mage. After Jackson let the sphere of light magic vanish, they bunched together, talking as quietly as they could.

"You have the lightborn with you." The male said as they ended their conversation. "Our elders desire for us to bring him to our shores."

"And why is that?" Daychaser remained composed and calm, even while the sharks began to swim around erratically in agitation.

"The lightborn brings honor and prosperity, none deserve it more than the siren." The older of the female's tone seemed to dare Daychaser to contradict her. "He is to come dwell with us."

"The lightborn doesn't bring prosperity or honor." Daychaser said firmly. "Honor comes from within, and prosperity comes from actions without. While I'm sure your façade has great power, the lightborn has his own agency in who he chooses to align himself to."

"Then why do you speak for him?" The male pressed.

"Because he can." Jackson said, letting his color spell drop, "and while I would like to learn more about your kind at some point, I'm afraid we don't have the time right now, we are needed elsewhere."

The sirens seemed taken aback, as if they weren't expecting Jackson to defend Daychaser.

"Our elders have demanded the lightborn return to dwell with our kind, do you wish to bring the rage of our façade upon you by your futile refusal?"

Jackson felt himself bristle at the smaller and scrappier female's words while Daychaser spoke up.

"Do your elders wish to bring the seas into darkness, and invite the anger of the Star of the Sea and the responsibility of the weakening of the oceans magic upon them?"

The siren went quiet, but after a few moments the male sneered. "You're bluffing."

"Am I?" Daychaser slowly swam up for a breath. "Surely your elders have sensed the great darkness growing in the oceans south of you?" He drifted back down to be eye level with the sirens, who took turns going up for a breath as he continued. "Not only that, but they should also be aware that the magic in these parts of the seas has seemed unstable, weak even. Do they wish to lose their connection to the very magic that allows your kind to so easily live below the waves? Do you wish to be stranded on your shores when your magic fails, unable to use the spells you use to travel quickly along the surface of deep waters?"

Jackson saw Draflor's mouth drop open in surprise.

"I didn't know he could read." Draflor gaped.

"I'm guessing he picked it up at Starkelp." Jackson grinned.

## SIRENS SONG

"Perhaps that is why your elders are so anxious for the lightborn to be forced to dwell among you?" Daychaser's tone was earnest. "Perhaps your powerful façade has become uneasy about the strange events that are changing the seas in your area, and hope the presence of the lightborn will protect your façade?"

Startide made a strange noise as the sirens shifted uneasily before the older of the two females came forward, looking more defensive than confidant. "The sirens demand the lightborn return to dwell with our façade, or we will bring him by force."

Daychaser seemed to sigh, and slightly widened his fins in annoyance. "So you have said, but I am afraid that your elders do not understand the gravity of what they demand—"

"Do you wish to challenge the power of the siren?!" The smaller female hissed, making Blade slash his fins in warning.

"Do your elders wish to challenge the power of the Star of the Sea, a breakoff group of the Fallen, creatures of great power who know the magic and secrets of the seas, and the Medians of the Sonaeko Nation?"

Daychaser's voice lost its calm tone and had taken a firm, but slightly fierce, edge. "If you are seeking honor and prosperity, then I suggest your elders begin rethinking what they wish to demand. Even as we speak, a group of the reformed Fallen are heading this way to meet up with us, and they remember the old magic of their kind that made them the most feared species in the seas before the Great Petrifying. Do your elders wish to try their power against them and others of great power?"

The sirens eyes had widened in fright at the mention of the Fallen and the whole group had begun slowly inching upwards in fear at Daychaser's words.

The older arrogant female's eyes slitted slightly as was about to speak when the male clashed his teeth together in warning.

# MYTHOS SEAS: MOVING SEAMOUNTS

"We will inform our elders of your message." The male said pensively. "Your words explain the deep calls of the Fallen that have occasionally echoed through our seas these last few days."

Daychaser quarked in confirmation. "Very good." He turned, swimming back towards Jackson and the others. He gave them a wink as he passed, before leading them away from the sirens who reluctantly turned to swim back the way they'd come.

Once the sirens were out of earshot, Startide gave Daychaser a shove with her snout. "Where has that been hiding all this time!?"

"You ever thought of being a diplomat?" Draflor asked, shaking his fins in disbelief. "You... that was impressive, to say the least, I wasn't aware you could read either! You used the info from my book really well."

Daychaser laughed as he gave Draflor a confused look. "Thanks, I think, but what's a diplomat?"

"I don't think I've heard of those either..." Zepherdust commented.

Spinescale groaned, slipping off Jackson's backpack when Draflor's eyes sparkled enthusiastically as he brought out a long scroll. "Oh great, do we have to hear another one of Draflor's overly long and complicated definitions again?"

"If so, my shiver and I will do our patrol up ahead." Blade grumbled.

"HEY! My explanations are not overly complicated, I don't like what you guys are implying—"

Jackson laughed softly to himself as his friends all began talking at once and slowly crept off to the side to activate his map spell.

While they continued to bicker, he quietly found the course he should take and, after giving the oblivious group a smirk, darted off with his magic. His sudden disappearance caused every-creature to suddenly stop and look around before Startide and Daychaser located him off in the distance.

"Jackson!? What are you doing?" Startide called.

"Escaping while I still can!" Jackson laughed as he increased his speed and took off into the blue. "SEE YOU AT THE POINT!"

"Huh, he's gettin good." Blade's eyes gleamed approvingly as he motioned for his shiver. "After the Sonaeko."

"Mavous, who was that boy?!" The Captain of the Fangcutter was pacing back and forth in his quarters. Around him were gathered many of the other old Venom Clan leaders, who had quickly come together for an emergency meeting.

"That doesn't matter to us right now, Captain." Mavous said firmly, slapping his hand down on the missive Jackson had thrown to him. "We must decide what we are to do about this betrayal this missive talks about."

"I knew the emperor was getting restless, but to destroy this many ships and their crews…" An old mage friend of Mavous's looked over the scroll once again, his old voice creaking slightly. "The power the Ironmamba left at Great Ghost Point must be immense for him to be willing to destroy so many of his own forces."

"Forces he suspects are not loyal to him." Another man pointed out.

"Not that he's wrong." Another captain, a woman in her forties, with long scarlet hair which was tied into a tight ponytail commented tightly. "Especially now."

# MYTHOS SEAS: MOVING SEAMOUNTS

"We mustn't let anyone know that we are aware of this." Captain Venmorul's face was tight. "We would be killed on the spot."

"Some of our men must know, at least those who we know we can trust." Another captain said. "And if we are to have the support of our men, they must understand why we are going to act against our orders."

"What should we do?" The redheaded captain asked, planting her hands on her hips. "We can't flee, or we will be hunted down, but if we stay, we are doomed."

"That is why we have assembled before we meet up with the other fleet. We must have a plan." Mavous said, tapping the scroll with his finger. "Any ideas?"

## CHAPTER ELEVEN
# THE TEST

Jackson and his group headed south for the next few days until they reached the outer edges of Great Ghost Point. At that point, they stopped to wait for Depthcall and her herd, who were supposed to meet up with them before they tried to go to the Stronghold.

While they waited, Startide, Daychaser, and Draflor spent a considerable amount of time trying to map out what they could of the waters surrounding the area. Zepherdust and Spinescale both spent a little time resting on a rocky outcropping where the group had decided to wait, while Jackson was dragged into defense training by Blade. The shark had insisted they practice as much as possible after he had received a message from Leavamentee with instructions.

"Depthcall is takin her salted time." Blade grumbled at the end of their third day of waiting along the edges of Great Ghost Point. Everyone had been growing restless and finally decided to head closer to the stronghold. They were currently moving further down the long thin stretch of rocky cliffs that lined its northern-outer edge.

"She will be here soon." Draflor didn't seem too worried. "Something must've come up that delayed her a bit."

"The sirens perhaps?" Startide offered. "They seemed quiet... determined."

"I doubt it." Daychaser shook his head. "I think the sirens were doing a lot of bluffing, and Depthcall and her herd wouldn't go into waters shallow enough to run into them."

Jackson yawned. "Can we please just find somewhere to rest for the night? I'm washed out."

"You ain't finished trainin." Blade said, earning him a long look from Jackson.

"I have trained on and off all day for the last three days." Jackson replied firmly. "I'm already worn out enough to pass out."

"Ignore him, Leavamentee only told him she thought you needed more training in self-defense, not that you needed to train till ya sink." Spinescale said, giving Blade a smug look. "I think somebody is just nervous and antsy, and training with you is easing his mind a bit." Blade slashed his teeth towards Spinescale in annoyance, but didn't respond, which made Spinescale's eyes widen a bit. "Wait, I'm right? I thought I was joking."

"We're gonna do patrol." Blade said curtly, swimming on ahead.

"Hm..." A hint of worry crept into Draflor's eyes as he watched Blade vanish into the darkening waters. "Jackson, I think we better try Oceaono and Stonecurrent again, or just Stonecurrent. I think there is something going on that Blade knows about and we don't."

Jackson didn't waste a second. "Stonecurrent?" He called into his communication crystal. "STONECURRENT!" He called more forcefully.

There was a glimmer from the stone before Stonecurrent appeared, looking troubled. "I hear you Jackson, where you lot at?"

# THE TEST

"We're at Great Ghost Point, waiting for Depthcall who is running uncharacteristically late."

"Two days late I might add." Draflor piped up.

"Whirlpools..." Stonecurrent muttered something under his breath. "Jackson, if she's not there yet, then she's been delayed by some things that Leavamentee and the medians sent her and her team to go find on their way there. She could be a few more days out."

"What kind of things?" Draflor was immediately interested.

Stonecurrent sighed, looking a bit upset. "Along their route to where they're supposed to meet you, there were a couple places where some dark energies had been forming the last few months. She and the team were going to stop to check them out. They were areas where some battles were fought after the Petrifying had occurred, and some ships had sunk there."

"Are Depthcall and the others alright?" Jackson asked.

"They're alright, that much I know, but I don't know what they found." Stonecurrent wasn't his normal positive self. "I didn't think they should stop there anyways, but Depthcall insisted..." He shook his head. "We've only received a message from her that they are fine, but she did mention something about the Dark One, and magic from a weapon tied to the Ironmamba that was acting up."

"Could that be connected to the Toxicshade?" Daychaser asked.

"I'm assuming so, but I don't know more than that." Stonecurrent sighed. "What have you found out?"

Jackson tried to hold back a yawn but failed miserably before Stonecurrent smirked a bit. "Let me guess, Leavamentee got ahold of Blade to have him do defense drills with you, didn't she?"

Jackson's eyes widened in surprise. "How'd you know?"

# MYTHOS SEAS: MOVING SEAMOUNTS

"She hasn't changed in the two and a-half centuries of me knowing her, and I don't expect her to change anytime soon." Stonecurrent laughed as the mischief returned to his eyes. "Draflor, why don't you and the others fill me in, Jackson you go find a rock to lay on and rest a bit."

Jackson nodded, another yawn threatening to break through his mouth while Draflor's magic reached out to Stonecurrent's form and kept it hovering in the water. As Draflor and the others began talking quietly, Startide led Jackson to a hidden area in the submerged part of the cliffs where he could settle down to rest.

After awhile, Draflor returned, and Jackson teleported the staff into his bag after a strong current sent it rolling towards the edge. With the staff safely tucked away, he flipped over, quickly falling asleep once again.

Jackson was deeply asleep when the Star of the Sea peeked out of his hand and suddenly darted off into the ocean. Time seemed to slow as it flew into the depths of Great Ghost Point, whizzing through an area where a multitude of shattered and sunken ships littered the seafloor. The star neared a giant, once beautifully carved, dome, which had been overgrown by seaweed and corals. It swirled around the thick layer of silt and dirt covering part of the dome, as if searching for something.

A large form suddenly shifted from its resting place when the star glimmered brightly next to its face. The movement caused soil and rocks that had washed against the dome to shift and crumble away. As the star flashed, a large serpentine eye snapped open to watch it hover over to a pair of sealed doors before it shot back to Jackson.

"A sleeping light is disturbed." The creature rumbled before it slipped away, a huge mass of the seafloor it'd been hiding under cascading off its scaly back. "More light must be brought to the day." As the great form moved away from the dome, more dirt and rubble came rolling off, causing a plume of dirty water to cover the area. "Before the Ironmamba's weapon wakes."

Jackson shifted uncomfortably as light flashed around him. He felt something smack into him and slowly sat up to see the Star of the Sea floating in front of him. "What's going on?" He asked tiredly, getting to his fins.

"Follow me, but leave the staff in your bag." The star said. "There is something you alone need to see."

"Where are the others?" Jackson asked as he quickly followed the star into the sea, the water around them slightly lighter in color.

"They are nearby."

Jackson stuck close behind the star once they entered Great Ghost Point as the morning sun gently illuminated the waves above. Jackson carefully wove around some large sharp rocks as the star led him along the seafloor. However, when he brushed past another stand of the strange looking rocks, they suddenly crumbled and Jackson froze, taking a nervous breath. "A-are these eggshells?"

"Yes, but very old ones."

Jackson quickly caught up to the star, casting many a nervous glance around him. "Are there any sea-serpents nearby?" His voice squeaked a bit in fright.

# MYTHOS SEAS: MOVING SEAMOUNTS

"There are many, this is their home."

"Then why are we here?" Jackson gulped when he noticed what he'd thought was an immense rocky outcropping ahead of them actually had scales.

"To find answers."

As they moved further into the sea serpents' territory, Jackson stuck as close as he could to the star, who seemed largely unconcerned. It completely ignored the shifting bodies of resting sea serpents as it and Jackson quickly moved through the nesting grounds.

Jackson let out a slow, calming breath once a large circular shape came into view up ahead. He lifted his head curiously when he saw the decorative runes of the Sonaeko where some soil and rocks had slid off the strangely shaped building. Clouds of silt and soil filled the water around the dome and Jackson thought he saw something move through the cloud, but when further inspection revealed nothing, he looked uneasily back at the dome.

"What is this place?" Jackson asked in a hushed voice as an immense, hidden form shifted. Jackson glanced to the side when the Star of the Sea flashed, a sphere of light flying out from its core to encircle Jackson and the entire area in bright light.

A loud gravelly voice made Jackson shiver. "To pass." The face of a giant sea-serpent burst from the dust. "YOU MUST PASS!"

Jackson screamed, dashing out of the way before a gigantic mouth snapped shut just behind him! He glanced over his shoulder as the serpent withdrew into the dust while it got ready to strike again. Jackson tried to flee further, but smashed into the bright blue dome created by the Star of the Sea and flipped around in shock. "What's going on?" He cried out as the star flashed.

# THE TEST

"A test." The star said, and Jackson swore he was being watched by many large pairs of eyes as the barrier gleamed. Jackson yelped when the behemoth sized head of the sea-serpent lunged out from the dust and he grabbed his pendant and held it out. "Shield guardian!"

The pendant flashed before the bright shield quickly expanded to a great size! The sea serpent's head smashed into the shield, making the creature pull back in surprise, one of its long fangs coming loose and drifting to the bottom. Jackson suddenly whipped around the shield, magic spinning around him before he sent a spiraling whirlpool flying into the cloud of dirty water. As the whirlpool increased in size the sea serpent paused, looking surprised. Jackson rushed forward, dashing around the distracted creature's head as the water began swirling around them!

Jackson's body crackled with energy as the creature flipped around when it noticed him! As the monster's jaws opened, lightning flashed from Jackson's hands and crashed into the snout of the sea-serpent just between its eyes.

The creature's roar shook the water as it whipped around while electricity crackled across its body and Jackson dashed away. As Jackson fired another bolt of lightning into the serpent, he forced the whirlpool full of dirty water through the barrier, clearing the silt from the water and leaving the serpent nowhere to hide.

The serpent hissed as it shook off the effects of the shock and laid its calculating eyes on Jackson while the water around it glowed with magic. Jackson braced himself when the serpent's hiss deepened. As the magic around the serpent intensified, Jackson swiftly formed a series of shields and barriers around him, fusing light, water, wind, water, earth and other elements into a quickly thickening sphere.

# MYTHOS SEAS: MOVING SEAMOUNTS

Jackson's muscles tightened as more magic poured from him while long, sharp teeth and powerful magical jaws formed around the serpent's head. The magical jaws swiftly formed into an even greater mouth so immense that it could swallow a fallen whale whole!

The serpent roared as it soared forward, and Jackson braced himself as its great magical mouth smashed into his barriers. The force blasted magic in all directions before the magical jaws and barriers shattered, sending Jackson spinning backwards!

Jackson quickly righted himself as the serpent dove forward, his hands flashing before the Star of the Sea swooped between him and the serpent! The serpent abruptly stopped, causing a blast of water to surge past Jackson and the star.

"Does he pass?" The star asked, hovered mere inches from the great beast's nose.

The creature pulled his head back, the lines of long, thick, slightly ridged fins folding flat. "Barely." It looked past the star to Jackson. "Waited long enough for a decent one, skinny though."

The creature gave Jackson a judgmental look before it turned. Its powerful body spun away before it coursed out through the barrier the star had formed around the area, vanishing into the cloud of silt beyond.

Jackson was left breathless and trembling, his body shaking even harder once the magical barrier the star cast faded away. As the barrier disappeared, it revealed a whole congregation of watching sea serpents who were eyeing Jackson intently. One by one, the creatures slowly turned away, either settling back onto the seafloor to rest or swooping off into another part of the nesting grounds.

# THE TEST

Jackson let out a few anxious gasps before his eyes flipped over to the Star of the Sea. "What was that about?" He demanded, giving the star a tart glare.

"The secret's here are guarded heavily by the sea serpents." The star explained as it floated down towards the dome. "There are few they won't test. We wouldn't have let you get hurt or killed, but we do try to honor the serpent's customs."

"What secrets are so important that they need to be guarded by sea serpents?" Jackson huffed, still very shaken by the whole event.

The star didn't respond as it went up to a very old set of doors and gently touched them, causing them to creak open. Jackson followed the star through the doors which snapped shut behind him, making him jump forward! *Ok this is just creepy, as if the sea-serpent attack wasn't terrifying enough!*

## CHAPTER TWELVE
# ENCOUNTER WITH HISTORY

With a small bit of reservation, Jackson trailed the star as it floated down a long hallway, its glowing form lighting the way. They slowly passed rooms full of books and magical artifacts that all seemed coated in a strange film of magic, making everything seem like it was asleep.

Entering into a large, darkened room at the end of the hall, Jackson watched curiously when the star dipped down to gently touch the center of the floor. There was a warm flash before light spread from the middle of the room, dancing up from the floor in spiraling patterns, allowing Jackson to see what the room held.

"WHAT?" Jackson looked around at the oddly familiar stone forms surrounding him. He crept forwards once he recognized some of the faces from old portraits of his Grandpa's family. "Is this, is this the place Auntie Ancie mentioned?" He whispered.

"It is. This is where part of your family came to wait for the return of their kin. This is the Sanctuary of Last Hope." The star gently flickered and seemed to motion Jackson over to one particular person. "There's someone I want you to meet."

"Meet?" Jackson asked. "How? They're all petrified."

# ENCOUNTER WITH HISTORY

"The magic in this chamber isn't the magic of the Great Petrifying, but it is connected to it." The star touched the shoulder of the young man, glowing brightly as pulses of blue magic ran over the stone encasing him. "Theren my old friend, we wish to speak with you."

The stone skin of the young man seemed to soften as his eyes fluttered open and he took a deep breath. He blinked when he saw the Star of the Sea and uttered a strange name Jackson didn't recognize.

"Prince Theren, my old friend, it has been a long time."

The young man looked around curiously. "Why am I awake? Everyone else is still frozen." His gaze stopped when he noticed Jackson. "Who are you? You look…" His eyes widened. "Like me and my brothers."

"This is one of your brother's descendants, your nephew. His name is Jackson."

Theren seemed lost for words before he shook his head and held his hand out to the star. "Can you fill me in on everything please, I take it we don't have much time?"

"That we don't." The Star "looked" over at Jackson. "Can I share some of what I've seen of your life with your ancient Uncle Theren?"

Jackson was too dumbfounded to do more than nod weakly before the star touched Theren's forehead. There was a soft glimmer before Theren gasped in surprise. "We've been asleep for two centuries?" He groaned a bit and sat back. "Great seas this is a lot to take in."

"Now you might know why I brought Jackson here." The star said.

"I think I do." Theren shook his head slowly, his silver tail shifting as he thought. "I think I better tell you about what I found out about the capital and what happened here first."

"You found out more about the capital after I left?"

"Yes." Theren looked back over to Jackson. "Jackson, Oceaono and the others don't know, but the capital has been damaged by Voidcul. Right before we helped seal shut the walls around the capital, she damaged one of the main towers that was used in casting the spell that was sabotaged by the rebel groups. If you're going to be able to cast the reversal spell, you'll have to make some changes in how you cast it to substitute for the damaged tower."

"Do you think part of the tower intact?" The Star of the Sea asked worriedly. "I was a bit out of it at that point."

"Yes, the lower half. However, it won't supply the amount of power you need unless you make a few tweaks, and if the remainder of the tower starts to crumble, you'll be in a heap of trouble if you don't have a huge amount of power."

Theren formed a diagram of a spell in the water in front of him. "While I think the spell the medians have been teaching Jackson should work, let me show you both the spell I've figured out that should also reverse the Great Petrifying. It'll be a good backup in case the tower has been damaged any worse, but it'll take a lot more power than the one the medians were coming up with." He frowned a bit as he looked at the diagram from his spell. "Hm… but the casting might need to be changed a bit on the music part just a bit."

"Music part?" Jackson asked, coming over to look at the instructions Theren was forming for the spell.

"I've found that very powerful spells often begin making musical sounds as they cast. You can focus on the purpose of the spell better when you work with the sounds…" Theren looked over and gave him a grin. "You're creating music with the magic, so to

# ENCOUNTER WITH HISTORY

speak. That's how the great white whales of the world portal can freeze entire swaths of sea to protect their ocean from invasion of wildweed lisheave. You could say the song adds soul to your spell."

"Theren is a highly talented spell caster." The star added when Jackson got a perplexed look.

"Really, I'm more of a spell writer or former." Theren shrugged bashfully, waving his hand a bit before he went back to work on changing a few things. "I'm not very strong when it comes to casting normal spells, but if I tweak them and make up my own, I can do pretty well for myself."

"Says the one who cast a spell strong enough to counteract and protect you and the others from the Great Petrifying. You're being modest."

"You helped me with that spell, and you know it." Theren smirked at the star. "Don't be cheeky."

Jackson's jaw dropped at Theren's teasing of the star, and both Theren and the star laughed.

"You haven't had the Star of the Sea with you very long, have you?" Theren grinned. "I had them both with me for a few years, you get close after that amount of time."

"To be fair, we haven't been in a place to speak with Jackson much." The Star admitted. "Our power has been focused elsewhere."

Theren's jaw dropped open before he stared at the Star for a moment. "It's even worse than you let on, isn't it?"

"I need you to teach Jackson this spell, and show us some other spells as well. I want to make sure I know them, so I can show him again or help him cast them later. I know you have a finful that will work for him." The star avoided Theren's question entirely.

Theren gave the star a long look. "If I'm ever freed completely, you and I are having a long talk about what's really been going on these last few centuries."

"Of course we will, you are still the crown prince after all. If you are freed, you must know your history so you can care for your people."

"Not that being the crown prince was originally my choice." Theren smirked thoughtfully.

Jackson's head was spinning a bit and he sat down with a thunk, shaking his head when Theren and the star moved over to check on him.

"You ok?" Theren asked. "You look a bit pale."

"I'm... ok." Jackson shook his head slowly, "just a bit overwhelmed." He weakly smiled at Theren. "It's not everyday you meet an ancient relative."

"If ya call me old, I'll cast a spell that will make your tail look like a shrimp's for a week!" Theren teased while he helped Jackson to his fins. "If you're up to it, let's hurry and work on some spells for a bit. I have a number I think you should learn and, of course, the one major one I need to teach you so you can reverse the Petrifying if that tower's not working right."

Jackson nodded. "I'm ready, let's do it!"

Jackson wasn't sure how long he and his ancestral uncle, who seemed to be in late teens or early twenties, worked on spells and talked. Theren was an ocean of information, especially on water magic, and Jackson loved every minute while Theren helped him figure out new spells and how to increase power to older ones.

Jackson had just successfully cast a practice form of Theren's reversal spell when the Star of the Sea stopped them, saying they had to finish soon. The news caused a crestfallen frown to cross Jackson's face.

# ENCOUNTER WITH HISTORY

"What's wrong?" Theren asked, looking winded. "I'm beat after all that, aren't you tired?"

"A bit, but it's been fun." Jackson gave a small smile, "and I really wanted to get it down better."

"Jackson has a remarkable amount of stamina when it comes to magic." The star praised, "and while I know he could learn much more, I'm afraid we're nearly out of time, and there is something I think Jackson needs to hear from you, Theren."

"I mean, other than everything, what else is there to tell?" Theren gave a rueful grin.

"I want you to tell Jackson about Voidcul, he only knows her as the Dark One, and we need to know more about what happened in the throne room."

"WHAT? You don't even know about Voidcul?" Theren looked alarmed. "The medians and guardians didn't tell you?"

"They've been hiding that from him for some reason..." The Star said. "Although, I think Stonecurrent would've told him, if he hadn't of found out the medians were keeping quiet about it."

"Why haven't you told him?" Theren asked pointedly.

"I'm currently trying to help keep the magic of the oceans stable, Voidcul has done a great deal to damage the balance of the seas the last two centuries, and—if I am being honest—it's taken a lot of energy to make time for this."

"Again, I think you are hiding the severity of what's going on." Theren gave the star a chastening look.

When the star didn't respond, Jackson cleared his throat a bit. "Uh, so who is Voidcul? And why's it so important for me to know about her?"

"I don't know if it's important to know about her personally, so much as know what she did, and how to defend yourself against her." A look of disgust crossed Theren's face. "She was an old

# MYTHOS SEAS: MOVING SEAMOUNTS

student of Koiwae's back in the day, before she turned against our nation. She's also the last living adult of her species, since she's responsible for the destruction of the rest of her kind." Theren sneered a bit in anger. "She completely wiped out all the other adults after the Petrifying, and I have no idea what happened to the eggs of the next generation of her species…"

A shiver ran down Jackson's spine and he gulped. "She sounds… horrible, what kind of creature is she?"

"A strange species that's half shark, half octopus or kraken, depends on who you ask." Theren frowned. "Her kind have very thick hides and hunt by shrouding themselves in dark clouds made from their ink, before lashing out with their tentacles and charging in with their gaping jaws."

Theren gave a thoughtful hum. "That normally isn't a huge problem, since her species normally only gets half the size of a normal human but Voidcul…" He shook his head. "Somehow found a way to increase her size and strength. I don't know how big she is now, but when she attacked us…" He shuddered. "She was the size of a small adult whitewing whale, and her hide was terribly thick, almost none of our spells could get through it."

He scowled. "To top it off, her clouds of ink were infused with dark magic, making them difficult to remove or clear away with the usual water spells." Theren suddenly snapped his fingers and gave Jackson a quick smile. "Wait, that won't be too big of a problem for you since you know light magic." A thoughtful look crossed his face as he nodded. "Even some low-level light spells should help you clear away her ink clouds fairly easily." Theren seemed to think. "I'd be mostly worried about her size and her shadow magic though, she knew some horrible shadow crushing type spells."

"I've dealt with shadow crushing spells in the past, so I might have a couple ideas for how to counter those." Jackson mused, "but

# ENCOUNTER WITH HISTORY

do you know how she's grown so large?" He was perplexed.

"That's kinda strange."

"The only thing I keep going back to, is all the magical artifacts she's taken and consumed." Theren sighed. "Right after the Petrifying, she immediately sought out as many powerful artifacts and weapons as she could find so she could try to steal their power, that's also why she is still alive I'm guessing." He looked over at the star. "She'd also gotten one of the Sun Spheres, didn't she?"

"Yes, but she's getting no power from him." The Star said. "I imagine he's been wreaking havoc on her internally the best he can, but he was cracked before she found him, and he wouldn't have had the time or ally needed to heal him."

"Sun Spheres?" Jackson asked.

"That's a lesson for a later date, but suffice to say they're the aspect stones for light magic and light aspects." The star interjected before Theren could answer. "Now Theren, is there anything else you found out I don't know?"

"Yes, we mentioned the throne room, and there are a couple of traitors inside who were there to sabotage the spell, and who were tasked with doing it again if someone tried to reverse it." Theren pointed to a satchel that was sitting next to a young woman Theren had been clutching hands with. "My girlfriend stored the papers in her bag that gave the names of the men and had a description of their orders. One of them was… well a member of the war council Father's friend, General Icoralos oversaw: the traitor is the one with a questionable earth heritage."

"I suspected as much, I never supported having him or those other two partial earth mages on the war council, there was something off about them from the very beginning." There was an edge to the star's voice. "I'll make sure he is taken care of before we work on reversing the spell, and I'll retrieve the papers, so we know who else to remove from the picture before we even attempt a counter-spell. Now is there anything else? My spell will end anytime now."

Theren's eyes lit up and he snapped his fingers again. "You're here in part because of the darkness around the stronghold, right? I don't know all the details, but I'm willing to bet it's somehow connected to Velocina, one of the watersnake colossals. I don't believe it's her personally, but I heard from some creatures here that something dark happened during a battle that involved her, which led to the colossals fighting each other and entering a mad rage. From what I could learn, she was the first one that entered into the rage state, and it happened during a battle with the Ironmamba's elite force led by the emperor and his brother." Theren winced when a pulse of magic rippled across him. "The spell?"

"It's ending." The star said ruefully as it pulled the documents from the satchel before they vanished away. "I'm afraid it's time for you to return to sleep with your loved ones."

Theren nodded sadly before he met Jackson's gaze and smiled slightly. "I wish we had more time… this is the first time I've had a younger brother." He ruffled Jackson's hair before going over to clasp his girlfriend's stone hand as some of his skin started to darken to a stone gray. He gave her a loving look before he looked back at the star and Jackson.

"Be careful, we'll be waiting to see the light of being awakened again, and Jackson." Theren's tail slowly became encased in stone. "I know you can do it, you're amazing for coming this far. Remember, that the spell is to restore what is lost, whether family, friends, or more. That's what's important."

He smiled, "and not just when it comes to this whole journey don't you think? Oh, and tell everyone 'hi' for me, it's been ages since I've seen any of them. Especially Draflor, he's matured a lot

# ENCOUNTER WITH HISTORY

the last two centuries." He then laughed as the stone traveled across his chest. "My father's gonna be so shocked when he finds out how many great-something grandkids he's got." He smiled. "May the Creator light your way." His face then darkened to stone, leaving the cavern deathly quiet.

Jackson took a shaky breath when the stillness of the room made the swishing of his tail seem to echo, and a few sad tears escaped his eyes. Seeing Theren's petrified form hurt horribly, and was a solemn reminder of the rest of Jackson's petrified family.

"Jackson..." The star's voice was soft, drawing the boy's attention away from Theren's stone form. "Come on, I'll lead you back to where your friends will find you, and I'm sorry, this isn't easy for any of us." Jackson thought he heard the star's voice catch a bit. "Don't forget Theren's words, he's the crown prince for a reason."

The star began to lead Jackson out of the chamber but paused. "I'm going to ask you to not tell the others where we've gone today, this place and those within must be protected. When you do talk about what you've learned, don't mention Theren's spells, and speak to Draflor, Stonecurrent, and Oceaono first, but don't tell anyone where it happened. Although, I suspect Draflor and Oceaono might figure it out. Their kin helped build this place eons ago."

Jackson was quiet as the star led him out of Great Ghost Point before it vanished into his hands. Quietly Jackson pulled the staff out of his pack to thoughtlessly twirled it around while he went over what he learned. He floated in the water silently for a while, oblivious as Draflor peeked out of the staff with a confused look before Jackson's other friends came rushing over with cries of relief.

"Jackson! We were so—uh..." Startide and the others slowed when they saw Jackson's expression while he looked off into the distance, spinning the staff slowly, still lost in thought.

"Um Jackson?" Daychaser swam over and let out a stream of bubbles, shaking Jackson from his ponderings.

"Huh? Wha..." Jackson shook his head. "Oh, hi guys, glad you found me."

There was a very long moment of silence.

"Ooookkaaaayyy." Spinescale came swimming over. "I think you better explain exactly what happened—and why you're acting stranger than a snake in a school of lampreys—or we're getting ahold of the medians and guardians to see if they know any healing spells."

"You do seem a bit..." Zepherdust swam up to give him a concerned look. "Spacy."

Jackson just shook his head while the others crowded around worriedly. "I'm ok, really. The Star of the Sea just wanted to show me something and it's just given me a lot to think about."

"What was it?" Startide pressed, an excited look in her eyes.

"I can't tell you," Jackson gave an apologetic smile. "At least not yet, I've been asked to keep it to myself for now."

Draflor looked behind Jackson towards Great Ghost Point before a thoughtful expression crossed his snout. "I might have a few guesses, but if the star asked you to not tell, I'll trust there is a reason."

"While searchin for ya, we got orders to head south." Blade coursed around Jackson, swishing his fins in a disgruntled way. "Depthcall'll hopefully meet us just south of the stronghold with her whaleguard and others."

# ENCOUNTER WITH HISTORY

Jackson nodded absentmindedly. "Ok, guess we're leaving now?"

Daychaser, Zepherdust, and Startide exchanged a long look before Daychaser finally laughed. "Jackson, by any chance did the star wake you up before sunrise?"

"Hm?" Jackson blinked and then blushed in embarrassment. "W-well maybe, but that's not why I'm zoning out!"

"Ooh really, you aren't just the faintest bit tired?" Startide teased, a big grin spreading across her snout. "You sure you don't need a little nap?"

"Hm... a nap might do him good, he does look a bit pale..." Spinescale chimed in. "I mean, more-so than usual."

"Hey, I'm not that pale!" Jackson retorted before a thought occurred to him, "but if you all insist, maybe I should go rest in my bag while we travel."

"Why ya givin in so easily?" Blade gave Jackson a once over while he swam around him. "What ya plottin?"

"Me? Plotting something? Psh." Jackson feigned shock. "I'm sure I haven't the foggiest Idea what you're referring to, but if I am, I'm not telling you what it is anyway." He gave his friends a wink. "Now if you'll excuse me, I'm apparently overdue for a few z's." He quickly teleported himself into his bag before his friends could stop him.

"When he gets out, we're all ganging up on him, right?" Spinescale asked.

"Oh yeah." Daychaser grabbed the bag.

"Also makin sure he's guarded at all times." Blade flared his gills in annoyance. "Don't want him vanishin again."

"Blade, if the Star of the Sea took him away to show him something, I doubt there would've been anything we could do to keep track of him." Startide said while Zepherdust helped Daychaser slip the bag over her dorsal fin and tighten it.

"It also would've been unwise for us to interfere with the desire of the Star of the Sea." A large male deeptyr said with a respectful fin flick to Blade. "I know Leavamentee tasked us with guarding Jackson with our lives, but we must be prudent about such matters sir."

Blade seemed conflicted but gave a slight fin flick of acknowledgement, although the troubled look didn't leave his eyes.

"So that's part of why you've been acting so strange." Spinescale exclaimed. "I was wondering why the rogue of the Jewel Isles was acting so seriously." She gave Blade a sly look.

"Let's move." Blade grunted, avoiding Spinescale's gaze. "Daylight's wastin."

"Ok Blade, you really need to get out of army mode." Spinescale's whole demeanor changed as she hissed in exasperation. "It's getting a bit annoying, like on old stuck shed."

Blade's serious look softened just slightly. "Until we're all safe, I'm in 'army mode.'"

"Ugh, it'll be the death of me!" Spinescale grumbled as she wrapped around Jackson's satchel while the group set off. "All this seriousness is getting so old."

"The excitement of saving the ocean isn't enough for ya, is it?" Daychaser teased.

"That's not what I meant." Spinescale was quiet for a while until Blade was out of soundshot. "But Blade isn't acting at all like himself, and you know it. Something's wrong."

Daychaser was quiet for a long time. "I know. It's like he knows something we don't and it's constantly eating at him."

# ENCOUNTER WITH HISTORY

"Or he's afraid of something and is hiding it behind Leavamentee's training." Startide added. "He's scared, and that's not a feeling he's used to having."

"But what could be scaring him so much that the rest of us don't already know about?" Zepherdust asked quietly.

The three friends were quiet for a bit as they swam. "I think we're all right." Daychaser finally said, "and I think we need to talk to Jackson about it, something's off."

"But how can we do that without Blade or the other sharks listening in?" Spinescale whispered.

"The key is strapped to Startide's dorsal-fin." Daychaser said with a sly grin. "We just need an excuse for Blade to carry it for a bit."

"I might have an idea how to do that…" Zepherdust said with a small smile.

## CHAPTER THIRTEEN
# TIME TO ACT

While the others traveled towards the stronghold, Jackson rested for a time until he teleported himself—without the staff—into the bag connected to Solarswell and began practicing the large array of spells Theren had shown him.

Every now and again he'd check the Book of the Sonaeko, which had added Theren's spells to its pages, just to make sure he was doing things right. He read over the music portion of the spell over and over again thoughtfully, hoping it would all come together if he needed it. He was also hoping he wouldn't have to use this new spell, as the one's the medians had taught him was much simpler and seemed… safer.

Once he started to run out of energy, Jackson put down the enchanted piece of paper he had been writing on. He let out a long sigh before he noticed the Toxicshade ship that was stranded on the shoreline of the small beach inside the bag. *I wonder what else we could find in there?*

He summoned the staff to him and Draflor immediately popped out with a slightly offended look.

"Mind telling me why ya left us in your old bag all by our lonesome?"

# TIME TO ACT

"Sorry, I was working on something that…" Jackson paused while he considered his words. "That's connected to what the star showed me. I didn't want to break my word to the star by letting you see what I was up to."

"Oh, well in that case you're forgiven, but next time tell me first before you vanish, please."

"Deal, you mind helping me look through the old ship again?" Jackson swiftly made for the half-submerged vessel.

"Normally I would, but I think somethings up." Draflor pointed up to the sunlight stones, which had dimmed slightly as an image appeared below them, showing Startide, Zepherdust, Daychaser, and Spinescale looking urgently into the bag.

"Do you think they want us to come out?" Jackson asked, readying his spell.

"Wait." Draflor held up a fin when Daychaser looked meaningfully between Startide, Zepherdust, Spinescale, and himself before he pointed his fin at the bag. "I think they want in."

Jackson blinked while Daychaser repeated what he did before. "Odd, but I guess it's worth a splash…" He teleported them in.

Immediately his four friends looked around anxiously, hurrying over once they'd spotted him.

"Oh, good currents, you figured it out." Startide said as they rushed over.

"What's going on?" Jackson tilted his head, confused. "Something wrong?"

"About that…" Spinescale said before they confided in Jackson what they'd been worried about.

"And to top it off, Blade isn't telling us everything Leavamentee is telling him, which is just strange." Startide said.

"He has been acting very secretive about it all." Zepherdust finished, looking concerned.

"There is something that we aren't being told." Draflor, after giving the staff—which was flashing wildly—a long, uneasy look before giving Jackson a sheepish glance. "Or at least somethings Jackson's not being told, although Stonecurrent and Oceaono are planning to tell him here soon."

Jackson was immediately on high alert. "Are the medians in trouble?"

"Or lying?" Spinescale suggested, a distrusted edge in her voice.

Draflor sighed. "Sort of yes to Jackson's question, and no to Spinescale's." Draflor shifted worriedly. "The medians wanted to confirm their fears, before telling the rest of us what was going on."

Jackson was quiet for a minute. "What fears?"

Draflor took a deep breath. "Why don't we ask Oceaono and Stonecurrent now?"

Jackson nodded and held out his arm with the communication crystal. "Stonecurrent, Oceaono, it's Jackson, we have a few questions about what is going on."

Stonecurrent and Oceaono's form immediately materialized above Jackson's hand.

"We were just about to contact you to talk about that very thing." Stonecurrent gave his version of a smile, although it didn't reach his eyes.

"What's going on?" Daychaser asked.

"And does it have to do with why Blade is acting so strange?" Spinescale added.

Oceaono and Stonecurrent both exchanged a surprised look. "Blade's been acting weird?" Stonecurrent asked. "Huh, well I guess if Leavamentee told him some of what's going on, it could be bothering him."

"What *is* going on?" Jackson pressed.

# TIME TO ACT

"We wanted to make sure we were right before we told you." Oceaono echoed Draflor's earlier sentiment, "and now that Depthcall and her team have confirmed our assumptions, that the Dark One is alive and has been creating dark pillars in different areas of the ocean: we were trying to decide when to tell you. Though I guess now is as good a time as any."

"Dark pillars?" Startide was concerned. "What are those?"

"It's actually a title for something that is created by corrupted magic that causes a great disruption to the environment around it." Draflor answered before either Stonecurrent or Oceaono could. "From what I gleaned from listening in on Blade's meetings with Leavamentee, these pillars are in the form of large strange misshapen orbs, made of thick strands of ink protecting a core of tainted energy."

Draflor pinched his fins against his side unhappily. "The dark pillars have apparently been created over a large area, with one major one in an undersea pass not far from Mythos Pearl, the capital of the Sonaeko. They've been causing enough damage that it's disrupting the balance of the entire ocean."

Stonecurrent gave Draflor an impressed look. "Still know how to eavesdrop with the best of them, don't you Draflor?"

"I didn't train for two seasons as a spy for nothing." Draflor grinned.

"If I recall correctly, the only reason it was for two seasons is because you hid the entire academy, grounds and all, so well they had to cancel the rest of your training." Stonecurrent's eyes gleamed a bit while he chuckled at the memory.

"Is it my fault if the nation's top spies couldn't find their own training headquarters?" Draflor's nervousness vanished for a moment as he smirked. "They still haven't found where I teleported the Sapphire Spyglass Tower!"

Oceaono pinched the shallow ridge between his eyes, letting out a slightly exasperated breath while he closed his eyes. "Stonecurrent, Draflor, if we could please stay on topic..." He met Jackson's gaze. "We've been suspecting there were dark pillars since before you returned to Starkelp Strand. Especially after you, Clearsong, and Draflor ran into that dark magic on your way back." He took a deep breath. "Though we weren't sure about the Dark One..."

He shook his head. "As I'm sure you noticed, before you left for Great Ghost Point, we asked Depthcall if she and her team would be willing to check a couple areas for us on their way there." He folded his arms behind his back as a dark look crossed his face. "We were asking her to investigate areas we feared there were dark pillars, and she found two of them before she and her team destroyed them both. One of which was connected to an ancient artifact that was acting up. Neither were very large, but the fact that they were even this far into the western seas is... foreboding." Oceaono was pacing back and forth. "And, as Draflor already heard, unfortunately confirms that there are larger ones around Mythos Pearl."

"What are we going to do then?" Daychaser asked. "It sounds like they'll pose a threat to us later on."

"We don't want your team to deal with these dark pillars." Oceaono said firmly. "Only Draflor would know how to deal with them, and we don't want your teams putting yourself in unnecessary danger."

"Ok, but who's this Dark One?" Startide asked.

Oceaono closed his eyes. "A powerful creature who... betrayed our nation..." He opened his eyes and looked behind him. "Right after the Petrifying she tried to destroy everything connected to our people in her efforts to put the seas under her control..." He shook

# TIME TO ACT

his head, "but we are doing what we can to make sure you won't have to deal with her, once you begin your journey across the Great Abyss, we were thinking of sending Jackson with a small team straight across the abyss to Mythos Pearl." Oceaono looked troubled "And sending a team led by Depthcall to lead the Dark One away before she realizes that someone is trying to enter into Mythos Pearl. We hoped it would buy you enough time to cast the spell, if it were possible."

"My mate was quick to volunteer for that," Stonecurrent looked concerned. "I'm still not sure how I feel about it."

Jackson saw his hands glow a faint blue and sighed, taking the hint the star was giving him. "Uh... that might be a bad idea, Voidcul is a lot more powerful now than she used to be."

Everyone was dead silent for a moment as Oceaono, Stonecurrent, and Draflor's mouths dropped open.

"How... do you know Voidcul's name?" Oceaono finally asked, giving Draflor a suspicious look.

"Hey! I might like causing mischief, but I wouldn't go against a direct request from you." Draflor actually looked insulted.

"Draflor didn't tell me, Theren did." Jackson said.

"WHAT?!" Oceaono shouted in surprise and began looking around wildly before his eyes bore into Jackson's as he whispered. "How could you have talked to Theren? He's still alive?"

Jackson was a bit taken aback by Oceaono's intensity, but nodded. "Well he's... kinda alive, he and the other Lost Ones are all petrified like the rest of the Sonaeko. The star took me to visit with him earlier, so I could learn more about what happened, and so Theren could teach me some other things."

"So that's where the star had you vanish off to earlier today!" Draflor crowed. "I knew it was showing you something interesting."

"Theren said to tell you all 'hi' before he was petrified again." Jackson ginned mischievously. "He also said you've matured a lot Draflor."

Draflor's gills flared out in embarrassment. He opened and closed his mouth a few times before he shrugged, making Stonecurrent below in laughter as he shook off his own surprise.

"The star still has plenty of surprises up its shimmer." The whale shook his great head. "I'm glad to hear that Theren and the others survived. I worried they had died long before this day."

Oceaono was silent for a long time. "I think you better tell me what Theren told you."

Jackson's hands flashed wildly, making him hesitate. "Well, what can I tell them then, just what you told me was ok?" He asked and got a few calmer flashes in response.

He looked up when Spinescale started to snicker. "Hee, you're starting to sound like Draflor!" She giggled. "It always looks a bit ridiculous."

Draflor gave Spinescale a long look, but Oceaono cut in before he could comment. "What can you tell us?"

Jackson explained what he'd learned about Voidcul, her damaging the tower, the involvement of one of the water snake colossals around the Stronghold, and what had happened in the Throne Room, but left out the spells Theren had taught him, per the star's request. Although Jackson hadn't the foggiest idea on why the star wanted to keep the spells a secret.

Stonecurrent slowly shook his head. "I think I understand why the star intervened, if you hadn't told us what you have, my mate and the herd would've headed into disaster."

"And we wouldn't have had the power we'll need from them to help cast the reversal spell." Oceaono was deep in thought. "This changes a lot; we must speak to the others about this at once." He

# TIME TO ACT

nodded to Jackson. "Thank you for telling us, but I better go, are you coming Stonecurrent?"

"I'll be there in a bit." Stonecurrent tilted his head in acknowledgment as Oceaono waved before he vanished.

"Might I have a private word with you later, Jackson?" Stonecurrent asked, and Jackson nodded. "Good, I have some things I'd like to go over with you. Until then, safe travels my friends." He vanished away.

"Well..." Draflor hummed. "That sure makes things more interesting." He looked over at Jackson. "You still wanna go look through that ship?"

Jackson and his friends went through the ship as best they could before Blade finally shook the bag enough times to get their attention. At that point, Daychaser, Zepherdust, and Startide left while the others kept looking through the ship, finding an assortment of weapons and a large assortment of magical crystals and gems.

"You'd think they'd have more papers that talked about their plans..." Jackson grumbled while he smashed open a locked drawer with an earth spell. "Finally." He pulled the papers out as Draflor came floating over, curiously peering over Jackson's shoulder while he read through them.

"What's that about an ancient weapon?" Draflor tapped further down the page with his fin.

"It only mentions something about a fang wielded by the Ironmamba Emperor's brother..." Jackson said, flipping to the next

# MYTHOS SEAS: MOVING SEAMOUNTS

page as Spinescale slithered over to listen. "And that the fang was a weapon that could destroy nations and beasts alike."

"I remember the Ironmamba had a finful of powerful weapons, but I don't remember what they all were…" Draflor looked troubled. "That, and I thought most of them had been captured or destroyed before that final battle when the colossals were rampaging."

"Apparently, you all missed one." Spinescale said as she crawled over Jackson's shoulder for a better look.

"Or it was one you didn't know about?" Jackson suggested as he reread through the missive, "and what is this about it needing to be awoken?"

"I don't know." Draflor's troubled look deepened as he looked back at the staff. "Solarswell, I know you're busy with what the medians asked you to investigate, but could you help us out here? I haven't the foggiest idea what this weapon could be."

The staff shone a beam of light onto the pages and seemed to read over them for a minute before it flashed and dimmed.

"I'll take that as a 'I don't know either.'" Spinescale said dryly.

"He doesn't know right now anyways." Draflor undulated his fins against his side in thought. "I'd ask Leavamentee or Stonecurrent, but they have their fins full right now…"

"But don't we need to know what's going on here?" Jackson asked.

Draflor sighed. "Our main purpose in being here isn't to involve ourselves in the war, we're supposed to see about the darkness surrounding the stronghold and get the last key we need to awaken the dormant power of Mythos Pearl."

"True, yet Jackson is involved in the war whether he likes it or not." Spinescale pointed out. "And if this weapon is connected to

# TIME TO ACT

the Ironmamba, it very well could be connected to the darkness around here."

Dralfor groaned and clamped his fins against his head in frustration while Jackson's mouth twisted in thought. "Didn't Stonecurrent mention that Depthcall had said something about a weapon tied to the Ironmamba acting up and contributing to one of the dark pillars they destroyed?" Jackson asked as his eyes hardened. "Uh... and we did hear the one Toxicshade guy talking about a power the Ironmamba left them that they were planning to release...."

"Could... this 'fang' weapon, or power, that the Toxicshade are after also be tied to the Dark One?" Spinescale wondered, looking concerned.

"We won't know more until we meet up with Depthcall." Draflor commented, looking like he was getting a headache.

"That's where you're wrong." Jackson teleported the papers into his own bag and rushed towards the broken-down door of the captain's quarters.

"What? What do you mean?" Spinescale asked as she tried to keep from falling off Jackson's shoulders when he hopped down from the ship onto the beach.

"We're supposed to be heading south and waiting for Depthcall, Jackson, remember?" Draflor said while Jackson jogged towards the water.

"I'm done waiting." Jackson said firmly, a determined look in his eyes. "There's something that feels wrong about all this, if that weapon the Toxicshade are after is somehow tied to Voidcul and the Toxicshade are trying to wake it I..." He went silent for a moment. "I'm worried about Mavous, and the old clans." He waded out into the water and dove under the surface, "and my aunt's relatives in the Fire Tribe's would be among those who are going to war."

# MYTHOS SEAS: MOVING SEAMOUNTS

"You're going to go against the medians orders?" Draflor eyed Jackson shrewdly. "Doesn't seem like you."

"Blade's orders were to wait for Depthcall, not mine." Jackson had a determined look in his eyes. "My orders were to meet up with the rest of the crew and head to the stronghold."

"Tell that to Blade, I'm sure he'll be thrilled." Spinescale said sarcastically.

"I've already had to fight a sea serpent today, I'm not afraid of Blade." Jackson whispered under his breath as he teleported them out of the bag.

He quickly grabbed his bag off a surprised Startide while Draflor and Spinescale stared at him incredulously.

"Y-you f-fought a sea serpent today?" Draflor stuttered.

"What's going on?" Blade asked as he and the rest of the group came swimming over.

"Jackson's planning to go on ahead to the stronghold." Spinescale said dryly.

"What?" Daychaser asked and everyone stared while Jackson started his mapping spell, magic shooting through the water as he did so.

"Orders are to wait for Depthcall." Blade said firmly.

Jackson nodded. "I know those are your orders, Blade." He continued his spell as he traced the direction to the stronghold, and where the missives indicated the Toxicshade might be gathering.

Everyone was quiet for a moment before Daychaser swam into the map sphere and looked Jackson in the eye. "What's going on?"

Jackson took a deep breath. "When I was talking to Theren, the Star of the Sea indicated things were worse off than even the medians realized." He looked over at his friend and met his gaze. "I'm worried that we might not be in a position to wait. The missives Draflor, Spinescale, and I just found mentioned the

# TIME TO ACT

Toxicshade are going to put their plan into effect once the last fleet of old clans joined up with the others at Great Ghost Point."

"Also, Depthcall mentioned that one of the dark pillars they destroyed was connected to an ancient weapon that was acting up." He looked back to the route he'd been marking. "In the missives we just found, it talked about an ancient weapon used by the Ironmamba that the Toxicshade plan to awaken. If their plan involves that Ironmamba weapon, they could put it into effect here in the next day or so... which is even worse if that weapon is somehow tied to the darkness growing around here." He didn't want to think of the endless number of bad possibilities of what that could mean.

Daychaser was quiet for a minute before he came over and tapped Jackson's route with his snout. "This route is too close to the siren; we should go this way." He used his own magic to mark a different path. "This way will take us slightly longer, but we'll avoid the siren."

Jackson smiled at Daychaser in relief as Startide came over and looked at the route. "I think it's a good plan. I take it this is where you think the Toxicshade ships are gathering?" She indicated a small circle Jackson had made with her snout.

Jackson nodded. "It's the only isle large enough to have fresh water, I don't think they've managed to gain a foothold on the mainland yet, so I figured it would be the most likely place."

"Sounds reasonable to me..." Zepherdust said as she glanced over the route.

Blade came over and sighed as he inspected the route. "This won't be fun to explain to Leavamentee." He said ruefully.

"Blade?" Jackson was surprised. "You mean you're coming with us?"

# MYTHOS SEAS: MOVING SEAMOUNTS

"I was your friend before I was Leavamentee's trainee." Blade gave Jackson a smirk, "and you ain't the only one tired of waitin, what's the plan when we get there?"

## CHAPTER FOURTEEN
# THE DARK PILLAR

The group traveled hard for the rest of the day as they worked their way carefully into Great Ghost Point, avoiding the area where Jackson knew there were sea serpents. Blade sent a message to Leavamentee, telling her to relay their change of plans to Depthcall but didn't hear back, which was only slightly terrifying.

As the group neared the island where Jackson thought the Toxicshade might be gathering, they slowed their pace uneasily. When they approached the shallows, they were faced with a huge number of vessels marooned around the isle, all of them heavily guarded and manned.

"Looks like you guessed right, Jackson." One of Blade's squadron commented while they swam under a large vessel. "There's ships everywhere."

"All of them with the Toxicshade's symbol." Startide added as they saw a large black, red, and purple flag waving at the end of a hastily built dock.

"Including a few mercenary groups too…" Zepherdust added with a disgruntled look in her eyes.

After a cautious inspection of the immense number of Toxicshade forces, Jackson led the group away from the isle and out into deeper water. He abruptly paused when a large ship that was trimmed in gold passed overhead and Jackson nearly growled at the sight.

"What's up?" Daychaser asked.

"That's the emperor's ship." Jackson ground out, giving the stilven metal encased ship a searing look. "If I could sink it right now, I'd be truly tempted to."

"Soooo why don't we just sink the ships?" Spinescale asked, giving the vessel a sly look. "Can't fight a war at sea if you're grounded."

"Two reasons." Jackson held up a finger. "One, stilven metal is extremely hard to break, even with magic." He flicked up a second finger. "Two, the Toxicshade would flood this entire area with poison if they thought someone was trying to sabotage their boats from below."

"Ookaay, reason enough for me." Startide quickly swam ahead. "I'm all for getting far away from these guys. I've already been speared once by humans as it is; I don't need to give poisoning a try."

"And I've already been stabbed by Toxicshade wreckage..." Zepherdust added wearily.

Jackson hesitated. "I can't believe I'm saying this, but I really wish it was darker so I could do a bit of spying..." He looked up at the clear sky. "Maybe I could look up a spell to summon some fog."

Draflor gave Jackson a look of mock alarm. "Who are you, and where is Jackson?!"

"Yeah, no kidding." Daychaser piped up. "Our Jackson would never want it to be dark."

Jackson rolled his eyes. "I don't want it to be pitch black." He looked over his shoulder at the ships behind them. "I just wish there

# THE DARK PILLAR

was a somewhat safe way to try and learn what exactly the Toxicshade are planning, and what it has to do with this weapon."

"I could go ashore and sneak around for information." Spinescale said.

Jackson bit his lip worriedly. "I don't know, the Toxicshade might attack you or try to kill you for your fangs or venom."

Spinescale's eyes flashed angrily. "If they try to kill me, I'll give them what for." She got a shrewd expression on her snout. "Koiwae, Falganous, and Leavamentee taught me a few tricks, I won't get caught."

Jackson exchanged a worried glance with Startide and the others.

"You sure you'll be ok?" Startide asked.

"Promise," Spinescale affirmed. "If it gets too dangerous, I'll dart back into the water and make my way to you guys."

"Two of my squad will stay here to help." Blade added, motioning to two of the darktyr with his tail. "They can help ya find us when you've finished."

"And I'll come too." Zepherdust insisted. "I can always provide an underwater distraction if you need it."

Spinescale hissed in agreement before she swam back towards shore, the darktyer following silently, swimming under Spinescale protectively. "Don't wait up for us, I might be there all through the night." She called back.

"We'll plan to meet up tomorrow." Zepherdust called back.

"Be careful!" Jackson called, an uncertain frown in his eyes.

"Then let's go see what's going on around the stronghold." Daychaser turned and headed towards the open sea. "We won't be getting anything done if we're waiting around here."

# MYTHOS SEAS: MOVING SEAMOUNTS

The team swiftly made their way out into deeper waters, stopping at a rocky outcropping where they could rest for the night. Early the following morning, Jackson woke uncharacteristically early and quickly dove back into the water before they all swam towards the stronghold. As they got closer to where the stronghold was located, they stopped when they noticed the water up ahead had turned a sicky black-red.

"It's a dark pillar alright..." Draflor whispered while they stared at the giant ball of ink as immense threads of red and dark black magic weaved through it. Jackson shuddered from the sickly, uneasy feeling the corrupted magic gave off as shadows seemed to reach out from the ink, turning the nearby waters cloudy and dark.

"Does that mean Voidcul's been here?" Startide asked as she looked at the barren, black stained seafloor below. "I can't sense a current here at all." She looked back at the orb. "It's like, the currents have died or something."

"I think we better reach out the Stonecurrent." Jackson raised his arm, only for Draflor to quickly shove it down.

"Not here, not this close!" His eyes were narrowed suspiciously. "Some dark pillars let their creator see and hear what's going on around them. Let's get further away from this one before we do anything."

Everyone quickly swam back a short distance, stopping at an undersea hill Startide located with her magic. Once they were there, Jackson, for good measure, secured his bag to the bottom of a large rock and teleported everyone into Solarswell's bag. As the others gathered around, he called out to Stonecurrent, who quickly answered.

The old whale looked a bit surprised to see everyone gathered together and gave Jackson an expectant look. "Well, I assume you have something to report."

"The stronghold is encased in the dark pillar just like the ones Depthcall has found." Draflor spoke before Jackson could, "and the currents around here have died because of it."

Stonecurrent was quiet for a moment as he thought, and Jackson was surprised he didn't question why the team was already there. "Then she did come out this far." He made a troubled bellow. "She must know that one of the keys is in that stronghold..." He sighed and looked up at Jackson. "You didn't get to close, did you?"

Jackson shook his head. "Draflor had us leave before we could."

Stonecurrent looked over at Draflor. "Was it big enough to allow Voidcul to see what was going on around it?"

"I'm not sure." Draflor admitted, "but it's big enough it's encased the entire top of the stronghold."

"Hm..." Stonecurrent looked over to Blade. "I want you to take Jackson's glove and swim around this dark pillar so I can see this thing. If it isn't big enough for Voidcul to see through, you all might be able to fight your way in before Depthcall gets there in a day or two." He turned back to Draflor. "I don't want you to destroy this one on your own, but if it's safe, you lot can make a break in it so a couple of you can enter the stronghold."

"Sounds good." Draflor answered as Solarswell flashed wildly. "Solarswell knows a spell or three that should work."

"Good, now Jackson, get us out of here so Blade can take me for a quick ride." Stonecurrent grinned. "I've been wanting to know how fast he could go for a while now."

"Huh, I'll take ya so fast ya'll lose your magic." The old cocky Blade was back.

Jackson teleported everyone back out of the bag and handed Blade his glove before the shark took off into the blue and disappeared. Jackson thought he heard Stonecurrent whoop in delight at Blade's speed and shook his head. *Only Stonecurrent or Draflor could make investigating a dark pillar a way to have a quick bit of fun.*

After a few minutes, Jackson went up to the surface with Startide—who was needing a breath of air—and carefully looked around. He paused when he saw a small, light vessel zip across the water towards them, powered by a magic power-crystal like the one Jackson's family used.

"What is that?" Startide asked after she and Jackson quickly dove under the waves when the ship flew towards them.

"It's a Fire Tribe ship." Jackson said as they sank deeper to watch while the vessel shot over them. "I think it's a scouting vessel. It's too small for battling."

"Does that mean something's happening?" Draflor asked while they watched it vanish across the waves.

Jackson shrugged nervously. "I don't know, but I hope Spinescale and the others meet up with us here soon..." He looked behind him as Blade returned, swiftly tossing Jackson his glove. Jackson quickly slipped the glove back onto his hand while Stonecurrent reappeared.

"From what I can tell, this one isn't large enough for Voidcul to see through," Stonecurrent said with a shrewd look in his eyes. "Which means we should be able to make a breach inside just large enough for Jackson to sneak through without too much trouble."

# THE DARK PILLAR

"How are we going to do that?" Daychaser asked as the group headed back towards the dark pillar. "I don't think any of us learned about those kinds of spells."

"Much of the work will be done by Solarswell and I." Draflor commented as the dark pillar came into view once again. "Although, that means Jackson will have to leave the staff and I out here with one of you while he goes in."

"You want me to go in alone?" Jackson's eyebrows shot up in surprise while he handed the staff to Startide.

"I think you should have Blade go with you." Stonecurrent suggested. "He won't run out of air if we have to take our time searching for the key." He motioned to the other sharks. "Though I'd suggest his squad form a perimeter around the area."

Jackson jumped when a loud boom from an explosion echoed from the direction the Toxicshade's island base was. He quickly flipped around while Startide sent out pulses of magic energy in that direction. "That can't be good…"

Startide's features tightened in concern when her magical sound waves returned. "It seems like the ships around the island have moved around a lot, many of them aren't even there anymore…" She closed her eyes as a second set of magical sounding calls reached her. "I think something happened around one of the docks. I hope Spinescale and the others are ok."

"Crashjaw." Jackson turned to one of the sharks, who was a similar species to Blade. "Could a couple of you lightning speed sharks go back towards the isle and see if there is anything going on? Then report back to us?"

"Sure thing, we'll report back soon." Crashjaw said, motioning to another shark before they took off towards the isle.

"I'll go too." Daychaser said quickly, magic forming around him. "We'll be back as soon as we can." He called as he shot off after the sharks.

"Not sure how I feel about ya tellin my squad what ta do." Blade gave Jackson a long look. Although Jackson swore he saw the shark's deep black eyes twinkle a bit in humor.

"Sorry, next time I'll just ask you to do it instead." Jackson grinned while the staff began glowing brightly behind him.

"Wait," Startide's eyes widened as an idea hit her. "Leave your bag here with me, that way when you find the key you can just teleport yourself out of there."

"Excellent idea Startide." Stonecurrent praised. "Then Draflor and Solarswell won't have to try to keep the dark pillar at bay for too long."

Jackson quickly took off his bag and hooked it onto Startide's fin while Draflor conversed with Solarswell.

"Get ready." Draflor said. "Solarswell and I won't be able to keep this open forever."

"Got it, Jackson, grab on." Blade came over and tilted to the side so Jackson could grab onto his dorsal fin. The shark's gaze hardened when Draflor's form began spinning wildly around the staff, becoming nothing more than a silver-gold blur while the staff glowed brighter and brighter.

A ball of energy formed over Solarswell as Draflor spun further and further away before he suddenly dove into the staff's orb. The staff pulsed brightly, sending a surge of magic flying past Jackson before a beam of energy shot from the orb and crashed into the dark pillar!

The dark pillar reacted violently as the bright energy swept through it, the magical ink splattering and whipping around in protest while the beam widened and formed into a large, bright

## THE DARK PILLAR

light-blue tunnel. The tunnel moved up and down for a few moments while Solarswell searched through the grime of the dark pillar, making more of the ink explode and pop as the tainted magic was hit by the pure magic from the staff.

The beam suddenly shivered for a second before it seemed to lock into place, a shimmer of yellow-white magic coursing down it.

"Found it!" Draflor called out. "Hurry."

"Hurry's my middle name." Blade's body tensed before he rocketed forwards, yanking Jackson into the tunnel of magic!

Jackson held on for dear life as Blade rushed down the tunnel, blasting up to the cracked doors of the stronghold. Blade suddenly whipped around mere moments before they got to the door, sending Jackson spinning forward from the sudden stop! The boy spiraled around in the water until he smacked into the door with a yelp.

"Oowwwwww...."

"Uh, sorry." Blade said, sounding a touch sheepish when Jackson grumbled as he pushed himself off the door, using a light healing spell on his bruised arms and chest.

"Can ya warn me next time, please?" Jackson muttered while he reached over to open the cracked door. He sighed in relief when it creaked open without any trouble. "I really don't want to break any bones this trip."

"Should'a held on tighter." Blade commented while he swam past Jackson into the building.

As he shut the door behind them, Jackson gave Blade an annoyed look, which the shark avoided by swimming further into the Stronghold.

"What we lookin for exactly?" Blade asked.

"The last key, which should be hidden in a room at the back of the stronghold." Jackson said, quickly swimming down a long, sloped hallway towards a large open cavern. Once Jackson got to the end of the hallway he abruptly stopped. "Oh spells."

"What?" Blade asked as he came up behind him. "Uh, nevermind."

Jackson and Blade both moved back warily when long strands of dark energy moved around the cavern before them, as if searching for something.

"What're those?" Blade asked when another strand of dark matter suddenly shot into the cavern through a hole in the wall.

"They almost look like tentacles…" Jackson whispered while one wrapped around a support pillar and seemed to tighten around it. After a moment the pillar trembled, and the dark magic dissipated while another tentacle came slithering through the water from a large crack in the ceiling.

"Look like they're lookin for somethin." Blade mused as another one reached around blindly.

"Maybe Voidcul didn't want anyone finding the key, so she's having the dark pillar try to catch anyone that gets in here." Jackson commented quietly while Stonecurrent appeared.

"She's thorough." Stonecurrent commented once he saw the tentacles. "Koiwae taught her well." His tone was rueful. "Like he did with all his students."

Jackson started a quick current spell but stopped when the tentacle nearest to them suddenly turned towards him. "Uh, I take it they somehow sense where magic is coming from?"

Stonecurrent was quiet for a moment. "Try another type of magic."

Jackson tried an earth spell and let out a sigh of relief when none of the tentacles responded. "So it's only water magic?"

"I think so." Stonecurrent agreed. "Which means I probably should leave, the magic you're using to contact me might attract them to." He looked over at Jackson. "You remember where the key is?"

Jackson nodded. "Yes, and I know the spells to get it."

"Good, contact me when you get out of here, I'll be waiting." Stonecurrent vanished away just as a tentacle seemed to sense something around Jackson and whipped through the water towards them.

"Time to go!" Jackson grimaced as he and Blade dashed into the cavern moments before the tentacle slashed into the hallway.

"Grab my fin, we're just headin to that door, right?" Blade pointed to a large broken door on the other side of the cavern with his snout.

Jackson shook his head as he grabbed Blade's fin and hung on tight. "Not that one, the one below it." He pointed to a smaller hatch below the door.

"Doesn't look like a door." Blade commented as he swiftly weaved around the other tentacles that were searching around the room.

"It isn't." Jackson answered, pulling his tail away when a tentacle got too close for comfort. "It's part of the stronghold's circulation system. It helps keep the water in the lower rooms of the stronghold clean and fresh."

Once they got to the hatch, Jackson searched around it for a moment. The hatch had long, half-circular sections missing that allowed water to flow through them, but no easy way to open it. He reached out with his earth magic into the wall next to the hatch, but pulled back when he felt the backlash of enchantments that were placed on the wall to help stabilize it.

"Hm." Jackson tried feeling around in the hatch itself with his magic instead. When he didn't find or feel anything out of the ordinary, he tried to magically manipulate the hatch, making a satisfied sound when the door shifted out of place slightly. With Blade's help, Jackson shoved it open just enough to squeeze through before they entered the tight tunnels of the stronghold's circulation system.

Blade stayed behind Jackson as the boy pulled out a small map he'd made to help him navigate the tunnel system. Jackson led the way through the dark tunnels, a small sphere of light magic dancing around his head while they cautiously worked their way further down into the cavern. Jackson suddenly froze and Blade flared out his fins when they felt the whole building rumble, as if shook by an earthquake.

Jackson and Blade locked gazes when there was a second rumble. "Should we try to go faster?" Jackson whispered nervously.

"Better believe it." Blade shoved Jackson forward urgently.

The two friends charged down the tunnels as quickly as they could, racing so fast they ran into the sides of the pipes a couple times on the sharper turns. Suddenly Jackson crashed to a stop at a fork in the tunnels, making Blade grunt in surprise.

Jackson promptly reached out and grabbed the pointed section of wall in the middle of the fork. After a quick look around him, he reached out with his water magic and twisted the middle section of the tunnel. The section clicked as it turned, creaking loudly before the middle section slid down to reveal a small entryway inside the wall.

Jackson hurried through the entryway into a secret room that was gilded in gold. The room was shaped like a large sphere, with lines of gold streaking up the sides of the walls until they met at a series of half-moons that curved around a sun symbol in the center of the ceiling. In the middle of the room—on a gold and sapphire pedestal—sat the last key, surrounded by a gently swirling mist of water magic.

# THE DARK PILLAR

As Jackson approached the globe shaped key, he noticed that the key was actually a miniature version of Mythos. Bright green, emerald pieces, that were outlined in gold, made up different continents, while the oceans were a deep sapphire. The polar ice caps were made of some sort of brilliant white crystal and there were even foggy sections of the globe that made it look like clouds were floating past.

"If you're gonna use a lot of magic, shut the door behind us." Blade interrupted before Jackson could start his spell. "Don't want them tentacle things followin us."

"Oh, right." Jackson hurried and closed the door behind them, just before another tremor shook the stronghold.

"Ya might want to hurry it up." Blade said as they heard something give way. "I don't like the sounds of that."

"Give me a minute." Jackson hurried over to the mist encircling the key, taking a steadying breath before he reached out to touch the magical fog. The mist reacted instantly to his touch and swirled up and around his arm until it was swirling around his whole body.

Jackson started the spell and held his hands out to his side. As the spell cast, he began spinning around, reaching out with his hands as if chasing the strands of the mist while they whipped about. Light blue magic formed around his fingers before spreading out to mix with the mist. His magic intermingled with the mist, making the mist quickly turn the same light blue hue as his magic. While Jackson continued to spin, the mist began pulsing different shades of blue before it suddenly condensed, as if being absorbed, swiftly getting pulled into Jackson's glowing hands before it vanished away.

"That was impressive." Blade said as Jackson held out his arms to stop himself from spinning.

"OOOoooo. Tell that to my stomach!" Jackson groaned, trying to keep the world from spinning around him as he reached out to shakily pick up the key and teleport it into his bag. The key disappeared just as something smashed into the doorway behind them while the whole building trembled and cracks formed in the walls!

"LOOK OUT!" Blade yelled, shoving Jackson out of the way when a huge dark tentacle reached out and slashed through the water towards them. Blade grunted as the tentacle slapped his tail and Jackson fired a blast of light magic into it, making the tentacle dart backwards before more dark energy seemed to pour into it.

"BLADE?!" Jackson yelled when the tentacle turned towards them, the dark magic forming into a set of huge, oily jaws.

"I'm fine, just get us out of here!" The shark turned and flashed his belly threateningly when the dark jaws reared back as the building shook once again.

The jaws suddenly whipped forward as Jackson quickly teleported both him and Blade away just before the jaws snapped shut around them!

## CHAPTER FIFTEEN
# THE WEAPON

"THAT was too close." Blade said as Jackson slumped onto the bottom of the seafloor in the larger bag.

"Way too close. I'm glad you thought to close the door." Jackson agreed as he tilted his head back and groaned tiredly. His head flipped forward when they heard a loud thumping sound and saw Draflor's panicked face as he whacked the bag with his fins.

"Better get back out there." Blade said, looking a bit shaken. "Draflor looks like a sardine in a shark shiver."

When Jackson and Blade reappeared next to the bag, Draflor and Startide shouted in relief.

"You're ok?!" Startide crooned as she shoved Jackson kindly with her snout. "We were so worried you got crushed!"

"Crushed?" Jackson and Blade asked at the same time, looking behind them to see a huge amount of dust billowing out from the dark pillar.

"The Toxicshade are casting spells at the dark pillar!" Daychaser rushed over with the sharks and Zepherdust hurrying behind him, while Spinescale was wrapped around one of his flippers.

"They seem to be after something on the other side of it." Zepherdust added her eyes wide.

# MYTHOS SEAS: MOVING SEAMOUNTS

"The magic spells they're casting caused the dark magic of the pillar to increase until it started crushing the stronghold." Draflor spoke up. "Although, the surge of magic also seemed to disrupt the magic of the dark pillar. I don't know why though."

"I know why." Spinescale unwound herself from Daychaser's flipper. "The Toxicshade are channeling the magic from the pillar into a spell they're using to try and wake that weapon!"

"What?!" Draflor's eyes bugged out. "Are they mad?"

"Was there any question?" Spinescale asked dryly before she continued. "I don't know what exactly this weapon is, but I did manage to spot a paper with an illustration on it, showing a large serpent with a long sword protruding from the middle of its mouth, instead of fangs. The picture also showed a man holding the serpent's tail as if he were using it as a whip or something.

"A serpent with a sword instead of fangs?" Draflor's eyes lost their focus as he thought. "Strange…"

"Worry about that later, let's get clear before the magic from the dark pillar goes whirlpool!" Daychaser pointed to the dark pillar with his flipper.

The inky mass lashed out in all directions while tainted magic shot out from its reaches.

"Go! GO!" Blade yelled when clumps of tainted, magical ink began sailing out from the pillar in all directions!

Jackson grabbed Spinescale and Solarswell before taking off with the others as they dodged through the clumps of ink. The ink seemed to sizzle and suddenly liquify as they got further from the dark pillar. Some of the ink globs burst like bubbles once they got beyond the reach of the pillar's magic, filling the water around them with clouds of murky, dark ink.

Once the group was safely out of reach, they turned to watch while the dark pillar seemed to disintegrate and fill the water around

# THE WEAPON

it with clouds of magicless ink. A couple seconds later, Jackson's glove began flashing wildly.

Stonecurrent, Oceaono, and to Jackson's surprise, even Koiwae promptly appeared, looking around wildly.

"What happened? Jackson, are you ok?" Stonecurrent asked before he saw where Jackson was looking and stopped. "What on Mythos? I thought I told you to not destroy the dark pillar."

"The Toxicshade are doing that, not us." Spinescale interjected. "They're draining the magic from the pillar to use to awaken the Ironmamba's weapon."

"What?" Koiwae looked horrified. "Why would they use tainted magic like that for a spell?"

"Could the weapon be tainted too?" Jackson asked.

"If it is, we have bigger problems." Oceaono looked nervous. "Anything tied to the Ironmamba would likely attack Jackson on sight. They hated the Sonaeko."

"Or anyone who fought against them." Stonecurrent added dryly.

"But if the Toxicshade cast a spell using the tainted magic from Voidcul's dark pillar, it could give her a boost of power." Koiwae ground out. "All the power they put into the spell could combine with hers."

"She's too far away for her to absorb the power from a spell like this Koiwae. I'm more worried about what her magic could do to this weapon." Oceaono looked a bit pale.

"There's a huge multitude of ships gathering behind the stronghold." Startide spoke up suddenly, her eyes aglow with magic. "And even more coming from the mainland."

"The Fire Tribes!" Jackson was on high alert. "They must know the Toxicshade are up to something big and are trying to stop them." He swam up to the surface to look across the waves and saw clumps of dark shapes indicating groups of ships further off, as well as a blinding purple glow coming from behind the collapsing stronghold.

Jackson dove back down. "I can see the magic from the Toxicshade's spell from here."

"You're going to try and stop them, aren't you?" Oceaono gave Jackson a droll look, his eyes dimmer than normal; he seemed tired.

"I want to see what's going on," Jackson admitted. "I have relatives caught up in this, but I don't know if there's anything we can do."

"Then hurry it up before they finish their spell and see if you can do something." Stonecurrent urged. "I know you well enough to know it'll be more of a pain to try and stop you, than it is to keep an eye on you while you put yourself in harm's way." The three creatures vanished away, although Jackson's glove continued to glow, letting him know they were still watching.

"He's not wrong on that..." Startide whispered to Blade and Daychaser, who both grunted in agreement.

Jackson gave his friends a sheepish grin as he cast a quick current spell and darted off, his friends only a few fin flicks behind.

As they flew around the huge mass of dark magic and dissolving ink, the dark clouds clogging the water seemed to thin and dissipate while more magic was sucked away.

When a huge mass of cloudy water suddenly seemed to clear, Jackson held back a yelp and jumped to the side when he saw an enormous stone snake coiled atop the remains of the stronghold.

"WHAT IN THE CURRENT IS THAT?" One of Blade's team shouted as the ink continued to clear away, allowing them to see the petrified snake's large, long fangs. The serpent's neck, head and fangs were stretched out as if it was striking at something, a tiny

# THE WEAPON

thin crest poked out from the back of its huge skull gleaming, and its eyes were slitted dangerously.

"It's one of the water snake colossal's." Draflor called, his eyes widening. "It looks like she was petrified while she was attacking something."

Jackson slammed to a halt, making Startide and Daychaser click-razz in surprise as they whipped around.

"What's wrong?" Zepherdust asked.

"Why'd you stop?" Daychaser added.

Jackson gulped as he looked at the giant snake. "Spinescale, did the drawing you saw look like that snake by chance?"

"Yes... but it was a bit different." Spinescale said uneasily.

"Spells, spells, spells!" Jackson shot off again while his friends exchanged perplexed looks.

"Ok, why are you saying 'spells' that much?" Draflor asked as they drew closer to the foreboding glow of the Toxicshade's ships.

Jackson gave Draflor a quick, sideways glance while he focused on closing the distance between himself and the fleets of ships up ahead. "How do you think the magic of the Great Petrifying will react if the Toxicshade are going to try and awaken that snake?"

"Oh dragon scales." Draflor turned a few shades lighter. "Ok, I get your point, even if they do awaken it, the magical reaction from messing with the Petrifying—"

"Would set off a huge blast of magic!" Startide twirp-clicked in alarm when she caught on. "It could petrify everything around here or destroy it."

"Stonecurrent, I know you guys are watching, how big could a blast like that be?" Jackson called as they neared the first of the vessels.

# MYTHOS SEAS: MOVING SEAMOUNTS

Jackson could hear a murmur of conversation from the orb on his glove. "It would still reach you where you are now." Koiwae called. "You must get even further away if they start trying to awaken it."

"Blade, I got a mission for you and your lightning speed sharks." Jackson called. "Go see if you can find where the old venom clan ships are." He formed a bright purple and light green symbol with his magic. "They'll all have flags like this flying underneath the one with the Toxicshade symbols."

"Got it, see you soon." Blade said before he and three other lightning speed sharks shot off while Jackson turned to Startide. "Koiwae? Can you tell Startide how far away is safe? Then Startide, I want you to check and see if the Fire Tribe's ships are out of the blast zone."

Koiwae appeared from the orb and rushed over to Startide as she began her spell, talking to her with quiet urgency. Jackson zipped up to the surface and shot out of the water, Draflor, Zepherdust, and Daychaser behind him while Spinescale hung onto his bag. Before he dove back under, Jackson saw the largest vessels of the Toxicshade's fleet gathered together in a semicircle, all facing the dark pillar.

On the second jump he could make out dozens of mages standing on the bows of the ships. All the spellcasters were focusing their magic into a giant crystal fang that was hovering in the middle of the semi-circle, just above a smaller vessel that would've been carrying it before the spell started.

During his third jump, Jackson caught a glimpse of the fang as more magic from the dark pillar was sucked into it. The tainted magic made dark stripes undulate across the fang's surface, a deep contrast to the medium purple, lime green, and reds of the untainted venom magic.

# THE WEAPON

"What is that thing?" Zepherdust asked after Jackson led them down deeper into the water.

"The Toxicshade's throne core." Jackson's face was tight in worry. "It can absorb great amounts of magic then it amplifies the magic it absorbs, so the spells people can cast through it are even more powerful than normally possible."

"Could you just teleport it into your bag? That could solve the problem, no core, no spell." Daychaser suggested.

"Bad idea." Draflor said. "If it's like the throne core used by the Sonaeko, it's alive, and quite aware of what it is being used for. It would likely destroy the bag, or it might figure out the spell used to teleport into the bag and use it for itself and its master."

"Ok, forget I said that." Daychaser said, giving Jackson a quick glance, "what's the plan then?"

Jackson looked over at Draflor. "Any ideas?"

"If I did, I could've helped out more in the Steelserpent War. The Ironmamba had five throne cores they were using against their enemies, that's why we had to summon the colossals. They were able to handle the power from those things." Draflor looked troubled and shook his head. "I got nothing, I have a feeling the Toxicshade's throne core would notice if we tried to interfere and attack us."

"Could you try to convince it that this is a bad idea?" Spinescale asked.

"It's helping out the Toxicshade and willingly absorbing tainted magic to awaken a powerful weapon," Draflor answered dryly. "Do you seriously think it's going to listen to something intelligent?"

"Ok, ok." Spinescale hissed a bit defensively. "Point made, don't talk to the thing."

"Jackson, from what Koiwae and I can tell, the Fire Tribes are trying to come up and attack the Toxicshade on the southern side." Startide called. "If the Toxicshade cast their spell soon, the Fire Tribes will be out of harm's way."

Jackson let out a tight stressed breath. "Ok good, and here comes Blade."

"The old clans are over that way, but they've been slowly movin away from the main group and back aways." Blade said. "You figured anythin out here?" He asked while Jackson and Draflor went to the surface and looked towards the ships up ahead.

"THAT WE NEED TO GET OUT OF HERE NOW!" Draflor yelled when the throne core began flashing wildly as more mages joined in the spell. Jackson saw some magic cannons turn to face the throne core before they fired into it, making it float even higher into the sky as it turned a dark purple black.

"Let's get out of here!" Daychaser cried before everyone raced after Blade and his squad, who swiftly led them towards where the old clan ships were gathered.

Jackson could feel the magic of the spell while it convulsed around the throne core, and he shuddered when the sky darkened above them. He skimmed the surface, looking over his shoulder to see more mages firing their magic from the long column of vessels forming a protective barrier around the ships overseeing the casting of the spell.

Jackson jumped when a sharp, pointed beam of magic exploded from the throne core, tearing through the air and the surface of the water before crashing into the crest of the watersnake colossal! There was a loud crackling roar as magic began wildly swirling around the snake's crest.

"Hurry! HURRY!" Startide screamed when the stone around the snake's crest began to shatter. Everyone strained to go even

# THE WEAPON

faster when they heard a deep foreboding humming sound as the magic from the throne core began to clash with the magic of the Great Petrifying.

The group barreled towards the old clan ships while the throne core seemed to falter for a second. The light within the core blinked as if it wondered if something wasn't quite right before it pressed on with the spell. As cracks quickly spread across the serpent's stone body and raced down its tail, Jackson and his friends reached the edge of the old clan fleets. As the first ship neared, Jackson reached out to grab the Ocean's Tear while he shot to the surface and activated his spells.

"Solarswell, Draflor, can you give me a boost?" He called as a large, protective current formed around him as he shot into the air. Solarswell flashed in response, only to darken when a loud, soul-shivering enraged hiss sounded through the water.

Jackson looked behind him and screamed. "NO!"

The spell holding the water snake colossal broke!

Everyone was thrown back when the magic around the snake exploded, sending a blast of energy that vaporized the water around the snake, destroying the stronghold beneath!

The throne core gave a single flash of fright before it was turned to stone and shattered. The blast of energy surged over the ships and crews around the stronghold, turning them into dark black stone that shattered and cracked before they began to sink!

Jackson and his friends were tossed about when the resulting tidal wave hit them, knocking Spinescale off Jackson's bag. The old clan ships behind them creaked loudly when they were thrown on their sides, the sudden movement tossing many of the terrified crews overboard.

# MYTHOS SEAS: MOVING SEAMOUNTS

Jackson righted himself and shot to the surface, flying into the air to watch in horror as the bright, flashing red eyes of the snake opened before it let out an enraged, roaring hiss!

"No, no, no!" Jackson whispered when he saw the snake's burning eyes latch onto the Fire Tribe fleets that had been halted in their advance by the blast. Another reverberating hiss echoed across the waves before the snake dove off the pile of rubble below its coils, racing through the water while hissing in rage.

"NO!" Jackson's tail flashed before he rocketed above the water as fast as he could, putting all his energy into his spells while he shot past the reeling forces of the Toxicshade. He barely registered the Toxicshade Emperor atop his personal ship: the horrid man shouted triumphantly as the snake slashed through the water towards the Fire Tribes fleets.

Pushing his spell to the limit, Jackson shot past the colossal when it slowed so it could draw back to strike as it came up to the leading ships of the Fire Tribe fleet. Jackson noticed the terrified looks of the men on board the ships while the snake coiled back to strike. He heard them shout as he whipped around in front of the main ship, grabbed his pendant in his hands, and nearly forced his Shield guardian out, pouring his and the Ocean's Tear's magic into the pendant as the snake lunged!

There was a bright flash before the shield suddenly appeared and burst to a giant size! The snake smashed into the shield with a crash powerful enough to send cracks shooting through the shield. Jackson cringed as the wild magic around the snake burned around the shield as the snake pulled back.

"You might want to look out behind you." Draflor said while the snake shook its head as if in a daze. "I think some of the fire mages don't know what you're up to."

# THE WEAPON

Jackson looked behind him to see some of the mages focusing on him with spells at the ready and he quickly darted down to the deck while the snake continued to shake off its headache.

The Captain readied her weapon as Jackson got closer. He quickly formed a symbol that his aunt—who was from the Fire Tribes—had taught him when she began teaching him fire magic.

The Captain lowered her weapon slightly when she saw the symbol, only to bring it up again when the snake hissed angrily and Jackson flipped about. As the snake's eyes opened Jackson looked back at the Captain. "I'll lead it off, you guys get clear!" He called, shooting into the air again while he pulled the shield guardian back into his pendant with a grateful "thank you."

He darted towards the snake's head as its eyes burned, hissing lividly once as it saw the fleet of ships before it. Magic glowed in its throat as it opened its mouth, only for Jackson to smack it across the snout with a water whip spell! "OVER HERE YOU SPELL BLASTED COLOSSAL!"

Jackson shuddered, slightly questioning his sanity when the serpent whipped around, its eyes latching onto him before it hissed. "Now would be a good time to run." Draflor's voice squeaked a bit before Jackson backflipped around and dove into the water, the snake's fangs slicing through the air behind him before it crashed after him!

Jackson dodged and dove while he led the snake deep into the depths before he turned up towards the rattled Toxicshade fleets. He balled his fists determinedly as he rocketed from waves while the serpent roared after him, chasing him as he soared over one of the emperor's personal ships.

As Jackson passed over the first ship, he heard it splinter and shatter behind him when the colossal crashed through it as it tried to catch Jackson in its jaws! The snake smacked another ship with its tail as it smashed into a third ship, which Jackson had charged under while he led the raging beast crashing through the fleet. As he fled, Jackson flew over and around every ship he could, the wooden vessels bursting into splinters while the magical energy flying from the serpent's scales melted through metal hulls as the beast charged after him.

As Jackson flipped around after a second pass through the fleets, his eyes locked on the emperor's personal ship before he scowled angrily and shot towards it!

As Jackson flew past, the emperor locked eyes with him for a single second and seemed to sneer, only for Jackson to form his tribe's symbol and throw it in front of him as the snake lunged. The wicked man's eyes widened in terror when he saw the symbol just as the snake crashed into the ship! As the snake's jaws crushed the front of the ship, Jackson dove into the water just as the Star of the Sea flashed out of his hands and touched his head.

Scenes flashed across Jackson's mind as he saw the water snake colossal before she became enraged. Her purple-red eyes were calm as she leaned down to lift some Sonaekian children up to a high ledge, a couple of the children rubbed the back of her head, making the snake rumble in pleasure. *"Velocina doesn't have a crest!"* Jackson heard the star call.

"JACKSON LOOK OUT!!" Spinescale cried as she formed a bright purple bubble of magic around her and shoved Jackson out of the way just as the snake's jaws snapped shut behind them! The snake whipped its head and smacked into them, sending them flying out of the water and splashing amongst a pile of wreckage!

## CHAPTER SIXTEEN
# SAVING SERPENTS

"SPINESCALE!" Jackson cried as he struggled through the water toward the limp snake. "Spinescale. Wake up, please!" Spinescale's eyes seemed to brighten for a moment. "You... r-really should watch your b...back you know that."

"What happened?" Startide, Zepherdust, and Daychaser surfaced, coming over worriedly while Jackson started a healing spell as he tried to find a way to heal Spinescale's injured back.

"Jackson," Spinescale's voice was deathly quiet. "I don't know if there is anything you can do."

"No, hang in there Spinescale, please!" Jackson whispered as tears stung his eyes while he tried harder, his hands flashing.

"Jackson." He stopped when her tail weakly wrapped around his hand. "Y...you have to..." She shivered in pain. "You gotta stop that thing, I'll be ok until you get back."

"I can't leave you like this." Jackson said before the sound of another breaking ship caught his attention while the colossal continued to charge around in rage.

"GO!" She hissed. "The Star..." Her voice died out and Jackson pressed his hands down further as he practically shoved healing magic into her.

"Jackson, she's still breathing." Draflor said quietly. "Leave Solarswell and I here, and we'll work on her. If you don't stop Velocina, she'll destroy everything."

Jackson looked over at Draflor. "You saw it too?"

"That's why I wasn't watching your back." Draflor looked ashamed. "I think the Star of the Sea was counting on me to do that, but I was curious and touched that Star so I could see what it was showing you. This is my fault." He looked down at the limp form of Spinescale. "Let me and Solarswell try."

"I'll stay and help too." Startide said gently. "Maybe I can help you guys by lending power to your spells."

Jackson finally told Daychaser to pull him away after he'd taken off the staff and laid it next to Spinescale on the broken part of the ship.

Once he hit the water, Jackson had to shake away the tears that hadn't come out yet and forced himself to swim towards the sounds of destruction up ahead.

"What do you need us to do?" Daychaser asked as he, Zepherdust, and the sharks gathered round.

"I-I need to get on Velocina's head." Jackson said, looking at Blade. "If you and your team can distract her, that would help."

"You got it. Let's move." Blade called out to the other sharks and led the charge towards the serpent, who had dove back under the water and surged after the fleet of old clan ships. Jackson and the others raced after them, hoping to head Velocina off before she reached the old clan fleets, which were fleeing as quickly as they could.

Jackson, Zepherdust, and Daychaser followed behind the sharks before they split off and Jackson launched himself out of the water into the air! Daychaser and Zepherdust followed by jumping into Jackson's magical water column and swimming up behind him.

# SAVING SERPENTS

"We got your back!" Daychaser called and Zepherdust barked in confirmation!

Jackson nodded as the serpent let out an angry hiss below them when Blade and his shiver dove into the attack. The sharks spun around the snake, lashing out with their attacks then dashing away before Velocina could get to close!

When the serpent whipped her head back out of the water and coiled as she prepared to strike once again, Jackson and the others dove! His jaw tightened once saw the small thin crest sticking out of her head and charged closer.

*It's not a crest, it's a sword!* Jackson gasped when the sword pulsed with magic, coinciding with a loud hiss of rage from the snake. Jackson shot down as Velocina readied her strike and grabbed onto the handle of the sword and yanked it back!

The hissing cry of pain and rage from Velocina made the very air shake, bringing tears to Jackson's eyes as his ears rang painfully! The serpent let out another cry as she wreathed around in the water while Jackson held onto the sword for dear life.

Somehow Daychaser and Zepherdust managed to dart forward and latch onto the sword with their jaws. "PULL!!" Daychaser shouted before they all yanked back on the sword which suddenly slipped loose, throwing the friends back into the air before they crashed into the water with a splash!

The effect on Velocina was almost immediate. Her flashing eyes dimmed and she stilled for a moment, breathing heavily as her eyes cleared while she looked around her. "What happened? Where am I?"

She looked around her in confusion. "Toxillio? Fanlioa?" She called, looking around her before she noticed Jackson and sighed. "Oh, dahling, thank venom there's a lightborn around here." She quickly came down to eye level with Jackson.

"Dahling would you be so kind as to enlighten me on my whereabouts. Last, I remember…" Her eyes hardened. "I got stabbed by that dastardly brother of the Ironmamba Emperor in the back of the head during a battle." She looked down to see the sword stuck in the mud.

"YOU!" She lunged forward, a coating of magic forming around her fangs. "You tortured me one time too many!" She opened her mouth to fire streams of poisonous acid through the water onto the sword, which began to shrivel and disintegrate away as she pulled her head back and made a satisfied hiss. "That'll fix you."

She looked back at Jackson as the sword sizzled away into nothing. "Dahling, now if you could be a sweetheart and please tell me where I'm at and what's happened?" She looked around worriedly. "Perhaps, I should try to reach out to the King, he would know what's going on."

"Um… are you Velocina?" Jackson stuttered.

"Why yes, of course I am." She got down to look him in the eye. "Where have you been the last fifty years?"

"Actually, miss Velocina…" Daychaser began only for the Star of the Sea to appear, making Velocina hiss in delight.

"Well, bite my tale and call me a cockatrice, it's so good to see you!" She gave Jackson another look over, "but when did you choose a new guardian? You and Prince Theren were getting on famously, as I recall."

The star hovered up to Velocina and flashed a few times, making her eyes widen before she tilted her head forward as the star touched it.

"WHHAAAATTT!?!?!?!" The water shook from Velocina's yell! "You mean I accidently started—and this whole—What?" She reeled, sinking into the water deeper while she processed what the

## SAVING SERPENTS

star had showed her, which Jackson suspected was just about everything.

"I... don't know what to say I..." She looked between Jackson and the star. "I'm so terribly sorry, I sure hope me going into a rage state wasn't truly the cause of all this, I..." She stopped, a horrified look crossing her snout. "Dahling, your friend Spinescale, we must get to her immediately."

"Oh spells, Spinescale!" Jackson cried and took off, sailing through the water to where he'd left the others.

When they came to where Startide, Draflor, and Solarswell were tending to the still form of Spinescale, Draflor looked up and tensed when he saw Velocina swimming up behind Jackson. However, he relaxed when she called out worriedly.

"Dahlings, let me try, us venom creatures must stick together you know."

"She's hanging in there, barely, nothing we tired worked." Draflor said as he moved back.

"It doesn't look good." Velocina said as she gently touched Spinescale with her great snout. "Let me ask her a question really quick, I can't do anything without her permission."

"How ya gonna ask her when she's out cold?" Blade asked.

Velocina chuckled. "Dahling, we colossals aren't your usual creatures." She touched Spinescale's head with her own before they both began to glow.

After a moment, Velocina seemed to smile and Spinescale was enveloped in a bright sphere of magic. Symbols flashed across the surface of the sphere as it lifted Spinescale into the air, the symbols spinning and changing all sorts of purples, greens, and reds. With much flickering and flashing, the sphere slowly descended back down to the plank of wood and vanished away, leaving Spinescale lying quietly on the plank.

# MYTHOS SEAS: MOVING SEAMOUNTS

After a moment she groaned, her wings weakly stretching out while her eyes brightened up. "Let's not do that again please."

"Spinescale!!" Jackson cried, scooping her up into a hug as he started sobbing, "I'm sorry, I'm so sorry!"

"Easy, you're crushing me." Spinescale wheezed, patting him with her tail. "It's ok, it wasn't your fault and I'm fine."

"And I think I'm the one that needs to apologize..." Draflor said quietly.

"I don't want to hear it." Spinescale gave Draflor a kind wink. "We all make mistakes."

Jackson wiped away a few tears as he let go of Spinescale who quickly slithered onto a plank. Draflor gave her an ashamed, but grateful, look.

"It's ok. I'm fine now, really." She looked around and glared at a piece of gold-rimmed wood from the emperor's ship. "And if that emperor guy is still alive, I'm gonna give him a bite he'll never forget."

"That settles it," Blade said, looking amused. "She's fine."

Jackson laughed, rubbing his puffy eyes while Draflor looked up at Velocina thoughtfully. "I never thought I'd see the day you took on a minossal."

"A minossal?" Startide asked. "What's that?"

"Colossal species can sometimes give a piece of their power to another creature; those creatures are called minossals: small creatures who can learn to use magic similar to colossal species." Draflor answered. "Usually, they train underneath the colossal that shared their power with them."

"I never intended to dahling." Velocina said, "but it was the least I could do, after all the trouble I've inadvertently caused."

Jackson jerked back when Stonecurrent, Oceaono, and Koiwae's forms shot out of the orb on his hand, making Velocina hiss happily. "Oceaono, Koiwae, Stonecurrent, dahlings, you're a sight for sore eyes."

"As are you, Velocina." Oceaono sighed happily, "and we're all relieved that you are still on our side."

"Oh dahling, I'm terribly sorry for everything you've been through. If only I hadn't been stabbed by—"

"It's ok Velocina." Koiwae interrupted. "We all know that the rage state is... complicated. I'm just sorry we didn't notice two-hundred years ago."

"It's all in the past, now we must focus on the future." Oceaono said. "I believe—"

Everyone turned when a loud whirring sound of magic resonated behind them. Jackson shivered as dark, tainted energy flew from the water into the air before it began to condense.

"The dark pillar is reforming?" Startide squeed in shock, "but how?"

"This is bad." Oceaono was alarmed. "If Voidcul's dark pillars can reform like this..." He looked over to Koiwae. "Koiwae, if she's this strong, could she break into the capital?"

"She's getting there." Koiwae was flaring his fins out worriedly as he paced around anxiously. "We have to get Jackson and the others there, and soon, or she'll break through and there will be nothing left!"

"Oh dahlings, I can help with that." Velocina said. "Once I rest a bit, I'm sure I'll have the strength to open a portal to the entrance of the Inner World along the abyss."

"That would help immensely." Koiwae nodded, flicking his fins approvingly, "but you must meet up with Depthcall and the others first."

# MYTHOS SEAS: MOVING SEAMOUNTS

"And I believe Jackson has a little business to take care of anyway." Daychaser said, giving Jackson a long look. "After we make sure the old clans are ok..."

"LOOK OUT!" Velocina suddenly cried, flipping around to whip a large black inky tentacle with her tail as the group scattered! The tentacle splattered from the impact, sending ink spraying everywhere while more tentacles began reaching out from the reforming dark pillar.

"Get clear of this place, it's too dangerous!" Oceaono called before he and the others vanished. Jackson and the others quickly regrouped before they fled the area while more tentacles reached out in search of prey.

## CHAPTER SEVENTEEN
# UNFINISHED BUSINESS

Mavous gazed out at the ocean from the deck of his wife's ship as the sun set. His uncertain frown deepened as he thought back to what he'd seen. The emperor's fleet was in ruins, his most powerful mages dead, and his personal army laid waste in a matter of minutes. He shook his head, which had begun to hurt from strain and overanalyzing. If that boy from the Growingstar Tribe hadn't given them the missive about the betrayal, they'd have been caught in the destruction.

"Would you like some spitfire juice, Mavous?" Venor asked as he walked up with Captain Venmoral and Captain Annasel, who had her bright red hair tied into a tight ponytail. "Might help with that headache."

"Thank you." Mavous gratefully took the cup Venor handed him before he took a long drink of the spicy juice. "What did the men find?"

"Not a lot that was intact." Captain Venmoral came over and leaned back against the railing at the side of the deck. "And no sign of the emperor or any of his personal ships."

"Our men couldn't stay long, not with that dark pillar that formed, it was attacking everything in sight." An older man with a bandage around his head commented as he came over with Captain Corian. "I'd hate to see the creature that made that."

Mavous shook his head as he looked out to sea, even from this distance he could see the undulating mass of the dark pillar rising from the water. "We've been trying for years to be free of the emperor, and in minutes his forces and the sources of his power are destroyed."

"A joyous day indeed." The old man said, raising his cup to the sky. "We should be very thankful the Creator had mercy on us."

"It is indeed a joyous day." Captain Annasel agreed, although she gave Mavous a worried look. "Isn't it Mavous, dear?"

"What's strangling your snake man?" Captain Corian asked. "You look like you're upset that the emperor and his forces were destroyed. You should be celebrating; I can assure you the rest of the fleet will be tonight."

Mavous sighed. "Didn't you all see him?" He leaned against the railings again. "That boy who gave us the missive? That boy single handedly stopped a serpent that could destroy one of the greatest fleets in the world and then made the beast vanish."

"I don't deny the whole thing is a bit strange." Captain Corian said, "but why worry about it? The boy was clearly on our side, one of my men saw him tackle that snake when it started heading towards us."

Captain Venmorul leaned forward slowly and huffed a bit. "He's the boy from the Growingstar Tribe, isn't he?"

"Venmorul!" Venor chided sternly while the others' eyes widened in surprise.

"I wasn't sworn to secrecy like you and Mavous, I think Greatcrower knew this would happen eventually." Venmorul retorted. "I'll take my chances."

# UNFINISHED BUSINESS

"That boy is connected to the Growingstar Tribe?" Annasel was aghast. "I didn't know they could use water magic."

Captain Corian huffed as he took another drink of spitfire juice. "Get why you seem so upset then; they were an interesting tribe."

"Who is somehow connected to what happened to our people." Mavous smacked his cup down. "I just don't know how, or what!"

"M-maybe I can help answer that f-for you."

Everyone turned when a young boy in a blue shirt, a bright green sash embroidered with the Growingstar Tribe symbol, dark blue trousers, bare feet, forearm length gloves, a blue headband with strange symbols tied around his head raised into view next to the boat. The boy also had a strange necklace around his neck, a bag slung over his shoulder, and a beautiful staff strapped to his back.

"What?" Captain Corian leapt back. "REINFORCEMENTS!" He roared.

"I w-wouldn't do that, if I were you." The boy said wryly while he stood in the air next to the boat.

"Oh and why not?" The captain challenged as some men started to appear on the deck with their weapons at the ready. "There's only one of you."

The boy sighed and closed his eyes. "One, I'm not here to fight, and two, you might not want to mess with my friends."

Everyone shied back when the boy was lifted higher into the air by none other than the giant snake who had destroyed the emperor's entire fleet. Men and women fell to the deck while others scrambled back as the snake leaned forward enough to let the lad jump off its head onto the wood planks.

"Thank you Velocina." The boy said while he tried to hide a tiny smirk as he looked around, his eyes settling on Mavous, Venor, and Venmorul. "I'm g-glad you're all ok; I have a f-few things I'm supposed to give you."

"Give us?" Captain Venmorul asked, looking stunned.

"WAIT!" Mavous rallied his courage and came forward. "Before anything else, I want to know what happened to our clans, I know you know about them."

Instead of answering immediately, the boy held out a stack of papers he seemed to pull from thin air. "I wasn't able to give these to you before. It wasn't the main thing on my mind, but these are the orders the emperor sent out years ago." He came up and handed the papers to Mavous as his thick necklace unwrapped from his neck, revealing the fine head of a winged sea snake who hissed warningly. "They cover everything about his plans to destroy your family, the Spherefangs, and his plans to blame my tribe for it."

The boy backed away when Venor and Captain Venmorul came up to quickly glance through the papers, their faces hardening as they did so.

"So our family, all our clans are all..." Captain Venmorul let the sentence peter out.

The boy reached out and flipped to the last few pages and tapped on them. "My grandfather found out about the emperor's plans and warned your clans." He met Mavous's eyes. "Your clans were able to escape before they could be killed. They're alive."

"Where are they?" Venor demanded.

The boy got a conflicted look in his eyes. "I can't answer that, but I know they're alive."

"Why can't you tell us?" Captain Venmorul gave the lad a suspicious look. "If you don't know where they are, how do you know they are alive?"

"Or are you lying to us for some reason?" Venor insisted.

An insulted expression crossed the boy's face as he gave Mavous and Venor a tart look. "Your mother's name is Calnoa, who is best friends with my great cousin Zelli, who is married to Toceth,

# UNFINISHED BUSINESS

who mentored you and your brothers in magic when you were younger and was the leader of your clans before passing it onto your brother Norven." The boy's insulted look deepened. "As if I'd disgrace my grandpa and great cousin Zelli by lying to you."

The men stared in stunned silence, completely shocked by the boy's knowledge of their clans and history. The boy gave them another tart look, a disgruntled huff escaping his throat while he looked back at Captain Annasel. "Could you have your men clear a bit of room on the deck please? I have something I know belonged to the old clans before the emperor took over your lands, and I'd like to give it back."

Annasel blinked in surprise, but waved her men back. Everyone jumped a bit when a magic cannon and a bunch of crystals suddenly appeared on the deck, making it creak from the sudden weight.

When Mavous and the others turned back to the boy, he was holding a small chest in his hands, "Y-you'll want to all get clear of this place, that d-dark pillar is continuing to grow and could k-kill you all."

He frowned as he turned to look at the dark pillar. "And my friends are w-worried more will be forming around this area here soon, t-thanks the emperor's meddling." He took a deep breath as he returned his gaze to the men while he held out the small chest to Mavous. "I was told to give this to you and Venor." He handed the chest to Mavous, "and if you see your clans again, please tell Toceth and Zelli that Jackson s-said 'hi,' and I love them."

A huge mass of water suddenly surged up over the side of the boat into which the boy turned and jumped into before it swept him off into the ocean. There was barely even a splash while the boy vanished just as mysteriously as he appeared, leaving everyone on the deck speechless in shock.

# MYTHOS SEAS: MOVING SEAMOUNTS

After a few moments, Mavous looked down at the chest and slowly opened it. He took a quick intake of breath when he saw the spiral crystal inside.

"It's Mom's crest." Venor whispered. "We can find Mom and Dad again."

"Only if I decide you're worthy to." The crystal said as it unwound into a tiny crystal basilisk. "Your mother gave me strict orders, for your sakes you'd better have kept your honor or I'm out of here." The little creature looked out to where Jackson had vanished.

"I like him, he knows just how to care for magical artifacts." It turned and gave Mavous and Venor each droll look. "You two better have learned how to do the same. I haven't forgotten how dusty I got when your mother was sick and left you in charge of tending to me, Mavous."

Annasel giggled as she came up behind Mavous and gave him a teasing swat. "I think you might be in trouble dear; you haven't dusted our quarters in weeks."

"You've already lost honor points and we haven't even got started on the real questions." The basilisk squawked. "Hope ya can keep up with my interrogation, or Jackson's getting another magical friend on his journey."

## CHAPTER EIGHTEEN
# GATHERING SHADOWS

The following night, the full moon was shining brightly overhead as the group traveled just under the surface. Blade was leading the team northeast where they were supposed to meet up with Depthcall and the other teams.

Spinescale's eyes sparkled mischievously as she watched Jackson brighten his biolumina spell once he'd noticed the sky growing darker. "You know, I've been meaning to mention something about yesterday…" She gave Jackson a sassy look. "I think someone's learning a flair for the dramatic."

"I'll take credit for that!" Draflor called out. "It's all the time Jackson and I spent together in Shieldguard, I've rubbed off on him."

Jackson pretended to focus on the map spell he'd conjured up. "I'm sure I have no idea what you are talking about. I just felt like the old clans would be less likely to try to attack or capture me if Velocina was there."

"Uhuh, which is why she lifted you up on her head." Daychaser added.

"I seem to recall that was her idea, not Jackson's." Startide gave Jackson a wink.

# MYTHOS SEAS: MOVING SEAMOUNTS

Zepherdust giggled. "And I'm sure Jackson would have gone up on his own if he needed to."

"Don't hurt to make an entrance." Blade said from up ahead.

"I wholeheartedly approved of his methods!" Draflor laughed, "and so did Stonecurrent when he heard about it."

Startide suddenly flipped around, and Jackson quit studying his map as he watched her sound the area heavily before she switched to her magic sounding. "Startide?" He ended his spell when he saw her features tighten.

"Something's following us." Her eyes slitted.

"Depthcall?" Blade asked, flipping around and slashing his tail, signaling the other sharks into action before they spread out protectively.

"No… but…" Her eyes widened when a familiar sounding clicking sounded out through the water. "Shadowtorrent?" She moved forward excitedly.

"Startide!" Shadowtorrent appeared through the water up ahead, a long wound down his flank visible as he rushed towards the group. "Thank the first currents I found you guys."

"What happened to your flank?" Startide hurried over to inspect the wound.

"I'll be ok, it's not that deep." He said gruffly, although Jackson swore the ex-killer whale was blushing a bit from the attention before he looked over to Jackson. "Depthcall sent me ahead, there's a group of sirens coming your way fast. They're after Jackson."

"What? I thought Daychaser had told them off long ago." Spinescale hissed uncertainly.

"I'll explain as we swim, we have to try and meet up with Depthcall and the others before the sirens catch up." Shadowtorrent's tone was urgent as the group took off.

# GATHERING SHADOWS

While they made for deeper waters, Shadowtorrent explained in hushed tones. "A faction of the sirens around here made contact with the Dark One through one of her dark pillars." He said. "Apparently, they think that forming a treaty with her will preserve their power in these waters. They've agreed to try and capture Jackson. In exchange, the Dark One will grant them a portion of her protection and power."

"Spells, as if we didn't have enough trouble already." Jackson grumbled while the sunlight vanished beyond the horizon. "We already had to deal with one dark pillar."

"Is that how you got hurt?" Startide pressed, still eyeing Shadowtorrent's side worriedly.

"Kinda, the rogue group of sirens tried to attack us when we were traveling through a shallow pass that led us here." Shadowtorrent said. "Depthcall found the dark pillar in the pass and attacked it, we didn't know there were sirens on the shoreline who would attack us as well. They caught us off guard."

"Let me work on healing you as we swim Shadowtorrent." Jackson said. "You shouldn't have open wounds out here."

Shadowtorrent shook his head stubbornly and moved further away. "I'll be fine, you need to save your power in case that group of sirens show up."

"How far away are Depthcall and the others?" Blade asked from up ahead.

"Not far." Shadowtorrent said. "Hopefully."

Spinescale gave Shadowtorrent a disbelieving look. "Hopefully?"

"They had to take a different route than I did." Shadowtorrent held himself proudly. "I was able to make better time, I'm faster than they are."

"Duh, you're an oroca." Spinescale quipped, giving him a snarky look. "Nothing impressive about that."

Jackson, Draflor, and Daychaser all exchanged amused looks.

"What you lot smirking over?" Spinescale hissed.

"Nothiiiing." Draflor said innocently before he vanished into the staff to evade further questioning while Daychaser snickered and whispered to Jackson.

"Just enjoying the show."

"Time for that later." Blade said as the other sharks tightened the perimeter around them. "I'm not likin how the sky is lookin, it's gettin too dark to the north of us, can't see the stars."

"WHAT where?" Startide sounded the area around them quickly before looking at the darkening sky. "Oh, I didn't even notice."

"Cause she's preoccupied with Loverboy instead of being on watch." Spinescale muttered under her breath while Zepherdust gave her a wry look.

"If the sirens find us, Shadowtorrent and I can run block from behind." Startide said, looking a bit embarrassed. "Blade and the sharks can protect Jackson from the sidelines."

Jackson held up his hands. "Wait, Shadowtorrent." He asked. "Do the sirens have any way to contact the Dark One?"

"Not that I know of, we destroyed their dark pillar." Shadowtorrent said, his fins beginning to glow a dark blue with his own magic as they hurried along. "Why?"

Daychaser's eyes widened. "Velocina?"

Jackson nodded. "She might be able to help out, she's just resting right now."

The group continued forward as the sky darkened, clouds thickening and pouring out over the ocean to the north of them. As they rushed ahead, Jackson felt a strange, unsettling feeling creep across his skin and kept looking up at the dark clouds uneasily.

"You sense it too, don't you?" Draflor asked quietly as he slipped up next to Jackson's head, and Jackson nodded.

"They're coming this way, aren't they?" Jackson whispered, trying to not worry the others.

Draflor nodded, glancing up at the mist, "and that mist isn't normal siren mist either."

"I can sound Depthcall!" Startide exclaimed. "They're just up ahead."

Jackson hesitated, looking northward before the cry of the sirens reached their ears and he tensed.

"LOOK OUT!" He shoved Daychaser out of the way of a long set of shadowy claws while Zepherdust, Startide, and Shadowtorrent darted to the surface when a series of shadowy orbs flew into the midst of the group. "Go, GO!" Jackson flipped around just before the dark slashes of a shadow spell sliced by his tail. "SWIM! HEAD FOR DEPTHCALL, GO."

Jackson grabbed Spinescale as he swept forwards catching Daychaser and the rest of the group inside a large current. He took off to where Startide had indicated Depthcall was, just as the shadowed forms of a host of sirens appeared rushing through the water with dark, vicious cries.

"Jackson we can handle the current, you block their attacks!" Blade yelled when another barrage of shadow attacks bore down on them.

Jackson nodded, flipping about as the sharks' touched fins, creating a surging vortex before Blade and the other lightning speed sharks shot off! The sharks yanked everyone along with them as Jackson threw out a multitude of bright spheres of light from his hands! The spheres raced off and crashed into the shadow spells with brilliant bursts of magic, disintegrating the shadow magic into nothingness while the remaining light spells barreled into the ranks of their pursuers.

Jackson could hear more and more calls and screeches as additional sirens joined in the attack, swarming towards him and his friends while they fled. Suddenly, the calls of the sirens were overpowered by the angry blasting bellows of the goliathan whales as Jackson and his friends darted into the midst of an army of magically gleaming whales, oroca, cadolin, sea lions, and a host of other creatures who closed ranks around Jackson and his friends.

"On my mark!" Depthcall shouted while the whales surrounded Jackson and the others. "GEYSER!" As one the whales flipped about, each one sending a barrage of glowing water blasts shooting out into the oncoming throng of siren which scattered with startled screams as the whales readied another attack.

"Swords of the icy north!" She called forming two huge ice swords next to her, the other whales following suit. "Freeze these bottomkillers!" The swords flashed as they spun out into the water and slashed into the scattering sirens, freezing both water and siren in ice.

"Sea lions! Fire the prey's revenge!!" Depthcall shouted as the huge chunks of ice cracked and creaked as they shattered apart while other chunks soared to the surface.

Avavo let out a loud cry before magical forms of seals and fish formed in the water around him and the other sea lions. The magical forms glistened before they shot off between the chunks of ice, swarming after the sirens who viciously tried to hold off the assault!

Among the cries of the battle, Jackson noticed the orb on his glove flashing and quickly touched it. "Oceaono? What's—"

"JACKSON!" Oceaono and the other medians appeared as well as the guardians. "Voidcul is trying to break through the Ironsong

# GATHERING SHADOWS

Pass, if she gets through she could break into the capital, you must—!" The medians all seemed to wince in pain, and Stonecurrent bellowed in alarm before he turned to Jackson. "HAVE VELOCINA TAKE YOU THROUGH THAT PORTAL NOW! If Voidcul makes it back to the capital before you get there, you might never get in!!"

"We'll form a barrier." Depthcall called as more ice swords formed around her. "Whales, defensive measures, buy us some time!" The whales all spun to the side and lashed out with their swords, spinning them around the group and freezing the water around them, forming a huge protective cone of solid ice.

Jackson teleported Velocina out of his bag while the others backed away to give the gigantic serpent room. The colossal took one look at the pained faces of the medians and the guardians alarm before she hissed understandingly. "One portal coming up dahlings, fill me in when we get there."

She twisted around, coiling her immense body into a spiral as she began to glow a host of different purples that flipped over one another. The magic from her body suddenly flew together in the middle of her coils, forming into a long, spinning whirlpool of magic. "Swim down through the top, I'll join you once you're through!" She called.

Jackson was practically yanked off his fins when Startide grabbed him in her jaws and took off towards the top of the circle before diving into it, the others following suit. Jackson's eyes slitted as they were engulfed by Velocina's magic, which spun wildly around them while the cries of Depthcall and the sirens sounding in his ears.

Then nothing, just empty, quiet, dark water.

Jackson looked behind him to watch as the rest of the group came flying through the portal. They were followed by the army of

# MYTHOS SEAS: MOVING SEAMOUNTS

ocean creatures before Velocina herself shot through, the portal closing the minute her tail left it.

"Where are we?" Daychaser asked.

"The entrance to the Inner World." Velocina looked longingly towards a tall white stone structure behind them. The rim of the entrance was made from the most polished of cream and blue stone that curved around giant white stone doors. The tightly shut doors were big enough for ten goliathan whales to swim through in a line without touching each other's fins. "The entrance to my home."

"And not far from Mythos Pearl." Depthcall urged everyone forward. "We must hurry." She gave Jackson a pleading look. "Could you try to reach my dear Stonecurrent and the medians?"

Jackson nodded and quickly called out to the guardians and medians only for the magic of the orb to crackle and flash before it went dark.

"That's really bad." Draflor was the most sober Jackson had ever seen him. "If you can't get through to any of them…"

"Perhaps Voidcul isn't preventing it…" Depthcall's voice was tight.

Draflor frowned at her. "She's broken through Ironsong Pass Depthcall, you know that's the only way she could prevent the medians from contacting us."

"I know, I just don't want it to be so." Depthcall shook her head as she went to the surface for a breath. "If she's at the capital by the time we get there, we will have to fight to let Jackson through to the entrance so he can open it."

"But…" Jackson whispered. "What about you?"

"We will show Voidcul what two hundred years of pain and rage can make a creature do dahling." Velocina's lips pulled back angrily. "I never liked her before her betrayal, I most certainly have no broken fangs about destroying her now."

# GATHERING SHADOWS

Draflor sighed. "Then it's time for me to actually be of more help."

"What do you mean?" Spinescale asked. "You're just a small little fish who can use spells of immensely terrifying scale."

"Which has been an immense help already." Zepherdust added, giving Draflor a reassuring look.

Draflor grinned a bit at Spinescale's attempt at humor. "I'm actually not just a fish."

"What do you mean?" Jackson asked.

Draflor didn't answer. "Solarswell? You gonna be ok without me now?"

Solarswell flashed a few times and Draflor made a sad huff. "Yeah, I'll miss hearing your annoying voice too. Maybe after all this, we can go over the rest of those lessons about the Nature Balance history you mentioned."

"Can someone please tell me what in the seas is going on?" Granitebow asked.

"Just wait." Depthcall counseled gently, giving Jackson a knowing look. "It might explain a lot of what you've learned about Draflor's past."

Jackson and his friends all exchanged perplexed glances while Draflor vanished. The staff suddenly flew from Jackson's back and started using its magic to draw in the water.

Everyone watched as the staff sketched a larger version of itself while a multitude of magical runes flew about in the water around it. When it finished drawing, the orb portion of the artwork suddenly began to grow bigger and bigger.

The orb flashed when the staff flew into the handle of its drawing before five beams of magic swirled up from its center. As the magic was absorbed into the giant orb it began to condense, forming into a large, powerful shape.

# MYTHOS SEAS: MOVING SEAMOUNTS

When the form suddenly flashed and solidified, Jackson gasped when a large dragon opened his eyes as his wing flared out. The dragon's lips pulled back in a snarl before he reared back and roared, sending waves of magic pulsing through the water. When the roar died down, the dragon locked gazes with Jackson and smirked.

"Draflor..." Jackson sank in the water a bit in shock. "YOU'RE A DRAGON?!"

Draflor laughed quietly. "It's a long story." He turned when they heard a rumbling cry and a growl hung low in his throat. "One that will have to wait."

Spinescale, Granitebow, and some of the other creatures had gone completely limp. "Draflor the jester is... a dragon..." Spinescale whispered, only to tense when a loud crash rumbled through the water, as if something was trying to attack a mountain.

"She's started her attack." Depthcall's voice was grim. "We must make our move." She locked eyes with Jackson. "You're taking the back. If we can, we will make an opening for you to sneak around." She turned to the others. "Protect Jackson at all costs."

Jackson winced at her words, but allowed himself to get pushed to the back of the group when they moved off.

He looked at the creatures surrounding him and took a deep breath, his lips tightening into a determined line. Around him, a couple squadrons of goliathan whales, a mass of oceanic knights, a colossal snake, a shiver of sharks, a herd of sea lions, multiple podpack of seawolves, a dragon, a winged sea snake, and a host of other creatures and magical items charged through the deep dark ocean towards a darker murky shadow in the distance.

## CHAPTER NINETEEN
# THE LAST LIGHT

The dark nighttime waters seemed to grow even darker as they closed in on their target. Jackson, through his magic, saw in the distance the murals and marks of the walls around Mythos Pearl, only for them to be covered in a murky mess moments later. Jackson looked up to see the light of the moon before there was another loud crash once something seemed to notice them.

Jackson shuddered when a deep angry groaning sound reached his ears.

"She's blocked our path there." Depthcall said grimly. "There's no way we can go around, or sneak Jackson through."

"As if I'd let you ruin my hard work!"

Jackson shivered as his friends braced themselves when dark clouds of ink billowed towards them, and large black tentacles shot out from the darkness.

Jackson tensed when a dark red eye opened, blazing with power.

"YOUR FUTILE LIGHT WILL DIE AWAY INTO NOTHING!" Dark magic shot into the water as giant black tentacles lashed out towards the army while Depthcall cried out orders to her

## MYTHOS SEAS: MOVING SEAMOUNTS

team! The whales' bodies flashed before the waters around Jackson were suddenly filled with goliathan whales.

"ATTTAAAAACK!!!" Depthcall screamed, charging forward as the whales bellowed in challenge. The army let out wild shouts as they attacked, bright magical attacks glimmering before they fired at the tentacles that lashed about them.

Velocina hissed angrily while Spinescale zipped over to her before they both shot towards a large tentacle, sinking their teeth into it as Draflor roared, bright magical blasts of energy flying from his mouth into the darkness! Blade and his shiver gathered together and attacked while Shadowtorrent and Startide came up under them to block the blast of dark magic from below.

Zepherdust and Avavo joined the sea lions and other creatures in their attacks while Jackson fired his light magic into the giant mouth made of ink that had borne down on him! The mouth evaporated before Daychaser and the other seawolves howled with their sounding magic, sending immense blasts that dissipated the inky tendrils attacking them.

As the Knights of Shieldguard fanned out around him, Jackson spun away before dark clouds of ink filled the water. He yelped when a tentacle slashed out to knock him aside, cutting him off from his friends who all called out in alarm while more ink filled the water, surrounding them.

Jackson saw a dark eye watching him closely while his tail turned gleaming white. The giant pupil dilated before five tentacles swung towards him, large dark hooks firing from their coils! Jackson grabbed his pendant in his hands and formed a glowing vortex of light infused water around himself. He barely felt the impact of the claws against his vortex before he flipped his hand out, throwing the glowing vortex at the dark eye!

# THE LAST LIGHT

There was an enraged roar of pain as his vortex hit Voidcul's head, seconds later she sneered before the water filled with dark shadows that condensed into large boulders.

Jackson held out his pendant, which flashed as his sword and shield golems flashed into view! As the sword slashed through some of the shadow boulders, the shield bashed into others, while Jackson formed glowing currents of water around him and sent them firing at Voidcul who suddenly vanished into her dark clouds.

Jackson tensed when a shadow suddenly swept above him, cutting off all light from the moon and leaving him in complete darkness. He felt panic grip him, causing his spells to falter before he was suddenly snatched up in a large tentacle that dragged him away as it coiled around him!

As he was dragged along, Jackson saw some of his friends struggling madly, Voidcul's coils wrapping around them tighter while Jackson was dragged further into the darkness. As the darkness increased around him, Jackson somehow caught sight of Draflor and Velocina. His two friends were each trapped within wreathing tentacles as the limp forms of other tentacles sank into the depths below them. He saw some of Depthcall's group had been captured in the grasp of Voidcul's coils while their comrades viciously tried to free them.

Jackson gasped when the tentacle tightened around his chest as Velocina sank her teeth deep into Voidcul's dark flesh. He heard Voidcul's enraged call of pain just before another tentacle appeared and smacked the snake across the head, making her release her bite while some of Jackson's other friends were dragged into view.

"I've wanted to take you out for centuries Draflor." Voidcul's voice slithered out through the water. "But when Theren and the others escaped me, I lost my chance to kill you and your friends."

# MYTHOS SEAS: MOVING SEAMOUNTS

She used her coiling tentacles to pull Jackson's friends and allies into a tight clump.

"No." Jackson gasped, watching as an enormous, horrible head appeared from the ink. The head was strangely shark-like, but thinner, and wrinkled like the skin of some large octopi. Voidcul's skin was abyss-black and only the red of her eyes gave them away when her head was suddenly encased in shadows. Her mouth opened wide, exposing rows of jagged, sharp, gleaming black teeth. "Now I shall enjoy finishing what I started!"

Jackson shuddered when the darkness grew deeper around him before Draflor let loose a blast of flamelike magic which Voidcul blocked with one of her tentacles. The magical flames incinerated the tentacle as she surged closer, an evil gleam in her eyes while she dragged Draflor and Velocina towards her gaping jaws, the others not far behind.

"NOOO!!" Jackson screamed, his tail flashing as he slashed through the entangling tentacles and—for the first time since he was little—charged into the darkness as Voidcul lunged!

Draflor braced himself for a heap of pain as Voidcul's teeth bore down on him, his suddenly heard a shout before a beam of light rocketed towards him. He roared in surprise when Jackson barreled into him, shoving him and Velocina aside as Voidcul's jaws crashed shut behind them!

"You only delay your death, I—" Voidcul's voice faltered when Jackson turned.

"YOU." Jackson's whole tail seemed to shine with light as it changed, taking a shape unlike any sea creature he'd seen as bright, golden streaks shot across it. His eyes flashed angrily as magic swirled around him while the sun peeked over the horizon.
"YOU'LL NEVER KILL MY FRIENDS AND FAMILY!"
Jackson's shout rang through the water, making Voidcul jerk back

when a bright seven-pointed star formed around Jackson before he shot forward! Jackson let out a yell as he slashed through a giant tentacle, while Voidcul anxiously formed dark jaws of magic that came flying through the darkness towards him! Jackson spun around the jaws as the glowing form of the star broke into seven bright points that fired into the water and crashed into Voidcul's body! The Dark One screamed as Jackson slashed the Staff of Solarswell down, creating a whirling vortex of light infused water that spun through the ocean around him, clearing out the dark ink and allowing Draflor and the others to break free.

"COVER US!!" Draflor shouted to the others before he and Velocina raced forwards. Draflor's claws shined with magic as he slashed them into Voidcul's side while Velocina smacked the dark creature across the snout with her tail. A multitude of magical snakes formed in the water around the colossal before they charged, smashing into Voidcul with bursts of magical energy and making her writhe in pain.

Bright swords of light flashed into view around Jackson before he lashed them out at Voidcul as he helped Draflor and Velocina back the Dark One down! Behind them, his other friends and allies charged in to tackle Voidcul's tentacles as they lashed about while others fired their attack into her sides.

Voidcul made a hissing sound of rage when Jackson sliced a deep gouge in her snout before she threw her head back. She let out a vicious scream as her remaining tentacles swept out to scatter the others away while her eyes flashed darkly.

"HERE IT COMES!" Velocina cried before dark beams of energy flew from Voidcul's body, making everyone scatter! The attack distracted Jackson, who dodged out of the way as tentacle swept passed him, only for him to hesitate when ink billowed into the water around him.

"JACKSON LOOKOUT!!" Startide screamed when Voidcul's gaping maw leapt over the boy's form. At the last second, Draflor and Velocina dove in, circling Jackson protectively before the Dark One's jaws crashed shut!

"NO!" Depthcall bellowed as Voidcul swallowed.

Voidcul was quiet before she grinned darkly, showing off her long teeth. She turned, her behemoth body quivering with a laugh as she sneered smugly. "The light of your nation has died, Depthcall, you'll never see your kind rise to power again." She laughed. "These seas are mine to rule!"

She was poised for another strike when her body suddenly shuddered, and her mouth closed with a snap. "What?"

Voidcul suddenly screamed in pain before her tentacles swept back to wrap around her middle. The dark magical ink around her fizzed out slightly as she threw her head back and roared when bright, magical lights blasted through her hide. Seconds later, a column of bright flame-like magic shot from her stomach before a second and a third followed, piercing through her thick hide like it was nothing more than kelp leaves.

As a blast of purple magic lit up her belly, Voidcul screamed. "NO!" She yelled as a set of glowing claws pierced through her sides and slashed around before Draflor came bursting into view. Draflor let out a roar as he swept free of Voidcul's jaws, Jackson clutched in his claws, and Velocina swirling around them protectively while Voidcul twisted around in agony. "NO! WHAT DID YOU—" She seemed to start to wither in on herself.

Jackson's pale arms held onto a large assortment of artifacts while a sphere that shone with the brightness of the sun spun around him. As Draflor swooped free of Voidcul's writhing tentacles, he turned to face her.

"You aren't so powerful without the artifacts you stole." Draflor snarled, "and you're defenseless from within. Your rule is over!"

Voidcul's eyes widened as her body continued to shrink and wither. "NO, I WILL NOT LET YOU WIN." With great effort she turned, opening her mouth to fire a dark coil of magic towards a distant, partially crumpled tower that was exposed by a breach she'd made in the walls around Mythos Pearl.

The dark coil hit the tower with a blast that shook the water while Voidcul's form shriveled away into dust as the tower groaned before more stone crumpled away.

"That tower is one of the one's used for spell casting." Depthcall said quietly while she gently helped lift one of her Whaleguard over to where the others were gathering. "If it crumbles…"

"Are you all ok?" Startide called as she helped Shadowtorrent swim up to the surface for a breath while Zepherdust aided Avavo in supporting an injured seawolf.

"We should be asking you that same question." Velocina said while Spinescale rushed in as Blade and his shiver helped each other over with Daychaser and Skycaller's help.

"I—ugh." Shadowtorrent winced "I'm fine, she just got my tail."

Depthcall's expression softened slightly once she saw part of Shadowtorrent's tail was badly blackened by shadow magic. "Here, I'll help you." She came up below him to lift him atop her head.

"Really I'm ok, it's just a scratch or something." Shadowtorrent insisted.

"Shadowtorrent." Spinescale said in the kindest tone Jackson had ever heard her have for the ex-dishonored oroca. "You're not ok."

Shadowtorrent went quiet. "It's that bad?" He asked quietly.

"I'll help stop the spread of the magic." Jackson said, teleporting all the items but the glowing Sun Sphere into his bag before he darted up to begin healing the wound. As Jackson's magic glistened over Shadowtorrent's tail, Depthcall carefully led the battered army towards the large gates of Mythos Pearl.

"You dove into the darkness." Daychaser looked over at Jackson with a flabbergasted expression. "The deepest darkness you've ever faced, and you dove into it."

"Don't remind me," Jackson shivered. "I'll be haunted by it for the rest of my life."

"But you're terrified of the dark." Startide whispered.

Jackson was silent for a moment. "Yeah, I am... but... I... I couldn't let that make me lose my friends and family." He took a deep breath. "You all mean more to me than any fear, darkness or otherwise."

Blade gave a thoughtful humph. "You're quite the kid."

Jackson gave a shy shrug as the group neared the wall of the city. He grimaced when an ear shattering crack resonated through the early morning waters as part of the tower started to give way.

"Why not go through the crack in the wall?" Blade suggested while the group struggled closer. "Be faster than tryin to open the gates."

"Good idea." Depthcall changed her course for the huge breach Voidcul had made while Shadowtorrent shook Jackson off.

"I'm fine now." He insisted. "Please, I just need time."

Spinescale opened her mouth to comment but stopped when there was another echoing rumble as more of the tower gave way.

# THE LAST LIGHT

Depthcall turned to Draflor "You and Velocina take Jackson, and whoever else isn't badly injured, to the Throne Room now! If that tower collapses, all is lost."

Jackson swam over to cling to Draflor's long neck. The dragon spread his wings before he swiftly soared towards the crack in the wall as many of the other creatures hurried behind him. Jackson blinked when the bright sphere floated up to his face before it vanished into his hands and his eyes widened a bit.

Draflor's powerfully thrusting wings flew them through the water as they cleared the last of the rubble and came up behind a huge stone coated palace.

Behind them the groaning and creaking sounds of the crumbling tower echoed through the water, sending out waves of magic. Jackson watched worriedly while ripples of magic swept through the sea around them as Draflor flew up to a large, beautifully decorated window which was coated in a shallow layer of stone. The dragon reared back, his glowing claws lengthening out and thickening before he slashed them forward, shattering the glass before he dove into a beautiful throne room.

*It would be more beautiful, if it wasn't all trapped in stone.* Jackson thought as shards of stone encrusted glass cascaded around them. As more rumbling shook the water, Jackson's other friends and allies—some of whom were helping Shadowtorrent—poured in through the hole Draflor had made in the ceiling.

Below them, Sonaekian men, women, and creatures were gathered around a large circular table that was engraved with seemingly countless runes.

A large, petrified orb sat in the middle of the table, and Jackson blinked when he saw a man who had been frozen in the act of jumping onto the table and slamming a long stout sword into it. Two

## MYTHOS SEAS: MOVING SEAMOUNTS

other men had been frozen as they lunged towards a man whose face made Jackson's heart momentarily stop.

"That's the King of the Sonaeko, Theren's Dad." Draflor explained, noticing where Jackson was looking.

"He looks a lot like one of my uncles." Jackson whispered when he noticed the king had been shoved back by another man with an evil expression marring his face.

The Star of the Sea suddenly shot out of Jackson's hands and whipped around as if in a rage. It swiftly flew over to shine a beam of light on each of the men who seemed to be sabotaging the spell. It then darted around like a blue lightning bolt, shining a light on a couple more people and creatures before it vanished into a different part of the palace.

"I have a feeling they won't be waking up anytime soon." Draflor went over and tapped the orb in the middle of the table which glistened faintly, despite being petrified. He motioned Jackson over just as the Star of the Sea came zipping back in to touch the orb as well.

Magic flowed over the orb, which took on a clear, pearly white color as the forms of the medians and guardians appeared, all of them anxious and nervous.

"Hurry Jackson, pull out the keys and place them around the Palace's Pearl." Oceaono winced when another loud crack made the water tremble. "We're almost out of time."

Jackson pulled out all three keys from his bag: The Lunar Seed, symbolizing the flora of the seas, the Key of Creatures Light, symbolizing the fauna, and the last key, the Sphere of Mythos. Carrying them in his arms, Jackson quickly placed each key in their slot around the orb in the center of the table.

The keys slid into place and Jackson felt the thrum of magic when energy poured from the keys into the table before it spread out

# THE LAST LIGHT

to the floor. White magic filled the runes in the room around them and the medians seemed to sigh in relief.

"Everyone who can, please help us by sending your magic into this pearl, it is the core of power for this palace." Seanel said as she and the other medians spread out their fins, arms, and flippers. "Jackson, enter the area in the middle of the table, right above the pearl. Start your spell there, do you know the spell you are to use? The one we've been teaching you?"

"Yes..." Jackson said hesitantly, wondering if he'd need to use Theren's spell as he moved to the spot Seanel had indicated. His hesitation was noticed by Oceaono and Stonecurrent, who leveled him with looks that demanded an answer while his friends began sending their magic into the pearl.

"I remember the spell." Jackson affirmed firmly before he closed his eyes and began the spell the medians had taught him. As magic spread from his hands, he felt his spell weave in with the magic of the medians, guardians, and his friends while the runes on the table below began to glow brighter. Small tendrils of illuminated magic spread up from the ground as light spread from the runes on the table to the lines that spiraled around the floor before they wound up the walls.

"It's working!" Jackson heard Docion whisper as the petrified people and creatures in the room were surrounded by spiraling orbs of magic. Jackson felt the magic spread from the room before a loud crack rang out, making him gasp in agony when a painful jolt of magic shot through him.

"Nononononono." Oceaono muttered loudly as the magic seemed to ebb, making Jackson lurch to one side when the quaking boom of the crumbling tower echoed in their ears.

"We have to stop! The spell will backcast if we don't." Falganous yelled as the magical energy began to spiral out of control.

"NO." Jackson yelled when he felt some of his friends back off. "I know what to do!"

"Jackson this is beyond your spell creating ability." Sharval shouted.

"It's not beyond Theren's!" Jackson challenged, quickly shifting to the spell Theren and the Star of the Sea had been teaching him. Beams of energy shot from his fingers, twisting him around as he called out to the magical aspects within him while the magic in the room coursed about wildly.

"You told me I could ask to borrow your power." Jackson called as the magic grew more chaotic, making him flip around wildly. "I'm asking to borrow all of yours now!"

"That much power in one body will kill you." The Earthcore warned.

"Then I'll split myself, like the goliathan whales do!" Jackson insisted while his body began to scream in pain. "Please, lend me your power, I'm asking help from all of you. I can tell we won't have enough power otherwise!" His face was tight as the world spun around him while the walls shook and groaned.

"It could still kill you." The Skyspiral said as the medians exchanged an anxious look. "Are you willing to take that chance?"

"Jackson, wait!" Oceaono called, swimming forwards like he planned to try to stop him.

"JUST DO IT ALREADY!" Jackson shouted, his head already screaming in pain as Stonecurrent shot forward to hold Oceaono back.

"Then borrow our power, Aspect Guardian!" The bright sphere of light, a Sun Sphere, called.

# THE LAST LIGHT

"This is his choice to make..." Stonecurrent told Oceaono firmly, though his eyes were sad, pained.

Jackson's body gleamed while he grabbed the Staff of Solarswell off his back, lifting it up towards the ceiling as the four Aspect Stones flew from his hands to spiral above his head. The stones crashed into each other before four more Jacksons appeared, each reaching up to grab an artifact!

There was a flash of light as the glowing forms of four strange creatures appeared in the water and swooped around the Jacksons. The five boys' eyes began to glow with magic as four of them brought their hands up to grasp the stones.

The wildly flying magic in the room was sucked into a liquid sphere of magic surrounding the boys before the magic suddenly soared towards the sky, raising the boys with it!

As they crashed through the ceiling, Jackson's copies released their grip on the stones and reached out to lock arms. They bowed their heads as magic whipped around them, growing brighter and more brilliant with every moment as the sun rose higher behind them.

Memories of his mom, Dad, Grandpa, family, friends both new and old, Theren and the Lost Ones, and the petrified creatures and people he hadn't been able to help, raced through Jackson's mind as the magic surged around him. His body glowing brightly, Jackson—the real one—opened his eyes to quickly look at each of the Aspect Stones and in a strained, but determined, voice said.

"I made a promise."

The sky itself appeared to rend as the magic of the spell seemed to implode, flying into the four boys who took a step back, unlocked their arms, and shot out across the world! Great waving ripples of magic flew around them, spreading through the sea, land,

## MYTHOS SEAS: MOVING SEAMOUNTS

and sky, churning the surface of the waves, and stirring the oceans depths.

A ringing melody sounded through the world as silt and sand billowed from the seafloor when the forms of petrified creatures were torn from their resting places and sent sailing into higher waters. Depthcall, and the other wounded knights and creatures watched in awe as the magic surged past them, healing their wounds and blasting away any remnants of Voidcul's reign.

Below them, the ashes of Voidcul's body were swept away as the hundreds of thousands of her species' tiny, petrified eggs flew into the glowing currents of magic. The stone encasing them vanished away as they hatched, the hatchlings letting out happy cries.

Stonecurrent bellowed loudly in delight while the shattered rubble of the broken walls and pillars of Shieldguard flew from the ground, solidifying into their proper places! His calls rang out all the more once the inhabitants of the hold jolted awake, the knights flying up into the water, alert for danger.

Outside the hold, the dead current glistened back to life, flowing quickly through the water and banishing the dark magic in the depths.

As magic swooped across the waters just southward, Clearsong and her herd watched in awe while Abysscourser let out a happy cry when one of Jackson's copies shot overhead. The copy gave the calf a little smile before swooping off towards the horizon and vanished from sight.

When the copy surged past Chasmringer and her herd, all of them stared in wonder at the magic spiraling around in the waters around them. A warm, grateful look crossed Chasmringer's eyes when her old eyes spotted the glow of Jackson's copy as he raced away.

# THE LAST LIGHT

Around Starkelp, the whipfins and other creatures who'd stayed behind watched as a lisheave jungle sprang to life, filling the water around the strand as seedlings awakened and began growing with wild abandon. Leavamentee made a satisfied humph as the sanctuary's magic healed and the creatures and people inside awoke.

At the Jewel Isles, Koiwae, Deepbite, Cora, Toxun, Thorra, Courser, and the Spherefangs all watched in awe while the magic surged across the islands as creatures great and small awoke from their slumber, looking around them in wonder.

In the canyons, Lorgeo roughly embraced his son as he and the others shook off the layer of stone encasing them, while the magic in the canyons cleared, purified.

As the magic shot past the Mistsurge Outpost, the remaining sea lions let out happy barks and calls, while deep in the depths an ophiotaurus cracked an eye open to watch the magic course by curiously.

In the waters beyond, Sandfang and Roughjaw exchanged an excited look with Delphashel and her pod while a group of shark pups and a few dolphin calves looked around at the magic in awe. Not far away, Startide's pod let out happy creaks and cries while her grandpodmother, Shalewave, got an approving and proud smile.

Not far inland, Farflight, his flock, and Darfang and the wild venstorn quivers looked around at the magic coursing through the sky and land in wonder. When they noticed Jackson's copy shoot past, many of them let out thrilled cries and went racing off towards the mountains.

Auntie Ancie bellowed with joy when the magic surged past her as she watched her dearly beloved mate and all her kin break free from their stony prisons. From her immense back, the Centels watched in shock while other turtle islands surged up from the sea around them, letting out reverberating bellows of gratitude.

At Great Ghost Point, the magic swept through and banished the dark pillar while the old venom clans watched with open mouths as multitudes of ocean creatures appeared through the churning waters. Many a shout rang out when numerous colossals rose from their entrapment, wounds healed and eyes no longer gleaming in rage.

As the magic passed by the Sanctuary of Last Hope the sea serpents there threw their heads back and roared in victory, greeting the copy of Jackson who blasted past.

Inside the sanctuary, Theren opened his eyes to see Jackson's copy grin happily at him before giving a quick wave. The boy phased out through the walls while the rest of Theren's family and friends blinked in confusion as they looked around.

"YOU DID IT!" Theren yelled, grabbing his girlfriend, Melony, and twirling her around before giving her a long kiss! "JACKSON DID IT!"

"Who are you talking about?" Theren's brother asked while he helped his wife to her fins. "Who did what?"

Theren couldn't stop laughing happily as he went over and shook his brother's shoulders. "JACKSON! IT'S BEEN OVER TWO HUNDRED YEARS! AND ONE OF YOUR DESCENDANTS JUST FREED US!"

"WHAT?" His brother pulled back while a middle-aged woman helped a man to his feet.

The woman looked Theren in the eyes. "Uncle Theren, what are you talking about?"

Theren was grinning wildly as he dove over and embraced the woman. "Nelva. Your great grandson, Spencer. His grandson Jackson just freed us!" He pointed when more magic came

# THE LAST LIGHT

swooping through the room, "and there goes the magic to free Father!"

As the spell continued to spread across the world, a second Star of the Sea and another glowing Sun Sphere came floating up from the palace's pearl to dance around the core Jackson.

"Jackson." A female voice said from the second Star of the Sea, making him open his eyes slightly. "Please, let my friend here hold the spell together, it is time to finish what you set out to do."

"My family?" Jackson's eyes widened when the second Sun Sphere floated over his head, and he felt some of the power of the spell shift.

"Yes, you've waited long enough." A male voice from the Sun Sphere said kindly while the Staff of Solarswell was lifted from his hands. "Go, they are waiting."

The second Star of the Sea floated over to touch Jackson's head before he was enveloped in light.

Seconds later, Jackson found himself at the entrance to the cavern his family was trapped in. He took a few tentative steps forward, drinking in the sight of friends and relatives he hadn't seen in so long, while magic crackled in the air around them. He saw his little cousin Jenny's stone form being hugged by her parents and siblings and spotted some of his other aunts and uncles. Jackson breathlessly wandered through the cave while the magic swirling in the air gently caressed his beloved family and friends, until he suddenly froze.

"Mom, Dad." Jackson whispered, his voice catching when he saw the stone forms of his parents and grandparents up ahead. Tears running down his cheeks, he ran as the magic swirled faster and faster.

"MOM! GRANDPA, GRANDMA, DAD!!!" Tears flew from his eyes while he raced towards his family and jumped toward them.

# MYTHOS SEAS: MOVING SEAMOUNTS

As Jackson's arms wrapped around his parents, magic suddenly surged through the cave as spheres of energy shot around and splashed into every stone person and creature while Jackson hugged his parents tighter.

"Jackson...?"

Tears were streaming from Jackson's eyes while he looked up to see his mom blinking, as if she were in a dream, before her eyes flew open. "JACKSON?!"

"YOU'RE OK." Jackson's dad exclaimed, clutching them in a hug.

"JACKSON!!" Jackson and his parents were knocked to the ground when his grandpa leapt over and engulfed them in a huge bearhug. Everyone cried and laughed tears of joy as Jackson's grandma came rushing over to join them!

"I missed you so much." Jackson whispered, happy tears trickled down his cheeks, while his family held him tight. "I'm so happy to see you."

"You made it back!" One of Jackson's uncles shouted as much of the tribe turned and hurried towards them.

"Grandpa told us you left to find a way to help us!!" Jackson's little cousin Jenny ran over, dragging her stuffed horse behind her.

"JACKSON!" Jackson's cockatrice friend, Farflight, suddenly swooped into the cave, landed on his head, and let out a happy crow. "You did it! You made it back."

Jackson and some of the others laughed happily as Farflight jumped off his head while Grandpa sniffled.

"Oh, I was terrified we'd never see you again..." His grandpa wiped his tears on his shoulder, still refusing to let Jackson go before he gave the boy a little shake. "You did it Jack, you did it!"

# THE LAST LIGHT

"How long has it been? Were you hurt? Are you ok?" His mother quickly looked Jackson over and he squirmed while she held his face in her hands, turning his head from side to side.

"MoOom." Jackson laughed as he pulled away while more of the family gathered around. "I'm fine, really, and it's only been less than a year. I have so much to tell you guys and I..." Jackson paused when the second Star of the Sea came floating over.

"I'm so very sorry to cut this reunion short." The star flashed in time with the words, "but it's time to return, the spell must be finished."

"What's happening?" Jackson's grandpa moved protectively in front of Jackson, whose form began glowing as magic began sweeping back towards the capital.

"Do I have to go now?" Jackson pled, hugging his parents tighter. "I won't get to see them until... until we travel back..." He gulped a bit. "I hope."

"Do not fret, Jackson." The star's voice was kind, reassuring, as a white feathered form flew behind her. "They will be coming back with us, as will your friends who have been guarding them." Jackson looked over to see that the entrance of the cavern was open and Farflight's entire flock and the venstorn quivers were staring inside the cavern incredulously.

"Where are we going? What is going on?" Jackson's grandma asked, giving Jackson a wondrous look.

"Now that you are together again." The Star of the Sea said in a happy voice. "I believe you could say you are going home!" Light that weaved and splashed like water poured out from the Star to swirl around Jackson's family and the creatures watching.

Jackson faintly struggled as he was lifted from his parents' arms, hanging onto their hands before his form began to fade away.

# MYTHOS SEAS: MOVING SEAMOUNTS

"I love you!" Jackson called, holding his mother's gaze as his form vanished from view. "I kept my promise."

The energy of the spell returned with sweeping waves and spiraling eddies of magic, bringing Jackson and his copies with it. As Jackson returned to the middle of the casting formation, he saw the stunning city of Mythos Pearl awakening from the grasp of the Great Petrifying as immense multitudes of creatures and people looked up in awe at the magic swirling around him. Coral gardens and lisheave jungles were bursting to life as the beautiful buildings, palaces, and a pearl white temple in the distance gleamed and glimmered.

When the second Sun Sphere moved away, Jackson felt a thread of pain shoot through him while the magic around him flashed with power. The magic quickly condensed into a shimmering orb, surrounding him and his copies before they slowly descended back into the Throne Room while the energy rippled over those trapped inside.

With one final flash, the orb touched the table as the king opened his eyes and watched in awe when Jackson's copies burst into bright magical raindrops. The raindrops cascaded into Jackson, who was thrown back as a pained yell ripped from his throat while the magic of the orb dispersed into the room! Startide, Daychaser, Spinescale, Zepherdust, Avavo, Blade, Shadowtorrent, Granitebow, Velocina, and Draflor rushed up to Jackson as his tail vanished before he collapsed, sinking onto the table.

The king jerked away once he saw the stone face of a man glaring at him in rage. After a moment, he shoved the stone form

# THE LAST LIGHT

out of the way and slowly moved forward, his golden tail sweeping behind him. He rubbed his head in confusion while he looked around, grunting in surprise when a Star of the Sea and a Sun Sphere came flying into the chamber. A huge number of oddly familiar looking people were being carried along behind them in a magical bubble as the men and women looked about in wonder. The king jumped when the magical form of his childhood friend, Oceaono, suddenly swept in front of him.

"Oceaono?" The king asked in his deep voice. "What's going on?"

Oceaono's form was shoved aside. "LET US OUT OF HERE!" Falganous and Fulrion demanded before they were tossed away by Seanel.

"Really you two, calm yourselves." Seanel chastened. "That's no way to address your king."

"We'll explain everything, old friend." Oceaono's looked exhausted but strong as ever, while he gave Fulrion and Falganous a tight look before he turned back to the king. "But please open the door so we can tell you in person, and check on Jackson."

The king reached out his right hand, sending a small teardrop of magic flying into the wall behind him before it quickly slid open.

The medians nearly fell out of the Median Chamber in their rush to escape their prison of two hundred years before Oceaono and the magical form of Stonecurrent swiftly rushed over to Jackson. Jackson's parents and grandparents started trying to swim over to Jackson when Oceaono hesitated a second.

"Jackson?" Oceaono asked as he came around in front of Jackson and gave him a gentle shake when he didn't respond. "Jackson, are you ok?!" He asked louder, shaking the boy anxiously.

# MYTHOS SEAS: MOVING SEAMOUNTS

Jackson lay limply for a moment, his body still until he suddenly grimaced, his chest lifting in a breath before he moaned. Everyone let out a relieved sigh as Jackson's features tightened. "H-hurts." He mumbled through gritted teeth. He weakly tried to get up, only for his eyes to fly open before he pinched them shut and tightened into a ball. "OWOWOWOWOWOWOWOWOWOWW!!"

"I have a feeling you're gonna feel that tomorrow." Draflor laughed in happy relief while Jackson groaned.

"Draflor…" Jackson ground out; his jaw tight with pain as his parents hesitated before they could reach out to embrace him. "Quiet! Even your… talking hurts."

Spinescale snickered. "Never thought I'd see the day Jackson told a dragon to be quiet."

Jackson winced before he cracked an eye open to give Spinescale a pleading look. "P… please stop talking… ears... hurts…"

"Here, let me help you Jackson." Seanel came over as little stars of magic twirled around her flippers. She sent the stars wisping into Jackson's arms, making him sigh in relief once his body began to glow.

"Thank you, thank you, thank you!" He whimpered once the agony engulfing his entire body began to lessen. "I thought the pain would never stop." He relaxed as the pain slipped away, that is, until he saw everyone staring at him. He quickly curled up into a nervous ball while his friend and family came up behind him.

Everyone turned when a commotion at the entrance to the Throne Room caught their attention before Theren and his girlfriend rushed in.

# THE LAST LIGHT

"FATHER!" Theren shouted happily as he dashed through the entrance, quickly swimming over to embrace the king happily while his girlfriend shot over to hug her mom and dad.

"Theren? How did you get here?" The king asked in bewilderment while the queen rushed over to join them.

Theren was too busy laughing happy tears to answer as he let his parents go and saw Jackson and his friends. "YOU DID IT!" Theren exclaimed, swooping over to grab Jackson in a big hug. "I knew you were a good one!"

"Your highness?" A man who had the tail of an eel instead of legs asked, interrupting Theren's celebration as he came rushing into the Throne Room. "What has happened, the entire city is worried and confused."

"They're gonna be more confused in a few minutes." Startide whispered to Daychaser and Zepherdust, who chuckled while Draflor leaned over to Stonecurrent.

"You have those recording crystals ready?" He asked in a whisper.

"**Draflor!** Who do you think I am?" Stonecurrent gave a teasing smile as the king came swimming over. "I've been recording since the minute you shattered the window."

Draflor paled. "Uh, can we not show that to my sire?"

"Oh, I better know everything." A dragon twice Draflor's size said as he came swooping into the room and Draflor winced, making Stonecurrent chuckle.

Oceaono let out a shout when his wife and children rushed into the room, and he charged over to scoop up his kids in a hug while he reached out to embrace his wife.

Jackson smiled while he stiffly tried to keep himself upright on the table as the king caught his gaze.

## MYTHOS SEAS: MOVING SEAMOUNTS

"Oceaono? Theren?" The king came forward, his slightly graying dirty-blond hair waving in the water as he took a deep breath. "Would you be so kind as to introduce me to your friends and..." He looked around at Jackson and his friends and family. "Perhaps explain what in the seas has happened."

Oceaono gave his wife a quick kiss while they came over to where Jackson's friends, parents, and grandparents were helping Jackson carefully get off the table. Oceaono's little daughter held her father's hand tightly before he picked her up in one of his arms.

"Your highness." Oceaono began as he swept his hand over all Jackson's friends. "While all these creatures deserve recognition, and to have their names known with honor among the Sonaeko and the Nations of Nature's Balance forever. I would like to begin with this young man here."

Oceaono gently—and somewhat reluctantly—put his daughter down before he came over. After a quick nod to Jackson's mother and father, he went and put his hands on Jackson's shoulders. "This young man, King Colthean, is Jackson and..." Oceaono choked up a bit. "Colthean, he is your fifth great grandson, and these people behind him are your descendants."

The king's face nearly cracked in shock and there was a gasp of surprise that echoed through the room. Draflor clamped his mouth shut with his claws as he and Stonecurrent's bodies began shaking with laughter.

"Y-you're..." Jackson stuttered as he looked up at Oceaono. "He is? I am?" He glanced back at his family. "We are?"

Oceaono nodded while the king tried to compose himself, failing miserably, until one of his councilors spoke up.

"Most noble Oceaono." A female siren-born spoke up. "If this young man is King Colthean's fifth great grandson, then how long have we been—?"

# THE LAST LIGHT

"Two hundred years." Oceaono said quietly while he looked soberly around the room. "For two hundred years, the Sonaeko and other Nations of Natures Balance have been petrified in stone. All but a few of us remained and..." He met Jackson's gaze and smiled. "Have long awaited this day."

"Sweetsalt..." Oceaono's wife whispered in horror. "You've been waiting for us for two hundred years?"

Oceaono nodded and his wife swept him up in a hug. "You've been worth waiting for." He whispered.

"I'll agree with that!" Theren said, going over to give his dad and mom another hug before he turned and grinned at Jackson. "And mark my words, every kingdom and nation who are a part of the Alliance of Natures Balance will know about you and your friends before the week is through!"

# EPILOGUE

The next few weeks felt like a wonderful dream for Jackson as he and his tribe were heartily embraced by their Sonaekian relatives. They spent many days wandering through Mythos Pearl, getting to know about their history and people as the nation worked to resettle into their daily lives.

Jackson spent a lot of time supervising his cousins, who had become enamored with Daychaser's pack, his dolphin foster family, and Startide's pod, who had all come to join them. Jackson spent a lot of time helping take his cousins on rides and play with Daychaser's new foster-brother and foster nieces and nephews and some of Startide's cousins. Toxun, Courser, and Thorra had also come to Mythos Pearl to join the tribe and Jackson was ecstatic to have them back!

Jackson also ended up returning Solarswell—and the magical bag Solarswell had made—to Queen Rillyka, his fifth great grandmother who had been Solarswell's guardian before the events of the Petrifying. To the surprise of many, the Book of the Sonaeko and the original Star of the Sea also returned to Theren, though the three other aspect stones insisted on staying with Jackson.

The sword and shield golems were also returned to the person they originally guarded, though the sword took a parting swipe at Draflor before Jackson handed them off.

# EPILOGUE

Afterwards, Jackson had felt slightly lost without Solarswell and the spatial bags, as well as the Book of the Sonaeko, which he'd accidentally tried to summon multiple times. However, at the end of the second week, he was surprised when the Sonaekian leaders presented him and his friends with a bunch of thank you gifts, including a special spatial bag for Jackson.

After two weeks, Jackson's entire tribe was escorted through a portal pool to the Jewel Island Sanctuary before boarding a large Sonaekian ship to sail to the Spherefang's island.

As they neared the harbor, his tribe was given wonderful welcome from the Spherefang's, who greeting their old friends with a fantastic display of magic and cheering once the ship came within sight of the docks. Jackson's grandparents were delighted to see great cousin Zelli, Toceth, and the other elders and Jackson was able to reunite with Deepbite and the kids he befriended and go swimming with them later in the safety of the harbor.

His tribe's stay with the Spherefang's was partly business. Many Sonaekian leaders and other delegates from the many different nations of the United Nations of the Nature's Balance Alliance came to visit and learn more about their changed world from both the Spherefangs and Jackson's Tribe. This left Jackson's grandparents and parents quite busy, and it wasn't until their final day there that Jackson was able to take his mother, grandma, and some of the rest of his family and some of the Spherefangs to see the coral reefs.

He, along with Startide, Zepherdust, Spinescale, Deepbite, and Daychaser, enjoyed watching the expressions of their families as they swam around the beautiful corals. Jackson noticed Spinescale had a small recording crystal tucked under her wing as she watched Donner get slapped across the face by the tail of a perturbed eel he'd tried to catch.

# MYTHOS SEAS: MOVING SEAMOUNTS

Jackson had the slightest suspicion Spinescale had been tasked by Draflor to record some of what was happening while he was helping with the Nature's Balance meetings: a suspicion later verified when he caught her sneaking the dragon a number of recording crystals she'd been hiding.

That night, as the clans held a final feast, Jackson was pulled aside by Mavous's mother, who happily told him that she'd been in contact with Mavous and Venor. They had kept their honor, and were planning to find a way to visit soon. She was hoping her sons would choose to stay, since things back in the Toxicshade's lands were still in turmoil after the defeat of the emperor.

Jackson was also able to meet Princess Oceamalia Suncrest, who turned out to be Theren's little sister, and learned she was only a year older than he was. He also found out that Oceamalia and her friends were studying at Jewel Isle under Koiwae, and the idea of studying under the wise Billowfin Guardian seemed to greatly interest Startide.

The morning his tribe was scheduled to leave for Starkelp Strand, Jackson and Oceamalia were pulled aside by Theren, who asked them if they'd like to be part of Theren's plan to propose to his girlfriend in a few months. Jackson was thrilled, as he had formed a close bond with his uncle Theren and his girlfriend, Melony, who had both taken him under their fins.

He'd discovered that Theren also seemed to enjoy causing a great deal of mischief, and in tandem with Draflor, Spinescale, and Daychaser, there had been a large number of pranks over the last couple weeks. This of course caused no small amount of mayhem every time Theren and Melony came to join Jackson's tribe on their trip.

At Starkelp Strand, Serphere and Longspar's pod took Jackson exploring around the regrown lisheave jungles all afternoon. That

# EPILOGUE

night, Jackson and his tribe gathered to watch the mystical sight of the glowing Starkelp under the full moon.

Jackson was surprised when on their third day at the strand a large fleet of ships, led by none other than Oceaono, came sailing in. Oceaono claimed he had been given orders to come to help in the reestablishment of the Starkelp Strand Sanctuary.

Although, after messaging Stonecurrent—who continued to meet with Jackson whenever he wasn't overseeing the rebuilding of Shieldguard—Stonecurrent, with his usual twinkle in his eye, mentioned that Oceaono's wife had begged the king to give Oceaono leave of his duties at the capital for an extended family trip. Oceaono had become so stir-crazy from two hundred years trapped in the Median Chamber, it was all his wife could do to keep him from taking them all on daily excursions around the entire island of Mythos Pearl.

Jackson, Startide, Zepherdust, and Daychaser were also delighted with a visit from their friends Sandfang, Roughjaw, and their new batch of pups. To Jackson's slight embarrassment—and Draflor, Daychaser, and Spinescale's great amusement—when Sandfang had proudly introduced all her new pups, she revealed that the last one, a little male, was named after Jackson.

Later, Jackson accidentally caught Leavamentee and her husband playing with the little pups when the others were off taking care of other things. He'd secretly recorded the old war veterans playing hide and seek and peekaboo with the pups, as Jackson was convinced he'd never believe he saw it, unless he watched it a second time.

Sandfang and Roughjaw pulled Jackson aside one night to tell him that he'd unknowingly freed them from their curse all those months ago. Jackson had ecstatically told Daychaser, Theren, and some of the others, who were more than a little surprised.

# MYTHOS SEAS: MOVING SEAMOUNTS

The whole event set the ball rolling for others of the sandtyr, darktyr, and deeptyr to be freed as well. Jackson couldn't be happier for his friends, especially when Sandfang and Roughjaw were both invited to be the first freed sandtyr to attend the academy at Mythos Pearl.

Blade and his shiver had come to join Jackson at Starkelp, where Blade revealed he was planning to stay and continue his training with Leavamentee and her troops. Shadowtorrent also expressed a desire to stay there and train as well until he could go to train as a knight at Shieldguard.

This revelation left Startide a bit torn, as she had plans to attend the academy at Jewel Isle with Princess Oceamalia and her friends in a class Koiwae taught. Koiwae himself had asked her to join his classes, and Jackson had never seen Startide so excited.

Zepherdust and Avavo also revealed that they'd planned to head back to help rebuild the Mistsurge Outpost and learn more about their magic. All this left Jackson feeling a bit sad, until Spinescale pointed out that now that the portal pools were working again, they could all visit each other whenever they wanted.

Jackson had hoped his tribe could go to Shieldguard Hold, but Stonecurrent insisted that they should wait until it had been properly restored to its former glory before they came for a visit. While the magic from the spell that had cleansed the Great Petrifying did restore the hold's magic and foundations, many of the buildings and grounds were still being repaired.

There was also a special team, led by Depthcall, who were overseeing the destruction of the voidblades used by Stonecurrent's brother to damage the hold. Granitebow and his brother had also returned to Shieldguard, and were part of a team working to build a bridge of understanding with the remaining Fallen and the numerous herds of newly awakened goliathan whales.

# EPILOGUE

After a month or more, Jackson, all his friends, and his tribe got ready to return to Mythos Pearl, where they would meet with the Council of the United Nations of Nature's Balance in their annual meetings.

A little while before they were due to leave, Jackson came into the building where his family had been staying to find a suspiciously smirking Draflor, Spinescale, and Daychaser waiting for him.

"Ok, what are you three planning this time?" Jackson asked suspiciously when he saw Spinescale quickly hide a recording crystal.

"Nothing." Spinescale said in a voice that implied that whatever they were planning, it was something big.

Jackson folded his arms and gave them each a long look. "Uhuh, and Daychaser's stomach doesn't rumble every time we go around the Jewel Island reefs."

"Oh, don't worry about it, Jackson." Theren laughed as he came in, his silver tail shimmering in the light. "I'm sure it's nothing too drastically troublesome."

Jackson gave Theren a disbelieving look while Daychaser came over and gave him a friendly nudge. "Come-on, there's something we want to show you really quick."

"But the tribe is leaving right now!" Jackson protested. "We have a big meeting we're supposed to be at. Remember?"

Theren chuckled before he swam out. "Don't keep him too long you guys. My dad wants him there for when the other leaders from the United Nations of Natures Balance show up."

# MYTHOS SEAS: MOVING SEAMOUNTS

"Don't worry, we'll make sure he misses everything!" Draflor called jokingly.

Jackson gave Draflor a dry look before he finally let out a short breath and shook his head with a smile. "Ok, what do you want to show me?"

"Actually, we want to see your recording of Leavamentee and her mate playing with Sandfang's pups." Draflor said, giving Jackson a huge, innocent looking smile. "Just for... you know... posterity's sake."

"Huh? Wait? How did you know about that recording?!" Jackson gave Draflor a stern look. "The only people I told about that were... oh..." He glanced back at the door. "THEREN!!"

"I think he's already out of earshot." Spinescale snickered and Jackson groaned while he pulled out the crystal.

"Fine, I'll let you guys watch it, but just really quick and then we gotta go! I'm going to be late." Jackson said as he got ready to magically start the recording until Daychaser suddenly spun around and slapped the crystal out of his hand with his tail. "HEY!"

"Go long Draflor!" Daychaser shouted, slapping the crystal over Jackson's head while the boy darted after it, only for Draflor to snatch it up with his tail and throw it to Spinescale.

"GUYS. GIVE IT BACK!" Jackson protested, chasing after his friends as they dove around the building, keeping the crystal just out of reach. The chase abruptly ended when someone loudly cleared their throat and Jackson and his friends flipped around to see Leavamentee hovering in the doorway, her flipper twitching impatiently.

"JACKSON, your entire tribe and the rest of your friends have already left!" She boomed. "I thought my training here would've taught you something about being on time. You're going to be LATE!"

# EPILOGUE

Jackson cringed "I know, but I needed to get my crystal back that Daychaser and—"

"None of your excuses!" She said impatiently, coming in and making a current of water shove him and his friends out of the doorway. "Get to the portal pool NOW. Or I'll have you doing drills for the next month!"

"Hop on." Draflor extended his wing so Jackson could swim up to grab onto his back, Jackson's recording crystal still tightly held in his claws. "We'll go faster if I take us all."

Jackson gave Draflor a sour look, but hurriedly swam up to grab onto his back spines while Spinescale intertwined herself around his backpack. Daychaser darted ahead of the others, making for the Portal Room as Draflor opened his wings and quickly flew through the water towards the portal pools.

"My parents are so going to kill me…" Jackson mumbled as they neared the portal, giving Spinescale—who still looked very smug—a tart look.

"You'll thank us later, these meetings sound **very** boring." Spinescale said innocently while Draflor swooped up and got ready to dive.

"What? But I'm supposed to be there I—"

Jackson's words were cut off when Draflor shot through the portal, bursting out the other end as he flew high in the air above Mythos Pearl. A sudden roar of cheering made Jackson look down at the most incredible sight he'd ever seen.

Draflor let out a roar of victory while he flew down towards the underwater city of Mythos Pearl, which was filled to the brim with people and creatures, who cheered wildly as mages sent beautiful patterns into the sky.

The shorelines were alive with animals and other races who cried out happily as dragons roared from the air while griffins, birds,

# MYTHOS SEAS: MOVING SEAMOUNTS

and other flying creatures let out wild cries. Elves and dwarves sent their magic rocketing into the sky while whales and other immense ocean creatures breached from the sea, letting out wild calls of joy and victory when Draflor flew past.

Herds of dolphins, porpoises, hippocampi, taurocampi, and capricorn porpoised out of the water around the whales as seabirds, ocean fairies, and other creatures flew through the air, calling happily as Draflor braced himself and dove into the sea.

As they splashed under the surface, Jackson saw the entire city was decorated with stunning decorations, and alight with glowing jellyfish and other bioluminescent creatures. Sonaekians cheered and waved when Draflor sailed past, the dragon aiming towards the palace, which was gleaming as bright as the sun.

Jackson had gone limp in shock but suddenly sat up straight, his eyes wide when he saw his whole family, including the Spherefangs, all gathered around a large area in the palace's coral gardens. His parents and grandparents all looked up at him proudly while Draflor landed in front of a tall monument shaped like a giant sphere while Daychaser shot past with a smirk.

"W-what's going on?" Jackson stuttered when Theren and Melony came over and urged him off Draflor's back. Meanwhile, Sonaekians, water creatures, and a myriad of other animals and races—many using magic to help them breathe underwater—clogged the waters around the palace as they came to watch.

Theren only laughed while he dragged Jackson over to where all his friends had gathered in front of the giant sphere monument. All his friends grinned widely when Jackson saw them. Jackson looked around in awe at his friends and family and saw the glimmer of multiple recording crystals from Stonecurrent, Draflor, Spinescale, and others before he nervously looked down a bit.

# EPILOGUE

"Surprised?" Melony asked with a teasing grin and Jackson nodded, watching while King Coletheon and Queen Rillyka came up to a large crystal that was floating in the center of the large circle that had been left clear of watching creatures.

When the king and queen came up and touched the crystal, Jackson watched in awe as it sent bright beams of magic flying through the water! Some of the beams even shot from the ocean's surface, going high into the air before they formed into images of the king and queen as the king cleared his throat.

"For two hundred years the United Nations of Nature's Balance have been trapped, sealed away with no way to escape." King Coletheon's voice rang out over the entirety of Mythos Pearl and the islands and seas around it.

"Today, we celebrate our return, and the deeds of those individuals who were responsible for the restoration of our nations." Queen Rillyka continued happily. "Henceforth this day will be set aside as a celebration for the Creator's mercy in allowing us to return to this beloved life, and to remember the brave deeds of those who freed us."

The queen raised the Staff of Solarswell high into the air as the king raised his sword. They turned as one, firing spiraling beams of magic into the giant circular monument behind Jackson and his friends.

Jackson and his friend all flipped around when the monument began to glow brightly before the outer layer of stone dissolved away, revealing a huge statue of Jackson and his friends.

Jackson stood in the center, right in front of Theren as they both held the Staff of Solarswell high into the air with one hand, while holding an open Book of the Sonaeko in the other. Stone figures of the Star of the Sea, the Earthcore, WindSpiral, and Sunsphere were suspended above the staff. Around them, all of

# MYTHOS SEAS: MOVING SEAMOUNTS

Jackson's friends, from Zepherdust and Daychaser, to Spinescale and Blade, were gathered around, with Draflor, Granitebow, and the medians and guardians behind them as Velocina's coils encompassed the whole group.

Jackson felt tears sting his eyes and the king and queen smiled when he rubbed them.

"This day shall henceforth be known as the Celebration of the World's Reviving!!" The queen called out happily. "A day of gratitude and joy, and to celebrate our freedom and chance to live our lives again. May the acts of these good people and creatures inspire and uplift those who hear them, for millennia to come!!"

The roaring cheer from the watching crowds made the entire island seem to shake as Jackson looked around in awe.

"Jackson."

Jackson flipped around when the king addressed him after the shouts had died down.

"Would you give us a few words?" He smiled. "You are after all, the guests of honor, without your effort none of this would've happened."

"M-me?" Jackson's voice squeaked at the idea of talking in front of so many people and creatures.

"You can do it!"

Jackson glanced back to see which one of his friends had spoken, but found them all giving him encouraging looks.

Tentatively, Jackson swam up to the crystal and watched when the magical images suspended above him changed to his own. "I..." He took a deep breath and closed his eyes for a moment. "Um, I'm very surprised and touched by this..." He glanced back at his friends and the monument behind him, only to look down a second before he glanced up and gave a small smile.

# EPILOGUE

"Someone much wiser than I once told me, 'great things aren't truly done alone.'" He looked over at Stonecurrent, whose smile deepened, "and I'm here, we're all here, today because of everyone who worked together to undo the Great Petrifying." He stood a little taller, "so let this day truly be one to give thanks, for the people around us, for our friends and families, for the Creator's love, and for all those of the good and light." He smiled brightly. "Because with them, we can do anything!" He raised his fist high as he remembered a phrase Theren told him was a cry used among the entire Alliance of Natures Balance as both a battle cry and a victory cry.

"TILL THE LIGHT PREVAILS IN ALL!"

Draflor reared back to let out a roar of victory, which was quickly joined by Daychaser's howl as the rest of Jackson's friends all joined in the cry. The cry quickly grew and grew, until every creature, person, and race joined in, making the very air and water quake.

"LET THE CELEBRATION BEGIN!" The king shouted once the cry ended, and music began ringing through the water and air!

People and creatures began singing happily to the music while Jackson gathered together with his friends.

"Well, we did it!" Daychaser exclaimed as the music grew louder and louder.

"But it sure took a while." Jackson's cockatrice friend, Farflight, clucked as he tried to steady himself, a magical pendant allowing him to breathe underwater dangling from his neck.

"And we're all here together." Zepherdust smiled as Avavo barked in affirmation.

"And you all better watch yourselves, because I'm the best dancer in all of dragondom!" Draflor joked, doing a spin in the water.

# MYTHOS SEAS: MOVING SEAMOUNTS

"HAH!" Spinescale quipped. "I think you mean the most embarrassing one, I'd beat you in a dance competition easy."

"Is that a challenge, sea snake?" Draflor responded, leaning down to look her in the eye while Granitebow chuckled.

"Bring it on, I'll take you any-day." Spinescale said, leaning forward to stare back at him while Deepbite shook his head tiredly.

"I think she's gotten even more sassy since she became a miniossal..." Startide whispered while Draflor and Spinescale began throwing challenges back and forth.

"She's got the power to back it now." Shadowtorrent pointed out wryly.

Jackson chuckled a bit before he looked around and frowned uncertainly. "Guess this adventure's finally over..."

"It is?" Daychaser asked with a grin.

"Don't think you'll ever be lackin for adventure." Blade huffed. "Not when ya got us around."

"I think you might mean that the other way around..." Thorra nickered, making Toxun and Courser snicker.

"JACKSON!"

Jackson looked over to see Kayla, Donner, Oceamalia, Theren, Melony, his mom, dad, grandparents, and some of his other friends and family waving him down.

"Come on! It's not a party if you don't start dancing!" Oceamalia called.

Jackson smiled, maybe this adventure was over in a way, but as he looked around at all his friends and family, he realized there would be a lot more adventures to come. To start with, his family still had to find a place to live, and he'd gotten offers from both Stonecurrent and Koiwae to come study under them. Jackson shook his head. There would be time to think about all that later.

# EPILOGUE

"Come on you guys!" Jackson grinned, grabbing Spinescale's wing and Daychaser's fin. As he dragged all his friends into the dance, Theren and Melony took the broadcasting crystal and began singing an enlivening and thrilling song.

"Let's GO!"

# GLOSSARY

ALURAN — (A-lure-an). An intelligent, lean, two-legged creature with a small head at the end of a long neck, and a short tail with a long-curved fin. Adults stand about five feet high and are usually different shades of brown or tan with green markings. Alurans lack arms but have long powerful legs and are often raised by many nations to take part in races and to use as messenger animals. They are incredibly fast, and few creatures can outrun them once they hit top speed. I just wish they were big enough I could ride one... my three-year-old cousins look like they're having a blast!

ANCIELLON — (An-see-el-on).

ASPECTS — Immensely powerful creatures that were created to safeguard and maintain the balance of the elemental magic of Mythos. While many mysteries surround them, it's known that there are different species assigned to each kind of elemental magic. They seem to intervene during times of crisis, but largely seem to watch from the sidelines, only helping when truly needed.

ASPECT STONES — Mythical gemstones that seem to have bonded with an aspect, allowing the aspects to work closer with and around humans and other races.

# GLOSSARY

**AVAVO** — A white colored male fur seal that Jackson and his friends met around the Mistsurge Isle Outpost. Avavo is a friendly and outgoing fur seal who becomes close friends with Zepherdust. He and Zepherdust stayed behind at the outpost after Zepherdust injured her flipper.

**BEAKED WHALES** — Also known by ocean creatures as deep divers or diving whales, beaked whales are an unusual group of whales with very pointed beak-like snouts. The males often have protruding tusks on the side of their jaws. There are many different species that vary in appearance, behavior, and size. The black-backed diving whales Jackson meets resemble a larger version of earth's Andrews beaked whale.

**BILLOWFINS** – Billowfins are a species of magical fish that was once plentiful before the great petrifying. They're deeply tied to water magic, something that is evidenced by their liquid-like fins and tails. The way their liquid-like fins move is considered calming and serene by many people, as are the billowfins themselves, since they were often very calm and thoughtful creatures.

**BLADE** — Tough, sarcastic, independent, curt, and a bit rough around the edges, Lashblade, or "Blade" as he prefers to be called, is the tough guy of Jackson's friends, not to mention the only shark. Being the only shark in the group doesn't hold him back any though. He lets his mind be known no matter what the situation, though he'll often watch quietly from the sidelines.

**BOOK OF THE SONAEKO** — A sentient magical book that holds the secrets of the long lost Sonaeko Nation. Jackson is able to summon it so he can learn more about the myriad of things the book

# GLOSSARY

has chronicled. It's like the water magic version of the internet... Well kinda, I mean it's different in that: the book's actually self-aware and has a bit of an attitude, there's no real search function beyond asking the book, and it has a particular hatred for bookworms... And no, I mean the magical Mythonian species of worm that sometimes eats books, not people who like to read books!

**CADOLIN** – (Ca-dol-in). Also known as seawolves, they are an aquatic creature that's a mix between wolves, dolphins and whales. They have four powerful flippers they use when swimming at a normal or slow pace and need higher maneuverability. They use their tails for long distance and high-speed swimming, but at the cost of maneuverability. Because of their unique magic, they are able to take a landform that changes their four flippers into long, powerful legs, allowing them to hunt on land and in water. Please note, they don't find it funny if you treat them like a dog or try to get them to play fetch, it'll end up with a game of chase... you'll be the one getting chased, and likely bitten... ask me how I know.

**CAPRICORN** — (Cap-ri-corn). A creature that's half goat, half fish or porpoise. They live in large herds led by the largest males. The males have long curved or spiraling horns while the females have shorter, sharper horns they use to protect their kids. They were once allies to the Sonaeko and helped keep invasive water plants out of coral gardens. Personally, I never know what to think of them, I mean, they have rectangular pupils! How do you know what they're thinking? Not to mention they keep breaking through my underwater fences and eating my seaweed patch...

**CAPTAIN VENMORUL** — A Toxicshade Captain that Jackson ran into during his stay with the cockatrice flock. Captain Venmorul

# GLOSSARY

serves in the Toxicshade's army. Despite this, he's loyal to the Old Venom clans and their ways, and doesn't put up with much of the Toxicshade's wicked behaviors and intents. He's good friends with Mavous and Venor.

**COMMUNICATION CRYSTAL** — Magical crystals used by the Sonaeko to communicate with each other over long distances. They're usually found in large towns, cities, outposts, or other places where the Sonaeko dwelled. They can vary in appearance, but are often shaped like large orbs, and many creatures refer to them as communication orbs. I've been wanting one for years, but the only one I found was in the ruins of a Sonaekian town... I felt a bit sheepish just taking it, and who knows who I might accidentally contact if I tried to use it!

**COURSER** — One of Jackson's old creature friends who was sealed inside a special crystal by Jackson's family. Courser is an excitable, high energy, and playful young aluran. Of Jackson's old creature friends, he's the youngest in age and perception and is perhaps the most childlike of the bunch. He loves to race and run, and has a slight obsession with fruit juices, and often got into trouble when he would sneak into the tribe's buildings to try and steal a sip.

**CURRENTS** — In the world of Mythos there are two types of currents, the currents of water that flow through every ocean, and the magical currents of water magic that course along with the actual physical currents. Many ocean creatures and water magic users can both send and hear messages, warnings, voices, and other more magical things on the currents of magic that flow through the seas. However, when the magic of the oceans is out of balance, the

# GLOSSARY

currents can fail in their flow or become hampered. If that is the case, please refrain from sending invitations for parties, holiday get-togethers, game nights, or sleepovers on the currents, or you might end up with a strange assortment of party-crashers...

**CURSE OF THE DISHONORED** — An ancient and severe curse placed on the Sandtyr, Deeptyr, and Darktyr as punishment for their destructive actions during a great famine. It shortens their lives, cuts them off from the good magic of the seas, and stunts their growth.

**DAYCHASER** — Responsible, determined, courageous, fun-loving, and a bit mischievous, Daychaser is one of Jackson's best friends. The seawolf is extremely protective of Jackson, who he sees as a brother, and is apt at taking charge, figuring out problems, and making decisions. He's got a huge appetite and is often on the search for something to fill his stomach, much to his friend's amusement.

**DEEPBITE** — Spinescale's clutch-brother. He's more patient than Spinescale and has a mature air about him and is highly interested in the Spherefang Clans. Unlike Spinescale, he prefers the feel of earth under his scales or the safety of the reef. However, don't' let him fool you, as he and Spinescale both share a prominent mischievous streak, trust me on that... last time I trust Deepbite when he and Spinescale come over for a visit...

**DEPTHCALL** — Stonecurrent's strong and good humored mate. Depthcall is an extremely loyal and protective whale who, like her mate, will do anything for her nation and people.

# GLOSSARY

**DISHONORED** — If a creature is dishonored, it effectively means they've chosen a path of darkness and evil. Dishonored creatures are cut off from the good magic of the world, though many are still able to use dark forms of whatever magic they could've used before. They are also able to somewhat hear things on the currents, especially if the currents are out of balance and weakened.

**DOCION** — (Doe-see-on). The large dark blue-gray dolphin median. He is perceptive, calm, composed, and patient. He is also a diplomat who specializes in working with interspecies communication.

**DRAGONTURTLE** — Immense turtles that have a host of dragon-like traits and can breathe a hot steaming blast of magical energy from their mouths. They're often cantankerous and dangerously smart and sailors dread running into one on the open ocean. One attacked my friend's pleasure boat once when he sailed too close to its favorite kelp patch... My friend survived, but his boat didn't!

**DRAFLOR** — (Drah-flor) A strange and magical creature who seems to be connected to a certain magical staff... he seems to be quite mischievous...

**EARTHCORE** — A strange, magical gemstone that seems to be the earth magic version of whatever the Star of the Sea is... what exactly are they?

**FARFLIGHT** — A young, loyal and protective cockatrice cockerel who has a strong friendship and bond with Jackson. He

# GLOSSARY

wasn't able to come with Jackson on his journey, but stayed to help his flock protect Jackson's petrified family. He's the son of Greatcrower and Greatfeather.

**FALGANOUS** — (Fal-gain-us). The dark green and orange dragonturtle median, his bite is worse than his bark, trust me on that.

**FULRION** — (Ful-rion). The dark brown leocampus median. He is an expert in many things, just not manners or patience. There might be a heart of gold underneath his huge mane of fur somewhere... maybe. I hope so, cause I'd really like to see it sometime!

**GALEBRINGER** — Daychaser's older sister.

**GOLIATHAN WHALES** — An ancient species of whale who were the protectors and guardians of the whales and the Sonaeko. Their wicked descendants became the race of whales known as the Fallen.

**GONE WHIRLPOOL** — Gone crazy, going wild, uncontrolled.

**GRANITEBOW** — A young male ex-fallen whale who Jackson helped in the depths of Shieldguard. He's become one of Jackson's friends, but is often off helping with other things and training with Depthcall and the goliathan whales.

**GREAT DIVERS** — Great divers, or great gray diving whales, are the Mythonian version of earth's sperm whales. The males are much

# GLOSSARY

larger than females are, and often migrate to select feeding grounds. Females form small herds with other females and their young.

**IRONMAMBA** — An ancient evil empire that started the Steelserpent War, the war which led to the disappearance of the Sonaeko nation.

**JEWEL ISLES** — A tropical island chain that Jackson and his friends ended up at after being chased into the whirlpools surrounding the islands.

**KOIWAE** – (Coy-way) The billowfin guardian of the Jewel Island Sanctuary. Koiwae is a wise, thoughtful creature who has looked over the Jewel Island Sanctuary for... many years. I wouldn't ask him how old he is though; however, I'm guessing at least two hundred and sixty, maybe more...

**LEAVAMENTEE** — (Leave-a-men-tee) You know the earth saying, "its bite is worse than its bark?" Well, that saying doesn't apply to Leavamentee. While she may be a manatee, trust me when I say her bite is much worse than her bark! Leavamentee is an experienced war veteran, and the current guardian of the Starkelp Strand Sanctuary. She's direct, curt, to the point, and savage when the need arises. Only Draflor seems willing to test her patience to its level. Me? I'd prefer just to stay a safe distance away, and keep on her good side.

**LEOCAMPUS** — (Lee-o-camp-us). A creature with the front half of a lion and the back of a shark, they live in large prides that dwell in seagrass prairies and other underwater habitats. The roars of adult males can travel for many whale-lengths underwater, helping the

# GLOSSARY

prides to establish territories and communicate with one another. However, those roars can also bust your eardrums if you're too close, so if a leocampus pride looks ready to begin singing the song of their people, you might want to put a bit of distance between yourself and them... If you don't... Well, I hope you have access to some good healing spells.

**LSHEAVE** — (L-ish-eave) A strange group of plant-like fish species. Are they plants, or are they fish? That is the question, but all I can tell you is that they're good eating, and they grow crazy fast when there's magic nearby... So. Very. Fast!

**LORGEO** — (Lore-gee-o) A elder of the sapphire golems. Lorgeo is a mysterious, blunt, and solitary character, and an expert on working with magical artifacts and enchantments. He was trapped in the canyons that lead out of the Jewel Island Archipelago during the events of the Great Petrifying and has remained there ever since.

**MAVOUS** — A Venom Nation scholar and mage who Jackson met when he was fleeing the Toxicshade on his way to the ocean. Mavous and his brother, Venor, are brothers to Chief Norven, the chief of the Spherefang Clans. Curious and well read, he likes to think things through, and is trying hard to find out the truth behind the disappearance/destruction of his people. He's married to Captain Annasel who is the Captain of her own ship.

**MISTSURGE OUTPOST** — A Sonaekian outpost inside Mistsurge Isle where Jackson and his friends stayed at for a time, before the magic in the outpost failed.

# GLOSSARY

**MOONSTONES** — Mythonian moonstones are magical stones innately tied to light magic. Like the moon reflects the light of the sun to provide us light during the night, moonstones use actual light to make light magic that can then be used by magi and magical creatures. They usually glow a soft white and look stunning in pieces of jewelry. I once had a necklace with a moonstone pendant... once... Actually, I got it back now, those nymphs finally fessed up after I called them out!

**NATURE EMERALDS** — Green gemstones that are connected to the magic of nature. They gather nature-based energy and magical power from the world around them, and can help make gardens flourish. I personally have two, one for my underwater garden and one for my land-based garden. No, they aren't for sale, don't even ask.

**OCEAN'S TEARS** — Teardrop shaped water-magic-based gemstones that pull magic from the water and currents around them. Magi and water magic wielding creatures can easily access the magic found in the gemstones, helping them cast larger and more powerful spells.

**OCEAONO** — (O-see-on-o). The sapphire golem leader of the Sonaeko Medians. Serious, calm, humble, and determined, he is a capable spellcaster and leader.

**OROCA** — (Or-o-ca). The honorable Mythonian version of earth's orcas and killer whales. The white markings and patterns are often more extreme and unusual then seen in earth's orcas and killer whales, and both Mythonian oroca and killer whales often get larger than earth species. The term oroca always refers to honorable

# GLOSSARY

members of the species, while killer whale refers to dishonored and wicked members, confuse the two terms at your own risk.

**PRINCE THEREN** — (Th-air-en) The crown prince of the Sonaeko, and the leader of the Lost Ones before they mysteriously vanished.

**ROUGHJAW** — Sandfang's mate. Roughjaw is a quiet, serious shark who is also good friends and allies with Jackson.

**SANDFANG** — A middle-aged female sandtyr shark who helped mentor Jackson when he first entered the sea. She's intelligent, impatient, firm, somewhat sarcastic, and doesn't like to waste time. She has a soft spot for Jackson, and was his loyal friend and mentor for the short time she taught him before they had to part ways.

**SANDTYR** — (Sand-tire). A brown to cream colored species of shark that resembles earth's lemon sharks. They have a long, large dorsal fin and can have a variety of patterns, from a scattering of speckles and spots to thin light stripes. There are two closely related species known as darktyr and deeptyr. Deeptyr sharks are a gray color, while darktyr are a dark bronze-brown with glowing green eyes, making them fabulous to have around during spooky holidays.

**SAPPHIRE GOLEMS** — (Saf-ire, gol-ems) An ancient species of gemstone or crystal golems that were members of the Sonaeko Nation. They're highly intelligent and powerful magic users whose bodies are always made from magical blue crystal in varying hues. Unsurprisingly, they usually love sapphires and often have jewelry or accessories made from them. While I'd never counsel you to bribe anyone, if you're already friends with a sapphire golem, it'd

# GLOSSARY

be wise to have a stash of sapphires on hand as gifts for holidays and special occasions.

**SEANEL** — (See-nel). The small but wise whale median and Oceaono's old friend and mentor.

**SERPHERE** — (Ser-fear) A older whipfin, and the wife of Longspar, mother of Flashtail.

**SHARVAL** — (Shar-val). The shark median. She is a large dark gray shark with a white belly and large scars running down her left side and is a war veteran and old friend of Docion. She doesn't say much, but when she does, you'd better listen.

**SIDE EYES** — Mythonian flounder, they are largely similar to earth flounder. Both their eyes are, unsurprisingly, on one side of their head, which makes finding a pair of glasses that fit right a horrible challenge.

**SIRENS** — Mythonian sirens are a shrewd, stubborn, and calculating species of humanoids. The tops of their black and gray bodies look remarkably human-like, but they have strong powerful tails instead of legs. They have human-like faces, but large, long fins instead of hair, no nose, and catlike eyes. They're able to use both shadow and water magic and often creature vivid mirages to confuse and scare other species. The one time I ran into them, their mirages about gave me a heart attack! I still don't know how they knew I was terrified of void manticores...

# GLOSSARY

**SKYCALLER** — Daychaser's childhood friend who he knew before he was separated from his podpack as a pup. Skycaller is a playful, smart, and quick thinking seawolf who loves to joke around and have fun. She may have a crush on Daychaser... from what I've seen anyway, and when I teased her about it, she blushed pretty deeply, so I'm calling it!

**SONAEKIAN** — (So-nay-key-an). A member of the Sonaeko Nation.

**SONAEKO** — (So-nay-ko). An ancient elementalborn nation that was known as the nation of the oceans and rivers.

**SOUNDING** — The term used by sea creatures that means echolocation, or the use of sounds to "see" the world around you. If that sounds strange, you should give sounding a try yourself, or maybe don't... Am I the only one who finds it weird that something can "see" what's going on around it by hearing it?

**SPACEKEEPER BAGS** — Extremely rare and special bags that are connected to large rooms, caves, or chambers that can be reached through the bag by special magical symbols and spells. People or creatures can teleport items and inanimate objects into the bag with those magical symbols. However, they can't teleport people or other living creatures into the bags without their permission or trust. They're also called spatial bags. I really want one... but they're way too rare, and I can't afford the price.

# GLOSSARY

**SPELL BLAST IT** — A phrase that basically means, "shoot," "drat," "dang it," "darn it," "oh come on," etc. Jackson usually shortens it to "spells."

**SPINESCALE** — A smart, sassy, and sarcastic winged sea snake friend of Jackson. Quick to state her mind, Spinescale gets to the point relatively quickly and doesn't like to beat around the coral. Despite that she's quite compassionate, curious, and wants to know more about the outside world. She has a poisonous temper and a big mischievous streak, enjoying scaring and pranking others.

**SQUALLRUNNER** — Daychaser's serious, firm, and slightly hardened father. Squallrunner is the lead seawolf in his podpack and takes the leading of his podpack extremely seriously after the trauma of losing Daychaser when his son was a pup. Since being reunited with Daychaser, his hardened and slightly cold attitude is starting to wear away, revealing a softer, more good-humored side to the old seawolf.

**STAR OF THE SEA** — A mythical, mysterious, and magical aspect stone that is connected to the magic of the seas and the Sonaeko Nation. It, along with a few other aspect stones have chosen Jackson as their guardian, but what exactly does that mean?

**STARTIDE** — A calm, serious, caring, and knowledgeable young oroca, Startide is one of Jackson's best friends and is the older sister of the group. Not afraid to put herself in harm's way to help others, she is also slightly impatient and easily frustrated. She has a passion for learning but doesn't always understand the way others view things, which gave her and Jackson's friendship a rocky start. She

# GLOSSARY

looks up to her grandpodmother, Shalewave, and hopes to lead her own pod someday.

**STEELSERPENT WAR** — An ancient war that resulted in the destruction of many nations and is connected to the Sonaeko Nation vanishing. It's also called the Great War and was started by the ancient Ironmamba Empire.

**STONECURRENT** — Stonecurrent is the wise, good humored, and somewhat jovial guardian of Shieldguard Hold. After Jackson and his friends freed him, he became a close friend, mentor, and father figure to Jackson and Jackson's friend Draflor. He was a strong Goliathan whale knight in his prime.

**SUNLIGHT STONES** — Magical gemstones that are said to be connected to the power and magic of the sun. They shine brightly during the day and dim during the night. They are often used in underground—or underwater—cities and buildings.

**THANK THE CURRENTS** — An ocean creature phrase that basically means, "thank goodness," or "thank heavens."

**THE FALLEN** — A immense race of evil predatory whales that are cousin species to the great divers. Before the Great Petrifying they were known as the Goliathan whales and were a powerful and honorable race of whales until they rebelled and turned against those they'd sworn to protect, thus becoming the Fallen.

**THE LOST ONES** — The last remaining group of Sonaekians to survive the Great Petrifying and the tumultuous next few years. It is

# GLOSSARY

unknown exactly what happened to them, the legends sung by the great whales say they returned to the sea and were petrified as well... but then how did Jackson's family get the Book of the Sonaeko and the Star of the Sea?

**THE SUN TOUCHING THE SURFACE OF THE SKY** — A sea creature phrase meaning noon, or the middle of the day. There are different forms of the saying, like "when the sun touches the sky's surface," but they all mean the same thing.

**THORRA** — An athletic, strong, dependable, and committed young palomino stallion. Thorra and Jackson grew up together, and despite the stallion being a few years younger, he acts like the older sibling Jackson, Toxun, and Courser never had. He's often very thoughtful and calm, and is the rule keeper and watchful "older sibling" of Jackson's old friends that were sealed away by Jackson's family. He's quite competitive, and when it comes to a race, he'll never say no.

**TOXICSHADE** — A corrupt and wicked empire that has been waging war with nations all over Mythos. They've placed a bounty on Jackson's tribe and are trying to destroy them.

**TOXUN** — Sarcastic, dry-humored, and determined, Toxun is the snarky brother of Jackson's old friends that his family sealed away. Despite his sarcasm, the venstorn is actually quite mature, and is a dependable friend, although a snide or sarcastic remark is usually not far away. Like Thorra, Courser, and Jackson, he loves to race. He's the son of Darfang and Servessva, but unlike his parents, he is able to speak normally, save for his words always end with long hissing S's.

# GLOSSARY

**VENOR** — Mavous's younger brother who is a Venom Nation Warrior. He's more impulsive and swifter to act than his older brother, though he's a man of few words, he notices much and is a good listener.

**WHAT IN THE CURRENTS** — What on earth? What? What in the world?

**WHIPFINS** — Whipfins are an ancient species of sea creature native to the lisheave jungles that used to grow around places like the Starkelp Strand before the Great Petrifying wiped them out. They have long, serpentine bodies, small, beautiful heads with big eyes, four flippers, and dolphin-like flukes at the end of their tails. They were calm and watchful species, that were known for being ecosystem engineers for their part in helping spread and care for lisheave jungles.

**WINDSPIRAL** — A strange, magical aspect stone that is the wind magic equivalent to the Star of the Sea. The one Jackson finds is connected to a female wind aspect, who is very kind and more soft spoken then some of the other aspects seem to be.

**ZEPHERDUST** — A light tan fur seal friend of Jackson. Zepherdust is a curious, considerate, courageous, but leery and cautious fur seal who was once very insecure and embarrassed about the color of her fur. Since meeting Avavo and the other Mistsurge Isle fur seals, she's grown in confidence and is more outgoing. Zepherdust helped Jackson, Daychaser, and Startide on the first part of their journey, before she had to stay behind at Mistsurge Isle due to a wounded flipper.

WANT TO SEE MORE OF JACKSON
AND HIS FRIENDS?

THEN KEEP AN EYE OUT FOR THE
FIRST BOOK IN THE ALL-NEW
SEQUEL SERIES

# MYTHOS SEAS
## BEYOND

# OF SUNSTONE AND SAPPHIRE

For more information on upcoming novels in the Mythos Seas series, please go to Mythosseas.com!

# CHAPTER ONE
# RACE TO THE SEA

Jackson was sleeping peacefully in the small cottage he, his parents, and grandparents had been staying in for the last few weeks. The small cottage was one of many that dotted the shoreline of a beautiful undersea city that gleamed in the distance as the sun peeked above the horizon. When something pounded against his window, Jackson mumbled in his sleep and tiredly rolled over, completely oblivious as the thumping sound started again.

After a couple minutes of angry pounding, all went quiet until a small creature shoved its way through a vent that let air into the room from outside. The animal fluttered over Jackson to the window, flipped up the latch, and shoved it open while Jackson snuggled deeper under the covers.

A huge head slowly slunk through the window, long white teeth gleaming in the faint light given off by a glowing shell hanging from the ceiling. As the immense creature opened its gaping maw its eyes flashed with anticipation before it reared back and—

ROOOOAAAARR!!!

"GAAAH!" Jackson screamed as he flew out of the bed, flopping onto the floor in a tangle of blankets and pillows while a silver and gold dragon chuckled smugly.

# MYTHOS SEAS BEYOND: OF SUNSTONE AND SAPPHIRE

"Draflor..." Jackson groaned as he tried squirming out of the blankets he was wrapped in. "Did you have to roar?"

"We've been pounding on your window for ten minutes, but all we got was you mumbling something about wanting more sweet cakes." Daychaser—Jackson's seawolf friend—grinned as he poked his head in through the window. He then shoved his way around Draflor's giant neck and waltzed over to grab a piece of Jackson's blankets in his jaws before he swiftly yanked back! Jackson yelped as he was spun out of the tangle of sheets and landed on the floor with a "umph" while his friends chuckled.

"You better hurry, you don't want to be late for your meetings, especially the one with the king." Farflight—Jackson's cockatrice friend—clucked from where he was perched on the back of a chair, while Spinescale came slithering up onto the windowsill.

"Yeah, pick up the pace sleepyhead, we're going to be late at this rate!" Spinescale, a winged sea snake, said with a grin.

"I'm up, I'm up!" Jackson said, swatting a pillow at Daychaser who laughed as he jumped back towards the window. "Now will y'all leave so I can get changed?"

"I think we'll have to get you a room in a different house..."

Everyone turned to see Jackson's very tired parents standing in the doorway in their robes. His dad yawned. "Getting woken up multiple times a week by the ruckus your friends make isn't my idea of fun."

"Ah, good morning Mr. and Mrs. Growingstar. Beautiful day, isn't it?" Draflor smirked, prompting Jackson's mom to shake her head with a tired grin.

"Good morning Draflor, everyone." She yawned too, while Jackson picked himself off the floor and began looking for his aquatic clothes. "Now would you mind telling us why you're all

# RACE TO THE SEA

waking up the entire village at this hour? Our meeting with the king isn't until well after breakfast."

"Oh, well that's easy. Theren was wanting to talk to Jackson about a few things, and we decided to get in a quick meeting with Koiwae and Startide beforehand." Draflor grinned. "As for waking up the entire village, is it really my fault the easiest way to wake Jackson is by roaring?"

Jackson's dad grumbled tiredly while Jackson's grandpa, who was always up early, came walking in.

The older man took one look at the assortment of creatures in Jackson's room and huffed in amusement. "Jackson, didn't I tell you to shut and latch that window of yours? Your friends really should start using the front door."

"I did! I don't know how they got it open..." Jackson gave Spinescale a long look. "Or do I?"

"Hey, don't blame me, it was Farflight who got the idea to go through the vents!" Spinescale exclaimed although her eyes gleamed mischievously. "Though I might try it next time."

"Alright you lot, out!" Jackson's mother chided, shooing the creatures off while giving a small smile to soften her tone. "Jackson will meet you outside once he's done changing and has grabbed a snack for the road."

"Next time, use the front door." Jackson's dad insisted. "Grandpa is usually up at this hour, and he knows exactly how to wake Jackson up." He gave the creatures a long, dry look while they started to exit out the window. "And he knows how to do it quietly." He added as Daychaser tried to hop out the window but missed his mark and had to scramble through the rest of the way.

Jackson rolled his eyes when some of his friends snickered as Daychaser flopped out of the window. His mom came over with an amused huff before she shut the window and latched it.

# MYTHOS SEAS BEYOND: OF SUNSTONE AND SAPPHIRE

"We'll now that that's over with." Dad yawned again and ruffled Jackson's hair. "I'm heading back to bed, I was up late trying to help plan the show for the next festival and I'm beat."

"Night Dad, sorry about the early wakeup call." Jackson gave his dad a quick hug.

His dad chuckled, patting Jackson's back while Mom grabbed Jackson's bag and put it on the bed for him. "It's ok Jackson, we're all still adjusting to our new lives here." He shook his head. "I still find it strange that your friends seem to see windows as doors though."

"From what I understand, most Sonaekian households use windows as doors all the time." Grandpa seemed amused while he watched Jackson grab a few things from his chest which he teleported into his bag. "Although, I understand why they use a lot of special glass that allows a person to see out of the house, but not in. Especially since most underwater creatures have a hard time grasping the concept of doors." He fetched Jackson's Sonaekian headband from its peg on the back of the door and handed it to Jackson, who quickly tied it around his head.

"Thanks Grandpa." Jackson smiled.

His grandpa grinned and nodded as Jackson's mother came over and gave Jackson a quick hug.

"Be careful out there today, ok? We'll see you at the meeting later, don't get so caught up in other things you show up late."

"Mom, we're going to see Theren." Jackson laughed and hugged her back. "He's a vital part of the meeting, he's the crown prince."

"I know, but you and your friends have been vanishing for so long lately while exploring Mythos Pearl." She yawned tiredly. "Just promise us you'll be careful and on time today, ok?"

# RACE TO THE SEA

"I will, promise." Jackson affirmed before his parents and grandpa left the room so he could change...

Jackson quickly slipped into his Sonaekian clothes and hurried into the dining area of the guest cottage he and his family were staying in. He happily grabbed a slice of flat bread with homemade starberry jam while his grandma came over and placed a glass of chilled belhurran milk in his hand. He smiled up at her and his grandpa, once again wondering at the change that had been wrought over them.

Along with the happiness that now seemed to overflow from his grandparents, they—and many of the other members of the tribe—were also looking a lot younger.

After his family had come to Mythos Pearl, his grandparents and the other elders and adults in the tribe were given the chance to receive a blessing of longevity, which allowed the Sonaeko and other races to live for a crazy long time.

His grandma's silver-gray hair was returning to its natural brown, and both her and Grandpa's faces and features were looking younger, like they were in their forties instead of... well however old they actually were.

"Your friends dragging you off for another adventure already?" Grandma smiled warmly as Jackson quickly chugged the glass of milk with a happy sigh.

"Yep, we're going to go see Theren, and apparently Startide and Kiowae wanted to speak to us this morning before the meeting." Jackson gulped down the last bite of bread.

"That'll be fun, you haven't talked to Startide for almost a week." Grandpa looked up from the scroll he was reading over. "How're her lessons at Starkelp going?"

"Last I heard they were going good, she said Koiwae's other students are amazing..." Jackson's voice wavered slightly.

# MYTHOS SEAS BEYOND: OF SUNSTONE AND SAPPHIRE

"Startide will always be your friend, Jackson." His grandma patted his shoulder encouragingly. "Just because she's making new friends, doesn't mean she'll stop being yours."

"It's just weird seeing her making new friends." Jackson admitted as he slung his bag over his shoulder.

"Try not to worry Jack." His grandpa smiled. "It'll all work out ok. You've all been through a lot together, and that forms a bond that's very hard to break."

Jackson smiled and nodded as he made his way to the door. "Thanks Grandma, Grandpa."

"See you later, don't be late for the meeting." His grandma called.

"I won't, love you!" Jackson replied and hurried out the door.

"Love you too!" Grandma and Grandpa called while Jackson jogged into the early morning light…

TO GET UPDATES ON FUTURE BOOKS, CONTENT, AND LEARN MORE ABOUT THE OTHER BOOKS IN THE MYTHOS SEAS SERIES, AND THE ALL-NEW SERIES, MYTHOS SEAS BEYOND!

GO TO:

MYTHOSSEAS.COM

WE'LL SEE YOU SOON!

## ABOUT THE AUTHOR

**JEREMY J. DAVIDSON** was born and raised in the beautiful, hot, and dry deserts of southern Utah, where he developed a love for warm weather, family, and creatures. Now living in the colder upper portion of Nevada's Great Basin, he still finds time to pursue his hobbies in writing, drawing, gardening, raising animals, and learning all he can about the amazing creatures of our world despite colder temperatures and snowy winters. He is the author of Mythos Seas: Call of the Coast, Mythos Seas: Alarm in the Archipelago, and the other books in the Mythos Seas Series!

Made in the USA
Las Vegas, NV
26 April 2024

89168143R00187